Moving Through

By Chase Will

Dons,

I hope you enjoy

the ride!

-CW

To Mom and Dad,
Thank you for always being there.

"The only people for me are the mad ones...."
    -Jack Kerouac

"That's how the light gets in."
    -Leonard Cohen

Part One

Chapter One

There's a stage here in Caedes, OH that's rarely used.

Our population's less than ten thousand, every other block seems to have a meth house on it, and the dozen or so pizza places and twenty-some churches all have a pair of deer antlers mounted somewhere on their walls. But for some reason or another, a wealthy alumnus of the high school, who managed to get out of this town and get rich elsewhere, bequeathed a small fortune to the city when he died…but only on the condition that it was used to build a mammoth stage in the middle of the horse track at the fairgrounds.

The stage is gargantuan, the sort of thing you'd expect big name rock bands to play on at packed music festivals, complete with footlights, overhead lighting fixtures, and a half-underground backstage area leading up to the stage through a short tunnel. Maybe that's what the wealthy benefactor had in his imagination: that a big enough outdoor stage would bring touring musicians through here and put our dead-end town on the map. For sure, it would've been a beautiful legacy for the man to leave behind.

It's kept under a series of blue tarps most of the year, though, except when it's used during the county fair and the school's annual Rock the Arts Festival. Every once in a while, there's an article in the newspaper about someone being arrested for having sex on the stage or defacing it with graffiti. The biggest act to ever perform on the stage was a country musician who'd made it big on a reality television show called *Sing Like You Mean It*, and although her show had the rust-speckled grandstands overflowing with fans from surrounding areas, she later called Caedes "a real shithole" in a *Country Crown Magazine* interview.

The stage is like a monument to failed aspirations. Someone summed it up pretty well with one spray-painted sentiment across the front of the stage: *"Welcome to Caedes! Aim low or hang high!"*

Grandpa told me about the stage three years ago, the same week I met him. Back when he was just an old man in a near-empty movie theater, loudly interrupting the movie I cut school early to see. Back when he was still alive and crazy as they come.

My family had just moved to Caedes from an even smaller town in Northwest Ohio, where Dad had been a shift supervisor at a meatpacking plant. The slaughterhouse in Caedes offered him a management job that would suck double the life out of him for significantly more money, which I guess he thought was a fair trade. Our house here is bigger than our old one, and Mom says we're more "well-off" than most people here, but that didn't mean a lot when I was entering a new high school midway through Freshman year.

It's not like I had many friends before we moved, friends who I could text when I was feeling lonely those first few weeks here. I stabbed a kid in the leg with a wooden pencil during math class earlier that year, but only because he kept jabbing me in the back with *his* pencil and the petite bald man teaching class—who didn't seem much older or more authoritative than any of us—wouldn't do anything about it. I got suspended, and the whole thing made me a bit of a social outcast, so moving four hours away to a new town didn't exactly make me cry.

Being that I was nearly invisible at the new school, it was easy to just walk out one day and catch a mid-afternoon movie at the theater. Worst case scenario, I thought, I'd get caught and the principal would call my parents, who I'm pretty much also invisible to most of the time.

The movie was called *Attack the Pack*, a star-studded Hollywood adaptation of my favorite book series from grade school. The books were actually pretty violent and depressing for something aimed at kids, and they were all about a vampire who takes a kid on as his apprentice and ends up starting a war with another vampire clan.

The movie, unfortunately, was flaming hot garbage. They absolutely mangled the plot of the series and ditched all the beautiful character moments by trying to condense *three* of the twelve books into *one* crowd-pleasing money machine, hinting at stuff like spin-offs and expanded universes and all that impure crap Hollywood does with adaptations. Worst of all, they even kept it rated PG, so all the decapitations, blood rituals, and cannibalistic monsters were either cut from the movie completely or rewritten by someone with no love for the source material.

Being the diehard fan that I was, I did my best to ignore the movie's cringeworthy awfulness. But it was bad. So bad, if fact, I was already zoning out by the twenty-minute mark and scrolling through Facebook on my phone, which is something I normally *hate* when people do. I thought I was still the only one in the theater. That was why I cut school in the first place, so I'd have the whole place to myself and wouldn't have to deal with rude people.

But then I heard a voice shouting from a few rows behind me:

"Can you believe the crap these Hollywood hacks pump out? Christ Almighty, I want to pull my eyes out of my head and stuff my ears with them!"

I turned around in my seat, thinking maybe if I made the rude person feel like an asshole they'd get embarrassed and shut the hell up. A wiry old man with a wrinkled face and scraggly brown beard grinned back at me.

"It's a disaster! An insult!" he ranted, upending a box of Snow Caps into his mouth and then throwing a handful toward the screen. "As soon as these jackasses get a whiff of whatever series you kids are throwing your allowances toward, they snatch the rights up and whore it out to make a few bucks! Don't you feel insulted by that, kid? Doesn't it piss you off?"

I smiled awkwardly, not sure if the old man genuinely wanted an answer. His eyes were lit up and wild, and he looked like someone who hadn't slept in days but was having too much fun to call it quits. I figured he was one of the town's many druggies. By that point in the schoolyear, I was already pretty sure everyone in Caedes was around three degrees of separation from an alcoholic meth addict.

I turned back around in my seat, and the old man kept right on talking to himself. On and on, he wouldn't shut up.

"The main character's supposed to be an Asian kid! Who's this pasty little Disney brat?" he complained. He kept breaking into his strange and nasally laughter, which sounded like a flock of seagulls being euthanized with a sledgehammer.

I finished half my popcorn and left the crappy movie. The old man called to me as I exited, "Smile a little more, kid! Life's not so damn serious!"

A few days passed. Over the course of those few days, I had my first real breakdown at the new school, which I suppose meant I'd finally adjusted enough to act like myself. Some inbred mongrel with a yellow snaggletooth and scruffy neckbeard threw his milk carton at me during lunch period, ruining the pages of the Stephen King book I was trying to read and soaking the front of my black Atreyu t-shirt. He laughed, and so did a few others, and he probably thought that was the end of it—throw crap at the new kid, he won't do anything!

But I grabbed the half of a cheesy burrito on my plate and smashed it across his face, apparently hard enough to give him a nosebleed. My retaliation must have been the only thing the teacher saw, because I was sent down to the principal's office and then suspended for three days.

Déjà vu. Only this time I wouldn't be moving to a new town; I was destined to be a social outcast in Caedes, too.

Mom and Dad both worked back then, so aside from getting my ass belted that first day home, suspension was pretty much just a vacation. So, I went to the movies alone all three days. The theater was small and only showed two movies, but I ended up seeing them both about six times, just for something to do instead of sitting in my room and letting loneliness slowly kill me. Matinees are only two bucks, anyway, and I stole some money from Dad's spare change cup.

Every few showings, the old man would be in the same theater as me. I was so miserable and lonely that the idea of sitting through a movie with an annoying person didn't bother me much. Crazy company was better than no company.

Sometimes there'd be others in the theater with us, and for the most part, they'd tolerate the old man's loud comments. A few times, people politely asked him to quiet down, and surprisingly, he stopped altogether and apologized to these people. But there were exceptions, like this one lady who dressed like the embodiment of Strong Christian Values and looked like she'd been born with a stick up her ass. This lady didn't even bother asking the old man to quiet down; she complained to the manager right away, and the old man was promptly warned to quiet down or he'd be put on the 'no sale' list. The lady half-turned in her seat and smirked, all smug and satisfied and suddenly the most unbearable person I'd ever seen.

The old man kept his middle finger raised toward her for the rest of the movie, even as he stared dutifully at the screen and munched his popcorn. He was already starting to grow on me, and before I left the theater, I asked the woman behind the concessions stand if she knew anything about him. I didn't know many interesting people at the time.

"His name's Edward O'Halloran," she said. She sounded exhausted, like someone who'd already died inside years ago. "He wrote some book a while back. Didn't do very well, I don't think. Is he bothering you or something?"

"No," I said.

"Was he doing the thing with the marionettes again?"

"Huh?"

"Sometimes he brings props with him. He puts on little shows if he thinks the movie sucks." She shrugged, gesturing with one hand like this was just a natural fact of life. "He knocks if off whenever someone complains. I think he's cracked or something."

I nodded, smiling to myself as I pictured the old man—*Edward*—marching a marionette up and down the aisle while others in the theater fumed quietly or made passive-aggressive groans.

When I got home, I spent the rest of the day scouring the internet for everything I could find on the old man. There wasn't much; he didn't have any social media accounts, which I assumed would be a riot. His book was called *A Day Away*, and it had mostly negative reviews online. One reviewer called it "self-indulgent and meaningless," and another reviewer wrote a ten-page essay about what little effect "the worst book ever published" had on him. A few people liked it, though.

I started reading the e-book that night, and it wasn't bad, it was just…dense. It was too literary or whatever, the kind of book you only force yourself to read so you can tell people you're "a serious reader." I soldiered through it until around chapter four before I gave up for the night, and I still had no idea what the plot was supposed to be. The main character breaks his ankle in the first chapter while wandering through a system of hidden caves in his back yard, searching for something he can't even put a name to and feeling more lost the further into the caves he gets. I felt lost just reading about it.

I kept going to the movie theater, less for whatever crappy movie was playing and more for the old man's antics. There was nothing particularly threatening about his brand of weirdness; he was oddly polite when I saw him talking to the woman behind the counter, and he always stopped performing the moment someone asked him to. But *only* if he was asked.

Sitting in the mostly-empty theater, a movie in front of me and a live one-man show behind me, it was like I was experiencing a new form of art, something everyone was invited to witness but nobody bothered to appreciate. I don't think there was anything mean-spirited about his performances, and I could tell he enjoyed making me snort with laughter whenever he'd make an obnoxious fart sound during "dramatic" moments in a movie.

Once he had a full conversation with himself using three different puppets made from paper bags, all of them arguing vehemently about the artistic merits of Tom Waits. Another time, he kept gasping dramatically and jumping in his seat whenever there was an explosion or any bad CGI effects on the screen. This was during *another* bad vampire movie that I won't even waste time talking about, and the only person in the theater other than us was a guy with a real 'pretentious film critic' look to him, something about the way he sat with one leg folded daintily over the other and his arms crossed tightly. As soon as I saw this guy, I knew he'd ruin our fun.

Just as I guessed, the guy kept doing passive-aggressive stuff like clearing his throat and sighing loudly while shifting in his seat. Finally, he shot up, shouted *"Goddamnit!"* and marched quickly toward the exit doors, huffing and puffing and swinging his arms in a way that made him look both extremely enraged and extremely flamboyant. The manager came in a moment later and booted the old man, but only for the day.

I got up from my seat and immediately followed the old man outside. I had to talk to him; it was like meeting a local celebrity, in a way, and I was actually a little nervous about it.

He was sitting outside the theater on a bench, smoking a large and smelly cigar. He grinned from ear to ear when he saw me approaching, and I could see his yellow and misshapen teeth.

"Now that one was a doozy!" he said, shaking his head as he took in a mouthful of smoke. "Did you see that guy's face? I mean, why go out into the world if you don't want to be entertained a little? I thought he was going to punch me in the face!"

He cackled to himself. He had a giant nose that stood out like a crooked pyramid in the center of his face, and his scraggly grey hair looked even greasier in the daylight. He had a small stack of his paper bag puppets on the bench next to him. I grabbed the top one, which had big googly eyes glued to it and a handful of purple yarn for hair, and I put it on my hand.

"What's the point, though, Edward O'Halloran?" I asked, moving my hand and giving the puppet a throaty growl for a voice. "Why are you such an asshole to people? Are you a meth addict or something?"

The old man must have been taken off guard, because for a second, he just stared at me unsurely, eyeing the puppet on my hand as he took another puff of his cigar. I knew using his name would jolt him a little, and that was somehow satisfying, sort of like an *"I know who* you *are and you have no idea who* I *am"* feeling of power.

He relaxed in his seat and propped one foot up over his knee as he addressed the puppet.

"There is no point, Mopsey," he said, smiling. "People live in their own little fantasy worlds, and it's fun every now and then to shake them up a little. Life's too short to be boring."

"Your book was pretty boring, though," I made the puppet say. "If you ever want to torture someone, make them read *A Day Away* by Edward O'Halloran. It'll bore them to tears."

The old man didn't smile at the puppet this time. Instead, he stared up at me with a sort of pissed off expression. I had a nervous feeling, like maybe I'd gone too far and had actually offended him. But I didn't rush to apologize; I had to know how far I could push him.

"Yeah?" he asked. "Well, who are you? King Shit of reading?"

"Pretty much," I answered, still moving the puppet's mouth. "Your book sucked, mister."

The old man's eyes shifted between me and the puppet. He started to smile, though.

"You know, insulting a writer to his face is a good way for a puppet to get stabbed to death," he said.

"And reading *A Day Away* is a good way to get bored to death," I said. "I'd take a good stabbing over a chapter from that book any day of the week. Set me on fire if you want; I'd rather fry in puppet Hell than read any more of your book."

The old man laughed loudly, looking between me and the puppet. He turned toward the theater doors, pushed a finger to one nostril, and shot a thick green snot rocket onto the glass. It hit the yellow smiley face and slid slowly down through the words "Smile! Cameras are recording!" printed below.

"You're here at the movies an awful lot, kid," he said, wiping his nose across his sleeve. "You're a little messed up in the head, aren't you?"

"You don't know anything about me."

"Nah, I've only known you for a minute and I think I've already figured you out," he said. He smiled, unrelenting mischief in his eyes. "Crazy can sense other crazy. You've got it for sure."

He went on smoking the cigar, and I let that comment sink in for a second. I'd seen him mess with so many people in the theater that I wasn't quite sure if he was messing with me now or if he was giving me a compliment.

"Is being crazy a bad thing?" I made the puppet ask. The old man shook his head.

"Crazy is the only way to get through life," he said. "The crazy ones find a way to keep going when others give up."

I thought about that. I was an outcast at school, and I was pretty sure I'd never fit in, nor did I have much interest in doing so. *Crazy.* Something about hearing it in one word made me feel proud, like I wasn't being judged at all but simply accepted.

"Hey," I said, taking the paper bag off my hand. "You want to get a piece of pizza? Fat Frankie's across the street is pretty good. I'll buy."

The old man waved a hand.

"Drop the charity, kid," he said. "I'm not homeless, you don't have to feed me. I'm crazy, not broke."

"No, I didn't mean it like that," I said quickly. "I just mean, do you want to go get food?"

"Haven't your parents taught you not to talk to strangers?"

I shrugged. "At this point, I think they'd be okay with me getting stabbed to death. At least I'm getting out of the house."

He laughed at that, shaking his head as he snubbed out his cigar on the bench and tossed it toward the parking lot. He splayed his hands, surrendering.

"Fine," he said. "But Fat Frankie's is terrible. It's Crowtown Pizza or nothing at all."

"That's fine."

"And you have to tell me your five most offensive jokes on the way there."

"I can do that."

"And they have to be *really* offensive jokes," he added. "If I don't get offended by the time we get there, I'm going to feel pretty cheated."

"Have you heard the one about the terrible author who wrote that godawful book?"

"I get the feeling you piss a lot of people off, kid."

"My name's not 'kid,'" I told him. "My name's Trey."

"Yeah? Well, I get the feeling you piss a lot of people off, *Trey.*"

We walked toward Crowtown Pizza a few blocks away, and I went on about what a drag his book was. He didn't seem bothered by my criticism, and when I talked I could tell he was actually listening, nodding along rapidly at everything I said or shaking his head wildly and saying, "No, no, no!" Always engaged, always quick with the cutting remark. He even made fun of my prematurely receding hairline—a completely stab-worthy offense—and I didn't get upset about it.

He wasn't just my first friend in Caedes. This my first *real* friend ever, I think.

And now it's three years later, 3 a.m. on a Sunday night, and the first person to truly accept me is already dead. If it wasn't for Grandpa, I would never have become friends with Sarah, Monk, Clive, and Kevin. Our friend group is small, and we only found each other because "Crazy can sense crazy." His name was Edward, and even though he wasn't related to any of us at all, we all called him "Grandpa."

And tonight, we're giving Grandpa a funeral that lives up to everything he gave to us.

Chapter Two

I'm almost to the graveyard now, and I'm pedaling as hard as I can. The streets are empty, all the lights are out in every house I pass. The wind whips at my jacket and pushes my crappy hair back from my too-large mongoloid forehead. I swear the only thing that's grown since high school started has been my forehead, and it makes me think of the time Grandpa playfully embarrassed me in front of Sarah by pulling my hair back and saying, "Look at that! You can land a plane on that window's peak!"

I laugh against the wind, standing and pedaling harder still. I feel tears burning at my eyes, and by sheer red-faced will I stop them.

Grandpa told us he didn't want tears at his funeral, only laughter and our usual bullshitting. He said so when he told all of us about the cancer. We were eating cheeseburgers and milkshakes on his patio, just the six of us, and Clive was playing some trash indie band on YouTube to torture Monk, who'd said something like "all music is art and all art is valid." Grandpa didn't even deliver the news sadly, the way an actor would say it on stage or in a movie. He stated it very plainly, and we all just stared at him for a few long minutes as the crappy music continued to play. He rocked in his chair, tapping one hand nervously on his thigh even as he forced a smile.

Listen, I don't want any of that sad ass funeral stuff, he said. *Dance on my grave a bit. Celebrate, smoke some weed, drink whatever beer's left in my fridge. But for real, don't get any dumb tattoos of my face or some 'inspirational quote' stuff, alright?*

I really hope Sarah doesn't forget the picnic basket, though I seriously doubt she would. It's a special basket, a giant black thing with twin wooden handles and a large bear painted on top with two cubs, all of them fading and hardly beautiful anymore. She's supposed to pack it with an assortment of fast food from downtown, the usual cheap crap we eat at our late-night gatherings. She won't forget about it. She cried when Grandpa passed her the basket from the bed in his house where he'd soon die alone, not a single one of us around to hear his last breath.

And that's only because of Grandpa's "real" family. Those sonsabitches who swarmed him like carrion birds the moment they found out he was dying, all the people who hadn't bothered to call him or visit him in years but think having a blood relation makes them somehow important. Figures, they waited until he was pumped full of medication to swoop in and take things over. I doubt he even knew who they were, yet they seemed to control everything from a legal standpoint once they arrived, and their cars disappeared from around his house the day after the "real" funeral.

I try shaking all the bad thoughts away, peddling harder and harder and letting the wind whip my crappy hair around. It's like an itch, all these mad and terrible thoughts. Every time I think I've scratched it for the final time it just comes back twice as bad when I'm least expecting it, and it gets so horrible that I cry if I dwell for too long.

The dead don't sleep in peace tonight—I'm not even at the gates of the graveyard when I hear wild laughter ringing out from the giant oak tree in the middle. It's the tallest tree in the whole graveyard, which is about the size of a city block with a slight hill on one side, and it has a few low branches.

Grandpa and I were the first ones to come here for late-night picnics. At first it was just something we did because I was having a really tough time sleeping one night, and I felt like it was the end of my whole world and I couldn't breathe or make much sense of anything. I went to Grandpa's house, because Mom said I was just being "overly hormonal" and too dramatic, and Dad, who would sometimes listen to me talk, was working third shift and didn't have much time for anything else lately. We walked and talked, and Grandpa let me vent everything that was eating away at my soul, stuff that I don't feel much like getting into right now because it doesn't matter much anymore and, frankly, it's embarrassing to think I was so wrecked about it in the first place. We ended up here at the graveyard, and something about the dead quiet was relaxing. It became our new spot—movie theater be damned—and when our little group grew, this is where we spent a lot of late nights. Sometimes it's midnight, other nights it's 3 a.m., but when one of us needs to vent, or if one of us just can't sleep because of our personal demons and various anxieties, we all show up. No questions asked.

It's perfect here; the cemetery's got an abandoned factory to one side and crappy low-rent apartments all around, this town's watered-down version of a true ghetto. We can make as much noise as we want and no one really bothers us, not as long as we keep it reasonable and watch for the occasional patrol car. Every now and then we'll see someone walking through here, either drunk or out of their mind on something else, and sometimes they'll be talking out loud to themselves or to God, crying about an instance where life's done them wrong.

I recognized a few of these people from school during our first few months of meeting up here. I'd tell Grandpa what I thought of them, even if I didn't know them too well. Sometimes Grandpa would invite these people to sit and drink with us, though not many accepted the invitation. More often than not, they'd ask to bum a cigarette and then sheepishly avoid eye contact as they walked away, as if they were embarrassed for us. *Only crazy can sense crazy,* Grandpa would say.

But a few of them *did* stick around, and these were the stray dogs who knew how bad the voices in your head can really get. Whatever was killing them so badly inside, they forgot about it for a chunk of time as they joined in drinking, smoking, arguing, singing, and all our usual madness...and before I knew it, I had a small group of friends gathering with us every couple of nights, people I might've ignored completely at school or outright hated if not for this strange way of meeting. We knew each other at a primal level, if you want to be real about it. Before long, they all started calling the old man 'Grandpa,' too.

The laughter from the tree sounds like Clive, and the unbridled volume of it makes me think he started drinking quite a bit earlier in the night. I can't really judge him for it, not with a dad like his.

I grin, pedal slightly harder toward the tree, and then jump off the bike and let it crash noisily into a nearby headstone, scaring the piss out of all of them.

"What's with all the giggling?" I ask. "Did Clive swear off smoking again?"

Clive grins, and a rock sails past my head in response.

"Well, well!" he says, splaying his arms at me. "All this stuff about *'Don't be late! Set three alarms if you have to, but don't be late!'* And look who the late one is!"

I give him the finger and unzip my backpack as I approach.

"Eat my ass," I tell him.

"Where were you, blowing your suit tailor?"

Kevin cracks up at that comment, and Monk—or, if you want your jaw broken, "Theodore Munkowski"—throws a crushed beer can at Clive's head.

As they jump down from the tree branches and walk toward me, I see how completely overdressed I am. I'm wearing a cheap black suit from Goodwill, and the others are wearing whatever black t-shirts they could scrounge up. Monk's wearing one with Tim Burton's *Razor's Edge* on the front, Clive's wearing his Led Zeppelin shirt with heavy sweat stains in the pits, and Kevin's just wearing a plain black t-shirt with creases still in it.

Grandpa wouldn't have had it any other way, though. I bet if he'd seen his "real" funeral, the one with all the laughable religious overtones and eulogies given by the handful of family members who bothered to even show up, he would've vomited in his casket.

I only bought this damn suit in the first place because I decided to go to Grandpa's calling hours, even after I told the others not to bother. I arrived about an hour after it started, which I thought would be enough time to let a nice crowd gather so that Grandpa's crappy family wouldn't notice me. But there was hardly anyone there; there were five rows of fold-out chairs, but the only four people in the room were all standing toward the back, away from the open casket at the front, talking over the sad and stupid music that Grandpa would've hated. Grandpa's family didn't charge at me when I walked inside, shooing me away the same way they shooed me from saying my final goodbyes while he was still breathing. They didn't seem to notice me at all, actually, and I sort of froze up when I saw the open casket with Grandpa's head propped up on a pillow and his face completely visible to me the moment I walked in.

It wasn't him. The person in the casket had all the same facial structure, the same bulbous nose and scrunched up forehead with permanent lines like college-ruled paper...but it wasn't him.

This doppelganger had a trimmed beard which had been dyed an unnatural shade of brown, and his hair was cut shorter and completely tamed. The corpse was just a canvas for someone else's art, someone else's depiction of what Grandpa *should* look like without so much as a memory to reference. If I'd doubted it before, I couldn't doubt it anymore: Grandpa's family didn't even know him.

My knuckles crack as my hand makes a fist. I take a deep breath and force a smile at the others. I don't want to be angry, not right now.

"Did you guys bring the stuff?" I ask.

Monk lifts a small grocery bag at his side and brings out a cigar and a can of chewing tobacco. Clive holds out a half-emptied bottle of Jack Daniels, likely borrowed from the back of his dad's cabinet. Kevin looks toward the ground, cheeks burning as he pulls a copy of *Penthouse* out from beneath his shirt.

"Cool," I say, bouncing uneasily on my toes as I look around. "So...where's Sarah at? Did she forget something or...something?"

I catch the quick and subtle glance between the three of them, the one they seem to think I never notice. It was a mistake telling them certain things when I was drunk.

"She's probably at Jordan's still," Kevin says.

"Did she call any of you?"

They shake their heads.

"I'll text her," Monk says. "She'll be here any minute, though. She wouldn't ditch on something this important." "Let's just wait up on her," Clive chimes in, putting a cigarette between his lips. "It's not like any of us have anywhere else to—"

"No," I interrupt him, holding a hand out before he can light it. "It's her own fault that she's late. If she's too busy with something else, well…we'll start without her, I guess."

Kevin nods and walks toward the grave, but Clive and Monk stare at me unsurely.

I keep that calm and fake smile on my face as I look around at all the headstones, telling my imagination to piss off as it forces me to watch images of Sarah cuddled up tight with Jordan, her lips breathing his breath, her bare thighs wrapped around his hips…

I walk toward the tree, and after a moment's hesitation, they follow me. Monk touches my shoulder.

"You alright, man?" he asks. His voice is softened and his brow is scrunched, communicating 'concern' the way only a goddamn theatre actor can. It's not insincere, though. Something about Monk is always sincere, no matter who he's talking to. It actually aggravated Grandpa sometimes, and he'd complain about not being able to get under Monk's skin because he's just too damn agreeable.

"Just tired," I lie.

"Be patient with Sarah," he says. "Let her do her. She'll show up."

I nod and start walking toward the tree with the others. No crying tonight. We promised Grandpa we wouldn't cry.

Grandpa was buried close to the gathering tree. He told me it's a spot he'd reserved when he was younger, before he met his wife of twenty years who eventually cheated on him and then died as someone else's problem. "A grave is the most important land a man can own," he told me. "It's where you get all your best visitors."

I stand at the head of the grave while the others gather at either side of me, all of us staring up at Grandpa's enormous special-crafted headstone and smiling at his final bit of performance art. This one must have required a lot of close friends in higher places. His name is engraved in the center of the eight-foot stone crucifix, just below a frowny face with horns on its head. On either side of his name, where Christ's hands would be nailed, there are wooden pencils sticking out from the stone.

Engraved below his name in a small metal plaque: "The One Who Cared."

The crazy bastard actually made it happen. He showed us the drawing he'd made a few days after the bad news, no doubt something to lighten the mood and get us back to our normal laughs, even though we all knew those laughs would never feel the same with the knowledge of him slowly dying. The pencils were my idea, because I knew it was the sort of vaguely offensive and stupid gesture he'd really like. The frowny face with the devil horns was Clive's idea, and that's where we knew we'd created something provocative and stupid enough to truly feel good about.

It'll be taken down within a few weeks, I bet. Some overly-concerned lady from one of the local churches— hell, maybe even my own mom—will see the silly thing as an attack on their personal beliefs, and they'll demand the city to remove it. I guess that's really the point, though. It'll get a reaction out of *somebody*, and for the rest of that day it'll feel like Grandpa's still with us.

Clive takes out his phone, and after I nod that it's time, he opens the playlist we all made together. I hold an open hand out to either side, and Kevin and Monk grab them.

When I clear my throat, they bow their heads, and Clive presses 'play.'

Our silence is broken as Buddy Holly's "That'll Be the Day" begins playing at low volume. I take another deep breath, ignoring what feels like an iron fist clenched in my chest.

"Death doesn't scare the crazy ones," I begin, "those brave enough to defy the whims of God and his angels and lead lives of their own choosing. This is something you've taught all of us, in your own way."

I slip my hands free and reach for the backpack at my feet. From the front pocket, I take out the wooden King piece from my chess board at home, and I hold it toward the giant crucifix as I continue.

"I couldn't even play checkers very well when I met you, but you spent weeks teaching me the rules of chess. I was confused by the board and all the pieces, and I'd move them into dangerous spots again and again, ignoring the strategies you repeated over and over. I lost games quickly because I was so eager to win that I always moved the big pieces first. You showed me how your king never even moved from his row. You told me that the king stays in the back so that he can train the smaller pieces with his wisdom. You said a lot of pawns die on their way to the other side, but the few who make it through the slaughter always come back as rulers in their own right. I'm not sure you really knew what you were talking about, at least not strategically. I looked online at video tutorials and 'how to' books, and none of them said anything close to what you were saying. But I think I understood what you meant, because it showed in the way you treated all of us. You never talked to us like we were kids, and you never dismissed us or talked over us when we went on and on about whatever was hurting us at any given moment. You listened when we talked. You pushed us to keep moving.

You were strange, creepy, loud, and brilliant. But more than anything else, you were our Grandpa."

I look over at Clive again, and he goes to the next song on the playlist as he trades spots with me, licking his lips and keeping his eyes toward the grass. "Street Fighting Man" by The Rolling Stones plays, and as Clive bows his head and gives his own silent eulogy, he rolls the butt of a cigarette between his fingers.

His goes on for a few minutes, and that's okay. We all agreed that there'd be no time limits to whatever we had to say, whether it be out loud or in our heads, and the most important thing is that we're genuine about making ourselves smile.

But even as I try to guess what memory Clive's reciting silently, a voice in my head speaks. *There were a lot of great memories,* it says. *And there could've been even more, if the world weren't unfair and God didn't take all the good people. What if you could've made his last days alive better?*

I picture Grandpa's family again, those greedy bastards. The invisible fist in my chest squeezes hard, and even as I try to smile again I feel a sort of dread: I don't know for sure that this is ever going to stop hurting.

Clive lifts his head, grinning wide even though his eyes are welled with tears.

He picks up the bottle of Jack Daniels from beside his feet, takes a deep swig, and then passes it around to the rest of us. When the bottle reaches him again, he pours some over the grave.

"Rest in peace, old man," he says quietly.

Monk is up next. As Clive moves from the head of the grave, he switches the song to "Knockin' on Heaven's Door." I can't remember if Monk picked this song or if Grandpa insisted on it for irony's sake. It's enough to make me grin for a moment.

Monk bows his head and brings both hands to his face. When he raises his head again, there's a black patch over one eye. Before any of us can question it, his mouth twists into a strange scowl and he hollers out:

"*Yarr!* Gather round, ye old scallywags, and hear the tale I'm 'bout to tell of the pirate laid to rest before ye! He had humor black as the devil's arsehole and heart as golden as a billion doubloons! His ship may've sunken whilst ours still carry on, but the cruel ocean mistress can only steal a man's body, never his spirit! Raise yer hooks to the man who'd sooner make us walk the plank than spend a single hour singin' songs of weak hearts! He may be swabbin' the decks of Heaven or Hell, but with a loud *'Yo-ho!'*, we sail on!"

The other three of us are trying our hardest not to crack up, which is doubly hard with Monk staring around with his hideous scowl, eyeing us each individually until we can't help but break into laughter. Finally, he breaks character.

"Seriously, Grandpa…you made us better than we might've been. I don't know that everyone gets to meet someone who cares about them the way you cared about all of us. Every bit of time we all got to spend together, whether it be here at the graveyard or playing pranks around town, was pure gold. You even came to all my shows and helped me prep every character I played. That meant a hell of a lot to me. You were a pretty harsh critic at times, and you definitely let me know when I wasn't one hundred percent believable, but the fact that you took it seriously made me want to do better at it. I hope they have theater, wherever you are."

He pulls off the eyepatch, holds it between both hands for a second, and tosses it on the grave. Then he reaches down at brings up the clipped cigar, which he lights with a few puffs and shares with me and Kevin. He hands Clive a can of Copenhagen instead, since Clive always throws up when he smokes cigars with us. We take a few puffs from the cigar while Clive puts a fat dip into his lower lip, and after a few minutes of smoking and spitting, we toss the remainders of these offering onto the grave.

Clive wipes his fingers on his jeans before shuffling to the next song on the playlist, and Kevin walks to the head of the grave as "Mr. Tambourine Man" starts playing. He pushes his glasses up and fumbles nervously with the porno magazine in his hands, cheeks flushed.

"Edward," he starts, "You probably know I didn't really like you all that much. You're the most deranged, foul-mouthed old man I've ever met, and I don't even know why—"

"Kevin!" Monk snaps, punching him in the shoulder. I hold a hand up, stopping them before they can go at it. I motion for Kevin to continue. He brushes his shoulder, glaring at Monk.

"Jeez, I was only kidding," he mumbles. "We can't all pull off a funny pirate character, you know."

"Just keep going," Monk says, twirling a finger impatiently.

"Well, what I was getting at was, Grandpa and I got along best when we were arguing over stupid crap. He was a friend, a really good friend, and he was always up for a good argument. I annoy people sometimes, I think, and it gets bad when you're afraid to speak your mind because you're afraid somebody's going to say you're being stupid or your thoughts don't really matter. But after knowing Grandpa for only a short time, I started speaking up more, telling people what I really think, arguing for just about any reason I could think of just because it's fun to point out all the ways something could be incorrect even if all evidence says it's right. I remember Christmas at your house, Grandpa, how we blasted old black and white movies in your living room while we all frosted cookies with you in the kitchen. One of the cookies was misshaped, and I knew it was supposed to be a tree, but you kept insisting it was a rocket ship. We were pretty drunk by then, and I knew you were just screwing with me, but we got in each other's faces, shouting '*It's a tree! No, it's a rocket ship!*' for like ten minutes while all the others laughed. I whipped my eggnog glass across the kitchen and stormed out onto the back patio, and I think I threw up while I was out there. When I came back inside, you threw a small red package with a big bow on it right at my head."

Clive snorts. "Damn near knocked your ass out."

"Yeah, no kidding, and I was super pissed about it. But he told me to shut up and open the damn thing. He said he got me in the gift exchange, and I had no idea there even *was* a gift exchange, so I was caught completely off guard and embarrassed. You guys were all in on it, because you're the absolute worst."

"Aww, ya love us," Monk says, pinching Kevin's cheek.

"I opened the damn thing up, and the whole time I was slowly tearing the paper and forcing a smile I was trying to come up with an excuse for not having a gift. I opened the box, and inside....was a rocket ship cookie cutter with the dough still on it."

He laughs, and as he wipes a tear from beneath his glasses he gnaws his lower lip. He twists the rolled-up magazine in his hands and stares at the headstone.

"That's one of my favorite memories with you. You always went the extra mile just to mess with people. And, you know, I was going to bring you one of the old magazines I stole from your basement, but..."

He smirks and unrolls the magazine to flip back the cover. Beneath, there's a collection of blank printer pages stapled together. Kevin flips through them all, looking victorious.

"I guess I got the final joke in, huh?" he says.

Kevin takes the lighter from Monk, and he sets the bottom of the fake magazine on fire and drops it onto the grass. We watch it burn, and the cover image of a pretty blonde with big tits and a small bikini slowly disappears.

The song finishes playing, and we stand together in silence. It's a heavy kind of silence, and it feels like we're all connected momentarily. It's soothing, sort of, and it makes me forget about the fist in my chest and the unbearable pain.

I'm smiling again, not even faking it this time, but there are teardrops trailing down my cheeks as I stare up at the blasphemous thing we all created together. I start to think about how much it's going to suck when the city inevitably removes the headstone and there's nothing left but just an average grave to memorialize Grandpa's far-from-average personality. There's no use in mourning the loss, since it's hardly much of a loss at all, aside from whatever money Grandpa sunk into commissioning the headstone and bribing its way into the cemetery. Still, though, it hurts to know there'll be a time really soon when it won't be here anymore. I had a similar feeling when Grandpa told us the bad news.

Clive clears his through loudly, obscenely, but I don't hold it against him because Clive doesn't cry as freely as some people do.

One by one, we step back from the grave. I kneel down, eyes closed.

"Thanks for giving a damn about us," I tell Grandpa.

I press the wooden chess piece into the dirt and then stand up again. I recite Grandpa's favorite prayer, the most holy of holy prayers he taught to any of us:

"Stay crazy, in life and in death!"

We're up in the big tree, and I'm taking the last pissy sip of my sixth Keystone when I hear Clive whistling from the branch above me.

"Well, it's about damn time she shows," he says. His voice is slurred, but mine probably is by now too. I drop my empty beer can to the ground and grab the tree beside me with both hands, looking first up at Clive and then in the direction he's staring.

I see a tall brunette riding her bike leisurely across the grass, weaving playfully between rows of headstones and smiling in our direction. She's wearing a short black dress under a gray Ohio State Buckeyes hoodie, and even though my eyes go first to the dress, I'm immediately distracted by the hoodie. She doesn't even watch sports. She *hates* sports, and there's no quicker way to lose her attention than to bring up sports. Is it Jordan's hoodie? Did Jordan get into Ohio State?

She slides to a stop and drops her bike beside mine.

"I know, I know, I'm late, and I'm sorry," Sarah apologizes, staring toward the ground and adjusting her backpack. "We were watching a movie and I accidentally fell asleep, and even though I *know* I set an alarm, it didn't go off!"

Clive burps loudly and throws his can behind him.

"Did Jordan know you had an alarm set?" he asks.

"He fell asleep too," she says. "I mean, it was a pretty bad movie. I don't know why I bothered with it."

"So there's no way he just, I don't know, turned your alarm off?" Clive insists.

"It's okay," I tell her quickly. I force a smile, trying to think of anything at all but her asleep on the couch with Jordan's arm around her, bare under the blankets, maybe sweaty. I'm drunker than I'd like to be right now and it's killing me in the worst way.

I grab the branch I'm sitting on and drop to the ground beside her—first on my heels, then on my ass. The others laugh, and I groan as I roll over. Drunk, drunk, drunk.

"Need a hand?" Sarah asks, holding one toward me. There's a streak of pink in her hair. She's kept it that way for two years, and she's talked about getting a pink ribbon tattooed on her wrist at some point, in memory of her mom.

I bite the inside of my lip, and even as she helps me up I'm hating myself inside. She's smiling, though, and when she smiles her dimples show and her green eyes seem to light up. She's wearing black lipstick tonight, along with her black nose ring and black ear gauges. Her smile makes me forget the crappy grey sports hoodie and anything it may signify.

"We started without you. Sorry," I mutter. My eyes shift between her smile and her feet. She's wearing knee-high black boots with lots of buckles and laces and a smiley face sticker on the outer heels. Damn she's beautiful. And I smell terrible.

"My fault for being late," she says. She takes off her backpack and pulls an 8x10 canvas from it, tilting it toward me with a sorta nervous look. "You think he'll like it?"

At first I think she wants me to judge a gift meant for Jordan, and a sick, vomity taste rises in my throat. But then I notice the dark colors of the oil paints, and my drunken vision suddenly becomes perfect as I study the picture they create. It's definitely a gift meant Grandpa.

The background is a dark swirl of yellow and orange colors, shades of red in various spots like a bleeding nighttime skyline. Black crows and ugly demonic buzzards are painted with blood and guts dripping from their beaks. Standing in the very center of it all, up to his knees in the mouth of some black-eyed demon with endless rows of razorblade teeth, is a pale and skinny man in blue jeans. His eyes are bloodshot, and even though it looks like he's trying to smile, the corners of his lips are weighed down by several large hooks with various-sized bottles and dripping syringes tied to the ends. In one hand, the man is holding a bottle of liquor. In the other hands, he's holding a gun with a smoking barrel.

I marvel at the painting for a long moment. I don't know everything about Sarah, not all the murky stuff, anyway. She talked more to Grandpa than she did to any of us, and I knew that if I ever snooped and asked Grandpa about the things they talked about, he'd probably look at me differently as a person or lose some respect for me. Everything I know about Sarah's losses comes from the people at school who talk an endless stream of horrible shit. Cheerleaders like Kylie Reed are the worst; she calls Sarah 'Little Orphan Annie,' and before Sarah and Jordan started dating, Kylie would sing *"It's a hard knock life!"* whenever she passed in the hallways.

Sarah can verbally eviscerate girls like Kylie in about three seconds flat, but the most I've ever heard about it from her was a passing comment one day when we were walking to Grandpa's after school. "I'd love to take a cheese grater to Kylie's ugly ass face," she'd said. "Maybe fix that crooked nose of hers." Other than that, the bullying's never seemed to bother her.

But she didn't talk to any of us on her dad's birthday last Summer, which was only a month after his suicide. And she stays pretty quiet on Mother's Day and around Christmastime.

"It's brilliant," I tell her. "He'd love it, I know he would. It's...amazing."

The way her smile spreads slightly wider tells me how much the small compliment means. I'm completely blindsided, however, when she throws an arm over my shoulder and hugs me tightly. I stand unsurely for a second, and when I hug her back I'm very aware of her chest against mine and I try not to think about it.

"I can't believe he's gone," she says, still hugging me. Christ, shoot me in the head if I get a boner right now...

I break the hug, reaching down to the cooler beside us.

"He loved you a lot," I tell her. "He was always *way* more talkative when you were around, if that's even possible."

The comment doesn't help the tears in her eyes, it just brings more of them. I feel something burning in my chest. I don't know if it'd be right to hug her again. One hug is fine. Two hugs...isn't there some sort of unspoken rule about a guy hugging a girl twice in a minute? Hasn't some prick in a movie already ruined that for everyone else?

"Well," she says, rubbing carefully around her eyes to avoid ruining her makeup, "I guess we'd better get on with it."

She looks toward Grandpa's headstone and sputters a strange sad laugh at the sight of it.

"Our headstone," she says.

I nod.

"Will you come with me?" she asks.

"Hell yes I will." I pat her gently on the shoulder as I open another beer. I guess that's good enough without being clingy as dog crap.

She walks toward Grandpa's grave, staring down at the grass the whole way. I stare at the back of her head as I walk behind her. If this were the first time I'd ever seen her, I'd never guess that chunks of her hair were missing less than a year ago from where she'd compulsively pull strands. Her eyes look older than when I met her, but not older in an ugly way, older in a way than tells you someone's been through some stuff that not everyone understands. Grandpa's eyes were similar, so maybe there's something about it that made them get along so well. I don't know if anyone outside our group knows just how bad it was for her last Summer, but I know any of us would choke the life out of anyone who'd talk bad about it. I at least shot a snot rocket into Kylie's hair when she wasn't looking, and that made Sarah laugh a bit when I told her.

I stand next to her with my hands in my pockets as she kneels silently with the painting against her chest. She bows her head and closes her eyes.

"Wait a second…wait…" Clive says. He's looking down at Sarah and then at her bike. "Where the hell's the picnic basket? With the food?"

"Oh shit," she says.

"You didn't bring the food?"

"It's at my house in the fridge," she says miserably. "I got everything earlier, and I meant to stop home and grab it before coming here, but I was already late because of the alarm not going off, and I forgot all about it."

"You were responsible for bringing the food," Clive says. He looks deadly serious. "How do you screw up that one simple thing?"

"Knock it off, would you?" I tell him.

"I mean it! We had everything planned out all nicely, and not only is she late, but she forgot the one damn thing she was responsible for!"

Sarah spreads her hands.

"I'm an idiot, okay? I messed up with the alarm and I messed up with the picnic basket."

"You're not an idiot," I tell her.

"We can hold off for a bit, if Sarah wants to run home and grab the basket," Monk says.

Clive waves a hand dismissively and blows smoke toward the ground.

"Forget it. It's not a big deal."

"Are you sure?" Sarah asks. "If you're really that hungry, I'll go back and get it. *Anything* to please the guy who's never messed up before."

"Get on with the damn prayer, will you?" he says. "I'm sorry. I'm drunk, hungry, and pissed off. You're fine."

Sarah holds a middle finger in his direction, and Clive burps.

"I'm sorry," she says to me. "I really did mess up the one thing you asked me for."

"I'm not hungry anyway," I lie. "Don't stress about it."

She bows her head again and starts with her silent eulogy, lips moving inaudibly. I feel weird about watching, so as she goes on with it, I listen to music in my head, flipping through imaginary stations and trying to find a song for the moment. Clive was supposed to play "The Macarena," because Sarah absolutely *hates* that song and I thought it would be a funny joke to play it anyway, and maybe it would get a laugh or even just a smile out of her. So much for that.

After a few silent minutes, she stands again and looks up at the devilish smile on the crucifix.

"I'll never forget you, Grandpa," she says. She rubs her hands nervously along the sides of the canvas at her chest. She opens her mouth, looking like she has more to add, but then she closes it quickly and just bows her head. She sets the painting at the foot of the crucifix, and then she stands there silently again, either continuing her piece or just lost in her thoughts.

"Are you going to hang out for a while?" I ask.

"Of course," she says. She wipes her eyes without looking up at me and walks toward the tree. "Can you give me a boost?"

I nod and weave my hands together, and when she steps onto them and balances herself with a hand on my shoulder, I lift her easily until she's gotten hold of a lower branch. I climb up after her, and we sit side by side.

From the branch above us, Clive clears his throat.

"For real, though, I'm sorry for being such a jerk," he says. "I mean it, it won't happen again."

"It's okay," Sarah says.

"Anyway, how's Anus doing?"

The others laugh at the inside joke, but I'm careful to not even crack a smile as she turns her head up at him and glares. I'm the one who made up the nickname for Jordan in the first place, and it's purely a miracle that she doesn't know it was me. Jordan's last name, 'Renus,' stretches an 'a' sound rather than an 'e' sound, so it sounds like 'Raynus.' Even if it were the other way around, we'd probably just nickname him 'Penis,' or something close to that.

"I haven't seen him lurking around the coffee shop lately," Clive continues. "Is he sick or something? Y'know, I just can't bear the thought of anything happening to poor, poor Anus."

"He's fine," Sarah says, smiling despite the pure venom in her stare. "Just busy getting ready for college. Oh!" She holds a hand to her mouth, looking alarmed. "Sorry for the c-word, I know that's a sensitive area for you. Plenty of others are working at the slaughterhouse after they graduate. It's really nothing to be ashamed of."

The smartass look evaporates from Clive's face, and Monk whistles toward the ground. It's an obnoxiously low blow, and I'm not sure if I'm laughing so hard because I'm drunk and everything seems funnier or because I'd laugh along with just about anything Sarah says.

I feel an ice-cold stream hitting the top of my head suddenly, soaking the back of my shirt. I yelp in surprise and nearly fall out of the damn tree before I look up and see Clive smirking with an upended beer can.

"Now it's funny for both of us," he says. I turn away from Sarah as I pull the bottom of my shirt up to wipe the beer from my face and dry my hair the best I can. My hair looks ugly when its wet, and the receding hairline is extremely visible. I run my hands through it a few times, giving it about as much volume as a dead radio.

Sarah slaps my shoulder.

"Hey, Monk said you're writing again!" she says.

I leer up at Monk, who stares off distantly like he didn't hear.

"Sort of," I tell her. "It's not very good."

"Did you show any of it to Grandpa?"

"A little."

"And?"

I smile. "He said it sucks a little less than my last story."

"Let me read it sometime. You never show me any of your stories."

"Yeah, you're welcome."

"At least tell me what it's about."

I shrug, lost for a way to put the idea into a simple sentence.

"It's...sort of a romance story," I say. I don't even sound confident to my own ears. "I mean, not like a traditional romance or anything, none of that fake stuff. It's....ummm...."

"It's about two gay lovers chowing down on each other's genitals in the desert sunset," Clive waxes poetically. "One of them is a tall banker with a terrible lisp—abandoned by everyone he's ever loved!—and the other's a grizzled drunk with a peg leg and an S&M fetish."

I shoot him a cold look.

"That's not my story, that's your dad's biography."

He whips his beer can at my head, but I duck and it sprays against a gravestone below us.

"Quit wasting the damn beer!" Monk shouts.

"Seriously, what's it about?" Sarah asks.

I shrug. "It's a horror story more than anything, but not the kind of hack-and-slash kind you see in movies, with a masked killer and a naked girl in every other scene. It's...I guess it's about addictions, sorta. Some healthy, and others....well...not healthy."

It's the quickest crap I can think of, because in my actual story the killer's a Catholic priest who dresses like a clown before raping and eating victims from the youth choir. It's a trash story, but Grandpa said every good writer wrote a hundred or so trash stories before coming up with something passable. This is nothing but a tally mark.

She doesn't ask me to elaborate any further, luckily. I can see her running the lame description through her mind and filling in all the details. She actually looks excited about it, but I don't know why, because whatever she's thinking of is probably a million times better than what I'm capable of writing.

"Is that what you're majoring in?" she asks. "Creative writing?"

I shake my head. "Grandpa said it's a waste."

"You'd at least be around other writers, though."

"Sounds horrible."

She laughs, and I feel her hand touch my knee. I look down, tasting something like candied bile in my throat, a sickening feeling of hope that the simple touch means anything at all. I think about putting my hand on top of hers, but her hand only lingers for half a second before she looks up at Kevin and pulls it away again.

"Can I hit that?" she asks. I have no idea what she's talking about, but when I turn I see Kevin exhaling smoke and then passing his bowl to Clive, who passes it down to Sarah. She offers it to me first, and I shake my head. I'm drunk, probably too drunk, and if I add anything else to the mix I'll do or say something stupid.

So they pass the bowl around, and I drink another beer and just watch the graves in silence.

"Let's get tattoos together," Sarah says. "Monk, would you get one with me if I went?"

"As long as it's not some lame inspirational quote, maybe."

"Trey?" she asks. "Would you get one?"

"Sure," I say. I don't look up from my beer can. I feel like crap all of a sudden, and I can't put a finger on why.

"Tattoos are expensive. Who has that kind of money?" Kevin says.

"Just let me do it," Clive says. "I know how to do a stick n' poke."

"Hell no."

"No, for real! It's really, really simple, and it'll cost, like, twenty bucks max for all of five of us."

"What the hell do you know about tattoos?"

"Trust me, all I need is some ink, a sterile needle—"

"*Again*," Kevin interjects, "What the hell do you know about tattoos? You don't think there's a reason people who do it professionally have certifications? You'll give us all gangrene or something."

"I'd let you do it," Sarah says. "For real, you guys. Grandpa's gone."

Kevin taps the embers from the empty bowl.

"Why do you always get so emotional when you're high?"

"I'm *not* emotional and I'm *not* high," she says. "Just listen, okay? It doesn't have to be a big tattoo, just something really simple we'll all have."

"Like a smiley face?" Monk asks.

"Yeah! Or a really simple tree design, maybe."

"There's no way in hell I'm going to college with a tree tattooed on me."

"What about a picnic basket?" Clive suggests. Sarah gives him the finger.

"Listen, guys," she says, "We're all getting tattoos. It's decided. We're getting tattoos, and Clive's doing them."

"Fine," Kevin says. "But Clive can't be drunk while he's doing them."

Monk blows lip music. "That's like asking a fish to stay out of water."

"Eat a dick, Jack Sparrow," Clive says.

I smile again, looking around at them all, forcing down the melancholy feeling that's in my gut for some reason. I look at Sarah, how beautiful and perfect she looks even in Jordan's ugly sports hoodie. I feel my heart doing something unnatural in my chest, like it's trying to reach up and take control of my vocal chords.

We go on for a bit longer, but I feel like I'm barely there for most of it. I'm falling asleep even as I'm nodding along and talking, but I keep drinking every beer they hand to me and looking past Sarah toward the top of Grandpa's headstone.

He's not under all that dirt, I don't think. He's not dead and buried. He never got cancer, and all that stuff's just a weird agreed-upon joke we're all taking part in, another prank, because pranks are what we're good at. If I text him right now, he'll text right back. He's not dead. He never went through all that suffering. It's not real. He's not gone.

"It's getting chilly out," Sarah says after a while. "I think I'm heading home."

I climb out of the tree first and help her down. Everything seems silent and lazy. I can smell the grass, and when I look around it all looks shiny and perfect because of the dew.

"Can I walk you back?" I ask. "I mean, not *walk* walk, but ride with you most of the way. Just to be safe."

She shakes her head as she picks her bike up.

"I'll be fine. I've got my knife," she assures me. "I need a few minutes to myself, anyway."

Her expression sinks a little as she gets on her bike and looks over my shoulder at Grandpa's gravestone.

"I'm sorry I forgot the picnic basket," she says again. "And I'm really sorry I was late."

"Seriously, it's okay," I tell her.

She shakes her head, and the way she pauses makes it seem like she's got more to say but can't find the words. I get it, though. I want to tell her something reassuring, something that'll make her smile and feel better and be able to get to sleep when she gets home to her Aunt Mary's house. I think of telling her how Grandpa called her 'The Goth Princess' whenever she wasn't around, or how he'd ask about her when it was just him and I, always making sure she was doing okay. It all sounds too lame for words, though, so I keep my mouth shut and just nod my head as I shift back and forth on my feet.

"Do you think you could take the painting home with you? For safe keeping?" she asks. "I mean, it took a lot of work to finish, and I figure you and Grandpa probably had the same taste in art, so…do you want it?"

"Hell yes!" I answer quickly, probably quicker than I should. She's never given me a piece of her artwork before, so to me this is the equivalent of being handed the original Mona Lisa, even if I don't know a thing about art.

She nods, and when she turns her bike toward the road she looks back at me for a long second before giving a parting wave to the group in general.

I watch her ride away until she's completely out of sight, and then I pick up the painting. I stare at it, mesmerized. These are more than just colors and brushstrokes, I think. It's pain, and it's a kind of dark, damaged, and angry pain that even Jordan probably doesn't get to see from her. She gave it to me.

"Trey and Sarah, sittin' in a tree…" Clive sings. "F-U-C-K-I-N-G…"

I look up and see him hugging the tree, nearly falling from his branch. He's smiling like an asshole, that dopey and drowsy expression.

I look at Monk. "Can you guys make sure he gets down from there okay?"

"Hell, I might need help getting down myself."

"I'll drive them both home," Kevin says.

"You're driving?"

He waves a dismissive hand. "I drive way better when I'm high."

I shrug, too tired to really care. It's the middle of the night; odds are, they won't be mangled in a horrible car accident. I take the last beer from Clive's bag and chug it as I put the painting in my backpack and pick up my bike.

"Are you going to make it back okay?" Monk asks.

I give a thumbs-up as I pedal away. Truth be told, I'm going to barf as soon as I'm out of view, but nobody needs to know that. Home isn't far away.

It's a slow ride home. Nobody's out, not even the odd third-shifters heading to the gas station during break. It's 4:30 or so, and I need to be up at 6:00 to get ready for school. This was a bad idea, drinking more than my fill. I could probably skip school, but I wore out my lucky streak during the week after Grandpa gave the bad news. The calls would go to Grandpa's house phone, because he'd helped me trick the school into changing the number on file. I'd skip every few days to go sit on the porch with Grandpa, just me and him, and talk about whatever he wanted to talk about. Every moment felt suddenly urgent, and I just wanted to make the most of it any way I could because I knew there'd come a time really soon when he'd be gone forever.

It's hurting like hell thinking of those days, even the great ones. He was old, but not so damn old that he should be gone already, and not from something like cancer. I pedal, pedal, pedal, and try to remember the time before he was dying, but all I keep seeing is the weak and pale shadow who asked me to help him lift his water bottle to his lips the last time I saw him. He was so weak by that point, nothing like himself, and he stopped letting us go inside the house because he was ashamed of the smells that wouldn't go away. Piss in his bedsheets. Vomit in the small wastebasket by the couch. A smell like rot coming from his skin. He didn't want us to smell death any more than we had to.

The fist inside my chest is growing stronger and hotter, and right now it's as powerful as I've ever felt it. It gets worse and worse the more I think about any of it, the good things and the bad, and even when I think about those days in the movie theater when it was just me and him, it crumbles the good memories like they're made of tissue. It's gripping my heart and my throat like it's trying to crush both, searing its fingerprints permanently into every bit of happiness that's left.

There's a wooden ladder against the side of our house. It's been there for a few months, and I'm pretty certain Dad knows I use it to sneak out through my bedroom window at nights but just doesn't care. Mom's the one who'll probably end up making a big deal about it at some point, but as long as our house doesn't get broken into and I don't go missing for days at a time, Dad won't make me move it.

I climb up to my room, and when I get inside, I go straight to the fridge and eat an entire package of deli salami. Dad has more alcohol in the cupboard above the sink, and I suddenly don't care if he knows I've been sneaking gulps or not. I help myself to the Jameson, and then to the Absolut, knowing damn well it could make this all worse but feeling like it could make it all better, too. Then I run to the bathroom, throw the door open, and puke it all back up.

I sit on my knees, heaving into the bowl. I just want to forget it all. I want to get so incredibly messed up that my brain breaks and I don't have to know how any of this feels anymore, because I've never felt anything this bad before and I don't know what else to do.

I flick the bathroom light on, and I'm momentarily blinded before my eyes adjust and I'm able to stare at my reflection.

I'm so ugly. And not just drunk-ugly. My face looks like something pulled from God's garbage disposal, and I'm just realizing it for the first time.

It should've been me who died, me who went through all that horrible stuff that Grandpa went through, stuff I'll never really know about. I spend so much time bitching and it all amounts to nothing, but he was a genius and a maniac who took care of the outcasts and lonely freaks just because he liked us. I can never be that; I can never be anything even *similar*, because I've been spoiled since birth and I don't deserve the air I'm breathing.

The fist in my chest clenches tighter. It burns so damn badly.

There's a bottle of bleach below the sink, and I feel like looking at it, so I take it out and sit on the floor with it in my hands. It's still half-full, and I think about what it would feel like if I swallowed it all. The thought makes me smirk for some reason. Yeah, I could take it downstairs, add some chocolate syrup from the fridge, shake it up really well, and have a very unique, very sugary suicide. There'd be a lot of questions when they find my body in the morning. Not so much *"Why did he do it?"* but *"Why did he do it **like this**?"*

I force myself to smile. Then I start to laugh. It's a real good one, too, and have to cover my mouth to keep from laughing so loud that I wake up Mom and Dad. I cry as I laugh, and the mixture of tears and laughter must confuse the hell out of the fist in my chest because it suddenly unclenches a little. I sit there sobbing and laughing, staring at the bleach bottle.

Grandpa would at least understand. He'd see the humor.

Chapter Three

I wake up to the sound of Mom's knuckles rapping loudly on my door.

"Trey, time to get up!" she calls. Then, before I can even open my eyes or move my forehead from the keyboard, she knocks louder. "Trey!"

"Give me a minute," I moan, slowly sitting up in the desk chair and wincing when sun hits my eyes. They feel ready to burst in their sockets.

I run both hands up and down my face as I stretch my back over the chair, dreading the moment I have to stand up and make it from the desk to the door. My mouth still tastes awful, and dried trails of puke are crusted on my pant legs from where I wiped my hands. I drank water like an absolute madman, but aside from a full bladder it's done nothing for me.

I finally dozed off maybe half an hour ago. The cursor on the screen is still blinking midway through a sentence.

I scroll up the page to compare where I started typing last night to where I am now. Somehow, I crapped out three whole paragraphs...maybe 200 words or so? It's not a lot, but it's magic. *A few bad paragraphs fix a bad night.* Another pearl from Grandpa.

Hungover as I am, there's a slight spring in my step as I shower and get dressed, and last night feels both far away and immediate, like it's just continuing with an alternate ending.

I'm in a good mood again, so I log onto Facebook and dick around for a few minutes, reading status updates from people I barely know and getting some solid entertainment from it. The news feed is like a psychiatric ward of unstable morons shouting through the tiny holes in their little glass window, and it's all pretty compelling in a freakshow sort of way. It's mostly selfies, pictures of people I don't like with smiles that are obviously fake and *oh-so-casual* expressions that scream *"LOVE ME! PLEASE, FOR THE LOVE OF GOD, SOMEONE JUST LOOK AT ME AND LOVE ME!"*

I'm no better, I guess. I don't post selfies, because I *know* how goddamn ugly I look, but even when I had Grandpa around to talk to, I'd still post long and over-sharing diatribes. Clive calls them my "menstrual updates," but I've seen him cry over girls before, too, so he can go straight to Hell.

I head down to the breakfast table with a pencil and notebook in my hands, hoping to scribble a bit more from where I left off last night. The story's hot garbage, but maybe Monk will give me some notes if it doesn't suck as bad as I think. The first thing I smell when I walk into the kitchen is coffee on the burner, and a primal urge takes hold of me as I rush to grab a thermos from the cupboard.

I sit across from Dad. He looks miserable, probably because of the switch from third shift to day shift. He's on vacation this week and trying to adjust to the change, likely with the help of some sleep meds. But he's been in charge of the third-shift crew since we moved here, and I know it's probably a crappy change. Mom said it came with more money, though, so I guess it's a good thing.

I take a sip of my coffee.

"Hey," I say, "Clive wanted me to ask you if he can borrow *Hysteria* from your record collection."

He wrinkles his brow at me.

"How do your friends know what records I have? I keep them in the office."

"We weren't in your office at all. He's really into classic rock on vinyl now, and I remembered seeing the cover when I was helping you put the shelves up. He can probably find it online, but Grandpa said music is truest on vinyl."

Mom looks up from her plate, looking surprised.

"Your Grandpa Jack? When did you talk to him?"

"Not Grandpa Jack," I tell her. "*Grandpa*. Mr. O'Halloran."

Mom rolls her eyes.

"I wish you wouldn't call that guy Grandpa. It's really weird."

"It's not weird. We all call him that, it's like...a nickname, I guess."

"Well, I'm sure he doesn't appreciate it. I think he'd rather you stick with 'Mr. O'Halloran.' It's polite."

I bite my tongue before I can tell for the fourth time since last week that 'Mr. O'Halloran' is dead, and that dead people don't prefer anything. The alcohol in my system has a voice of its own, and it's dying to scream at her that she doesn't know a thing about 'Mr. O'Halloran,' and that 'Mr. O'Halloran' would probably think she's a stuck-up mid-40s lady who needs to pull the stick out of her ass.

Dad looks back down at his plate, wolfing down his breakfast as the ceiling light reflects off his bald head.

"So can he borrow it?" I ask.

"Hell, I don't care. Tell him if he scratches it, though, he'd better be holding a gun when he returns it."

"Also, did you get a chance to look over his work application yet? It's been like a month, and Summer's—"

"Trey," Dad snaps, "Can I please just eat my damn breakfast? Huh?

"Sorry," I apologize. He glares at me for a second, but I make sure I'm not the first to look away. It's a trick I learned, and if I completely fail as writer, which I probably will, I can always host a National Geographic documentary titled *Avoiding Conflict with Dad When He's Pissed.*

He sighs and shoves a broken piece of turkey bacon in his mouth.

"I'll get back to Clive the first chance I get, alright? It's the absolute last thing on my priority list, but I'll get to it. If he wants the job so bad, why doesn't he ask me for it himself instead of making you his lackey? What the hell's wrong with your generation that you can't bother to take charge?"

I don't answer. Another lesson for the potential documentary: don't answer Dad's rhetorical questions about your generation. Clive's not usually nervous about talking to people, but Dad's an exception to almost anyone's bravery.

"And speaking of work," Mom says, "I want you to mop the kitchen and vacuum the downstairs as soon as you get home today. You made a mess last night, and I'm not your maid."

"I'll take care of it," I tell her.

"And I want you to scrub the bathroom upstairs."

"Fine."

"And if you blah-blah-blah-blah-blah-blah-blah blah. Blah-blah-blah. Blah."

I nod my head automatically to whatever it is she's saying, but my mind's already in another world as I stare down at the blank page from my notebook. The only thing I'm interested in cleaning up is this damn piece of crap story. How did the Catholic priest come to dressing like a clown in the first place? The part about eating his victims can be explained pretty easily, I think, but dressing up as a clown while doing it is a little too stupid.

"Blah-blah-blah?" Mom asks.

"MmmHmm," I answer."

Maybe he knew a clown when he was a kid, and he looked up to him? Sounds too convoluted. Stupid. Lazy. Grandpa would probably crumple the story up and tell me to do better.

"Blah?" Mom asks.

"MmmHmm…"

Maybe he doesn't need to be a clown after all. Priests are scary enough, and their fake smiles and funny robes are clownish enough to have a similar effect.

"Blah?"

"MmmHmm…"

My pencil's moving now like it's on fire as the story seems to open itself up a little—

—and then I'm staring down at Mom's hand as she slams it down on the page.

"Repeat back to me what I just said," she demands. I'm too hungover and too irritated to explain that I'm seventeen, and seventeen-year-olds don't need the *'scary parent'* treatment. I can't even glare back at her without my eyes aching. I blink slowly, unapologetic as I dare, and jerk the paper back from beneath her hand. She stares at me a moment longer and shakes her head with a dramatic sigh.

"I swear," she says, "it's like you have A.D.D. or something."

I scrape the remainder of my breakfast into the trash and walk back upstairs, still groggy as hell but awake enough to resist crawling back into bed. I walk over to the tank next to my desk and pull back the black sheet as I squat down to grab the jar of dead bugs from the floor.

"Wakey-wakey, Hector," I coo quietly, smiling to myself as I remove the screen covering the tank and give the small jar a shake. Nothing happens for a moment, but then a large and hairy brown leg peeks out from under a strip of bark I'd pulled from our tree. I tap the glass gently, and the rest of Hectors body appears as he scurries eagerly to the other side of the tank. I reach into the jar and pull a dead cricket out with a pair of long tweezers, and then I lower it near the water dish in the middle of the warm potting soil. You're not supposed to feed live insects to tarantulas—small as they are, they can really put up a fight and sometimes overcome larger predators, especially if you put more than one inside the tank. I only know this because Grandpa told me when he gave me Hector.

'And don't overhandle the damn thing,' he said. *'You wouldn't like it if someone grabbed you constantly and played with you like a toy, would you?'*

I watch as Hector approaches the dead prey, advancing slowly as if testing it. They're not very smart pets, and Grandpa said even a cockroach is more entertaining than a tarantula, but I'm a big fan of spiders even if I don't know much about them.

To my disappointment, Hector doesn't even touch his food after a few minutes. I watch him move around the tank a little, until finally he goes back underneath his strip of bark. Maybe he's molting; Grandpa said spiders go through a shedding period, and they're especially sensitive during that time. Or maybe he senses Grandpa's gone, and he's mourning too.

"I love you, bud," I tell him, and tap the glass.

I take a thermos of coffee from the kitchen before walking to school. I could bike there, but I'm just in the mood for a long walk. I'm going to be late anyway.

I take the long way to the high school. The way that takes me past Grandpa's house. I stop out front, and for a brief good moment I admire the wreckage.

By anyone's standards, it's a shithole. But it was *our* shithole. The cement patio—with rusted aluminum siding and a roof half-stripped of its black shingles—is cracked, and where there used to be a small stair there's just a vacant spot with weeds growing through, just like the sidewalk leading to it. Someone trimmed the grass recently, but that seems to be as far as their effort went because the trimmings are littered in clumps across the yard. Otherwise, the house looks untouched and abandoned. The shiny black Ford Focus that his family of vultures arrived in is gone. Judging from the overfilled mailbox I'm guessing they're gone for good. Thank God.

The package I left with the glass chessboard inside is still on the porch, weather-beaten and unopened. I feel anger bubbling up again just from looking at it. They never even bothered taking it inside. It's just been sitting out here for weeks.

They're gone now, I remind myself. It's no use thinking about how they blocked us from seeing Grandpa or screwed up any comfort we could've offered him. The house is ours again, at least until it's eventually sold, and it brings a bit of a smile to my face just knowing there are no intruders polluting the rooms with their outsider smells. It makes me feel somehow reassured, like not everything's dead and taken away yet.

I was running late when I stopped, but now I'm definitely going to be late. I walk toward the patio, feeling like a holy man walking to Mecca. I move slowly, waiting for the blinds in Grandpa's upstairs window to open a crack and show his still-living eyes. It's stupid and hideous wishful thinking. But I wait for it anyway.

The door handle is locked, and after trying it a few times, I decide to knock. I wait a second, and that second feels like forever as air in my lungs feels somehow restricted and the fist returns and gives a light squeeze.

He's not really dead. Any second, he'll answer. This has all just been a cruel and terrible dream.

Nobody answers.

I stand there stupidly for a minute, waiting and waiting and finally giving up hope. I think of Grandpa's old van, and as I hold onto that thought for refuge I walk back to the garage behind the house and look through the filthy brown window at the monstrosity inside. It's still there, untouched by the vultures who probably mistook it for worthless.

Grandpa told us how he built it the year he met his wife, sometime in his late forties. He'd been poor as hell, even poorer than he was when we all met him. But he needed something for getting around, so he bought this beat-to-hell green van with a cracked windshield that he'd never repaired, a windowless back section, and seats that smelled like cat urine and old age. Handyman that he was, he covered the front seats with two halves of an old tablecloth fastened with a few layers of tape. He gutted the back of the van, and rather than install new seats, he welded the bottoms of a few folding chairs to the bare metal floor and glued some wood paneling to the walls.

He said he used the van to run stack deliveries for a newspaper, so it always had that very specific smell of paper and ink, another part of the van's charm. But when he asked the woman from the jewelry store downtown out on a date—the woman who would later, for better or worse, become his wife—this was the vehicle he picked her up in. For some damn reason, he said, she didn't run for her life. Maybe that's why he loved her for a while.

I look at the old van a few minutes longer, smiling as the terrible thoughts fade a little.

I walk fast the rest of the way to school, and by some strange miracle, I'm only two minutes late.

"Please rise for the saying of the Pledge of Allegiance."

Everyone in the classroom rises to face the flag in the corner, crossing their hearts like they've been trained to and obediently speaking the words with Kevin and the other announcer on the TV.

Monk and I sit and smirk at them all. We're on the far side of the room, away from the teacher's view as he continues playing solitaire on his computer.

"Pledge this," Monk snorts, grabbing his crotch. A girl in the row next to us—some straight-A honor roll girl named Katy Livingston, I think—shoots a glare back at him as she carries on with the oh-so-heartfelt pledge.

The pledge ends, and the class sits back down to resume their idle conversations as Kevin and other kid continue with the announcements. You learn pretty early on in high school that half the stuff on the morning announcements doesn't pertain to you at all, not unless you're like the aforementioned straight-A honor roll girl, so there's really no point in listening.

Monk and I, however, listen *very* intently as we play our daily game.

"*Touch of Class* won't meet this Tuesday afternoon," Kevin says on the screen.

"'*Touching ass won't beat honest poon,*' got it," Monk affirms loudly, turning Travis McCoy's head from across the room. Travis doesn't even smile, but I grin like an ape and listen for the next one.

"Students in Mr. Kauffman's class must pay their lab fees before—"

"'*Students must pray on their knees to whores.*' How very insightful, Kevin," I say quickly. Monk shakes his head.

"You interrupted the sentence, no points granted."

"C'mon, that was pretty funny."

"Terrible, just terrible," he says.

Vincent Gardner, a fat kid in the row next to us, makes a sour face.

"Grow the hell up," he says. He shakes his head at us and then goes back to his daily game of *Magic: The Gathering* with the half-twig-half-human in front of him.

The other announcer continues.

"Attention all members of the Talented and Gifted Group, there's been a change to this week's schedule."

I wait for Monk to take the bait and rhyme 'group' with 'poop,' or something even stupider. But then I look at him and see that the humor has left his face and he's watching the screen with complete interest. I remember his one flaw as a human, the big and ugly thing about Monk that I just *can't* bring myself to forgive...

Monk's been a member of the T.A.G. group since before I met him. It's not something I hated about him at first, because he'd be crazy *not* to join a group that gives him a chance to sharpen his acting skills in front of actual audiences. But Jordan created the group, and he's a complete prick to Monk, limiting his segments at every year's Rock the Arts Festival and constantly pointing out small flaws in his acting where there are none. The festival is one of the only places T.A.G. puts on a show each year, and it's by far the biggest audience they get. But nothing's subjective in Jordan's idea of "art," and from everything Monk tells me, he tears apart every act that goes on stage.

The announcer continues, "There will be a short meeting after school today to discuss plans for the annual 'Rock the Arts Festival.' This meeting is mandatory for all members who plan on participating."

I throw my pencil at Monk, bouncing the eraser off his temple.

"There go *your* afternoon plans. Little Actor Boy needs to report to Dear Old Uncle Anus."

He shrugs. "He probably just wants us to tell him what we're planning on doing. He does this crap before every show."

"Oh? And what are you bringing to the table that Jordan won't destroy?"

"I'll think of something."

"You should do that scene from *The Godfather*, like at last year's festival," I say, and I clear my throat before summoning the raspy voice of Marlon Brando. *"I never wanted this for you, Theodore."*

The bell cuts me off before I can make his face any redder, and the doorway floods with students rushing toward their first period classes. The two of us shove our way through the crowd, and Monk walks with me to the end of the hallway before branching to the right.

"I'll meet you guys at the movie theatre as soon as I'm out," he promises, and then he's lost in the sea of bodies.

I make my way forward on my own, looking for Clive's face as I start down the staircase toward English class. Clive sits a row and three seats away from me, with a pair of flounder-faced volleyball girls and a kid with really bad acne seated between us. You'd think College Prep English would be a wannabe writer's favorite class, but there are two simple words that make the class a living hell. One of them is 'Mrs.,' and the other is 'Renus.'

The moment I reach the third floor I spot the blonde-haired witch waiting outside the classroom. Her arms are crossed over her white cotton sweater with the giant volleyball in the center, and she greets passing students with a thin smile. To all the girls, especially her athletes, she gives a sweet "Good morning," and she even compliments the occasional girl on the jeans they're wearing, undoubtedly bought from the 'Anorexic and Dying' section of Wal-Mart. To the boys she either says nothing at all or scolds them with "Hurry along!" or "Don't glare at me, mister!" No matter what it is she's saying, though, her tone of voice doesn't really change—she speaks as softly as a teddy bear hailing from the enchanted forests of Gumdrop Mountain. If you listen to her voice for too long, you'll likely have an aneurysm.

Mrs. Renus has been dying to coach the Volleyball team, and everyone knows she's just waiting for the Spanish teacher Ms. Ross to either croak or forfeit the job willingly.

Jordan strides past me toward the classroom, towering over everyone else in the hallway. He's built like a linebacker, at least that's what I've heard sports-savvy teachers tell him. But a full inch or so of his height comes from his gelled-up douchebag hair, and he only *looks* sort of muscular because he wears shirts that are so stupidly tight it makes you want to cover him in gasoline and set him on fire.

He's holding hands with Sarah, and as he talks with her about something that's making her laugh, I notice something terrible.

Sarah's wearing a pink t-shirt. And not just any pink t-shirt, but an American Eagle pink t-shirt. She's never worn anything remotely close to that, and seeing her in it is like seeing a beautiful turtle stuck in a plastic ring.

First the damn sports hoodie and now a pink t-shirt...

Jordan lets go of Sarah's hand and kisses her quickly on the lips before she continues down the hall without him.

She doesn't even notice me standing there, and as I watch her head bob along I think of running after her to quickly say hi, and maybe jokingly give her crap about that sad, sad t-shirt. I still have a minute or so before the bell.

For some reason I shoot down the idea. When I turn to walk toward class I see that Mrs. Renus is watching Sarah too, only now her eyes have switched from those of a teddy bear to those of a deadly cobra poised to strike. This cheers me up greatly.

"Why, hello Mrs. Renus!" I say, extra-extra-cheesy. "Swell weekend, I hope? Broom still riding okay?"

She gives me a one-of-a-kind smile, a very tight and un-glowing kind that says, 'I could slit your throat right now and not lose sleep over it.'

"Get to your seat, Trey, or I'll mark you late," she says, not even bothering to sweeten the venom in her voice. I shrug and stroll past her.

Funny enough, when Mrs. Renus did the "random" seating arrangement at the beginning of the quarter, Clive and I both ended up much closer to her desk. I'd like to say we've used this power for good—that is, annoying the hell out of her all the more vigorously—but it's really just a pain in the ass, because now she watches us like a hawk and jumps into our conversations at the end of every class period. Lately, our ongoing conversation has been whether or not an ugly skin tag on the right side of a woman's mouth is a sure sign of witchcraft.

I'm shuffling through my folder for my set of *Beowulf* notes when I feel someone rap their knuckles on the back of my head. I grab my sharpened pencil tightly before turning around, but the flash of anger goes away when I see it's just Clive standing behind me.

"Holy shit," I say quietly. "What happened to you? Did you *sleep* with that bottle last night?"

He holds up a middle finger, yawning as he plops down and pushes the desk back a few loud inches. Mrs. Renus's head turns toward us, but she's in the middle of a conversation with one of her special girls.

"Seriously, you look terrible."

"So do you," he says. His voice is quiet and groggy, like he's struggling to stay awake. He smells, too, which wouldn't be a big deal if his sweat wasn't pure alcohol.

"Did the others get you home last night?"

He waves a hand dismissively. "I don't need a babysitter."

"I told them to make sure you got home. You didn't sleep in the tree, did you?"

"I didn't sleep at all," he says. Christ, his breath must be flammable.

"What did you do?"

"Went for a walk. Went down to the slaughterhouse for a minute. Threw some rocks into the runoff creek by the rubber factory. Got some coffee at Circle K."

"Why didn't you just skip school and sleep it off?"

His eyes are scrunched and exhausted, and I can tell he's getting pissed at my questions.

"My dad's home all day, and I'm already on his shit list for forgetting to feed the dog. Shut up a second, would you?"

I nod and turn back around in my seat, and he sits slumped over around his face and his grey hood over his head. He definitely finished off the alcohol last night, and even though it's really not my problem, I feel bad for it. Maybe he's suffering like I was suffering last night, but at least I got a little bit of rest. I *told* Monk and Kevin to get him home...

The bell rings, and everyone moves to their seats as Mrs. Renus closes the door. I continue digging for my notes, hoping like hell there isn't a pop quiz today because I haven't read any of this week's chapters.

From the corner of my eye I see Clive lift his head. Neither of us are friends with the two volleyball girls seated in front of us, and I'm pretty sure neither of them wants anything to do with us, either. But for some damn reason, Clive reaches out and touches the shoulder of the girl in front of him.

"Taylor," he says. She half-turns in her seat, just enough to show a disgusted look as she pushes his hand away.

"Do you want to go to a movie with us later?" Clive continues. "Me and Trey and some others are going."

"Leave me alone," she says. She wrinkles her nose and recoils a little before a slight smile touches her lips. "Oh my God, you smell like shit!"

He doesn't seem to hear her, though. He tries his best at a charming smile.

"I'm just saying, none of us have ever talked, and I think you'd really like talking to us before one of us is dead. Does that make sense? I would really hate to die someday without you talking to me just once."

Taylor's got her phone out now, and she's recording his drunken slurring as she eagerly taps the girl beside her. They're both staring at him now, mocking him.

"Why do you smell so shitty?" Taylor asks. "Can't your dad afford running water, or do you have to bathe in the creek?"

"Look, there's puke on his sleeve!" the other girl says, jabbing a finger toward him.

"Leave him alone," I say. They either don't hear me or don't give a damn. I grip my pencil tighter as I stare at Taylor's puffy freckle-covered face.

The rest of the room is already quiet, and when I turn my head I see Mrs. Renus walking in our direction. Taylor doesn't even bother putting her phone away.

"Why are you wearing something with puke on it? Don't you own any other clothes?"

Clive stares toward the floor, silent. He gnaws his lower lip, and I can see his jaw trembling. I don't think he even hears what they're saying; he's lost somewhere else in his head, and I know how much that sucks.

"I believe I heard the bell ring, ladies," Mrs. Renus says. Taylor points excitedly at Clive.

"He's drunk! Look at him!"

"He's not even in the right seat," the other girl adds.

Mrs. Renus sees Clive's pathetic form. Like a raven swooping down on a mouse, she sets her pale claws on his shoulders. He jumps at the touch, loudly moving the desk again as he nearly falls out of the seat. The rest of the class laughs, and I think of how much I'd like to stab them all, one by one, right in their bastard faces.

"You're not looking well today, Mister Lange," she says, sweetening her voice again. "Do you need to go to the nurse's office?"

He shakes his head, trying to turn back around in his desk as he reaches under his seat for his notebook.

"I'm fine," he says.

"No, no," she says. "I really think we need to have this checked out. Look at you, you're burning up! Is it a fever, Mister Lange?"

I know she smells the horrible stench, but she's putting on a show while the girls snicker. I know where this is going and what will happen if Clive gets sent home. I'd never tell Clive this, because he'd straight-up kill me if I even hinted at it, but everyone knows what a monster his dad is. He'll bust Clive's face in if he gets sent home. And this evil, evil witch *knows* it.

"I think you'd better go down to the nurse's office," she says.

Terror floods Clive's expression, and his mouth drops a fraction as he shakes his head wordlessly. The girls are still recording, and the rest of the class is gawking at the scene. I want to jump in somehow, say something to his defense, anything to keep the witch from feeding on him further. But her hunger's just begun.

"Be reasonable, Mister Lange," she chides him.

I stand up.

"I'll take him to the office, Mrs. Renus," I offer, trying to sound helpful rather than desperate. "I'll make sure he doesn't trip down the stairs or anything."

Once we're out of the room, I'll sneak Clive down to the second-floor exit and take him home from there. We'll both get in trouble for cutting class, but I don't care.

"I don't believe I asked for your help, Trey," Mrs. Renus says. She's already grabbed the tablet of hall passes from her desk, and as she scribbles, Jordan stands up from his seat on the other side of the room.

"I can escort him there," he says.

"I'm okay," Clive says. "I swear to God, I'm just tired. I'm not sick or anything."

Mrs. Renus doesn't even respond. She pushes her lower lip sadly out at him as Jordan walks over and extends a brotherly hand in his direction.

Like a cornered animal, Clive's expression quickly changes. It all seems to come together at once for him, the ugliness of it all. His lip quivers as he looks at Taylor, and with a quick slap at her arm, her phone goes flying toward the wall.

"Hey!" she shouts, rushing to grab her phone. I glance down and see the uncracked screen is still recording.

"Screw you," Clive says, and he smacks Jordan's hand away as he stands on his own. He glares at Mrs. Renus, who just watches with her arms crossed. "Screw all of you!"

"There's no need for such language," she says. "I think you'd better serve three days of detention once you've been all sorted out."

Clive leans forward and spits in her face.

The reaction from the class is immediate—they go 'ooh' and 'oh shit,' waiting for Hell to break loose as Mrs. Renus shouts in disgust and hurriedly grabs a Kleenex. Jordan rushes at Clive like he's going to knock him out, defending Dear Mommy.

"Enough!" Mrs. Renus shouts. "Clive, get out of my classroom and down to the nurse's office right this instant!"

Clive stares at her like he's going to say something else, but his mouth just moves silently. There are tears in his eyes, but for a fleeting second, he looks far from pathetic. Taylor's no longer recording, and no one in the class says a word.

He storms out the door and slams it behind him.

Mrs. Renus looks ready to explode. In a videogame, I think this would be where the final boss takes its ultimate ugly form and starts slaughtering indiscriminately. Instead, she just sighs.

"Notes out, everyone," she says calmly, and walks toward the front of the class. A few people groan, because their entertainment's over. Screw those people.

The rest of the class is boring as ever. Mrs. Renus lectures on and on about Beowulf's heroic journey, and even though I'm moving my pencil across the page like I'm taking notes, my mind's wandering and I can't reel it back in. I really, really wish they'd listened to me and taken care of Clive last night. He's a wreck over Grandpa. We all are. If they'd forced him to drink a little water, or maybe convinced him to sleep it off in the caretaker's shed...

I force the thoughts away. It doesn't matter. Done is done. Clive will probably be okay.

Instead, I think about my story and the murderous history of the nameless Catholic priest. I still don't know much about him, his backstory, or anything substantial. I need to work harder, because Grandpa would really hate me if I didn't distract myself from the pain somehow.

I re-read *A Day Away* last year, and it was a whole lot better than I remembered it. I told Grandpa I want to write as well as he does, and I'm going to make him proud.

I pick up where I left off at breakfast. The priest isn't a religious nut or anything like that, using the bodies of his victims for some freakish cult ritual. That sort of thing is overdone, I think. I can't figure out the logic, though, and my head hurts trying to make sense of it. Why would a priest dress as a clown at all? What's his motivation for killing people? Even in bad fiction, no character can just exchange his cross for a knife just like—

Wait a second. The knife...

'Yes?' Grandpa's voice asks.

An experienced killer would keep it hidden somewhere clever, wouldn't he? Somewhere nobody would look.

'You're getting warmer.'

The cross! He'd keep the blade hidden inside the lower part, and the top part would be the blade's handle! He'd be able to carry it around all day in plain sight, and nobody would ever find the murder weapon.

But why's he killing people in the first place?

Damn.

I'm back to the crappy pondering stage again, but at least I know a little more than I did at breakfast. As I begin to write the information down for later reference, the lecture finally ends, and Mrs. Renus writes our homework assignment on the board. The room begins buzzing with conversations again.

Without Clive in the room, I don't have anyone to talk to. I don't know any of these other people, and I don't think they have any more interest in me than I have in them. Sometimes it's enough just to listen in on their conversations, because as lame as they all are, their drama is sometimes hilarious. I sieve through the dull stuff like who's dating who and what was on TV last night, and I'm quickly able to tune into the really good stuff, the very hush-hush stuff that I have to strain a little to hear.

One of the girls in the front row apparently thinks her boyfriend, who's a varsity quarterback, is cheating on her with Vanessa McCoy, who everyone knows had an abortion last year.

Cy Wilson, the boy who was caught masturbating in the third-floor bathroom two weeks ago, is asking someone else if they've ever had a burning feeling when they piss.

My ears perk up with real interest, though, when I hear Jordan's less-than-discreet voice from the other side of the room. He talks with the annoying arrogance of a politician. I turn my head just enough to see who he's talking to, and I see the usual suspects: a bull-headed kid who could probably fit an entire watermelon in his mouth and three girls who somehow always end up seated near him.

Jordan's leaning back in his chair with one hand spread out on the desk in front of him, putting his big golden class ring on display.

"Did I tell you guys I started writing that book I've been talking about?" he asks them.

"A book?" one of the girls asks. "I didn't know you write."

"That's so amazing!" says the other girl. I think her name's Karina, and her constant unwarranted enthusiasm tells me she'd slit Sarah's throat to have Jordan all to herself.

I say into my hand, "You don't freaking write."

I'm driving the point of my pencil into my notebook, staring down at the small black hole I'm making.

"Well," Jordan says, lowering his voice, "I've had this big idea for a book series in my head for a while now, and I think I've finally got it all straight. All I really need to do is just get it down on paper and send it off. It's part of my process."

"That's not a freaking process," I mutter. Jordan's expression is practically audible, and somehow I know he's sitting there with his eyes slightly downcast, acting modest while also feeding on the unwarranted adoration like a gel-haired soul sucker.

I picture him sitting at a keyboard, and I sneer to myself. He'd never make it to the end of the first paragraph. I doubt he's even read an entire book in his life.

"Actually, I really didn't want to say anything," he continues, "but my mom says she has connections with an editor in New York. She thinks he'll at least take a look at it once I get the first draft on paper."

"Oh wow!" says one of the girls.

"I'll get to say I knew you back before you were famous," says the other.

I mutter, "You lying goddamn sack of dog—"

"What?" someone asks.

Oops. I spoke too loudly that time. The girl two seats to my right, next to the empty seat where Clive had been, is looking at me.

"Did you say something?" she asks.

"No."

"Oh," she says. She starts to turn back around in her seat, but then something catches her attention. "Is that Rob Zombie on your shirt?" she asks excitedly.

I look down, not really knowing what shirt I pulled from my dresser.

"Oh my god, I *love* Rob Zombie!" she says. "Have you ever been to one of his shows? I mean, he's sort of freaky, but I guess that's fun, you know?"

"Sure."

"Do you like Machine Gun Kelly at all?" she asks.

"Hell no," I snort automatically. She looks completely taken aback by the reaction, and I feel a little ashamed for it. "I mean, he's alright, I guess. I really don't know much about rap music. Eminem's pretty good, though."

I really have no interest in her or any possible conversation with her. She's a nice enough person, I think, and she helped organize a blood drive last quarter. But despite all her kindness and good enough looks, all I'm suddenly able to think about is Jordan and his goddamn *editor in New York...*'

So, I look back at my notebook and just let the unfinished conversation hang. After a few seconds I see her finally look away again, and even though I know she thinks I'm a jerk now, I feel relieved.

I try listening back into Jordan's conversation, but it's no use. I sit there stabbing at my notebook, trying and failing to get back into my story. The minutes drag by, and all I can do is sit silently and wish Clive was still here.

There's a stray dog at my mind's door, a mangy little hellhound with rotting meat in its crooked and misshapen teeth.

If Jordan's mom really can hook him up with an easy path to publication...what then? What the hell do I really know anyway? Grandpa's the only writer I've ever talked to, and the only advice he gave me was *"write!"* He never said much about a process outside of that. Maybe Jordan really is holding a bestseller in his mind and he'll get it out perfectly the first time he puts it on paper. Maybe I'm wasting my damn time actually *trying*, losing sleep over one stupid idea and letting it bother me at all. Maybe…

I kick the imaginary hellhound in its side and slam the door on its paws. I'm overthinking this. Jordan's just an asshole.

The bell rings, and once again the doorway floods as everyone hurries to their next class. I'm one of the last ones up, gathering my things with a sort of languish that I blame solely on being hungover and not at all on any sort of depression. I trudge forward, pushing and shoving, and my books are suddenly knocked from my hands as some jackass throws an arm between my body and someone else's to rip ahead of the pack.

People storm past me as I kneel to pick up my books and papers. Rather than crawl between their feet and risk getting my fingers smashed, I wait for the flood to pass, completely disregarding anyone whose path I'm blocking.

The crowd starts to dwindle when suddenly a hand runs up my back and through my hair, and I see Sarah walk past me with her tongue stuck out. Jordan's arm is tied around her like a second belt, pulling her along as she calls back to me, "Better work on that grip, butterfingers!"

I smile at her, offering only a stupid wave because I don't have anything witty to say. Jordan turns his head barely, and when his serpent-green eyes meet mine, he grins. His hand slides gently down Sarah's back, and with a quick wink in my direction he squeezes her butt.

She turns to hit him on the shoulder, and he backs away innocently from her futile attempts while she laughs and calls him something I can't even hear.

I'm frozen, unable to remember for a moment why I'm even on the floor. My heart's beating wildly behind my ribcage like a prisoner banging against his cell bars, and all I can do is stare at the spot where Sarah and Jordan disappeared. All at once I feel like everything in the world is against me and there's nothing I can do to stand up, and the iron fist is squeezing my heart mercilessly.

Maybe it's the alcohol still in my system, but my mind stops interpreting thoughts with words alone. Images are flashing in my mind like a weird movie with everything but the violent parts cut out of it.

My hands must know about these mental pictures as well, because when I look down they're both curled into fists.

Chapter Four

There's about twenty or so members in the T.A.G. group, and they're all gathered across the auditorium stage when I sneak in and hide behind some curtains. Most of them are sitting on the choir risers, all business and no play in their expressions as they talk with utter seriousness. Others are either standing around the concert piano and chatting idly or dangling their legs over the edge of the stage and playing on their phones.

I'm disappointed, really. Walking into the room, I half-expected to see virgin sacrifices to The Holy God of Bullshit.

I peer out from behind the curtain, searching for Monk's face. He's not hard to spot, being the only giant in the group. I find him standing by himself on the opposite side of the stage, holding a thin red book in front of him and gesturing wildly with his other hand as he seems to argue with himself. I hold back laughter as I watch his expression repeatedly change as he contorts his face into anger, sadness, anger, fear, anger, laughter. He reads lines from the book out loud, whispering all the really angry parts but still looking as if he's yelling.

Is he warming up? Is that what this is? Whatever it is, it's disturbing as hell to watch, but I think maybe I can use some of it for the pastor/clown/cannibal character.

School's been over for nearly fifteen minutes when Anus finally strolls onto the stage. Sarah unglues herself from his hip when they reach center stage, and she hurries to stand next to Monk.

Jordan announces his presence by clapping his hands together and whirling dramatically to face them all.

"Alright everyone," he says, grinning widely as he begins to pace. "As you know, The Rock the Arts Festival is less than a month away. I don't think I need to remind you all of last year's major flaws..."

He looks toward Monk, who doesn't give him the satisfaction of looking away.

"But I think this has the potential to be a really great show," he continues. "I will say this, though: if we want T.A.G. group to continue next year, we need to start working harder at putting on a *show*! I won't be around next year to help you younger guys, but let me tell you, this half-assed stuff we're putting on just isn't going to cut it. I'm only saying this for your benefit. We need to think *bigger*, and we need to work *harder*!"

He claps his hands for emphasis, and his audience nods obligingly as his eyes pass over them. As soon as his back is turned a few of them stick up their middle fingers. One of them cocks an invisible shotgun and fires it at him repeatedly.

Jordan lifts his nose a fraction as he lets his words sink in, pulling the gentle look of a parent explaining to his kids he only beats them because he loves them.

"You guys, I'm just so proud of all the work we've done together, and I really want my final show with you to be amazing. Is everyone excited?"

"Yippee," a girl on the risers says flatly.

"With all that said, it's high time we get to planning. Theodore!"

Jordan looks at Monk, who just blinks back at him. I can see Monk's jaw moving slightly behind closed lips. He hates it when you use his real name, and if he wasn't one of the few people who actually liked this group he'd make damn sure the mouth it came out of stopped working entirely.

Good, I think in a Darth Sidious voice. *Let the hate flow through you...*

"Do you have an act planned for the show?" Jordan asks innocently.

"Yeah," Monk says. "I'm doing a scene from *Razor's Edge*, the Broadway play."

"*Razor's Edge?*" Jordan asks dubiously. "Correct me if I'm wrong, Theodore, but isn't that a musical?"

"It is," Monk says. "But the whole point of being here is to get better, right? I won't grow as an actor if I don't push myself out of my comfort zone."

"Hmm." Jordan winces, tilting his head with a look like he's picturing disaster. "I suppose your heart's in the right place, but I think maybe I should see you try it out before I give the thumbs-up. Fair enough, bud?"

Monk nods, not looking the least bit demoralized. He'll do any damn thing he sets his mind to, with or without Anus's stamp of approval. Jordan claps his hands again as he looks around the room.

"Who else has something for me? Anyone? Clyde, I know last year you did a great stand-up act, but if it's okay with you, I—"

"Excuse me," I interrupt, stepping out of the shadows. Monk's not the only one who knows drama and how to use the stage; they all turn and look in my direction, and I swear to God, the lighting above me actually changes. I look around at everyone with my best impression of a kind smile, cocking a hand at a few of them as I walk toward the group.

Jordan spreads his hands with visible annoyance.

"We're in the middle of a meeting," he says. "What do you want?"

My kind, warmhearted, not-at-all-genuine smile doesn't falter. I'll give Monk a lesson in acting they don't teach in that thin little book of his.

"I'm sorry to interrupt," I say, "but I heard the group is planning another talent show for the festival. I've always loved the shows you've put on, and I was hoping I could join."

Off to my side, I see Monk looking at me incredulously.

"I mean," I continue, "I've been working nonstop lately on developing my storytelling skills, just nothing but writing and rewriting and stressing every single day. But I heard some people say you're really, *really* good at storytelling, and I figure I could learn a lot from you."

For as much as I'd prefer hacking my dick off with a broken beer bottle over sucking up to Jordan, I stare at him like he's my idol, waiting for him to take the bait. The look on his face tells me it's working. It's like I just asked for his autograph or something. He looks at me unsurely, waiting for a punchline.

But he *is* the punchline. If he wants to talk himself up like he's Mister Bigshot, that's great, he can go nuts with it. But I'm going to take this group from him, and I'm going to do it from the inside. Give me one show, one chance at doing anything whatsoever on stage, and I'll embarrass the smarmy douchebag with how much better I am. Maybe I'm not a great writer, but whenever Grandpa was bold it always seemed to work out for him.

I almost burst out in laughter imagining what must be going through Monk's mind right now, watching me sell out to the scum of the Earth. I tell myself not to look over at Sarah, but her reaction is all I can think about, and before I can stop myself I'm glancing in her direction.

And that's what screws it up. Jordan follows the direction of my eyes and then looks back at me, and I'm busted.

"Sorry, Trey," he says, shrugging helplessly. "If you'd asked me earlier in the year, maybe I could've mentored you a bit, but membership is already closed, and we can't start accepting people into the group when we're so close to a show date."

"That's not true," Sarah says. "You let me join less than a month before a show, remember?"

"That was different," Jordan says. "*You* actually have talent. Hell, you paint *and* you dance. You're multi-talented, babe."

"You said the group is only sanctioned by the school as long as it offers open membership to anyone who wants to join. Regardless of when the next show is," she insists. "Otherwise, why keep posters up around the school telling people to audition?"

It takes all my effort not to smile at Sarah's support. She doesn't look at me, but instead stands in Jordan's eyeline. She looks perfectly innocent, one hand on his elbow as she waits for an answer. Oh, she's good…she's really, *really* good.

Jordan's eyes move between me and the floor. In my mind I'm already celebrating, because as soon as I get home I'm going to write the best damn story I've ever written and rub it in his face.

"Okay," he concedes. He blows a calm breath toward the floor as he sets his hands on his hips. "You can join. But you have to audition, right here and now." He gestures to the center of the stage and starts to back away. "Give it your best shot."

I feel a sudden coldness like dead fingers crawling up my back.

"What?" I ask.

"Give it your best shot," he repeats, twirling a finger impatiently. I look around the room for support, at Sarah and then at Monk, but neither of them jumps in to save me this time. I wanted a chance, this is it. They want me to create a story on the spot.

I feel sick, like I'm going to throw up, and all the confidence I had walking into the room is gone and the tables are turned. Jordan's the one who going to make a fool out of *me*, and I made it happen.

"We haven't got all day, Trey," Jordan says, and the smug bastard actually looks at his wrist even though there's no watch. "I mean, if you can't do it, just say so. No need to embarrass yourself. I'll be happy to tutor you outside the group."

Hatred overtakes panic as I look into his eyes. God, I hate him so bad. If I could kill him and get away with it, I would, and I'd be doing everyone in this school a favor. They'd name a holiday after me, probably. Hell, some of them might even name their firstborns after me.

No matter what I say right now, it's not going to be good enough. If he can find a way to tear Monk's acts apart all the time, he'll tear whatever story I tell to shreds, because that's just who he is and he's the one in charge. How the hell does Sarah stand him? She can't honestly love him, not real love, at least if love is what I think love is and everything I believe isn't a damn lie. Is it magic? Is it drugs he's putting in her drink that makes her go to his house every night, change her style and her whole way of thinking for him? He's a complete dickhead, everyone knows it, *she* even knows it, so why in God's name…

My breath catches in my throat, and I smile as I latch onto the first idea that comes to me. I have no choice. I run with it.

"Okay," I begin. I clear my throat and start to pace anxiously. "You all know the Garden of Eden, right?"

A few of them answer, but most just either nod or stare at their phones.

I continue: "This story's set far outside the beautiful Garden of Eden, just after God banished Adam and Eve from Paradise forever because of their sins and stuff. And there was nothing but a dark, desolate, horrible wasteland outside of Eden, just like the bible says. But there were more creatures than just the two scared humans—there were evil, twisted beings who'd risen from Hell itself through the cracks in the Earth.

"Outside the golden gates, Adam and Eve stood clutching each other, listening fearfully to the maddening sounds of chirping, buzzing, scratching, and horrible, horrible laughter from the evil creatures inhabiting Earth at the time…"

I'm looking around as I speak, and I see a few of them losing interest already. Monk and Sarah and a few others are listening attentively, but that's not enough. I'm losing the audience. I feel like I'm going to throw up.

The piano's right beside me, and with the spirit of Grandpa taking hold of me I make the bold choice: I slam my fingers down twice on the leftmost keys, snapping a few of them away from their distractions with the low and reverberating sound.

And then I throw my head back and laugh a deep and demonic laugh; it's the monstrous laugh I've heard haunted house performers use, the full-tilt madness kind of laugh I've never let loose before.

"And as Eve listened," I continue, pacing again, "a spell came over her and she was put into a trance. These weren't noises meant for human ears, and not even angels could withstand the horror of these sounds. She didn't stand a chance of refusing their beckoning demands, and she succumbed immediately to what these noises told her to do."

They're all listening now. I don't see a single damn phone out anymore, and I feel electricity moving through me as I continue pacing, some strange and awesome magic.

"She took a sharp stone from the ground and slit Adam's throat from ear-to-ear," I say. "His blood showered across her face and covered the dry cracked soil all around them, and as he fell forward into her arms, carrying her with him to the ground, he looked at her with absolute betrayal in his eyes. But beneath his anguish, she still saw pure love as he touched her face one final time. She screamed and cried with his corpse in her arms, but there was no one around to hear her weep. Where Adam's blood spilled, there grew a long and thorny rosebush, and it wrapped around her until she and the corpse were given a small shelter, and the shelter seemed to protect her from the terrible sounds and their demands.

"The creatures of Hell which ruled this desolate wasteland were presently at war with each other. One side was led by an angel named Basilia, who'd fallen from Heaven long before Lucifer ever did, and although Basilia's face was still as beautiful and holy as the day God made him, he reeked terribly from the stench of Hell that followed him permanently. His face was perfect, but the rest of his body was morphed. He had the long tail of a snake with a scorpion's deadly stinger on the end, and the hind legs of a leopard, and the rest of his skin was blackened and shedding like scales. His wings were burned off, but what he lacked in flight he made up for in venom which seared the veins of his prey while he decapitated them with the deadly pincers that replaced his right hand."

I pause and take a deep breath. Coffee, alcohol, and all the sexy fantasies in the world have never given me this strange sort of rush. My vision's going black around the edges, but I don't feel weak, I feel powerful, and I can feel the energy coming from every pair of eyes in the room looking at me.

"The other side of the war was led by Taral," I say. "He was an angel sent from Eden to defend the gates from demonic wrath, but as soon as the fumes from Hell touched his body they transformed him, and God disowned him as he would with any other abomination. Taral remained loyal, though, and stuck to his duties. Unlike Basilia, Taral's demonic mutilations didn't spare any of his beauty—his robe was tarnished and blacked, fused to the festering sores on his skin as his back was hideously contorted into a large hump and his teeth grew so large and sharp that they pierced his cheeks and kept his mouth permanently shut. Eight spindly legs sprouted from his torso, and when he moved on them his human legs dragged behind him. But despite his horrid appearance, Taral had no venom in his still-holy soul, and his only defense against the demonic hordes was to swat them away repeatedly. It was purely by a miracle that any demons at all gravitated toward his side of the war. Maybe they were inspired by him, maybe they were just mindless and bloodthirsty and happy to kill alongside any larger beast that supplied them with targets.

"So, as Eve sat under the safety of the twisted rosebush, she watched helplessly as the sun lowered and the legions of nocturnal creatures became louder in their approach toward the gates. As he rose from his burrow in the cracked ground to fight his nightly war, Taral immediately spotted Eve, and he momentarily forgot his duties as he approached her. He'd never seen these strange new creations before, and when he crawled closer to get a better look at the woman's naked flesh, the two of them marveled at the terrifying beauty of one another. Taral saw the corpse she held and recoiled at her wicked deed.

"It was then, though, that he realized what the Lord had put into these new creations that made them better than any other creature. This woman looked terrified and ashamed of the corpse she was trapped with, which told Taral she still had a semblance of innocence left within her, no matter what her reasoning was for being outside the gate. He contemplated this deeply, and he felt a strange sense of mortality that was new to him. He knew, right then, that his own death would come someday soon, and there'd need to be a new protector of Eden's gates."

Jordan starts clapping, slow and sarcastic.

"Great work, Trey, real brilliant," he says. "Blasphemy and loads of story holes. Real nice work. That'll really go over well with our audience."

I pause, mouth already opened to continue with the story. I feel frozen there for a moment, unsure what to do.

But then Sarah touches Jordan's shoulder, and when he turns toward her she glares at him.

"Shut up, babe," she says. "I want to hear the rest."

He looks at her for a second, and then back at me. Finally, he throws his hands up in surrender and sits back down, looking less than pleased. Sarah nods to me, and I feel my energy renewed.

"Taral explained to Eve the best he could how they could help each other, telling her that by helping provide Eden with a new protector she would be providing a great service to the future of humanity, and in exchange he could offer her protection from the beasts which would otherwise tear her apart. Eve quickly agreed, and as the sun fell over the horizon, Taral spun a much stronger shelter made from his own webs and the bones of his enemies. It was decided that he would bring her only the best meat from the demons he slaughtered so that she might live.

"So Taral put his seed within Eve, and he defended her night after night from the hordes. But those who escaped his wrath went back to tell Basilia of the strange cocoon they'd seen not far from the battlefield, and how they'd seen a face staring out from within. One night, after hearing many of these rumors, Basilia himself came toward the gate to see this strange sight, and while Taral was distracted with his fighting, he chewed a hole in the web shelter and peeked his head inside. When he saw the scared woman and the corpse she still held onto, he knew she was another fallen creation of the God who'd cast him out. He smiled and considered killing this precious thing of Taral's just to spite him…but then a better idea occurred to him.

"He saw the woman was pregnant, and rather than crush any hope of Eden's new protector being born, he decided to add a touch of his own malice to the unborn baby. He dipped his venomous tail into the blood that covered the battlefield, and when he pierced Eve's womb he tainted the life she carried within her and all future generations. Never again would there be total purity in the world, and never again would he need to wage war against these gates. The evil in all future generations would balance out the goodness, and every descendent of this woman would be cursed with pains far greater than their pleasures."

I end the story on that line, lowering my voice and leaving the room hanging in total silence. Nobody speaks; those who aren't staring at me still are looking solemnly down at the ground between their feet like they're seeing the story for themselves. I see Monk and Sarah watching me with proud looks, and it makes me shake inside like a muscle spasm that won't quit.

The silence is broken when Jordan coughs into his elbow and clears his throat loudly. The corners of his lips move upward into an artificial smile as he walks toward me.

"That was good," he admits, somewhat reluctantly. "I would've probably done a few things differently, and I can definitely see why you'd come to me for help. For one thing, I'm just not buying the tone you're creating, and the characters are all a little over-the-top. It felt too sloppy, if we're being honest, and—"

"It kicked ass," says a girl on the risers, looking up from the floor. A few others mutter their agreement, and even better than the powerful feeling this praise fills me with is the utter defeat on Jordan's face. I've won the crowd, and he knows it. I've knocked that smug look right off his face.

"So I'm in now, right?" I ask, confidence rising still as my smile stretches wider. He meets my eyes for only a second, and from that single look I can see he'd rather stick his hand in a garbage disposal than stay on this stage any longer.

"There's another meeting tomorrow," he says. He moves his jaw a little, then adds, "But I'll have a long list of things I want edited for the show. There'll be old people in the audience, and I don't want you offending them with all that sick stuff."

With his two cents chipped in, he turns toward everyone else and continues taking stock of all the other acts for the show. I walk over to stand with Monk and Sarah, smiling with shameless pride. I feel invincible, like I've discovered some superhuman part of myself that's been waiting since birth to be tapped.

It didn't suck too bad, I hear Grandpa say. *Attaboy, kid.*
For at least a moment, I feel alright.

Chapter Five

I lead the way as the three of us walk across town toward Schiff's Matinee and Pizza Shop, shortcutting through yards and alleyways. I'm still smiling, and the electric current under my skin is still going strong.

"And you said *I* was the traitor!" Monk says triumphantly. "Hypocrite!"

I let him go on and on, listing off every time I'd talked badly about T.A.G. group. I'm sure he knows why I was really there, which is why he finally shuts up when Sarah walks beside me.

"There's no way you made all that up on the spot," she says, eying me suspiciously. "You had to have at least had part of it memorized."

"Nope," I say, grinning. "I just opened my mouth and let it flow."

"Write it down!" she urges, slapping my forearm. "You can sell it to a sci-fi magazine, or you could even make a short film out of it. There've been entire religions based on less, haven't there?"

"*The Gospel According to Trey*," Monk reflects. He shudders at the thought.

I know how impossibly self-indulgent I'm being right now, listening to their praise and feeling like someone completely new. I'm nothing special. The story's nothing special. But I feel Grandpa walking beside me, telling me ecstatically how damn proud he is of me and clapping his hands like a maniac. Sarah and Monk keep going on about the story, but it's Grandpa's ghost that I can't stop listening to. I'm not crazy, because I know he's not *really* here talking to me. But it feels good to think about the madman I knew from those first days at the movie theater rather than the dying man who was quickly stolen by cancer.

"We have to pick up your sister, don't we?" I ask Monk. He nods gravely.

"We won't be late for the movie, though," he promises. "Dad's got the car for work, and the dance studio's right along the way. We just need to dump her there."

"I don't mind your sister," Sarah says.

"Nothing but a giant pain in my ass."

The movie theater's only twenty-some minutes away by foot, and the elementary school's just a little out of the way. Katy's actually supposed to be in the seventh grade by now, but she got held back last year for behavioral issues after she took a pair of scissors from her teacher's desk and chopped off a handful of another girl's hair. Monk's parents threw a fit over it, and apparently the other girl's mom actually drove to their house to complain about the incident and demand that Katy be given "swift and severe punishment." Monk's mom is about as old school gangster as it gets, though, and Monk says she told the woman *maybe* Katy wouldn't have reacted that way if the other girl had parents who taught them it's not okay to taunt someone every day about the birthmark on their face.

Monk relayed the story breathlessly to Grandpa while we were all on his porch, and I swear to God, Grandpa fell out of his chair laughing. *'Your sister's one of us, alright,'* he said. It really is too bad Monk never brought Katy around, because Grandpa definitely would've gotten a kick out of her.

She's already outside waiting by the time we get there. The elementary school's been out for a little while, and she's sitting alone on a bench with her phone in her hand, volume turned up loud with some show on full-blast. Monk swipes the phone out of her hand as he walks by.

"Let's go, brat," he says. "I'm taking you to dance practice today."

"Where's mom?" she asks, throwing her backpack over one shoulder and rushing to follow. "Give me back my phone!"

"Mom's busy, don't worry about it," he says. He doesn't stop walking or even look back at her as he speaks. She sees me and smiles.

"Hey Trey," she sings.

"Shut up and walk," Monk says.

She grimaces, causing the thumb-sized pink birthmark to peek out from beneath her blonde bangs, and hurries to walk beside Sarah.

"Why's he being such a jerk today?" she asks, and then stares at him as she whispers loudly, "Is he on his period?"

"Shut up," he growls. He walks faster and tells me, "Just don't acknowledge her, alright? I swear to God, I want to throw that little brat down a stairwell sometimes."

I smile, entertained as ever by his hatred for his sister. He's also said to me before that he's going to kill the first little kid who speaks a bad word about her, and he's coached her to drive a foot between the legs of any boy in her class who tries to touch her, so I know the hate doesn't run too deep.

Sarah and Katy walk behind us, talking about who-the-hell-cares. I can't hear them anyway, because Monk's going on about the notes Jordan gave after the meeting, asking him to reconsider the idea of doing a song from a musical.

"*'I just don't want you to end up embarrassing yourself!'*" he mimics, giving his voice a girlish falsetto. "What a piece of trash."

"You're the one who puts up with it," I point out.

"What choice do I have? There's no amateur theater in this crappy town. It's this or nothing at all."

I pry him away from his raging bitchfest, because I'm honestly bored hearing about it. We start talking about baseball, even though I don't care about sports and he knows I don't care, but at least he calms down.

Then Katy runs up beside us, followed closely by Sarah.

"I have something for you!" she says.

"Piss off, we're talking," Monk says.

"I wasn't talking to *you*." She opens her backpack and pulls a book out from inside. "I was talking to Trey. He's the reader, not you."

She holds the book toward me. *A Clockwork Orange.*

"I've read that," Monks says, a little defensively. "Why do you have it? That book's not for kids. It was too weird for me, even."

"Mom gave it to me. She says I'm advanced for my age and only *you* got dad's stupid person genes."

"You know Mom drank when she was pregnant with you, right?"

"Mom says you have an underbite, and that it's a sign of Down syndrome."

"You don't even know what Down syndrome is, you little brat," he says.

I look at the book's cover while they bicker, and I start leafing through it. It's a pretty thin book.

"I haven't heard of this one," I say. Katy's scowl turns quickly back into a smile as she looks from Monk back to me.

"It's weird," she says. "I'm almost halfway through, but I don't think I'm going to finish it. Sarah told me you like weird stories, though, so you can have it."

I look back at Sarah. She shrugs.

"You'd like it, alright," Monk says, pushing Katy with one hand toward the empty street. "I watched the movie, and it's right up your alley with all that weird stuff. It's set in the future or something, and apparently it got banned by a bunch of places."

"Cool," I say. "Thanks, Katy."

"Maybe when you're done reading we can talk about it," she says. And then she dances her eyebrows at me.

"Stop that!" Monk says. "Stop being a little creep!"

We reach the plaza a few minutes later, and by that time we've regained a comfortable distance between our conversations. The dance studio's on the corner, inside a remodeled old insurance building, and the movie theater's just on the other side of the plaza.

"The movie gets out around five-thirty-ish," Monk tells Katy. "If you're not out here when we walk by to pick you up, I'm leaving you for kidnappers."

"That's two hours from now," Katy whines. "Dance class only goes for an hour."

"Fine, then just come to the theater when you're done. Wait around inside the lobby or something."

"Can I have money for popcorn?"

Monk doesn't answer; he's already walking toward the theater with his middle finger held up behind him.

"Bye, Katy!" Sarah says, and we start to follow Monk.

I can see Clive on the other side of the plaza, sitting against the wall outside the theater with a spit cup in his hand.

"Did you hear about what happened to him earlier?" I ask as we walk.

Monk nods gravely. "That little bitch Taylor's been showing the video around school all day."

"Why didn't you get him home last night?" I ask. "I thought you said you were going to, but maybe I misheard."

He furrows his brow at me, annoyed.

"I *did* get him back. We got him inside and everything. Lucky his dad wasn't there, all the noise he was making."

"He must have left again, then," I tell him. "He said he was out all night."

"We're not his babysitters," Monk says. I look across the lot and see that he hasn't noticed us yet.

"It was Taylor's damn fault," I say. "Taylor and Mrs. Renus. Clive was already upset, and they took it to a whole new level."

"I heard he was drunk and acting like an asshole," Sarah says. Monk rolls his eyes.

"Well, damn, I wonder who *that* came from."

"Jordan was in the room. He said Clive was a mess when he came in, and that he spit on his mom."

"Jordan would do anything to stir crap up. You know he hates Clive."

Sarah stops in her tracks and holds both arms out to block us.

"Did he or did he not spit on Judy?"

"Judy?" Monk asks.

"Mrs. Renus, I mean," she says. "Did he spit on her?"

"You're on a first-name basis with Jordan's mom? She doesn't even like you, you know she doesn't. You're not good enough for her perfect widdle baby boy."

She waves a dismissive hand.

"Fine, don't answer the question. It's only because you know I'm right and Clive was being an asshole. Talk about Jordan all you want, he didn't do what Clive did."

"I mean, yeah, Clive was pretty sloppy drunk," I admit. "But seriously, if you'd seen how Mrs. Renus was being—"

"You're saying I would've spit on her?" she asks.

"No, but you would've been pretty pissed off."

"Taylor was recording him," Monk adds. "How would you feel if someone stuck a camera in your face while you're drunk?"

Sarah throws her hands up, looking exasperated.

"That's *his* fault for coming to school like that," she says. Then she makes this crazy sound as she shakes her head, sort of like a quiet laugh but much more unsettling. "He should've stayed home, okay? That's all I'm saying. Better yet, he shouldn't have drunk so much last night. He's been sloppy drunk before and he knows how he gets. You both know I'm right."

"Fine, you're right," Monk says calmly. "But our friend just died, okay? Maybe he's taking it a little hard."

"And alcohol helps *so* much," Sarah says. She looks full-on pissed now. Across the plaza, I see someone staring at us as they exit the tobacco shop. "I *know* how hard it is, alright? Don't talk like I'm being insensitive, because I'm not! Did acting like an asshole bring Grandpa back? I mean, wow! Is he here right now and I'm just not seeing him?"

We're both silent. Sarah stands there with her arms spread, looking around sarcastically.

"Is he here?" she asks again. "Seriously, maybe I'm wrong. Maybe we just need to get drunk and *that'll* fix everything. *That'll* bring him back. I mean, damn, it brought my mom back when my dad got drunk and shot himself, didn't it? Let's all just get drunk, and do whatever stupid shit we want, and blame alcohol and grief for everything!"

I see the tears in Sarah's eyes. They're barely there, but her face is red and I can tell she's holding something heavy inside. Even as she continues to smile wildly like she's proving some grand point, I see that this isn't the moment she's really living in. I don't understand it at all, and I don't know where she is, but I know it's somewhere in her head that I know nothing about.

"No," I tell her. "Grandpa's not here."

"And doing stupid shit isn't going to bring him back, is it?" she insists.

I shake my head. "No. You're right, okay? Clive spit on Mrs. Renus and he got what he deserved for it."

She turns away from us before wiping her face.

"I'm sorry," she says quietly. "I don't know where that came from."

"Don't apologize," Monk says. "Just take three deep breaths, alright? Do what you've got to do."

She takes a deep breath in…and releases it. In…release. In…release. I don't want her to be in whatever place she's in right now, because I've seen her break down like this before and she's been stuck in that place for days, drained of all happiness and almost completely nonverbal. It's a wound, that's how Grandpa described it. Physical wounds scab over and heal, but mental wounds are always there, and they can re-open from the slightest touch and make past events feel fresh again. All I can think to do is hug her to try to bring her back, hug her like a big dumb idiot even if it doesn't help at all.

"I'm sorry," she says again, face against my shoulder. "I messed up. Grandpa died, and I made it all about me."

"You didn't mess anything up," I tell her. I hold her for a second, feeling her shaking as she takes more deep breaths. Monk stands between us and the street, looking toward the lot. Nobody's going to pass by and make some mean comment while he's standing there, not if they've ever seen him sprint after a bastard.

She pulls away after a minute. Her eyes are red.

"Let's go," she says.

"You're sure?"

"I'm fine," she says, and she starts walking again toward the theater. Monk and I follow behind her, silent. She takes her phone out as she walks, but I can't tell if she's texting someone or just scrolling through Facebook. I really don't want Jordan to come and pick her up, if she's actually texting him, not after I *just* had that feeling like I'd taken him down. He'd calm her and make her feel better, make her feel loved and supported. But *we're* here for that.

Clive stands up when he sees us coming, and he digs the chew out of his lower lip and throws it aside.

"The movie's about to start," he says. "What took you guys so long?"

"We had to drop Monk's sister off," I say.

"Well, are we going in or not? I've been sitting out here like an asshole for like twenty minutes."

"Back up a bit," Monk says. "Tell us what happened. Why aren't you a dead man?"

"Why would I be?"

"Your dad didn't find out what happened?" I ask.

Clive shrugs, looking toward the theater. He draws a cigarette and lights it up.

"I got a week of in-school suspension, that's it," he says. "I went to the nurse's office and she smelled alcohol on me. The principal called my dad, but he's working thirds at the rubber plant and there's no way in Hell he's getting up for a phone call."

"So he doesn't know yet?"

"Oh, he knows," he says. "The principle just kept dialing and dialing, and he nearly had a damn hemorrhage shouting at me about underage drinking. It was like one of those dumbass commercials they show before the morning announcements. Anyway, my dad finally came, and after *he* got an earful from the principal and the nurse, he gave it right back. He's pissed as all hell, but I think it's mostly because he got woken up. It's not like he doesn't know I drink."

Sarah holds two fingers out, and he passes her the cigarette. It's the first time I've seen her smoke in a while. She draws in deep and blows a thick cloud toward the lot.

"You should be at home sleeping," she says. Clive clutches his heart.

"Aww, you care," he says. She flicks the cigarette at him, and he grins as he picks it up again. "Dad told me to get the hell away from him for a bit. Said we'll have it out later, once he's off work. That'll be a fun way to start tomorrow."

"You don't have to go back," I tell him. "You can stay at one of our places."

He shakes his head.

"I'm not scared of him," he says. "He knows I'm not. The only reason I don't kick his ass is because he's my dad."

"You're so full of shit," Sarah says.

"Full of coffee," he corrects her. "Are we going into the damn theater or not? I want to check out the girl behind the counter."

I look toward the glass doors and see the empty lobby and lone worker sitting behind the counter, reading a trashy-looking book with a bare-chested man on the cover. I don't know her name or anything, but I think she goes to the community college just outside of town. She has one of those faces that's cute but not quite sexy, really plain and round in a way that makes her chin somewhat masculine. She has big tits, though, and I can practically see them reflected in Clive's stare.

"You don't have a chance with her," I say. He shrugs.

"That girl's going to have my babies someday."

"Right after your bedsheets," Sarah says. He gives her the finger and lights another cigarette.

"Do you guys actually feel up for a movie right now?" Monk asks. "I'd really rather go get food or something."

"There's a pizza stand right inside, dick-for-brains," Clive says.

"That pizza sucks. All the pizza in this town sucks."

"Let's flip for it," Clive says, reaching into his pocket. "Heads we go in, tails we do whatever. I don't care."

They bicker for a second, and Clive starts flipping a quarter, chasing it as it rolls off toward the curb. I look at Sarah, and that image of Grandpa walking beside us becomes fresh in my head again, and I think of that first conversation he and I had right out here on this bench. He wasn't a sick and helpless dying man back then, just an old guy with madness in his eyes. He brought us all together, in the graveyard and at his house. Last night was ugly, today's been ugly, and Grandpa wouldn't have any of that if he were here.

"Put your quarter away," I tell Clive. "I've got something else we can do."

"Yeah?"

I look toward the town, thinking it through…how bad could it really be if we get caught? I don't know if I believe in God or anything like that, but I believe Grandpa's stubborn enough to push Death aside and guide us through this one thing.

"Are you gonna tell us?" Sarah presses. Her voice sounds normal, but I know in the back of her head she's still thinking those terrible thoughts about her dad. That's how it works; a person can be both fine and not fine, and pain like that sticks in your chest like napalm. I've seen her and Clive both struggle today, and even if I'm faking it too, I feel like I'm speaking on Grandpa's behalf now.

"We need to take back what's ours," I tell them. "Grandpa's family came when he was sick and they took him from us. They're gone now, and there's no one watching the house."

"We can't just break in," Sarah says.

Clive nods. "Yes, we can."

"Grandpa's neighbors knew us all better than they knew Grandpa's daughters," I say. "They might even think one of us is actually related to him. It wouldn't seem strange at all if we're seen going inside."

"I might even know where his spare key is," Monk adds.

It's quiet for a second, and I know there's no way they're going to shoot down the idea now that it's in the open. They miss the place just like I do. They felt the same hurt when it was taken away from us and we were turned away by those outsiders.

From the corner of my eye I see movement inside the theater, and when I look I see the girl behind the counter staring out at us with her book lowered.

"It'll be great," I tell them. "And it might be our last chance. I don't know who owns the place now, but someone's going to come along and start boxing everything up. Grandpa would want us to enjoy it while we can."

Sarah's staring out at all the cars in the lot, but I can see a smile starting to surface.

"Let's go," I say, and I start walking, waving them along. "Someone text Kevin and tell him to meet us there, he should be part of this."

They start following. Clive's the last to give in, and when I look back I see him staring at the girl behind the glass.

"Screw it," he says, shaking his head. "It's just another dumb remake, anyway."

Grandpa's house is on the corner of Ogontz and Columbus Avenue, just a few blocks from the theater and not too far from my parents' house. I'm excited the entire walk there, because we're finally going *home*. I know it was never our real home, but it's where we all belonged. My heart's pumping, and the big stupid smile on my face won't go away.

"Kevin's said he's on his way," Clive says, once we get close. He's carrying two plastic grocery bags filled with chips, energy drinks, cookies, and all sort of bad food from the Circle K along the way. We all pitched in for it, and I'm carrying a two-liter of Coca-Cola that should mix well with whatever's left in Grandpa's cabinets. There's no telling yet what his daughters took from inside, but I doubt they'd be low enough to take his dozens of opened liquor bottles or the beer in the fridge.

We stop when we get to the sidewalk leading to the porch, and we just sort of stare at the place.

"Well damn," Monk says. "There it is."

"Go find the key," Sarah says. He walks toward the back yard.

I walk toward the porch, the same place I was at this morning. The package is gone. Somebody must have finally seen it sitting there for weeks and decided nobody else was going to claim it. The thought doesn't sting as much now as it would've before.

Monk comes back shaking his head.

"The key's not there."

"Check under the mats," Sarah says. "Or in the mailbox, maybe."

"It won't be there," he says. "There's a hollow stone turtle out in the garden, that's definitely where it was. His family probably took it with them."

"Crap," I say. "What about the basement door?"

"It's got that chain around the handles."

"But it's wooden, though. We can just break the handles off."

Sarah shakes her head. "If neighbors hear us breaking something they'll definitely call the cops."

We're stumped for a few minutes, standing there awkwardly while a few cars pass by. Clive sits on the plastic rocker.

"You think maybe one of the windows is unlocked?" he asks. "I mean, who really thinks about locking their windows?"

I wait for Sarah to object, but instead she tries moving the window closest to us. It doesn't budge.

"I'll try around back," Clive says. He jumps off the porch and runs toward the back yard, and the rest of us, inconspicuously as possible, start trying the other windows around the house. Kevin's car pulls up while we're doing this.

"Locked out, right?" he asks. He stands at his open driver's door, ready to bail.

"Go help Clive search the back yard," I tell him.

"No need," Clive says, coming back around the side of the house. He's holding an old looking wooden ladder over his head, puffing a cigarette between his lips.

"Where did you find that?" Sarah asks.

"Garage. It was unlocked."

He sets the ladder against the side of the house, just below the upstairs bedroom window. He starts to climb.

"What are you doing?" Sarah demands. "You're going to get us caught."

"*'Look like you belong and nobody thinks otherwise,'*" Clive recites, still climbing. "My dad said that once. Pretty he was stalking my mom's boyfriend at the time."

"Charming," Sarah says. The ladder creaks and wobbles beneath him, and she adds, "If you fall and break your neck, we're leaving you for the cops."

"*Har-har.*" He reaches the window, and when he pushes the bottom it immediately gives, and he pumps a fist in the air. "I'm a genius!"

"Whatever," Sarah says.

Clive climbs inside and closes the window behind him.

"I'll put the ladder back," Kevin says.

We wait on the front porch for a second, watching the street and the neighbors' houses. Nobody's looking out at us, and I honestly doubt they'd care even if they did. In a town like this, you could spend a whole day noisily ransacking someone's house and the neighbors won't get involved. I still think we could've just broken the basement cellar door.

The front door finally opens, and Clive bows.

"Thank you, ladies and gentlemen, thank you," he says. We walk past him into the living room, taking off our shoes at the doormat just as Grandpa would've demanded. There's already dirty footprints all over the place, but they're from Grandpa's kids and not Clive.

It's dim and eerie in here, and the only light's coming from behind the closed blinds. I can't put a name to the smell, but the whole room smells dirty in a way I haven't experienced before—something like faint body odor mixed with a strange sterility that makes me think of hospital sheets. The garbage in the kitchen is overflowing, and I hear the sound of a box fan upstairs.

Standing here with that smell all around me, I feel my arms break out in gooseflesh as I think about that terrible mixture of smells and why it bothers me so much. This is the place where Grandpa died. This what death smells like.

Bedsheets and a pillow are still on the couch, where I'm hoping one of Grandpa's daughters slept and not him. They wouldn't do that to him, I don't think, because nobody's that evil. I can't help but hate them, though. They couldn't even take out the trash before leaving or bother to clean the house a little bit.

Sarah flips the wall switch, and the lights come on. The electricity hasn't even been shut off. I doubt the water's been shut off, either.

"I'll take these to the fridge," Kevin says, grabbing the two liter and bags. He rushes to do so, eyes downcast. Everything about the room has a heaviness to it, a weird and undefinable weight, and death's presence is like a crashing wave.

We walk around in silence, inspecting the room for missing items and finding almost nothing out of place with the exception of the television and the Blu-ray player. Grandpa's daughters probably thought those were the only two valuable things in the house, and it makes me almost laugh thinking about it. The walls are covered in far better things, things that they'll never even try to see the beauty or value in.

I look around at the array of portraits, paintings, and the arsenal of weaponry decorating the room without rhyme or reason to their arrangement. It's an eerie feeling, looking around at the handiwork of a dead man and knowing that his own hands placed everything just where it's at and moving it would be almost like undoing a part of him that's left. That last part hurts, because I know that eventually *all* these things will be moved by someone, probably auctioned off or thrown into a dumpster.

I'm actually more elated right now than I've been in days, even more so than when I was on stage. As I look around at all these items I feel like I'm swimming through time. It's a museum in here, and I look around at all the best displays with a buzzing sort of dazed feeling.

On one wall is a framed print of the Mona Lisa, painted over with large cartoonish eyes and a sloppy wet dog tongue sticking out of her mouth.

Fastened to the ceiling is a larger portrait of God in Heaven holding an index finger toward Adam, but Adam's giving him the middle finger.

Beside the empty spot where the television was, a broken store mannequin with a Richard Nixon mask over its head stands covered in splattered paintballs of various colors.

And then there's the weaponry spread throughout the room, displayed almost everywhere you can look. Shotguns, pistols, battleaxes, a longbow, throwing knives, samurai swords, a large mace with fake blood covering the head, a musket with a rusty bayonet on the end, screen replica lightsabers and blasters...

I wish I'd asked him about each and every item when I had the chance, all those times we were all in this room together. I want to know where he got them all, the stories behind them, where he found them and what was going through his crazy mind when he saw them.

Sarah folds the bedsheet on the couch and sets it on the arm along with the stained pillow without a cover. Hanging from a wire above the middle seat is a skinny black dagger with a red jewel in the center, something his unwanted guests either didn't see or didn't bother to remove before sleeping there. Grandpa wanted an actual sword hanging there—his gag version of the Sword of Damocles—but the ceiling's too low, so he settled for the dagger.

Clive smiles and takes down a double-barreled shotgun. He points it toward Kevin as he re-enters the room.

"Yoo-hoo," he calls, and pulls the trigger just as Kevin turns. Kevin flinches at the dry click it makes. "Gotcha, sucka'!"

Sarah swipes the gun from Clive's hands.

"Are you a child?" she asks. He shrugs and pulls a throwing knife from where its buried in the drywall.

"I bet I can knock an apple from your head," he says. Sarah smirks as she puts the shotgun back.

The mood in the room starts to change, slow as it is. It's haunting in a refreshing sort of way, like we're all back in a better day and Grandpa's just upstairs. Any second he might enter the room, maybe wearing old pillows taped to his chest and an umpire's mask over his face, and he'll grab a dull rapier from the wall while demanding a "duel to the death" with one of us. I know he's gone, but I also know he's just upstairs and playing an elaborate joke. I don't know what I know, only that it's both reassuring and painful.

There's still beer in the fridge, both *real* beer and also some fruity spritzer stuff that I know didn't belong to Grandpa. I pass out the cans while Sarah pours from the half-empty pitcher of iced tea.

"It's still good," she says. She stares out the back window above the sink as she drinks, looking lost in her own private moment. I want to stand there with her and drink some of the tea, the very *last* bit of iced tea that we'll ever have in this place. I leave her alone, though. Instead, I walk alone toward the small unlit hallway that connects the living room and first-floor guest room to the staircase.

I look up the stairs. I know he's not up there, but I'm afraid of what I might see. I don't know how I'll react to seeing all that medical gear that carried him to his final moments, the IV stand with heavy bags hanging from hooks and the tubes that pumped medicine into his veins. I never actually saw him hooked up to these things, but it's the first thing I picture when I think of him on his deathbed with sunken eyes and unnaturally pale skin, fingernails overgrown because his terrible daughters probably didn't bother to trim them.

The stairs creak as I walk slowly toward the landing, and I pray over and over, *'Please, don't let that stuff be there.'*

When I get to the top, I pause before turning the corner and looking into the room, bracing myself with a deep breath.

It's just a bed, though. No IV drips, no oxygen tanks, nothing else that immediately betrays the indignity of Grandpa's death. The bedsheets are crumpled toward the foot of the bed, and the pillows are stacked where his head rested to watch the small box television on the opposite side of the room.

It's colder up here than I remember, quieter than what should be possible. The silence is accentuated by the absence of the air conditioner Grandpa kept near his writing desk, one that always made a ticking sound like a timebomb ready to go off. Instead there's just the fan going. The blinds next to his bed are open where Clive entered, and a little bit of sun shines into the room. It still smells like Grandpa in here—Old Spice, cigar smoke, and Jack Daniels. There's a faint undertone of something else, maybe urine. Whatever he went through in his last days, I hope his daughters at least had the decency to help him to the bathroom.

A horrible image invades my mind before I can stop myself: Grandpa's lying in bed with the bedsheets at his feet and a large wet circle around his groin, calling weakly out for help even though he doesn't *want* to need help for something like this, crying because he's absolutely helpless for once in his life and he's never experienced that feeling…

I swallow a hard lump in my throat. I don't cry, though. I feel like he's watching me right now, and he's the one who told us not to cry too much.

His dresser drawers have all been pulled out, and his clothing is strewn across the floor. The savages and their disrespect. Did they at least wait until he took his last breath to start searching for valuables?

I kneel down and start folding things, moving mechanically and feeling somewhat distant from reality. I pull up a stained white undershirt, and it uncovers a rectangular black jewelry box. I hold the box for a second, running my fingers over the engraving of a rose on the top. I open it.

It's a box made for rings. There are a dozen or so slots, and most of them are empty. I look over the leftovers, all the rings that weren't even good enough for scavenging thieves. They're all manner of silver and gold, some of them thin and barely visible aside from their glass jewel, others large and gaudy with strange designs on their sides.

I take each one out, turning them in my fingers and trying a few on. As I do this, I imagine Grandpa telling the stories behind them:

'I was a big collector, Trey. A big, big collector,' my imagination says. *'I got a few from when I used to travel the world, I got some others from the ladies I used to sleep with during my backpacking years when I was about your age…Christ, kid, the women I met, you should've seen them! This one here was given to me by the captain of a ship I sailed on—Daniel was his name, I think, and he was a real bastard fighter in the ring. But I beat him fair-n-square, and I got his wedding ring as a souvenir!'*

I laugh, thinking of his voice narrating these strange and wonderful stories. None of it's true, or maybe some of it is. Maybe these are all just rings he bought cheap and wore for style, just afterthoughts with nothing special to them.

I settle on one ring in particular. The band is sterling silver, I think, and it's decorated with a small pair of angel wings on either side of the large black stone in the center. There's grime all over the inside of the band, and the stone itself has a large scratch through the center. I try it on, and it feels *right* somehow.

I think of Grandpa's ghost in the room, watching me do all this. Is he sitting on the edge of the bed, or is he floating above me with a large white spectral tail, sarcastically moaning *"Boo"* over and over again?

I suddenly feel like I'm wearing a biblical artifact, and I'm unworthy of it. I take it off and start to place it back in the box. But even when it's back in its slot, my fingers stay on it.

Would he want me to take it? If this place was already ransacked for valuables, everything else will probably get thrown out. I feel like I'm graverobbing just by thinking of keeping it, because even if he's gone it was still *his*, and I don't even know what this small collection meant to him.

'Take the damn thing,' I think of him saying. Or maybe he really is saying it. I can't tell. Maybe the coldness I feel on my back is his presence or maybe it's just a regular cold spot.

Tears sting my eyes, thinking of all this. Kneeling here right now, here in this room where we blew cigar smoke from the window while watching TV with Sarah and the others sitting on the bed or the floor, claiming one last bit of Grandpa to hold onto and keep as a reminder…it feels too real.

I walk back downstairs, looking one last time at Grandpa's deathbed. I take the ring with me.

Sarah's sitting on the couch with a bag of chips next to her, drinking her tea as she watches a movie on her phone.

Monk's hopelessly strumming an out-of-tune acoustic guitar while Kevin throws knives at the bottom of an overturned table with a target painted on the bottom.

Outside, Grandpa's van roars suddenly to life. I look out the window and see someone in the driver seat, and I grab a knife from the wall.

"Get the hell out of there!" I shout, running outside with the knife raised. If it's the ungrateful daughters again, come to steal more of Grandpa's things, I swear to God I'll stab them to death.

Clive's head pokes out from inside the van.

"Calm your tits," he says. "I'm just checking it out."

I lower the knife, slightly embarrassed. The van idles noisily, growling like a great big beast awoken from hibernation.

"Where did you find the keys?"

"They were under the floormat," Clive says. "He didn't even keep the thing locked."

I shrug. "Who the hell would bother stealing it?"

He gets out of the van and stares at it, rubbing his lower teeth with one finger and the other hand rested on his hip. Kevin and Monk walk outside behind me, the latter holding the guitar by its neck like a bludgeoning weapon.

"Damn," Monk says, lowering the guitar.

"You think it'll still ride?" Clive asks. He looks lost in thought.

"The tires look pretty flat," Kevin says.

"Yeah, they could use some air. I bet it's fine otherwise, though, right?"

"I can't see why it wouldn't be," Monk says. "Grandpa drove it around sometimes. Why does it matter?"

Clive doesn't answer. He opens the van's side door and stares into the back with a strange smirk.

"No reason," he says.

"Bullshit."

He reaches inside and cuts the engine, silencing the beast. He stands there holding the key, nodding to himself.

"Just an idea, that's all," he says, and he turns and walks past us inside. Kevin follows after him. Clive says something to him in a low voice, and they walk down into the basement.

"That can't be good," Monk says. We go back inside, and he starts strumming the guitar again, muttering lyrics to himself as he walks around.

Sarah smiles when I sit down beside her.

"How are you doing?" I ask. She shrugs noncommittally. I nod, and we stare at the small screen in her hands.

I don't know what the movie is, some crappy comedy I haven't even heard of. I don't interrupt to ask, though— Sarah puts her head on my shoulder, I reach for the bag of chips, and we watch the movie in silence as I sip a can of beer.

Clive and Kevin come back upstairs, and all throughout the movie they throw knives across the room at various targets, adding knew holes between the hundreds of old ones. Bored with the guitar, Monk smashes it against the wall, and he looks down at the pieces for a long moment. There are several other guitars in the hall closet, each as worthless as the last, bought solely for the purpose of smashing because *'Everyone needs something to smash sometimes.'* Monk's lips move slightly as he stands there, and he smiles at whatever he's saying, looking somehow both somber and amused.

I feel it too. Grandpa's still here with us, watching us enjoy the place one last time, moving around the room and talking to each of us even though we can't see him and only hear what we need to hear. This might be the last time any of us feels at home anywhere ever again, and I just want this moment to last forever.

Chapter Six

Four hours later I'm up in my room reading the book Katy gave me, thinking about Grandpa's house and trying to distract myself from these thoughts any way I can. It's silent in my room, but I hear the crickets outside, the occasional passing car's radio, and the sound of the downstairs television. Mom and Dad are babysitting my ten-year-old cousin Nicholas and his friend Connor, two kids mischievous enough to put Bart Simpson to shame. Part of me thinks about going downstairs to see them all, maybe watch them quietly from the kitchen table while I struggle to read, just so I can be near them all and enjoy their presence. I feel strange, filled with these stupid sentimental thoughts that I wish I could swat like bees. I hold the book with one hand, folding the cover back like I do with every book even though it ruins the spine, and I lie in bed with one foot in front of me and the other on the floor.

We stayed at the house for a few hours, right up until Monk got a call from his mom and caught hell for forgetting his sister at the theater. Kevin drove him to get her, and the rest of us walked together for a minute before splitting our separate ways. I wonder how they all felt, leaving the house behind us like that. I think maybe we'll go back, but I doubt it. The house was ours again only momentarily, and if we go back it won't be the same. It'd be like trying to squeeze water from a dry rag.

My mind wanders repeatedly as I slog through the first chapter. It's a good book, and if I was in a better mood I'd probably tear through it in a single session because, just like Monk said, it's right up my alley. I imagine Sarah lying next to me, her head rested against my shoulder like it was during the movie. I can feel her weight there, and I can feel the gentle tickle of her hair against my arm.

I set the book down, giving up on it for the time being. I sit at my desk and try writing a few paragraphs, but everything that comes out suddenly feels mediocre and empty no matter how many times I erase and restart. I surf the internet, first checking out band websites and movie trailers, then Facebook and Twitter and anywhere else where I can be deluged by mindless whining and casual-pose selfies. I feel anger, sweet anger, but it's not enough to make me stop dwelling on thoughts of Grandpa's house and Sarah's warmth against my body, and when I'm done scrolling I just feel worse than when I started.

I start watching a movie, a godawful remake of a western Grandpa showed me once. Nothing is kept sacred, and the first shootout in the opening scene ends with a big CGI explosion rather than the dismissive line of dialogue from the hero to the bad guy as he escapes on the back of a passing wagon. The tough-as-nails villain was short in the original movie, and he had a big moustache and stubble down his neck, but everyone in this terrible remake is played by a dolled-up twenty-something, and it seems like each of them has a reason to be shirtless at least once so they can show off emaciated bodies with visible abs.

Grandpa would've hated this movie, and as I watch I try to fill in the gaps where his commentary would be. I can't hear him, though, and my fruitless attempts only highlight his absence.

I'm lying on the floor, listening to Bruce Springsteen on my phone and muttering the few words I know, when there's a knock at my door. The handle turns very slowly—a warning to close any websites I might be on and zip up if I need to—and Dad pokes his head in.

"Hey, there's pizza downstairs if you're hungry," he says. I shrug. Bruce is singing about his glory days. Is this one of my glory days, sad as hell and out of my mind? God, I hope they pass me by.

"Okay," I say. I stare up at chipped paint on the stucco ceiling, counting the cracks. Dad just stands in the doorway, and I can't tell if he's looking at me or looking around at the mess on the floor.

"The kids want to watch a movie, too," he says. "Your cousin's really into those superhero movies. Might be something you can bond over."

I shake my head. "I'm alright."

"Hmm."

The song stops, and there's one of those annoying commercials that you can't skip. I stare up at the ceiling and listen to Jake Gyllenhaal talk about a pill that helps with fat loss. Dad's still standing in the doorway.

"Did something happen at school today?" he asks.

"Nope."

"You're sure?"

"Yep."

He waits there for a better answer. Seventeen. There are seventeen individual cracks in the ceiling. Some of them look like crooked smiles on eyeless faces, and the spots where paint's chipped away are like mouths stuck with surprised expressions.

"Talk to me a bit," Dad says. He walks further into the room, and then I see him standing over me, blocking my view of the audience in the ceiling. The commercial ends, and another commercial begins.

"I'm fine," I tell him. "Just tired."

"You know you can talk to me, right?" he says. He always says stuff like that. Grandpa never said it; when I wanted to talk, I talked.

"There's nothing wrong," I lie. He sighs like he's annoyed, and that makes me smile for some reason. When he sits down on the edge of my bed, I know there's no chance I'm getting out of this. I turn off the commercial and sit up.

"Listen," he says, "I know it's been hard for you lately, and I get it. You lost a friend. You think I don't understand, but I do."

"MmmHmm."

"I know that Edward guy meant a lot to you and your friends, and that's really great. I've lost people before, and I know how it is."

I look up at him, at his serious expression that makes his forehead wrinkle as he sits with his elbows on his knees and his hands clasped in front of him. I don't know what he's expecting.

"I don't want to talk about it," I tell him. He sighs again, grimacing and spreading his hands.

"Alright," he says. He's silent for a second. "What about Summer?"

"What about it?"

"Have you given any thought to what you're doing for work?"

I shake my head.

"You need to find something soon," he says. "It's already April, and companies are filling those Summer positions."

"I know."

"Believe me, you're going to get to college and wish you'd made all that extra spending money. You think I'm wrong, but I'm not."

It's by pure willpower that I don't drive my head through the wall behind me. I shrug.

"I don't know, I guess I could do McDonald's or something."

He shakes his head. "You don't want to do that."

"Monk worked there before, he said it wasn't too bad. Just a lot of stupid people with stupid complaints."

"And you really want to deal with those people all day long?"

"It's just an idea. I don't know."

"What about the slaughterhouse? You said you want me to hire that other friend of yours. Why don't I see about getting you in there, too?"

"The slaughterhouse?" I ask, disgusted.

"It's just a job, not a career move," he says. "And I think it'd be good for you. Plenty of people in your class are probably going to work there permanently, and you're going to do something else with your life."

"So?"

"I'm just saying, you'd get that experience and it'd build some character. There's a lot of nice guys working there, and I could introduce you to some of them. I'd probably have you on the packing floor, so you'd be standing there all day boxing the meat up, but you'd go to college with a lot more money in your pocket than a fast food job would get you."

I picture it in my head, standing in front of a moving conveyor belt for eight hours every day and doing the same repetitive movement over and over again. It doesn't sound terrible, really. There are worse things I could do. I could be a lifeguard. Sarah did it for half of last Summer, and she got fired for hitting a Sophomore kid in the face when he tried following her to the bathroom. Maybe staring at bloody pig parts every day would do something for my mind.

"You'd better decide soon, kiddo," Dad says. "I can get you in there, but if I do, I need you to be committed to it."

"I guess I could do it," I say. "But I don't want to work full-time or anything. I still want to be able to hang out with my friends and stuff."

He laughs. "You need to get the hell over that right now. You're almost eighteen. You need a damn job, and I'm telling you I can get you a good one. Do you want it or not?"

I throw my hands up, defeated. "Fine."

"And I'll see about getting your friend in there, too." I stare miserably down at the floor, and when Dad stands up again, he pats my shoulder. "Maybe you'll finally pay me back for all the drinks you've been stealing."

I look up at him, surprised. He just smiles.

"Did you think I wouldn't notice?"

"I'll stop drinking," I tell him. He waves a hand and makes a sour face.

"You don't have to lie to me," he says. "You think I don't know better, but I was your age once. Just go easy on it, would you?"

I nod.

"I mean it," he says. "There was a full bottle of Jameson down there last week, and it's nearly gone. You're too damn young to be doing that."

"I'll take it easy," I lie. I smile up at him. It's the fake ass smile that I think I'm pretty good at, at least when I need to be. It's the understanding look that I think says, 'We're bonding, and you can trust me.' Maybe he sees through it, but he nods anyway and leaves the room.

I blow a deep breath toward the floor. Summer jobs. Hooray.

Get a job. Get some money. Get fat. Get dead. I feel the clock ticking

I hear Grandpa groaning in my head. *'Quit your bitching,'* he's saying. *'You want to be a writer, you need some of that horribly boring real-life crap.'*

His voice brings a smile. I look down at the ring on my hand. Yeah, it's not so bad. Fun is fun, but money is a necessity. Jordan's got money. How else does he buy those stupid sports hoodies that he lets Sarah wear? That's got to be something.

Another hour goes by, and after a little while I hear the superhero movie playing downstairs and smell popcorn. I'm hungry, but I can't make myself go eat. I listen to more music, some Bob Dylan. Grandpa didn't like him much, but I think he's alright, at least in small doses. "Blood on the Tracks" is a good album, maybe the only one I've listened to all the way through and genuinely felt something from. I'm just in that weird sort of mood, and I can't shake it.

Sarah's probably painting, because she's been talking lately about how she needs to take it more seriously and make a nightly habit out of her work. She might be with Jordan, but I seriously doubt it; I picked up on something, sitting so close to her and feeling her heart beat, and I don't think she wants anyone near her tonight, especially not someone she claims she loves. Monk's probably rehearsing his lines for the show.

I decide to go for a walk. There's really no plan to meet tonight, since we all spent so much time together already at the house and don't want to risk tainting that catharsis with another average night in the graveyard. I always feel better during a long walk, though, and even if I hate this whole damn town sometimes it feels oddly comforting at nights.

So I go downstairs, glance momentarily at the movie in the living room while I put my shoes on, and I head out the door.

My first stop is the Circle K a few blocks from here. The raspy-voiced lady behind the counter with tired and half-dead eyes never cards any of us, so I make sure she's the one working before I go inside and make a beeline for the cigars and then the coffee. The cigars here aren't any good, not even as good as the poorly-rolled cheapos Grandpa bought sometimes, but I feel nostalgic for that awful taste.

"Eight-forty, sweetie," the woman says. I hand her a ten, and when she gives me my change I start to shove it into my pocket, but then I reconsider and put all of it into the glass box near the lighters, one of those boxes with a smiling cancer kid on the front and a short message about how small donations can make a big difference. It probably won't help even a little bit, but it makes me feel good for a few minutes as I clip the cigar in the parking lot and walk leisurely toward the train tracks. The further I walk and smoke, the more I smell the overpowering rubber odor from the nearby factory. The houses around here look more pressed together than houses in other neighborhoods, and most of the lawns are overgrown or chewed-up-looking, ruined by large dogs kept on short chains. They bark at me as I stroll by, and when they charge toward the sidewalk and are jerked back by those tough chains, I feel bad for the little idiots.

The windows here are mostly covered, either by blinds that are missing entire rows or American and Confederate flags that look ruined by age and smoke. Some houses I pass have lights on in every room, and I see small silhouettes moving around behind them. The town has the biggest rubber factory in the Midwest, but it seems like nobody here can use a condom properly, and these kids are probably doomed the moment they're born. Or maybe I was just born lucky, not born into a rich family but at least born with some hope for leaving this place.

I walk on and on and on, and the depression eating away at my chest doesn't get any better. It hurts in a way that I think it's supposed to hurt, but it also hurts in an extremely stupid way that makes me feel like a jerk for feeling it. It's not all about me; Grandpa died, and he was going to die whether I was in his life or not, regardless of what he meant to me or Sarah or anyone else. But walking through the neighborhood like this, I want to put the blame on someone else, hold someone accountable for the sickness he went through and make them explain why it happened to *him* and not to *them*. Selfish, selfish thinking from a selfish, selfish little bastard.

"Shut up," I say out loud. I try to make my voice sound like Grandpa's. "You're just whining now, kid."

I walk faster, halfway through the cigar with lukewarm coffee spilling out over the lid and down my hand.

I turn back the way I came, directionless until I come to the train tracks again. I walk down the tracks, distracting myself from these idiotic, selfish thoughts by watching my steps and warily avoiding a twisted ankle. It starts to sprinkle as I walk, and there's a few flashes of lighting in the sky that make me think God or Grandpa is trying to say something helpful. It doesn't last, though; it stops sprinkling after only a few minutes, and by that time I've already turned off the tracks and toward Main Street.

After a few minutes of walking down the empty street and looking at the many papered-over storefronts, I see a familiar face up ahead sitting on a bench outside the courthouse. Grandpa called him Jim, but everyone else calls him Crazy Jim because he reeks of piss and has the face of a half-smashed Jack-o-lantern that's been left outside too long. My heart sort of leaps in excitement at the site of him.

"Hey Jim," I say as I approach. He's staring down at a crack on the sidewalk, his lower lip pushed out and revealing a few brownish teeth. He jumps when he hears me, and when he turns he stares at me unsurely.

"Who's that?" he asks. He looks like a blind man squinting to see, but I think that's just how his face looks. It's exciting, talking to him one-on-one for the first time after hearing only stories from the town. The piss smell is real, so maybe the crazy is real, too.

"My name's Trey," I tell him. "We haven't met before."

"Trey…" he says, nodding to himself. He licks his lips, shrugs, and looks back toward the ground.

"What are you doing out here?" I ask. He shrugs again, and the silence lingers a moment. I tap the lid of my coffee nervously. "Can I sit?"

"Free country," he says. I take a final puff from the cigar and throw it toward the street.

"Are you having a good night?" I ask. He shrugs. He doesn't even look up from the ground. "Mine kind of sucks. A friend of mine died."

"A friend?" he asks, finally turning his face up to look at me again. "I didn't hear about no kids dying."

"It wasn't a kid," I tell him. "His name was Edward. Edward O'Halloran, actually."

Crazy Jim winces.

"Edward O'Halloran's dead?" he asks.

I nod, and even as the sickness in my stomach stirs again I feel suddenly excited at the idea of someone else knowing him, someone I can talk to who isn't part of our close friend group or Grandpa's family of vultures. I just want to hear *someone* talk about him and listen to me spill all this junk in my head.

Crazy Jim sucks his throat in, throws his head forward, and spits phlegm on the sidewalk.

"Good riddance," he says. "He ain't right none."

"What do you mean?" I ask, staring at the yellowish glob.

"He ain't right none," Crazy Jim repeats. "Spends all his time hanging out with kids, acting the fool all around town like some sort of jackass."

"That was just him having fun," I explain. "He did it to get a reaction out of people. He never hurt anyone by doing it."

"Somethin' wrong with a guy like that, you ask me," Crazy Jim says. "Especially someone who hangs out with kids. He ever touched any of you?"

"No," I tell him. He waves a dismissive hand.

"If you say so," he says. He stares down at the ground again, watching a crack in the sidewalk like he's waiting for something to rise out of it. Any happiness I felt in meeting him has quickly gone away.

"He wasn't like that at all. You don't know anything about him," I say. "You sit around here smelling like piss and creeping everyone out, what gives you the right to talk about him that way?"

He shrugs.

"Huh?" I demand, and I push him so hard that he nearly falls off the bench. He doesn't seem fazed by it; he sits up, adjusts his stained blue jacket, and looks back at the ground. "He was my friend. He would've given *anything* to anyone who asked, and he actually gave a shit when nobody else would. You don't know anything about him, and you run your goddamn mouth like you're an expert on everyone. Who the hell are you, anyway? Huh?"

I'm expecting something—he'll say something profound, maybe, or he'll tell me something about an exchange with Grandpa long before I ever knew him. He's got to give me *something*, because that's all I'm dying for and the fist in my chest is squeezing again, harder than before.

But he doesn't say anything. The son of a bitch just shrugs.

"Screw you," I tell him. I stand up and start to walk, and my hands are shaking like it's colder out than it was before.

"Wait a minute, wait a minute," he says. When I turn around he's sitting with an urgent sort of look on his face. It gets my hopes up.

"Yeah?" I ask.

"Do you have a couple bucks on you?" he asks. "Five, ten bucks, maybe?"

I stare at him for a second, disbelieving. I know it's not right, but my mind's telling me that if I hit him and leave him bleeding on the sidewalk, nobody in town would really give a shit. They'd pretend for a day or so, probably, but nobody would go looking for any answers.

I push the anger down. "I don't have any money."

"A cigarette, maybe?" he asks. "I saw you smoking a cigar, do you have any more of those?"

"No," I tell him. He scrunches his face at me like I've offended him.

"I'm not some damn beggar," he insists. "You don't have to lie. I just want to go buy a beer down the street."

"I don't have any money," I repeat. He spits on the sidewalk.

"You damn liar," he says. "You take up my bench, you push me, and now you see fit to lie. I ain't ever done nothing to you."

He throws his hands up, then hunches back toward the ground, staring at the same crack in the sidewalk. I walk away, and the further I walk the less I feel the anger boiling inside. I laugh, and if someone drove by right now they'd probably think I was nuts.

Crazy Jim isn't crazy after all. He's just a stupid asshole. Another of Caedes' finest.

I walk and walk, on and on, past the downtown area, past the plaza and the movie theater, around the bend toward the factories, and finally toward the cemetery. I'm not going to find anyone to talk to, not anyone I can push all these horrible thoughts onto and feel some sort of relief from. So I talk to myself the whole way, at first just under my breath, whisper-shouting and then just shouting. I'm not great company, though, because no matter how much I talk I don't feel any better, and I actually feel angrier and more ashamed.

I make sure to keep my face toward the ground when headlights from a passing car blind me momentarily. Then the car honks three times as it passes, and someone shouts my name from the passenger window.

When I turn around, I see Grandpa's van flying down the road.

"Hey!" I shout, running after it. The driver honks again as they speed off, throwing handfuls of paper out the window as they round a corner. There's no way I'm going to catch up, and I'm already panting for air as I buckle over and stare at where the vehicle disappeared.

There are dozens of flyers face-up on the sidewalk. I follow the trail, picking them up as I go and seeing that each of them has the same picture. When I round the next corner, I see them littering the entire street ahead, blowing in the gentle breeze and covering the chewed-up front lawns of dilapidated houses.

I smile, still with tears in my eyes and a raw feeling in my throat. Suddenly everything feels somehow right in the world, and as I hold one of these flyers between my hands I feel the familiar electric current moving under my skin, reanimating this depressed walking corpse like Frankenstein's monster.

The pornographic picture that takes up most of the flyer is in black and white, but even with dampness from the road smearing sections of it, the faces in the picture are crystal clear.

Mrs. Renus's smiling face is superimposed over the head of a kneeling woman surrounded by naked men, each of them visible only up to the waist and each of them with their pants around their ankles and their erect members in their hands. The woman in the picture is completely naked, fully displaying her enormous fake tits and the short C-section scar that runs through her bellybutton and down toward her bush. There's a cut in Mrs. Renus's photo that makes the mouth look opened in a very cartoonish sort of way, and the hands of the woman are each grabbing onto one of the surrounding members that seem to be mid-fire.

Below the picture, in bold: **For a Good Time Call the Renus Household!**

I follow this trail of flyers, picking them up and throwing them down again, feeling my smile grow wider and wider as the trail stops every few blocks and then picks up again with a stray flyer blowing down the street ahead. I see a few people on the sidewalk as I rush madly through the town, completely giddy. A few of these people look disgusted, but most of them are laughing their asses off and taking pictures with their phones.

I look online as I walk faster and faster, and I already see a slew of status updates on social media, walls and walls of comments from everyone in the school, several of them with pictures of the flyer. It's too much, and the more I scroll through these comments the funnier it is to me.

I try to call Clive as I run home, but he doesn't answer even after four tries. I follow the trail, feeling like a kid at an amusement park. After half an hour of running breathlessly through town, I suddenly find myself back in Grandpa's neighborhood. I stand in front of his house, smiling still even as I buckle over at the waist and struggle to catch my breath. I look over toward the house, and though I don't see the backside of Grandpa's van poking out from the driveway, my mind's already racing too much to care.

My phone rings, and when I see Clive's name on the screen, I answer.

"Holy…shit…" I wheeze. I hear the loud sound of an open car window in the background.

Clive laughs, and then confirms: "Holy shit."

Chapter Seven

The next morning at school begins with retribution.

At first everything's perfect: Monk and I are laughing our asses off during homeroom as we listen to people go on and on about the flyers. They're all over the place near the factory, and although Clive and Kevin only printed a few hundred of them, several photos of it have already flooded social media and it's been circulated thousands of times.

A few of Mrs. Renus's varsity volleyball girls do their best to stomp out the growing fire. Debbie tells Annie that she was out all night picking up the flyers and throwing them away before the wind could take them, but Kyle tells Vincent that he made a bunch of copies as soon as he grabbed one off the street, and he's planning to spread them everywhere he can. It's loud as hell in the room, and I bet it is in every homeroom in the school. Monk and I are so busy eating it all up that we don't even bother playing our game when the announcements come on.

The announcements are extremely brief, anyway:

"There will be a mandatory assembly in the gym following homeroom," Kevin says on the screen. I can't tell if he's laughing inside just like we are, but he keeps a serious face as he reads from the paper in front of him. "All students and faculty are required to attend."

"His eyes are still red," Monk notes, squinting up at the screen. I nod.

"It was good shit," I tell him. Monk and Sarah didn't come out last night, but I met Clive and Kevin out at the graveyard for a little bit. As we settled in the tree and Clive delivered his loud and proud declaration of victory, Kevin shared a joint. I didn't bother with more than one puff, but the two of them smoked away as they retold their story over and over, trampling each other verbally as they eagerly added the most mundane details of what they'd done.

Grandpa's van is gone; after throwing flyers by the handful all around the factory side of town, they took the van down to the football field and left it parked behind the bleachers where there aren't any cameras. It'll get moved eventually, and once it's towed away it'll probably be gone forever. But that's alright, because Grandpa would be undoubtedly proud of its final ride.

Mr. Shepherd, our substitute homeroom teacher, is standing at the front of the room with large and fearful eyes, crossing and uncrossing his arms and doing his best to shut everyone up about the "reprehensible situation." He's an adorably small man, the human equivalent of a yapping chihuahua, and even as he shouts for silence, it's clear that he's out of his depths.

"I'm warning you!" he keeps saying, but at least half the class goes on talking, and the beautiful fire keeps burning, burning, burning.

The bell rings, and we all walk down to the gym, where we're given a long and vicious speech from Principal

Jones. He's a goddamn giant, fully bearded with perpetually angry beady eyes and short-cropped black hair. He's been principal for an even shorter time than I've lived here. When my family first moved here I heard some pretty screwed up stories from when he was the American History teacher. If these stories can be trusted, he once lost his temper and picked a student up, desk and all, and held him over the fourth-floor stairwell until the kid finally pissed himself in fear.

"Quiet!" Mr. Jones roars, and with that, he manages to do what none of the other faculty members could. There's perfect silence as he stands glaring at us from the gym floor.

He talks on and on, and I do my best not to smile as I duck my head and listen. I glance around the room and see that Sarah's seated with Jordan, one arm around him and rubbing his shoulder as he stares around the room, face red and angry like he's waiting for the culprit to present himself. Sarah probably knows it was Clive, but even if she's playing the supportive girlfriend role with Jordan, I doubt she'd sell any of us out.

Mrs. Renus is nowhere to be seen, but all the other teachers are lined up behind Mr. Jones. They watch us all with grave disapproval as he makes his idle threats to whoever was responsible for making and distributing the flyers. These threats tell me what Clive already guaranteed: nobody knows who did it, and even if they know, they don't have proof. We live in a piss-poor hick town, and even as he tells us that the police are involved and that they'll find the responsible parties, all I can think of is drug dealers in town who seem to get away scot-free without much effort.

It's beautiful—so, so beautiful. I can almost hear Grandpa laughing along with us.

After a thorough berating and not much else, the assembly finally ends. Mr. Jones tells us that anyone caught distributing flyers from the incident will be suspended, and the same consequence goes for anyone who so much as talks about "that shameful, disgusting act!"

And then the day goes on as normal, or at least something resembling normal.

I'm humming to myself, happy as hell and picturing Mrs. Renus's mental breakdown in my head. Clive really went all-out with his revenge, but she's pissed off enough students that I doubt he's even at the top of her suspect list. She's probably making herself crazy thinking about it, and that makes me so, so happy.

I have Algebra II first thing today, and it's dead silent the entire time Ms. O'Reilly lectures. She glares around at us while we work on our assignment, listening for any talk of the incident.

The next two classes are pretty much the same. Kevin's in my Spanish IV class, but he doesn't talk to me at all and keeps a disinterested poker face throughout the class. Bummer, but not unexpected.

I get to 4th Period Journalism class. There's still a spring in my step on the way there, and I swear not a single thing can wreck this little bit of euphoria.

Surprisingly, though, Mrs. Renus is at her desk.

When I enter the classroom, expecting to see another timid little substitute teacher, she's glaring at the doorway, watching as each student enters and communicating a nonverbal death threat that shuts us up invariably. Her stare lingers on me as I walk toward my seat, and I can't help but look toward the floor, even after all that internal laughter.

"I expect complete silence," she says when the bells rings. No one challenges her, and I see some of them avert their eyes as she looks around at all of us. "Anyone who breaks this expectation will be sent to the office. No exceptions."

She looks deadly, not at all broken or humiliated like I pictured her in my head. I look around the room and notice the only person missing in Jordan, who's usually her T.A. for the period. She must have let him go to study hall today instead. Hell, I can't imagine how awkward it must feel to be him right now, knowing everyone in the school saw your mom's face superimposed onto a porn star. That, at least, makes me grin a bit.

I think about Clive as I listen and take notes from her lecture. Poor Clive, trapped in a tiny room on the second floor with cubicle walls around him, nothing to do all day but stare at those walls and go insane. The movie *Shawshank Redemption* comes to my mind, and I picture myself sneaking him out through sewage pipes below the room. It's a stupid ass thought, I know. Realistically, I could probably walk right into the I.S.S. room and talk with him for a few minutes before getting kicked out.

While we all work, Mrs. Renus walks between the rows of desks, never letting her head drop or showing any cracks in her expression. *'I'm still here,'* her expression tells us. *'Test me, you little shits.'* She pauses to look over a few students' shoulders as they write, and when she sees Katy Laird texting below her desk, she snatches the phone from her hands and drops it in the trash without slowing her step.

"Office. Now," she says. Katy looks from the trashcan to Mrs. Renus with a look of utter betrayal before standing up, digging her phone out of the trash, and slinking out of the room with her head hanging low.

A few students stare. Mrs. Renus looks around at us, nostrils flaring as she forces a calm smile. They quickly look away.

Twenty minutes later, I need to piss. She's been walking around like a dictator, head held high with an unshakably calm smile and a green pamphlet of hall passes in one hand. She's sent three people to the principal's office already, and she's flipping through the stack of hall passes while she walks as if it's a kill trophy. I look around and see everyone with their eyes toward the floor or their notebooks, not so much as daring to look in her direction.

Screw her.

I take a deep breath, and then I stand and walk toward her.

"Sit down, Trey," she says before I've even reached her.

"I need to use the bathroom."

"You should've gone before class. Sit."

But I don't sit; I refuse to sit. I refuse to so much as look away as she turns fully toward me.

"I really need to go," I tell her. "I'm being serious."

She shrugs. "Too bad."

My fist tightens at my side. I keep my cool the best I can. If she wants to play games, I'll play games.

"Listen," I tell her, "It's going to start smelling real bad in here if I don't get to the bathroom. If that's what you want, fine."

A freckle-faced boy in the front row snorts, and I see a few others sneaking a look in our direction. I smile at Mrs. Renus, mirroring her fake-ass calmness. Her nostrils flare again, and I imagine her skin breaking away like bits of eggshell, revealing the scaly witch-demon with black eyes and rotted teeth.

Her left eye twitches. She tears a pre-signed hall pass from the pad.

"Be quick," she says.

I start walking toward the door, feeling pretty self-satisfied and somehow heroic. Then I hear someone's books fall from their desk, and there's a sort of collective gasp from a few people before Mrs. Renus's footsteps charge loudly across the room.

I turn and see her walking toward the mess of papers on the floor as a shaggy-haired kid named Brandon works quickly to collect them. But the papers are all over, each of them the same, and Mrs. Renus only needs to reach the one closest to her feet. She holds the drawing in front of her, and all at once the entire calm façade drops from her face. She stands there speechless.

"What is this?" she asks. The authority has disappeared from her voice, and she looks frantically around at the mess of loose papers still on the floor.

I take a step back inside, cocking my head to see toward the front of the class where Brandon kneels collecting the papers with a look of pure mortal dread. I can barely see the drawing on all the pages, but I make out Mrs. Renus's photo from the yearbook. There's a large dialogue bubble coming from its mouth and a title written below in bold: **'The Glob Guzzler!'**

The hurt in Mrs. Renus's eyes is nothing compared to the rage that quickly comes to conceal it. She charges toward Brandon.

"Who made this?" she demands. "Did you do this? Did you make this, you little bastard?"

A few people are laughing openly now, and she whips her head around to glare at all of them in turn, eyes wild and crazed like she's finally broken. Brandon backs away from her on all fours, scrambling to collect the papers and wiping tears from beneath his glasses.

I leave the room, eager to be away from it all before I get caught up in her rampage. I walk quickly down the hall, folding the pass in my hands as I go and trying to feel a sense of joy that I know I should be feeling.

But I saw the hurt in her eyes, the pure desperation and helplessness. Somehow that ruins it for me, and all at once I feel like trash for laughing at her suffering in the first place.

A voice in the back of my mind tells me I'm wretched and horrible for celebrating a single thing about Clive's prank, and I can't shake a mental image of Mrs. Renus crying in her home, forcing herself to overcome this horrible embarrassment and show her face at the school.

All morning long I've been storing nasty comments in my head, rehearsing them to myself in preparation for some big showdown moment where I can tell them to her and watch her crumble. But seeing her like that, nearly crying and vulnerable like an *actual human*, it makes it hard to hate her like I want to. Hell, it makes me feel sorry for her, and that thought's like a foreign object jammed into my brain, ruining everything.

I shake my head as I continue walking, wondering if this moment of shock will wear off and leave me to my much-deserved enjoyment of her humiliating downfall. I reach into my pocket and touch the ring I took from Grandpa's house. He would've found this hilarious, I bet. I'm not an asshole for laughing. I'm not a bad person, not really.

I use the bathroom just like I said I would, but I've already decided I'm not going back to class. She's so messed up from the pile of drawings that she won't even notice I'm gone. I have my notebooks with me, and that's really all that's worth grabbing.

I'm craving a cigarette so bad right now. I don't smoke when I'm sober, but I really want one all of a sudden. I bet Clive will have some. Maybe he'll even sneak out of the ISS room and have a smoke with me, and I can forget all these horrible feelings of 'empathy.'

A livelier, self-assured bounce is in my step as I reach the locker bay and walk toward the stairwell. I stop when I see two Sophomores walking toward me. One of them's a fat kid dressed in ill-fitting skinny jeans and the other's a little brat with patches of red stubble checkered around his acne.

The fat one's holding a big camera from the tech lab, and he points it in my direction as I walk toward them.

"I'll shove that camera up your ass," I warn him.

"Cut!" the skinny kid shouts. He crumbles a few pages in his hands and throws them at the other kid. I recognize him now, I think. Kevin's tutored him before, and he calls him Smelly Mac.

"Wait," he says, and he runs after me as I continue down the hall. I groan, preparing myself for the soupy unwashed smell Kevin's described.

"Leave me alone," I tell him.

"We're filming a promo video for the Rock the Arts Festival," he explains. "Mr. Kauffman wants us to get comments from a few people in the halls. Can you just say something for us?"

"Sure," I tell him, turning again. "You smell like sewage, and your parents don't love you. See if you can use that."

I start walking again. Mac says something, but I'm already heading down the stairs toward the second floor, smiling to myself again.

The door to the ISS room is shut, and through the glass pane in the door I can see a wrinkled old teacher sitting at her desk and watching the three students sitting in their enclosed cubicles. I watch for a second, then decide there's no way of sneaking in.

I sigh and walk down the hallway toward the upper auditorium doors. There's nothing going on in there until after school, since the choir kids only do their crap in the afternoon and the band brats have their own room to practice in. I've come here before whenever I've cut class, and it's a comfortable place to just sit and nap for a bit, maybe mull over a story in my head. Once I walked in and saw a Freshman kid sitting alone in the back row and playing with himself over his jeans.

The lights are off when I discreetly crack the door open and look inside, and only the red glow from the exit signs in the wings is visible.

But I hear someone groaning from inside, a low sort of moan like someone with a hand over their mouth. I pause as I squint my eyes. I poke my head in, careful not to let more than a sliver of light into the room. From the left wings by the stage near the first-floor exit, I see a figure moving.

I smile, sneaking with ninja-like stealth into the room and shutting the door quietly behind me. I take my phone from my pocket with the bright screen kept tight against me. I lower the brightness and open the camera, one finger hovering over the 'record' button. The flash won't come on until I press the button, and I have to put a hand to my mouth to keep from laughing as I picture the look on some asshole's face when I shine the flash on them and watch them flee.

I get closer, all the way down to the lower half of the auditorium.

"Quiet," I hear a girl's voice whisper. Someone mutters a response.

My stomach lurches. I feel a horrible chill as I stop in my tracks.

That voice…

Leave, Grandpa warns me. *You don't want to see this, kid.*

But my feet keep moving. I can't control myself, and even as the feeling in the pit of my stomach grows worse,

I keep moving forward until I reach the dividing wall separating me from whoever's on the other side.

I flatten myself against the wall, listening to the sounds. The muffled groaning continues, along with a wet sound that's barely audible but somehow magnified in my mind like it's coming through a speaker.

You don't need to see this, Grandpa's voice insists. *It's going to hurt, so just turn and go.*

I peek my head around the dividing wall, barely able to keep my own breathing silent.

Even with the faintest red light illuminating the two figures, I can tell who the one on their knees is, and I watch her head moving in front of Jordan's waist. His eyes are closed. One hand is against his own face and the other against the back of a girl's head, running his fingers through her hair.

Temporary paralysis prevents me from looking away or even blinking. Every bit of me is pleading to regain control of my body, and the fist in my chest is suddenly returned and punching my heart over and over as I watch this sick level of Hell I've wandered into.

An angel somewhere must be begging for mercy on my behalf, because suddenly I'm able to move.

I hit the staircase and run, no longer muting my steps but fleeing as fast as I can toward the upstairs doors. I hear someone behind me shout as I run. Someone else curses, and there's a panicked sound of movement from where I'd just left.

I can't see the seats around me in the auditorium, but I feel a thousand invisible eyes watching me with wild laughter, mocking me as I explode through the double doors and back out into the bright light of the second floor, disoriented and sweating and feeling like death.

I run down the hall, and I keep running until I end up collapsing in the hallway outside the shop class doors. I drop my notebooks and sink against the wall, breathing hard and ragged, sick as I've ever felt and unable to collect my thoughts. All I can do for several minutes is sit there with my head in my hands and fight back tears as the image of Sarah kneeling in front of Jordan plays over and over in my mind with horrible clarity.

Chapter Eight

"*Their deaths are justified! Tell you why, Mrs. Lovens, tell—*"

"Wait, wait, wait! Hold it right there, Theodore!"

Jordan sighs heavily as he storms toward the center of the stage where Monk stands mid-pose with the straight razor he'd whipped from his pocket. Monk's expression goes flat as Jordan stands in front of him with his arms crossed.

"What the hell is that?" Jordan demands. Monk raises an eyebrow.

"It's called acting."

"No, *that!*" Jordan waves a hand toward the razor, looking appalled by it. "This show's sponsored by the school, Theodore! Just what the hell makes you think you can bring a lethal weapon on stage? Are you seriously retarded?"

I can see Monk's teeth grinding back and forth behind his lips as he closes his eyes and takes a calm breath inward. Even from my seat on the choir risers, I can see his anger rising just below the surface. Stacy Miller, who gets a lot of crap for having an autistic brother, bristles visibly at the word 'retarded.' The whole group's been patient with Jordan today, not making a single joke about his mom or mentioning anything from last night. I'm hoping Monk loses control and snaps Jordan's neck like a goddamn glowstick.

"What would you prefer I use as a prop instead...*sir?*" Monk asks. "I've never heard of a vengeful barber slitting someone's throat with a banana, have you?"

"Something else!" Jordan yells. "Anything else! Anything but a damn razor, you idiot! You know what..."

Jordan digs into his pocket and brings out a mechanical pencil.

"Here," he says. "This can be your prop. It'll get the point across well enough without risking any sort of accident."

Monk grimaces as he takes the pencil, and I imagine the several "accidents" going through his mind right now. *Stab him,* I pray silently.

"Fine," Monk says, and he folds the straight razor and tucks it into his jeans pocket. "May I continue?"

"No," Jordan says wearily, rubbing his mouth with one hand. "Come to think of it, there are too many other problems. The whole thing is terrible."

"Problems such as...?"

"You say the word 'shit' a little into the song," Jordan says. He makes a face like he's picturing utter disaster— riots in the streets, performers lynched indiscriminately by angry mobs. "If you want to keep the song, you need to change that, too."

"You want me to *change* an award-winning musical?"

"Yes! Just say 'filled with spit' or 'filled with wit' instead. No one cares about musicals, anyway."

The comment nearly sets Monk on a rampage, and I see the anger breaking through. *Do it,* I think. *Rip his throat out, and stomp on his corpse.*

Monk manages to choke back whatever he's about to scream, and he allows his favorite musical to take a second purging.

"Anything you say," he says. "May I continue?"

"From the top," Jordan says, backing away again toward his seat. Monk takes another deep breath, stares down at the pitiful replacement in his hand, and starts the act over.

I stare at Sarah, who's sitting in the front row of the auditorium with her feet up on the seat and a drawing pad in her lap. She looks completely engrossed in whatever she's drawing, and it makes me wonder if she disappears into her work the way I disappear into mine, if pencil strokes and brushstrokes are as therapeutic as keystrokes and paragraphs.

I hate her. I hate her for what I saw, and I hate myself for wandering into it.

My throat tightens. I picture all the times she sat next to me and Grandpa on the back porch of his house, drinking pop and smoking cigarettes with us as we talked for hours about crappy people, new movies, and how much better our lives would be someday.

Sarah and I talked once about what sort of parents we'd be someday, how we'd stop ourselves from messing up our kids the way we've been messed up. I don't remember a whole lot about our solution, but I remember she said her kid was going to be named Charlie. Charlie, Charlie, Charlie. I made a stupid joke about chocolate factories, but she laughed at it anyway. Grandpa went inside, and we stayed out on the porch together until sunrise, just the two of us.

All those long talks, all those nights watching crappy b-movies together when Monk and the others were too busy to join… All those moments really were *just* moments.

I watch the colored pencil moving in her hand. My insides feel like a fire-gutted church.

Monk wraps up the song with a loud and melodramatic bellow, down on his knees with both arms raised toward the ceiling. Sarah sets down her drawing pad and shoots to her feet, clapping wildly for him. A few others join in, but most of them are just looking down at their phones.

"Good enough, Theodore," Jordan says, looking less than impressed. He twirls a finger impatiently and then looks at me. "Trey, why aren't you moving? I told you you're up next!"

I set down my books and walk toward center stage. My hands are in my pockets, because I can't lose control and choke him to death if my hands are in my pockets.

When I tell the story this time, it's an unenthusiastic mess. I can't remember most of it, and I meant to write story cues on an index card but haven't been able to focus on a damn thing all day. I slog through it the best I can, not giving a damn as the few attentive people in the room quickly lose interest. I can't even picture the story anymore; all I see in my head is Sarah on her knees with Jordan's hand in her hair.

A few people clap obligingly when I finish. I walk back toward the risers, and Monk moves to sit down beside me while Clyde takes the stage and does his overly-sanitized stand-up routine.

"You feeling okay?" he asks. I shrug. I feel him staring at me for a second, but I ignore him. He walks away, and I'm sitting alone again. I feel myself shaking like it's freezing cold, but when I raise my hand in front of my eyes it's perfectly still. I want to smash my head against something.

Clyde's act is suddenly over, and Jordan's standing in front of him on the stage and rattling off a series of notes. He writes on the clipboard he's carrying, looking so goddamn official and pretentious and unholy.

Why you? I wonder. *What's so special about you?*

If I tied him up, gouged out his eyeballs, and stripped away every bit of skin and muscle, would his skeleton be much different than anyone else's? Was he born with gilded bones, or the markings of some celebrity god in his marrow, markings that blessed him so thoroughly that he's freely given *every goddamn thing* the rest of us are too filthy to receive?

I'm breathing harder, and I don't want to calm myself down. Anger feels better than self-pity or braindead emptiness.

I could smash Jordan's knees in with a baseball bat. I could cut his face off and wear it like a mask, and I could taunt him while he screams by talking an endless stream of bullshit about the new book I'm working on, my perfect plans for after high school, all the girls I'm going to cheat on my faithful girlfriend with in college, all the literary agents who'll be lining up to suck my dick the moment Mommy points me in their direction.

I could twist his head off his shoulders and hold his bleeding neck hole to my ear like a conch, listening for the fabled 'Sound of the Brilliant Masterpiece.'

Or maybe I could just mutilate him a bit, that would be alright. Just one long and deep gash across his face—that's all it would take to ruin his whole life, I bet.

I dwell on it for a few minutes, thinking of all the horrible things I'd never do even if I had the opportunity. I know I'm too weak. Maybe everyone's a ruthless murderer in their head. In reality, I'm still a loser and Sarah's never going to want me the way I want her. I'll always, always, always be this way no matter what goes on in my mind or what I *think* I can do about it.

I shake my head and rub my eyes, but I still feel myself mentally descending, and I can't tune out from it. I pull my phone from my pocket and pop my earbuds in, and I close my eyes and rest my head in my hands.

Someone shakes me before the first song ends.

"Hey," Sarah says. "Your story was different today."

She sounds so disappointed, like she actually cares about me or our friendship or any of the things I thought were real but were all just in my head.

"It sucked anyway," I mutter. She frowns and sits down beside me. I look between my feet.

"I thought it was good," she says.

I shrug.

"You look like there's something wrong," she says. "Are you hungover?"

"No."

"You're telling me you weren't out drinking with Clive last night?"

"No."

She shakes her head and draws a deep breath. I'm pretty sure she's about to go on some rant about Clive and what he did and how wrong it was. I put my earbuds back in.

"Hey!" she says, swatting me. I take an earbud out.

"What?"

"Are you serious right now?"

"Well, what do you want?"

She frowns again. Her lipstick is crimson today. I wonder if she had to reapply it.

"I'm not pissed at you, okay?" she says. "I know Clive did the flyers, not you. Don't be so defensive."

I'm holding back a scream. I gnaw the inside of my cheek and stare down at the risers.

"I think the meeting's almost over," she says. I don't even have to glance up to hear Jordan still giving notes to poor Clyde. "You want me to get you a pop?"

I shake my head. "I'm okay."

"Something's bothering you."

"No, it's not. I'm fine," I tell her.

"Fine," she says. She's quiet for a second. She nods and taps her fingers on top of her drawing pad.

"I made you something," she says, opening up the pad. "I started on it last night. I was going to show it to you later at the graveyard."

I open my mouth to make some bland and dismissive comment about whatever it is she's showing me, something cruel and overly-critical and Jordan-like, because apparently that's what she loves, not all this 'Trey' stuff that I'm full of.

But I glance over at the sketch and stop myself in time. I turn toward her, and she hands me the pad in both hands like it's a baby wrapped in a blanket. I stare at it, and it's like a sprinkler system putting out the fires in my lungs.

"You made this?" I ask. She nods, pleased with herself.

"Like I said, your story was good," she says. "I got a little inspired by it."

"It's…really, really good," I tell her.

I suck at words, terrible writer that I am. The sketch is better than 'good,' it's absolutely brilliant, and it makes everything I've mentally discarded feel suddenly real again. Like God waving his holy hand, it rebuilds everything I thought was destroyed.

"That's what he looks like, right?" she asks, moving closer to me. "I tried to remember all the details, but I feel like I missed something."

"No, it's perfect."

"The good guy was the one with the spidery legs, right?" she asks. "I remember you said he was ugly and deformed, but it's just a sketch, so I didn't go into too much detail."

"You nailed it," I tell her. I stare at the drawing, the picture that came *out* of my mind and *into* Sarah's mind and is now here in her drawing pad. I feel elated just looking at it, and for some reason my mouth takes this as a cue to keep talking.

"I can't believe how talented you are," I tell her.

"It's not that good," she says. "It's just a sketch. It's not even done yet."

"Remember the other night you were talking about us all getting matching tattoos?" I ask. "I think we should get this."

She laughs, taking the pad back.

"I'm glad you like it."

"I'm serious," I tell her. "Do you even know how good you are at this stuff? Nobody else can make something like *that* and just call it a sketch, something they just threw together because they were inspired. You're really, really good. You know that, right?"

Her smile fades, and she looks at me for a second like she's waiting for something else, some kind of "but" or "if only" or some other crappy qualifier. Seeing that expression makes me instantly regret saying anything, and I look back down at my feet as she closes the pad and taps her thumbs against the cover.

"Thanks," she says. I nod.

It's quiet between us again. A girl from the group does a long dance routine, some strange and whimsical ballet number. My left leg is restless.

"What are you listening to?" Sarah asks. I shrug, and hand her one of my earbuds as I put the other in my ear and restart the song.

It's the first song from Michael Stanley Band's *Heartland*, "I'll Never Need Anyone More." I watch her expression, anxious for the verdict. She nods along, and I think I see a smile.

"Interesting choice," she says. She reaches for my phone. "Gimme."

I hand it over, expecting her to shuffle through whatever other music I have on there, searching for Marilyn Manson, Rob Zombie, or some other band that she already knows. She skips through a few songs on the album, though, and I'm pretty sure she's sold on it.

"My dad blasted this band all the time when I was a kid," I tell her. She nods, and I decide to shut up, because I know that look. She's lost in the music, hypnotized by it the same way I was after a million or so times hearing it. Or she's just faking it for my benefit.

What I don't mention, and what I'll *never* mention, is that the song "Rosewood Bitters" was practically a lullaby for me as a kid, and that I still mumble the words to "He Can't Love You" and "All I Ever Wanted" to myself in the shower, holding a shampoo bottle in front of my mouth like I'm holding a microphone and rocking out to the music my dad still probably thinks I hate. Too much information, I bet.

"You like it?" I ask.

She nods. "Can you text me a few of those?"

"Hell yeah."

The rest of the meeting goes by pretty quickly. The last couple of acts finish, and Jordan gives a very brief speech to the whole group about how it's all "coming together, even if a few of you clearly don't care." It doesn't get under my skin. Earlier today feels so distant, and I'm someone else again, someone better.

When Jordan's done spewing his usual semi-acidic word vomit, everyone gets up to leave, and Sarah walks toward him with her drawing pad under her arm. I watch her energy change again as she stands talking to him. It's something about her eyes: she looks suddenly vulnerable in a way I've never seen her, and even though she's smiling I see her searching for something from him. He barely even looks at her as she says something I can't hear, he's far too busy flipping through his fruity little clipboard and grimacing at whatever's on the pages. She might as well be invisible, but she's still breathing him in like air.

It's disgusting.

She walks down toward the first row of seats where she left her books. I start toward the opposite exit. A few steps from the door, I see one of Clive's flyers on the floor. It's stepped on and dirty, but I pick it up and smile.

"Jordan," I say, walking back toward him with the flyer held out. I feel so damn invincible, so damn sure. "You missed one."

He looks toward me and sees what I'm holding. His face contorts in an ugly grimace, and he snatches the flyer from my hand.

"It's actually a pretty good picture."

"Fuck off," he says under his breath, glancing toward Sarah.

"You know," I say, "Maybe you should give your mom some notes."

"Excuse me?"

"I mean, she came in today to show that she's not bothered by all this, right?" I ask him. I scrunch my face the same way he does when he's giving his notes. "Do you really *believe* her act?"

The look on his face says he wants to hit me really, really badly. It's the same look I've seen on his mom's face when Clive and I push it sometimes. But Sarah's walking back toward us. He wouldn't dare.

"Maybe she got what she deserved," I say quietly. Sarah's back on the stage, and I tilt a hand at her as I turn my back to Jordan.

And then I walk off toward the exit, feeling like a goddamn champion on a throne made of clouds.

Chapter Nine

"There's only one thing faster than a hot, sunny mid-March day in the city of Inspiration, and that's the tempo at which Father McAlbertson's knife went in and out of the frontside of his prisoner as she hung with her wrists bound by heavy chains. Her name was Leslie Dotson, and she screamed bloody murder through the gag in her mouth, but nobody came to her rescue. She was all alone. He watched the life leave her eyes as he drove the tip of his blade into her naked chest one final time, and when he was certain she was dead as she could be, he licked his lips and stood tall, feeling the holy spirit kiss his hands through the blood they were covered in. 'And now,' he thought, 'to break the bread of your body.'"

I stare off into the carpet as I finish reading the opening paragraph of my story. My foot won't stop tapping, and I'm sweating through the pits of my shirt.

"Is that it?" Monk asks. He's sitting at my computer chair, hunched over with a wide grin.

"So far," I tell him.

"Damn, man, it's not half bad."

"Really?"

Kevin shrugs from the floor.

"You've got a few run-on sentences," he says. "And also, it's sort of a lot at once. Don't you think you should start the book out a little slower? Maybe ease into the horror stuff?"

"No, screw that!" Monk says. "A story *needs* to start off with a hell of an opening! What, you want him to start off describing the flowers or something? Maybe spend a little time discussing each character's sleep cycle?"

"I'm just saying, it's a lot at once," Kevin insists. "It's not my story, so ignore me completely if you want, I'm just saying it's a turnoff for me."

Monk shakes his head. "You're worse than Jordan, you know that?"

"He asked for notes, and that's my note."

I nod.

"Kevin's right. Thanks, Kevin," I tell him. I turn a page in my notebook and make a show of writing the note down, pretending I'm not screaming a little on the inside.

Clive sits up on my bed. He still has his boots on, and there's dried mud caked on the bottoms.

"Do you know what happens next, or what?" he asks.

"Still working through it," I lie.

"We should really get back to studying," Kevin says, grabbing his book off the top of Hector's tank. Clive snorts and whips a pillow at him.

"Screw that," he says. "I want to hear the rest of the story."

"It's not ready," I tell him. He puts a cigarette between his lips as he opens the window and climbs out onto the roof.

"Whatever, man, just wing it. None of us read, anyway. We don't care if it's choppy."

"Let me just send it to you when it's finished," I tell him. Below Kevin's comment, I discreetly write *'too choppy?'* Clive shrugs.

"You damn artists," he says, shaking his head. "So precious about everything."

Clive has a bruise on the left side of his face, and it's dark and ugly as any I've seen on him. None of us have said anything about it, but it was the first thing I noticed when Clive met up with us earlier. He went to school that way, too, but I seriously doubt the teacher in I.S.S. said anything about it to anyone. A bruise like that doesn't mean anything when none of the teachers would give you water if you were on fire.

"I like how twisted it is," Monk says. "I mean, priests are supposed to be the good and pious guys, the holiest of the holy and stuff. You'd never stop to think maybe a couple of them are messed up in the head."

"It's almost cartoonish, though," Kevin says. "Don't hate me or anything, but it's like something out of a b-movie."

"I like b-movies," I tell him.

"Then it's great," he says. He continues working, biting his lip as he scribbles something out. I write in my notes, *'b-movie bullshit?'*

"Let's go do something," Clive says from outside.

"We're studying," Kevin says. Clive blows lip music.

"I mean, let's go do something fun. Want to go mess around at Wal-Mart?"

"I think you've had enough excitement," Monk says. "Not that I disapprove. Screw Mrs. Renus."

"Mrs. *Anus*," Clive corrects, grinning apishly. "And hey, only half of it was my idea. Thank Kevin for making it possible."

"I just showed you basic photoshop and where to print everything," Kevin says. "Legally speaking, I have *nothing* to do with how you chose to use that knowledge."

"You drove the van," Clive points out. When Kevin doesn't look up again, he grins. "Come on, would it kill you to say you had fun?"

"Where did you guys print all those flyers?" Monk asks. "I mean, my dad buys all the computer ink in our house, but I know it's expensive."

"We used the school printers," Kevin says.

"You liar."

"No, for real," Kevin says. He looks up from his book. "The cameras are never on in the hallways. Security at our school's a joke."

"How do you know they're not on?" Monk asks. Kevin shrugs.

"It's just a guess. I mean, if they *were* on, Clive and I would be in serious trouble by now."

Clive's smile disappears. "You said they weren't on. Like, *for sure* weren't on."

"And now we're sure they aren't," Kevin says. "We wore masks, anyway."

"Damn," Clive sighs. He takes another long drag from the cigarette.

"Just listen, okay," Kevin says, setting down his book. "How many times has bad stuff happened in the hallways and nobody gets in trouble for it? You remember last year somebody wrote 'faggot' in Sharpie on Kyle Derbins' locker?"

Clive nods.

"What I'm saying is, if the cameras were always on and someone was always checking them, whoever wrote it would've been caught right away. But they weren't. Ergo, the cameras are probably just for show."

"But how did you get into the school?" I ask.

Kevin lifts his butt from the floor and reaches into his back pocket, drawing out a key ring.

"I got a copy of the school key last year from Mac. Pretty sure he stole it from a janitor and copied it."

"Yeah, I've heard a few people have copies," Monk says, nodding. "I guess they never thought they could get away with using it."

"That's the thing," Kevin says. "If everybody knew how bad the security at our school actually is, they'd do stupid stuff that would give the school a reason to actually use the cameras. That's why I didn't let Clive throw the flyers all over the hallways, because they would've known someone was inside the building after hours."

Monk smiles at the floor, shaking his head.

"Our school's so poor," he says.

"No kidding," Clive says, climbing back inside. "The moral of the story, I guess, is that justice was served. I'm not saying it's God's will or anything, or that I'm some sort of divine hero, but justice was served."

"Sarah's totally going to kick your ass," I point out. He shrugs.

"She'll get over it. Probably."

"Speaking of which," Monk says, checking his phone. "Where's she at? She never responded to my message."

"Probably with Jordan," Clive says.

For a brief and horrible second, I picture Sarah kneeling in front of Jordan in the darkness of the auditorium, and I bit down hard on my cheek.

"She's on her way," I tell them. "She texted me a little while ago. And she's bringing food."

Clive throws his hands toward the ceiling.

"Alleluia!" he cries.

"Seriously, though, you might not want to be yourself when she gets here," I warn him. "She's probably pissed at you."

"I'll manage."

I shrug and go back to working on the stupid English paper that's due tomorrow. I'm supposed to be halfway through reading *Fahrenheit 451* by now, but I've mostly been reading chapter summaries online and half-assing my way through everything. I doubt I'm the only one.

She shows up half an hour later, and by that time we're down in the living room and Clive's browsing through Dad's record collection in the office. He drones on and on about his theory of music prodigies of the past versus those of our time, all about how he was born in the wrong era and he'd give his left nut just to *glimpse* the 1970s in all its glory. We don't even bother pretending to listen as we eat leftover pizza from the fridge.

"Jesus," Sarah says, walking through the front door. "This again?"

"For ten minutes now," Monk says, grabbing the last cold slice from the box.

"Will you just shut up and *play something* already?" I ask.

"Give it a second," Clive says, throwing a dismissive hand. He pulls *Led Zeppelin II* from the shelf, and I reach for a couch pillow to whip at him.

"Pick something else. *Anything* else," I tell him. "I'll make you a damn playlist filled with Led Zeppelin if you want, but I'm so, so sick of that album!"

"Hear, hear," Kevin mutters.

Clive grins. "Awww, a playlist!"

Sarah sets a bag of tacos down on the kitchen table and digs into one. Red sauce drips down her mouth.

"I was thinking on the way over here," she says between bites. "What would you guys think about Jordan coming out with us one of these nights?"

Clive's search through the records halts abruptly.

"No," he says.

"*Hell* no," Monk emphasizes.

"I'm being serious," she says.

"So are we," Clive says. "I'm telling you right now, if he comes within a hundred yards of our tree, I'll cut his head off and send a recording to his mother. Test me."

"First of all, screw *you*," Sarah tells him. "And second, he was already there. We went for a walk after school."

The pizza nearly falls out of my hand.

"You took him to our tree?" I ask. I imagine Jordan standing in front of Grandpa's headstone, grimacing at the strange design and muttering critical notes to himself, maybe making Sarah laugh with some cutting comment, changing her more and more.

"He wanted to see it," she explains. Clive and Monk are staring daggers at her. "Look, I was having a shitty day, okay? I was thinking about that time we all played tag in the library, and I remembered how Grandpa laughed when I ran straight into that librarian, how fun that whole day was, and… I don't know, it just sort of spiraled from there. I wanted to keep thinking about all those good memories, but every time I thought of his face, I started to cry."

I nod. "I get it."

"We sat on Jordan's porch talking, and when I told him all about the tree and what that place means to us, he said maybe it would help to just go there for a while."

Clive shakes his head. "You shouldn't have taken him there."

"I don't feel I have to explain myself to you," she says. "Listen, you guys, I know you're completely dedicated to hating Jordan, but it's really immature and I want you to knock it off. He's not a bad person."

Monk laughs bitterly toward his feet.

"Okay," Sarah says, "I can understand Monk hating him, maybe, but the rest of you guys? Seriously, what has he ever done to any of you?"

"He's just *him*," Kevin says. "There's just something about him, it's instinctual. I can't help it."

"Well, try. Before Grandpa brought us all together, would any of us *really* have hung out?"

"It's different," I tell her. I'm still staring down at the counter, trying to listen to what she's saying and be completely objective, but also unable to shake the sick image of Jordan comforting her in front of Grandpa's grave.

"How is it different?" she insists. "Grandpa said it over and over again, 'Crazy can sense crazy.' I know Jordan better than any of you, and I'm telling you he's one of us. You're all just seeing what you want to see, and it's not fair to him."

I shake my head. "You're wrong."

"Sarah," Clive says, hands splayed helplessly, "If Jordan shows up one of these nights, I really, seriously can't guarantee I won't do something terrible. I know you think I'm a piece of shit or whatever for that thing with his mom, but I'm telling you, I'd straight up kiss that witch's feet before I put up with even a *second* of Jordan ruining our nights."

Sarah chokes the air in front of her with both hands, looking exasperated.

"You're all a bunch of jackasses," she says. She throws the rest of the bag of food into the living room, and Clive pounces at it. "Where's the bathroom?"

"Did the taco move right through you?" Clive asks with a smirk. She doesn't even acknowledge him.

"Next to the basement steps," I tell her. She walks off, and I look toward Clive. "Don't be such a dick," I tell him. He waves a dismissive hand.

"She knew how we'd respond," he says. He waves a soft taco at me. "You just want to bang her, that's why you're not pissed."

"Keep your voice down," I tell him.

"Are we going to Wal-Mart or what? Seriously, you guys, I'm getting bored."

Kevin grabs the bag from him. "Give me a few minutes, I'm almost done with your Algebra."

"You're doing his homework?" I ask. He shrugs.

"For twenty bucks, yeah. The hardest part is dumbing it down."

"Otherwise they'll catch on," Clive says.

I walk back upstairs while they eat. My shirt feels sweaty, and even though the pits aren't soaked I decide to change. My hair looks crappy, too, and when I go into the upstairs bathroom to fix it I notice a red bump on the upper left side of my forehead. It's not even a pimple yet, and it'll probably go away on its own, but I stand there in front of the mirror and scrub the absolute hell out of it, thinking only about Jordan standing with Sarah in front of Grandpa's grave, sharing a nice little moment while Grandpa listens from below.

When I walk into the hallway I see Sarah standing in my bedroom, kneeling down in front of Hector's tank. She smiles up at me when I walk in.

"Why didn't you ever tell me you have a tarantula?" she asks. "Can I take him out?"

"I think he's molting," I tell her.

"Crap." She taps the glass a few times, and when Hector doesn't come out from beneath his shelter, she stands again. "Your room's actually pretty nice."

"You sound surprised."

"I figured your room would be a complete mess," she says. "I mean, that's how mine is all the time, so I guess I figure everyone's is like that."

She walks toward the desk, looking around at the posters with an appraising sort of look. She points at the one above my bed, a theatrical poster for *Attack the Pack* that's frayed on the corners from being torn from its tacks and re-hung too many times.

"I remember that movie," she says. "You liked it?"

"It's alright," I lie.

"I fell asleep halfway through. I remember it wasn't very good."

"The books were better."

Her eyes catch something on my desk, and she turns toward me excitedly as she seizes it.

"Is this a *poem*?" she asks incredulously. "You write *poetry*?"

My heart races with sudden terror.

"Please don't read that," I beg, reaching for the piece of loose-leaf. She holds it out of reach, dancing her eyebrows as she ducks under my arm.

"*'Like a carpenter's nail bent out of shape, my love remains unused,'*" she reads loudly. "*'And like a hammer broken from endless swings, my heart feels hurt and abused. I—'*"

Before she can read any further, I shoot for the back of her legs and pull them out from under her. She falls toward the floor with a surprised shriek, catching hold of my shoulder on her way down, and I snatch the page from her hand. I start to stand, and she dives on top of my back, reaching for the paper. I give in almost right away; I let myself crumble beneath her, and I feel the warmth of her body against my back as she wrestles me for the page. She crawls over me, laughing and pushing my head away. I let her almost reach it before I stand up suddenly, tear the page to little bits, and throw it into the metal wastebasket. She smiles as she pushes herself up onto her elbows.

"A little defensive?"

"It was just a rough draft," I tell her. I feel my cheeks burning, and I adjust myself discreetly before pulling the computer chair toward me and sitting.

"Clive said something about going to Wal-Mart," I say. She climbs to her feet, and smirks back at me as she walks out of the room.

"You can tell us all about your future as a poet on the way there," she says.

I ball up a piece of computer paper and throw it at her, and she smacks it back it me. I sit there for a few long seconds, just replaying it all in my head and wondering if it happened at all. Sarah was in my bedroom. Her body was on top of mine. I could smell the lavender scent of her shirt.

I don't come downstairs for another few minutes. My skin feels on fire, and there's a big stupid smile on my face that I can't fight down. The others are already outside, and the front door is wide open. I grab the empty pizza box and drop it in the recycling bin outside as I follow them toward Kevin's car.

"Dibs on driving!" Clive calls, swiping Kevin's keys.

"Now hold on!" Kevin shouts. "I just got the damn thing, and my mom'll throw a fit if anything happens to it!"

Clive blows lip music.

"I said I'll *drive* it, not crash it into a ditch. Besides, I'm an awesome driver."

"I'll drive," I offer quickly. Kevin wrinkles his brow at me.

"When did you get your license?" he asks.

"I didn't. Not yet, I mean."

"There's no way in hell I'm letting you drive my car."

"Come on," I insist. "You'll be right there riding shotgun. It'll be educational."

He lowers his eyes uncomfortably, wincing.

"Let him drive," Sarah says. I feel something in my chest flutter, but I manage to keep my stupid grin from spreading wider.

Kevin looks down at his keys, then sighs.

"Fine," he says. "But if anything goes wrong, I'll literally murder you. *Literally*."

"It'll be fine," I promise him. I smile toward Sarah, but she's already getting into the back seat with Clive and Monk. I get in the driver seat and adjust the mirrors.

I haven't even taken my permit test in over three months, and the last time I took it I knocked over two cones while parallel parking. As long as I don't have to parallel park, everything will go fine.

"Keep it under thirty, alright?" Kevin says. I nod and start the car.

My foot barely touches the gas pedal, and the car lurches forward, nearly rear-ending the neighbor. Monk's face hits the back of my seat as I slam on the brakes.

"Sorry," I tell them. Kevin takes a deep breath, one hand moving restlessly on his knee.

I adjust pretty quickly to the car's sensitive touch, and after a few minutes I'm cruising around comfortably with one hand on the wheel, feeling like a seasoned pro. Hell, I could get my license anytime I want, I just don't see the point in getting it. A license is no good if you don't have a car of your own, and there's really no point in getting your own car in a town this small. The only reason people at school get one is for attention, and I bet most of them can't even afford to fill their tanks.

Then again...it's oddly relaxing. There's something powerful about it, something that makes me feel like a little less of a screw up, like maybe I'm someone with his whole life figured out. I let my mind wander a bit as I take the long way toward downtown.

I look at Sarah in the rearview mirror. I'm picturing a million different things that feel simultaneously real and unreal, memories that the two of us haven't even experienced yet. I picture us sitting cozy in a dark living room, her head on my shoulder and her fingers interwoven with mine, one thumb tracing the inside of my palm as I trace counterclockwise circles gently just above her waist and feel the warmth of her skin.

There's a naked feeling, but we're naked with our clothes still on. *Emotionally* naked, the sort of naked that everyone thinks they know about but can't really describe until they've felt it, and I'm actually *feeling* it in this daydream. I only know about this feeling because one of the characters in Grandpa's book talked about it, and he called it "a feeling like someone's running their fingers through your soul, mixing all their wet paint with yours and finishing the picture you never knew you were working on." The rest of Grandpa's book was a little boring, but that description really stuck in my mind.

The Wal-Mart parking lot is empty with the exception of a few cars. On either side of the mega-store are several smaller storefronts, each of them either dead or dying, and a large woman in a purple sweater stands smoking a cigarette outside of the boutique salon on the far-left side. I see her looking at us when we pull up, putting on a welcoming smile and stubbing her cigarette out against the brick wall beside her. I avoid looking at her, feeling guilty for reasons I can't exactly pinpoint, and I have the sudden urge to pick a different spot a little further away from her store so as not to get her hopes up. But the others are already opening the car doors and walking, so I turn the car off and keep my head down as I walk after them. When I look in the woman's direction, she's already re-lit the cigarette, and she continues staring toward the dead lot.

We walk past the old greeter in a wheelchair, a shriveled and hunched over man who's been given a too-large smock and a hat with a smiley face pinned to the front. He rasps a lukewarm 'welcome,' and I stare distantly toward the checkout counters, feeling something like cold fingers moving up my back. I don't look behind us to see if it's actually Grandpa sitting there playing a long con on us all, faking dead all this time only to let his familiar voice give him away. I wait for him to call after us, maybe pull two paper bag puppets out from inside the smock and have them put on some quick show that will make us all laugh.

Stupid, stupid thought. The inside of my cheek feels raw from biting it.

"You want a slushy?" Sarah asks. The others are walking ahead of us. Monk's singing loudly over the music playing from the speakers, bellowing some musical I haven't heard before and don't really care about.

"I left my wallet at home."

"I'll get this one. You can owe me."

I shrug.

"Sure," I say.

We walk toward the drink stand beside the bathrooms. The lone checkout clerk notices us, but he looks up from his phone for only a second before losing interest. We fill our giant Styrofoam cups and she pays for them both, and then we walk after the others. I watch her from the corner of my eye, wondering what it means or if it's even supposed to mean anything at all. I suck the drink down so fast that I get a brain freeze, and then I leave the cup on a shelf as I walk by it.

"Are you going to any concerts this summer?" I ask. Stupid, stupid question, but she tolerates it.

"Probably at some point, yeah," she says. "Jordan wants to go to some country music thing in Columbus, but I think I'd rather shoot myself in the head."

"Nah, shoot him instead," I say. She shoves me playfully. I feel encouraged by it.

"You know what we haven't done in a long time?" I ask.

"What?"

"Played 'Last Man Standing.'"

She grins. "Is that a challenge?"

"Sure."

She looks behind us, where a woman in the book aisle pushes her shopping cart idly back and forth while the toddler in the front cries nonsense. Other than the woman, we've only seen two other customers in the store so far, and neither of them were people we know.

She eyes me suspiciously.

"You'll push me down as soon as we start," she says. I shake my head.

"We'll have a momentary truce, and honor it until it's just us," I tell her. I nod toward the others ahead of us. "And look who the easiest target is."

She looks ahead at Clive, who stopped to grab a bouncy ball from the giant mesh cage near the toy section. She smiles, eyes lit up deviously as she sips from her straw.

"No limits?" she asks.

"No limits," I agree.

"Awesome." She takes the lid off her slushy. "I go high, you go low?"

I nod. "Let's get him."

Sarah charges toward Clive, and with a loud battle cry she raises the drink overhead. Clive turns around just in time to see the cup coming toward him, and she smashes it over his face, covering him in bluish liquid. He recoils, eyes gone wide as he watches her race away with her middle finger held triumphantly up behind her. I barrel into him, and he smashes hard into a shelf full of Barbie dolls.

"Clive's out!" I call, running after the others. Clive's shouts a loud curse, and Kevin sprints toward the women's clothing aisle when he sees me running after him.

Sarah's already after Monk, but he expertly dodges her as she goes in for the shove, spinning and grabbing a nerf ball from a shelf. He laughs maniacally as he throws it, box and all, toward my head. It crashes into a poorly-dressed mannequin beside me, knocking an arm loose.

"Trade off!" Sarah calls, running after Kevin as he pulls bag after bag of socks and panties off a shelf and starts throwing them. She bats one out of the air, pursuing him relentlessly as he flees toward the Electronics section.

I nod and run at Monk, who lowers himself into a Sumo wrestler stance and waves me forward.

"Oh, hell no," I say, and I turn tail and run toward the deli aisle.

"Face me, coward!" he shouts, stomping loudly in my tread as I weave between displays. I stay as low as I can, heart pounding as I move stealthily and pull a flowery pencil dress from its hanger. The last time we played, Grandpa pretended to slip and fall near the front of the store, and it took a few minutes for anyone to boot us all out. He's not here now, so we have maybe a minute until someone shouts at us.

"Kevin's out!" I hear Sarah call from across the store.

Monk turns toward her voice, and I seize my opportunity—I open the bottom of the dress and run at him with it raised overhead like a poacher's net. I almost get it over his head, but he hears me coming when I'm within just a few feet of him, and one of his mammoth arms smashes into my side. I fall toward the ground, knocking over an entire shelf of stacked graphic t-shirts. But I manage to catch myself before my body can hit the floor.

"Oh, bullshit!" Monk shouts. I'm already rebounding, though, and without wasting a second, I charge back at him.

And then Sarah hits him, leaping up onto his back like a tiny goth spider monkey and taking him quickly to the floor as he shouts in surprise. I laugh my ass off as Monk pulls a circular rack of shirts down to the floor with him, and Sarah hurries to her feet, eyeing me next.

"Hey!" someone shouts. I see a short man step out of an office near the front of the store, someone who looks less than five years older than us but at the same time tired and ancient. He walks toward us with an authoritative gait, not bothering to rush but relying on his high and mighty station as Lord of the Store to keep us pinned to the spot.

"Split!" I shout, and I bolt for the exit as Monk runs toward one side of the man and Sarah runs toward the other. The poor guy nearly falls over himself, spinning on his feet and seizing only air as he tries to grab hold of us all at once.

"Get back here and clean this mess up!" he shouts, but we're already past the checkout counters and pausing only to watch Clive as he runs up behind the man and slaps him on the ass.

"Run!" he shouts, eyes filled with gleeful madness.

We make it out to the car without anyone on our tails, and Kevin's the first to reach the driver's seat. We pile in the car and take off, and as I look through the rear glass I see the little man walking out the front of the store, hands on his hips and utterly defeated.

"Damn, I needed that!" Sarah says from the front seat, throwing her head back and running her hands through her hair.

"I need a damn shower," Clive says. He pulls off his soaked shirt and holds it out the open window to wring it out. Kevin turns in his seat, attention pivoting between the backseat and the road.

"Tell me you didn't get any of that on my seats!" he says.

"It washes out."

"Goddamn right it does, because *you're* washing it out!"

An oncoming car blares its horn. Kevin jerks the wheel in time to bring us to the right side of the road.

"Don't get us killed, Kev," Sarah says. I see her hands clutching the door handle beside her in a death grip. It makes me smile for some reason.

"So who won that round? Technically, I mean?" I ask.

"Oh, I totally won!" Sarah says, turning in her seat. "I got all three takedowns, you got none!"

"I at least got the assist," I argue. "I think that makes it a tie."

"*One* assist versus *three* takedowns?"

"It merits a tiebreaker."

"He's got a valid point," Monk says.

"Oh, whatever!" Sarah says, shaking her head. She's smiling, though, and when she turns back around in her seat I see her look at me in the side mirror. She looks away quickly. My fingers tap restlessly against my knee.

"What kind of tiebreaker do you have in mind?" she asks.

I feel both brave and anxious for a second, and my guts turn as I think of the flirtatious words I could say, the confident and suave suggestions of someone better. Monk nudges me, but I can't move the words from my mind to my tongue.

"Never mind. You totally won that one," I say instead. "I'll get you next time, though. Count on it."

"Promises, promises," she says, and she half-turns in her seat so that I can see her dance her eyebrows.

Clive reaches over and flicks my earlobe. When I turn to look at him, he raises a questioning hand at me like I missed something crucial. I open my hands at him, knowing damn well what he means but pretending I don't.

"No, no, no. I absolutely object to the ruling," he says, leaning forward toward the center of the car. "I think we need a clear winner here. I think we need to see a one-on-one match between Sarah and Trey. First one to pin the other for a three-count wins."

"I think that's a great idea," Monk says, grinning like an idiot. "Trey, don't you think that's a great idea?"

I don't say a damn word, I just look down at the floor between my feet and wish I could disappear. I hear Sarah click her tongue.

"How about it?" Clive says.

I sneak a quick glance up, and once again I see Sarah's eyes move quickly away.

"What the hell?" I hear Kevin mutter. I look up and see we're about a block away from the cemetery, and the sun's glaring right at us so that I have to squint to see what he's staring at.

Then my eyes adjust.

"What's he doing here?" Monk asks.

"I don't know," Sarah says. She starts to roll her window down, and Clive reaches forward to stop her.

On the sidewalk up ahead, walking away from the tall wrought iron cemetery gates with his hoodie pulled up over his head, I see Jordan walking with his hands shoved down into his pockets. He's walking quickly, head down low like he's fleeing a murder scene and avoiding suspicion. I know he lives up in the hills, miles away from this side of town.

Something evil and wretched is clawing at the inside of my stomach, some virus suddenly hellbent on destroying me from the inside out.

"When you left here earlier," I say quietly to Sarah, "did Jordan stay behind?"

She shakes her head. "We went back to his house afterward and watched T.V.," she says. The feeling in my stomach worsens for some reason, and I feel a horrible urgency.

"Pull over, Kevin," I say quietly.

"What are you going to do?" he asks.

"Just pull the damn car over!" I snap at him. He slows the car down, and before he's even at the curb I throw my door open and rush out, breaking into a sprint with unholy adrenaline.

Monk shouts something behind me, but I block him out and continue sprinting, entering the cemetery before any of them can even come close to reaching me. I go toward our tree, expecting to find something horrible awaiting me.

He's cut the damn thing down, I think. *Or he spray-painted it. Or he carved something about Grandpa into the side, something slanderous and cruel...*

He messed with our spot somehow, I know it, and I'm going to cut his fingers off one by one and make him eat his own bastard hands.

But to my surprise, there's nothing wrong with the tree when I arrive.

I circle it a few times, looking for the smallest visible flaw, anything that suggests he so much as touched it. The only minor change that catches my eye is near the very bottom of the tree, carved into the bark closest to the ground and highlighted with red sharpie: ***Jordan + Sarah 4Ever.***

I cringe at the hideous cliché, but at the same time I have to laugh at myself. I hear the others approaching quickly through the gates, calling after me, and I wonder how the hell I'm going to explain why I bolted out of the car like some action hero wannabe.

I take a deep breath inward, hoping to save face.

And then I smell it.

It stings my nostrils, a familiar stench I didn't notice right away. I walk toward Grandpa's grave, taking slow steps and praying I'm mistaken.

I'm not.

In front of Grandpa's gravestone, right above where he's buried, is a fat log of human shit. It's lying beside a half-crumbled flyer, maybe the same one I handed to Jordan after the meeting. The flyer's apparently been used as toilet paper.

I don't even know how to react. All I can manage to do is just stare at it, watching a lone fly land and move across it.

Sarah reaches me first, panting heavily and grabbing my forearm.

"Trey, what…"

She loses the words; the smell hits her, and when she looks at Grandpa's grave and sees the desecration, I watch the flood of emotions in her expression, but the most prevalent isn't even anger.

I don't give her time to say anything or defend Jordan's innocence. I rush past her toward the gates, walking in a daze at first but slowly building toward a dead ass sprint as control slips away from me. Monk sees me coming, and when he reaches out to stop me I knock him aside and keep moving.

I run toward Jordan, less than a block away from me.

I don't know what exactly I'm screaming, only that the words spilling out of me feel like a swarm of bees in my throat as my feet continue to pick up speed. My fingers curl inward as I think of how I'm going to dig my nails into his eyes sockets and smash his head into the asphalt until his teeth are nothing but slinters in his face.

This is it. This is the moment he dies, and I'm going to be the one to kill him.

I scream louder, and he turns toward me suddenly. I feel drool running down my chin, and when I see the panic in his face and he starts to run, I laugh hoarsely.

I catch up to him easily, and I grab him by the back of his hoodie and pull him toward the ground.

Clive and Sarah are somewhere behind me shouting words I can't understand. It might as well be in another language for all I can hear.

All I want is Jordan dead, dead, dead, nothing but roadkill on the sidewalk.

I grab him by the throat, and he punches me hard in the face just below my left eye. I feel the sting, and I fall back in recoil, but before he can crawl out from under me I seize his throat again and stab his chest with an empty fist, forgetting somehow there's no knife in my hand.

He kicks and punches, and my face hurts like hell as he lands blow after blow, screaming all the while for me to get off of him, making all the demands he's in no position to make. Doesn't he know today's the day he dies?

He manages to turn onto all fours, climbing to his feet, and I wrap an arm around his throat and twist his head as hard as I can while he throws his elbow repeatedly into my ribcage.

Before I can hear the oh-so-glorious sound of his bastard neck snapping, someone pulls me off of him, and I'm suddenly lying down on the sidewalk with Clive's knees in my chest and Kevin fighting to pin down my wrists.

Through all the tears in my eyes and the blinding red hatred, I see Jordan get back to his feet and stand over us for a second, huffing as he touches his throat with one hand. Sarah appears, and when she shouts something at him, he shoves her away and rushes forward to kick me in the ribs.

"Your friend's a fucking psycho!" he shouts at her.

Monk rushes at him.

"Get the hell out of here," he says. When Jordan doesn't budge, Monk grabs him by his hoodie and throws him back like a ragdoll. "Now!" he roars.

Jordan doesn't wait for a third invitation—he disappears, running for his life toward the end of the block, looking back at us only once. I lean forward and watch him, screaming death threats and fighting to free myself as Clive and Kevin keep me down.

I can't even stop screaming, though I don't even know what's coming out of my mouth, nor do I know what's real or if there's someone still hitting me or how the hell I got from the sidewalk to the backseat of Kevin's car.

All I can feel is pure hatred for everything and everyone, and I'm falling out of reality and into a living hell.

Chapter Ten

They throw me into the backseat of Kevin's car, and I explode everywhere, nothing but blood and guts and bones splattering everything and everyone.

I'm clawing and punching at everything in sight: the seats, the windows, even Monk and Clive's arms as they try to restrain me from opening the door and jumping out onto the streets. The world's moving faster and faster through the window. I can see the signs we pass and the cars moving in the opposite direction—they're all mocking me, taunting me, cheering for that son of a bitch and what he did.

The knuckles on my right hand are bleeding badly from punching the window over and over, and the back of Sarah's seat is streaked in red hieroglyphics that seem to spell death: death to me and death to everyone and everything I love and care about, everything that makes life worth living, every dream and every bit of hope that anything will ever get better.

I'm *screaming*, screaming so goddamn loud that even I'm tired of hearing me and want someone to shut that other passenger the hell up. My body's not mine, and I watch it flail desperately as my head is suddenly shoved under one of Monk's arms and the world turns momentarily upside down. I'm quaking, unable to catch my breath or see anything clearly or do anything but scream.

"Jesus Christ," Grandpa says next to me. I see him in only a blur, but I smell the cheap cigar odor as he holds a paper bag puppet toward my face. "You've finally snapped, haven't you?"

Then it's just Clive sitting there. He grabs my legs, throwing himself overtop of them to stop me from kicking Kevin's seat. I moan miserably, trying to make words but suddenly as stupid and helpless as a stoned toddler.

Horrible films are playing on loop in my head, a picture show of pure damnation.

I see Grandpa slowly decaying, trapped in the body that's betrayed him and unable to even get out of bed to pour himself a glass of water, eyes always tired like he's been awake for days even though he's only been able to sleep on and off for weeks. He's alive but at the same time lifeless, just a dead person wearing the shriveling and overripe banana skin of the person he was, and there's not a damn thing I can do to help him or make him laugh or convince him everything's going to be okay. I can hear him crying painfully in his sleep, but I can't get to him in time or pry away the ghost in the black hood that's standing over him, skeletal hands choking him while a sneering hellish face mocks his anguish. I'm glued to the floor, pinned below this shadow's heavy boot, and all I can do is watch as it pulls Grandpa apart and takes away his humanity before it takes away his life. I turn my head to look away but there's suddenly water everywhere around me, rising to my lips as I lie there so that I can only suck brief gasps of air as Grandpa slips further and further away. I look around for something to seize hold of, something to pull myself up off the floor, but there's no loving hand in sight, only bastards everywhere in the darkness. They all smile and mock me, filling their hands with rocks to weigh me down further.

I want to hit the stop button on everything. I want to unwrite this horrible script we're all obeying and tear it to shreds.

My foot suddenly collides with the driver's seat, and I hear a passing car blare its horn as we're all thrown sideways and the car's tires squeal.

"Calm him the hell down!" Kevin roars. Clive shouts something back, and suddenly I can't move my legs—I'm trapped in bed just like Grandpa, sick and dying and surrounded by nothing but vultures and demons.

"It! Won't! Stop!" I scream, but none of them seem to listen. To them I've just lost my mind, and no matter how much sense everything suddenly makes to me there's nothing I can do to make them understand it.

Monk says something to Kevin, and the streetlights outside in the sunset seem to zip by faster and faster as I try to tell them everything I see, speaking a language none of them speak and throwing my head backward against Monk's chest out of sheer frustration.

After either a few minutes or several hours, who the hell knows, the car finally stops and the passenger door behind my head is thrown open. I'm pulled backward out of the car, and the limbs of treetops overhead fill the pink sky like veins in a bloodshot eye.

"Up this way," Monk says. They stand me upright and walk me along a dirt path, talking all soft and rational, patting my shoulders while they restrain my wrists. I'm not screaming anymore, just mumbling to myself and squeezing my eyes shut as my feet move reluctantly onward. When I open one eye, I see the silhouette of a deformed man with spidery legs. I can't hear what she's trying to tell me, but I can tell whatever war he's fighting is nearly lost.

They lead me up a steep hill, and it seems to go on and on forever. I look ahead and see Sarah wiping her eyes, stealing only the occasional look back at me. She's looking down at her phone, and there's a wall of text on her screen that I can't read. I feel sick to my stomach, and when my feet stop moving and I drop like dead weight in their arms, they continue to guide me upward.

Keep moving, kid, I hear Grandpa say.

But he can't be talking, because he's *dead*, dead from a disease he didn't deserve, and now there's a steaming turd on his grave.

We suddenly arrive at wherever they've been leading me, and Monk tells Kevin and Clive to let go of my arms. I'm not prepared for it, and I stagger forward a few steps before falling to my hands and knees, still trembling uncontrollably. I retch toward the ground, trying to puke up the large lump that feels like a burning coal cauterizing my throat. I try to lift my head, but I might as well be trying to lift a bowling ball with a twig. For a long moment I just lie there on my stomach, clutching handfuls of dead leaves and dirt from the ground beside me.

The wind whistles through the treetops overhead, and as I listen I'm able to bring my head upward a little and look at the shaking world around me. They've taken me to the middle of a large clearing in the woods, and I hear grasshoppers making noise somewhere in the distance.

"C'mon, Trey. You've gotta get the fight out of you," Monk says. His voice sounds like it's coming from the far end of a long tube.

I manage to get one knee beneath myself, and I grab onto his arm and climb slowly to my feet. I look around for evidence of the horrors I imagined, spots where the ink's bled through from the other side of the page into reality. But it's just my four friends around me, three of them standing at my side while Sarah stands a few feet away with her phone still in her hands, both thumbs hammering anxiously at the screen.

I stagger forward a few steps, looking around at everything. I recognize where they've taken me, and it's so oddly comforting that the feeling of absolute rage abruptly fades, leaving a void in its place like freshly-mauled flesh that's yet to bleed.

Just up ahead is a wide opening with a short metal bar separating the edge of the woods from a long drop toward State Route 83, the road leading out of town. Dad and I went hiking up here once during those first few weeks, and we stopped at the edge of the cliff to get a good look at the picturesque town below. Dad told me on the way up how he only knew about this place because someone at the factory told him about a woman who'd jumped to her death here. She was a therapist.

Sarah screams, and throws her phone toward the trees.

"That bastard!" she says, palms pressed to her eyes. When she pulls them away I see tears, and she looks so utterly lost and helpless. "I trusted him!"

"Can only *one* of you break down at once, please?" Monk asks. He puts a hand on my shoulder. "I used to come up here to vent, back in the eighth grade when my dad went away for a while. You can throw an absolute shit fit here and nobody'll bother you."

He stomps toward a tree and rips a thin branch away, then he starts beating the tree trunk with it.

"Screw Jordan," he growls between swings. I watch him club the tree over and over again, sending loud echoes toward the town below. "Shit!" he shouts, and he throws the stick aside, heaving. His hands tremble at his sides, and I watch him stare down at the spot where Jordan's broken corpse should rightfully be.

Sarah picks up her phone and storms back toward the car.

"Kevin, give me your keys," she says.

"Stop flipping out," Monk tells her.

"No! He needs to tell me face to face why he did what he did!"

"I know you're upset," Monk says. "We all are. He crossed a line."

"Crossed a line?" Sarah asks, and what's surely meant to be a scream comes out as a choked laugh. "I told him things I've never even told any of you, things I never thought I could tell anyone! I thought...*shit!*"

She brings her hands to her face, and then she turns her back to us and takes a few steps toward the car. I can hear her muffled crying as she fights to keep it hidden, and I watch her back as she trembles like a leaf in the wind.

"Whatever you say to him, it's not going to do any good," Clive says quietly. He's sitting with his back against a tree, head tilted back as he runs his palms over his eyes. "If you go to his house, you're just going to look like the crazy one. His mom will even call the police, and tomorrow all anyone will know is his side of things."

"You're the one who did this!" Sarah shouts. "It's all your fault he messed with Grandpa's grave like that!"

"No shit!" Clive snaps. "Yeah, it's my fault that he went as far as he did, but *you're* the one who trusted him when all of us told you not to!"

"Screw you!"

Sarah storms at him and punches his side, and when she draws back to hit him again Monk and Kevin rush at her and pull her back.

"You have no right to say that to me! No right at all!" she shouts, pushing futilely at their arms. "He said he loved me! He said he'd never do anything to ever hurt me, and that I meant everything to him!"

Monk pulls her further away, ducking his head back to avoid her elbow as she thrashes around.

"Neither of you did this," he says. He lets go with one hand, and he catches Sarah's wrist as she starts to run at Clive. She turns around, drawing back like she's going to hit him, and he reaches out and grabs the other wrist as well. "Look at me," he says. She shakes her head, lowering her face and crying freely now. "Look at me! Sarah, you didn't make this happen. *Neither of you* made this happen, okay? He did it, and it's done now."

Her forehead falls against Monk's chest, and she stand there half-collapsed with her wrists held up at either side of her. Monk hushes her, rocking back and forth on her feet in a strange and depressing dance. He lets go of her wrists, and she hugs him weakly.

"I swear to God I didn't know he'd do that," she says.

"Of course not."

"I trusted him!" she says. "I thought he was a good person. All those nights we'd talk and he'd listen to me cry, I thought I was seeing something about him nobody else saw. I'm such an idiot."

Monk pushes her away gently, enough to look her in the eyes.

"You trusted him because *you're* a good person," he says. "You're not an idiot. He is."

He takes a deep breath, and it seems like he's going to say something else, something that fixes everything with a tidy and heroic monologue. But he doesn't say anything. He reaches up to wipe tears from his own eyes, and he looks like he's fighting a scream.

"I just want him to look me in the eyes and tell me how he could do that," Sarah says. "If he never really loved me, and everything he ever told me was all just a lie, I want him to say it! He owes me that much, right?"

Her shoulders rock up and down as fresh tears come. Monk pats her shoulder, staring down at his side.

"I'm an idiot," she repeats. "I don't know what I'm doing. I never know what the hell I'm doing! How does everyone else know what they're doing but I don't know a goddamn thing?"

Nobody answers. She pushes away from Monk and walks toward the cliff. She rests her hands against the metal bar, leaning against it as she squeezes her eyes shut. She bites down hard on her lips, and her entire body heaves as she tries to hold everything in and take deep breaths.

"You're right, Sarah," Clive says from the ground. His arms are crossed over his knees and he's hiding his face. "I'm the one who took it too far. It might as well have been me who did that Grandpa's grave."

Kevin shakes his head.

"Shut up," he says. Clive looks up, and Kevin fidgets unsurely on his feet. "I mean, it's not like any of us could've known he'd do something like that."

"I'll tell you one thing," Monk says. "I'm sure as hell not taking any part in that show of his. I'll put up with all sorts of crap from Jordan, but this is it, this is where I draw a line."

"You have to do the show," Sarah says. She turns toward him, and when she tries to force a smile it only highlights her sadness. "Don't drop out of it. Don't you dare give him even that much."

"He'll probably kick us out anyway."

She shakes her head. "Let him try. You've worked too hard on your act to just give it up. You too, Trey."

I feel her arms close around me, and I see in her expression she's doing everything she can to appear brave and encouraging even if she's dying inside. I feel sick thinking about it; the very last thing I want to do ever again is sit on those choir risers and listen to Jordan's pretentious notes about everyone's acts. Even that crappy story I've been telling feels tainted now, along with any notion I've ever had of being something I'm not.

I tell my arms to reach up and hug her back, but they don't obey. My body's a ship filled with mutineers, two-hundred-some bones all telling my sanity to piss off with its directions and walk the plank.

We should hunt him down. He can't get away with what he's done. He needs to suffer somehow. He needs to feel shame, or whatever semblance of shame a bastard like him is capable of feeling.

Even my own imagination laughs at the pitiful thought.

Sarah moves away from me, walking aimlessly through the trees and taking deep breaths, trying to maintain that fake smile even when it repeatedly breaks and her tears continue.

I look around at them all, feeling rage come back again in full force as I watch defeat choke the life out of them. In my head, I'm saying something that makes sense of it all, some brilliant writer bullshit that can make it all go away, something that'll save us from this hopeless feeling. But nothing comes to mind. Not a single damn thing. I can't even think of what Grandpa would say to us right now.

In the space of an hour, it's all become horribly clear. He's not here with us, not physically and not spiritually. He's truly gone, and every time I've thought I've heard his voice in my head, comforting me and pushing me onward, it's just been a desperate ventriloquism act. He's dead, and not a single person outside the five of us even cares. The world's always been an ugly place. He just made us forget that for a while.

"Someone should go clean up his grave," Kevin says. Nobody answers him, and he puts his hands in his pockets and leans his head against a tree.

It stays like this for a while, and I can't tell how much time's actually going by. I sit at the edge of the cliff looking down at the town with a dried-up condom near one of my feet, and every few minutes I hear one of them moving behind me or sniffling. I don't even want to look back at them—I feel so useless, so ineffectual and powerless, that I just want to stay here and die. There's nothing any of us can do. I hear Sarah crying behind me, and in my head I'm bashing Jordan's face in with both fists and making him apologize for doing what he *knew* would hurt her. It hurt seeing the two of them together, and it hurt watching him change her little by little, but nothing hurts like seeing her look so destroyed by his betrayal. She really loved him, and he didn't even give a second thought to hurting her.

The sun's almost down. In the distance, I see the lights from the slaughterhouse and the rubber factories turning on. We make our way slowly back to Kevin's car: heads hanging low, eyes rubbed red, and throats choked half to death by invisible hands. When we get there, I pause before climbing in after Monk and Clive. Sarah's already sitting up front with her face in her hands, and when I re-open her door she looks up at me. I force myself to smile, because all I want in the world right now is to give her back whatever feeling of security Jordan gave her and then took away.

"It's going to be okay," I say. I'm only talking to her, but when I look away from her eyes I see the others looking at me too. I feel the heaviness weighing me down inside, and the hand that's been pulling apart my insides is scratching its name in my guts as I see that none of them believe my words any more than I do. I feel stupid again, lower than I've ever thought I could feel. I nod around at them, unable to channel whatever spirit Grandpa filled us all with. I take a deep breath, squeeze Sarah's hand in mine, and mumble again as I climb into the backseat, "It's all going to be okay."

*

The ride back into town is silent. I'm still burning alive inside, but I push everything down and stare out the window at the occasional passing car as we get back on State Route 83 and drive past the park, back toward the cemetery on the other side of town. Time's been flowing like blood from arterial spray, but now everything feels congealed, nearly dry and blackened and starting to flake away.

When we get back to the cemetery, Kevin pops the trunk and takes out an empty Wal-Mart bag. We walk back toward Grandpa's grave. I thought maybe we'd be lucky and the caretaker would've already seen it, and maybe he'd have it cleaned up and disposed of. No such luck; the fat log of shit waits to greet us like an ambassador from Jordan's ugly soul.

I take the bag from Kevin, stick my hand inside, and pick it up.

"We should throw it at Jordan's house," Clive says. He's staring at the bag as I double-tie it, hellfire in his eyes.

"No," I tell him.

"Why not?" he protests. "He deserves it. We could pin him down and make him eat it and it still wouldn't be even."

"I wouldn't stop you," Sarah says quietly. Her eyes are still puffy from crying.

Again, I don't know what to say. I know there's something I desperately want to communicate to them, something that'll concisely explain what's in my head and make them all understand. I can't find it, whatever it is.

I jump on the idea of revenge with absolute vigor: Maybe Jordan's got a dead relative lying around here somewhere? I could be as righteous as the Lord Himself and deliver biblical justice, maybe dig his grandmother up and leave her on his porch one night with a sign taped between her hands reading, *"Give Gammy a hug!"*

But we can't do anything like that. We can't even call the cops, or tell anyone at the school, because nobody gives a damn about any of us and they give even less of a damn about the guy who took care of us when nobody else would.

Jordan wins.

"We'll get him back," I tell them.

"When?" Clive asks. And then, almost pleading, he adds, "Why can't we go get him right now?"

I shrug. It's easy enough to picture all of us going to Jordan's house in the middle of the night, maybe breaking in through his bedroom window and standing in a circle around his bed with duct tape, ropes, and an assortment of sharp knives and blunt objects. It's something that might've happened in one of the movies Grandpa and I watched at the theater, one of those rare and beautiful cinematic moments that make you almost believe in justice.

But we can't do it. Jordan knows he'll get away with this, and if we tell the truth he'll just lie, lie, lie about the whole thing. And the ones who matter—the ones who decide who's innocent and who's guilty—they'll side with him in a heartbeat.

I try to hear Grandpa's voice from below our feet, telling us the grand plan that'll feel just like one of our old games, making a joke of the whole rotten thing and lifting the burden from our backs with a dismissive joke.

But I don't hear a damn word from him.

*

PART TWO

Chapter Eleven

There's a game Grandpa and I played once, about a week before Sarah came along and then all the others.

We were walking home from the movie theater, and I was feeling terrible for reasons I couldn't quite understand. I woke up that morning feeling like the whole world was ending around me, and no matter what I did to shut my brain up, I just felt worse and worse as the day went on. Grandpa was my friend, sure, but I still felt like an alien in school and couldn't help but feel something was wrong with me.

Grandpa wasn't the type of person to ask if something was bothering you. I was either mad or upset about something almost constantly, anyway, and if I really wanted to vent or talk about it he was all ears. But he knew better than to pry or force me to talk. People who tell you that you *have* to talk are rarely the ones who care.

We walked along the railroad tracks, and he balanced on one rail as I walked in the center.

"I'll tell you what," he said, after a while of my silent brooding. "I'm going to teach you a new game, kid. You up for it?"

I shrugged. Games didn't even feel interesting to me anymore, and neither did music or movies or other things that would normally make me happy. I was so, so hopelessly miserable.

He drew a handful of peppermint candies from his jacket pocket and threw them at my head.

"Huh? You up for it?" he repeated.

"Fine. What's the game?"

"It's a real good one, I promise," he said. "You look like you're about four bites deep into a shit sandwich, not gonna lie to you."

"I'm fine."

"Here's how you play," he continued anyway. "I want you to drudge up all the horrible, nasty, life-wrecking thoughts you can think of. Be real clear about them, too. Really feel that pain, alright?"

"Why the hell would I want to do that?"

"Humor me and just do it, would you?"

"Whatever."

I thought about school and how alone I felt even when I was in rooms filled with people. I thought about girls who were hot but almost always indifferent to me, and how I already knew I'd rather die alone someday than join any of the cliques of athletes and ass-kissers.

I thought of the girl in my American History class with the brunette hair and nose ring, always dressed in black and always looking just as lonely as I felt. She'd just lost her mom to cancer, and I wanted to hurt everyone who made cruel jokes about it and made her even more miserable on her first day back at school.

"Pissed off yet?" Grandpa asked.

"Uh-huh."

"Good," he said. "Now here's the hard part of the game, the part you're *really* going to struggle with. You ready?"

I nodded.

"Okay," he said. "I want you to force yourself to smile."

Something like invisible claws were pulling apart my insides. With all these awful thoughts brought to the surface at once, I felt like I might never smile ever again.

"I can't," I told him. Then added, "This game blows."

"Yeah, yeah. Keep playing, alright? It doesn't have to be a real smile or anything. Just force yourself to smile."

"Fine."

Forcing the stupidest and most sarcastic smile I could muster, I stared at Grandpa. My teeth and gums were bared, and my eyes were wide like a total maniac. Grandpa nodded.

"There you go," he said. "Now hold that smile for another ten minutes or so."

"Seriously, this game blows."

"Just hold the damn smile, would you? You'll see."

"Fine."

We finished walking the tracks and started heading through town toward Grandpa's house. A lady passed by us, walking her dog. She looked freaked out by my smile and quickly averted her eyes. Cars passed by, and I made sure to aim my unrelenting smile directly at the drivers. Keeping the smile on my face and making strangers uncomfortable became a game of its own, and Grandpa nodded in silence. He even joined it with his own crazed smile, waving excitedly at passerby.

"Well," he said when we arrived at his porch, "you still feel bad?"

"A little," I admitted.

"Good enough. Think of it as fertilizer for your mental crops. Real good stuff grows from pain."

I went inside and grabbed a beer from the fridge. I didn't feel much like drinking, but the cold can felt good in my hands as we sat out front for a while.

"How do you win the game?" I asked. "I'm just going to feel bad again later. It's not like I can fake a smile forever."

"Sure you can," he said. "We're prisoners to the things we can't smile at, Trey. Either misery owns you, or you own your misery. You win by getting through it."

I didn't end up drinking the beer. We just sat on the porch together, and each time a car or neighbor passed by the house, we'd show them our big and idiotic smiles. And it worked, little by little; the smile was only fake until it suddenly wasn't.

A week later, as if by some divine destiny, Grandpa and I got our first permanent addition to our late-night graveyard chats. She was out alone on her bike, clearing her head with her own private version of the smile game, and she must have heard us talking loudly underneath the tree. I saw her stop at the edge of the graveyard, a slender silhouette staring back at us for a few long minutes as we carried on. I knew it was Sarah before I even saw her face approaching. It was like I felt her before I saw her, and the moment was pre-arranged by God himself.

Seeing my face, even though we'd never really spoken before, must have eased her a bit. She looked beat down and drained, and she didn't talk a whole lot to either of us that first night. She stayed close to my side, though, wary of Grandpa at first. But twenty minutes in or so, she seemed comfortable enough with both of us to laugh along.

She was one of us. At school, she started talking to me more and more. We sat together at lunch, and making her smile every chance I got became a mission that made everything else bearable.

Then we found Monk, then Clive, then Kevin. Rather, they found us. Our late-night meetings at the graveyard were like a beacon to the lost, the crazy, and the broken.

I didn't need the smile game anymore. I felt like I finally belonged, and I didn't have to be anyone but myself.

*

For the next week or so following the desecration of Grandpa's grave, I play the smile game. I'm rusty at it, but I do my best to hold that damn smile on my face. It's my only defense against the sudden onslaught of unfair events.

It starts the next day at school. Monk and I are silent during the morning announcements, though he mumbles a few sarcastic comments to himself and tries to pull me in. I feel like I'm in a daze. Things seem both real and unreal, like I'm living in memories instead of moments and I'm actually lying dead somewhere far away.

The final announcement of the morning, read by Kevin: "Trey Matthews, please report to the principal's office immediately."

Down on the second floor. In Principal Jones' office. Jordan and his mom are both already waiting there. Jordan has a look on his face like an abused puppy, and he makes a show of averting his stare when I enter the office.

"Mr. Renus here tells us you attacked him yesterday afternoon," Jones says when I'm seated. "Is that true?"

I nod. "Right after he shit on my friend's grave, yeah."

"Language, Mr. Matthews."

Jordan looks at me with his hands splayed innocently, then he looks back and forth between Jones and his mom.

"I never did that!" he says. "Why would I ever do anything like that? That's absolutely disgusting!"

Mrs. Renus glares at me.

"I've had trouble with Trey and his friends before," she says. "They've had it out for my son all schoolyear, and I want it stopped. I want this boy suspended."

Jones looks at the three of us, deliberating silently. He toys with a paperclip, unfolding and refolding it repeatedly.

"This seems to be a bit of a 'he said, he said' situation," he says. "Being that this all allegedly happened off school property, and there's no proof of either scenario—"

"Look at my son's neck!" Mrs. Renus screeches. "Trey just admitted to it! And now he's covering his tracks with an outrageous lie!"

"Regardless," Jones continues, "suspension doesn't quite fit the circumstance."

"Look at his neck!" Mrs. Renus repeats. "Suspend this boy immediately! He's obviously a bully and a danger to my son's personal safety!"

Jordan lifts his head, trying desperately to look meek and innocent.

"I don't want Trey suspended," he says quietly, making his lips quiver as he looks at the principal and then at me. "I mentor him in the Talented and Gifted group, and he's part of our show coming up at the festival. It's possible that he just lashed out at me out of frustration. He works so hard at being good, you know? He's really an inspiration to others in the group."

Jones nods. Suddenly it feels like the two of them are teammates, bonding over their leadership struggles.

"Honestly, I'm willing to forgive Trey for what he did to me," Jordan says. Then he looks at me directly, and I can see the hint of a smile in his eyes. "All I really want is an apology. That's all."

Jones splays his hands at me, seeming satisfied.

"Well, that's easy enough," he says. "Mr. Matthews, do you have something you want to say to Jordan?"

The smug bastard looks so self-satisfied underneath his 'victim' mask. He sold the act perfectly. 'Victim' sells. Facts don't.

"Well?" Mrs. Renus prompts.

I nod. I force a smile, a real big one. I play the game.

"I'm sorry you're such a lying piece of shit, Jordan," I tell him. "And I'm sorry you'll get what you deserve someday."

I get detention for the next three days. I smile through that, too.

I play the smile game again the next day, when rumors about the breakup spread around the school like a plague. Everyone knows what happened. Nobody gets the story right.

"I heard he broke up with her because she's emotionally unstable," a girl in homeroom tells her friend. "Like, she literally goes on and on about her dead dad and stuff."

"Give me a break," her friend groans. "I bet she played the 'tragic victim' card all the time to get whatever she wanted from him. Girls like her don't deserve guys like Jordan."

"Right? I mean, I know her parents are dead and stuff, and that's totally sad, but she's just a train wreck of a person. He didn't need to be her therapist."

"Jordan's got a heart of gold, though. He probably thought there was a real person in there somewhere."

"Underneath all that skanky goth makeup? Not likely. Hurt people hurt people, and Sarah's damaged goods."

Monk's not here today. I text him, and he's home sick. If he were here, he might say something to them so razor-sharp and deadly that their heads would fall off their shoulders and bathe us all in their blood. I want to tell them they're wrong about everything, and that Sarah broke up with *him*, not the other way around, and that *she's* the one who trusted too much. But truth doesn't matter to these people.

I force a smile, and I try my best to tune them and everyone else out for the rest of the day. In every story I hear, Sarah's a terrible person and Jordan finally saw through her. In one variation, she has another boyfriend from a different school, and Jordan caught the two of them together.

When the bell rings and we all head toward first period, I pass one of the girls in the hallway and shoot a snot rocket into her hair.

I play the smile game again a few days later, when I walk toward my third period class and see Sarah kissing Jordan on the lips in the hallway.

It's a passionate kiss, so completely over-the-top and hellish that I swear I feel my heart stop beating completely. Jordan's arms are around her waist, and he smiles like he's the happiest boy on Earth as she whispers something in his ear and then goes in for a second kiss.

They part, and I stand there feeling dazed as Jordan walks off in the opposite direction and Sarah walks past me. She sees me there, and her eyes are suddenly downcast and guilty.

I don't move from that spot. The bell rings, and I'm late. Then I'm two minutes late. Then I'm twenty minutes late. I lose the ability to function, standing there and trying to work logic in my mind, unable to add up everything I just saw and how it fits with everything that's happened.

Smile through it, I hear Grandpa say. *It doesn't have to be a real smile.*

I do it. And it's the ugliest, saddest smile I've ever felt.

I play the smile game again throughout that same day. I'm still thinking about Sarah and what I saw, flashing back and forth between now and a few days ago, the vast difference in what was said versus what was done.

None of us have met up to hang out since that day at the graveyard. Sarah seemed so wrecked last time I saw her. So utterly *anti*-Jordan. She'd finally seen him for who he truly was, and something was actually *right* in the universe.

And now she's back with him.

I rehearse my same crappy story at the T.A.G. meeting after school. She's by his side the entire time, and their hands are practically inseparable. Everyone knows they're back together, and everyone suddenly fawns over how happy they both look, even the people who never seemed to care. This is the romantic ending to a teen soap opera, after all.

I force myself to smile. In my head, I'm dragging a razorblade from my wrist to my elbow.

I play the smile game again five days later. It doesn't feel like it's really been five days, because no matter how I try to distract myself, my thoughts keep returning to Sarah, and it feels like that moment in the hallway never actually ended.

I get to school. I remind myself as I walk into homeroom that I'm still playing the smile game, and that it's imperative that I win, and that at some point smiling won't hurt so much.

"What's so funny?" Monk asks. He sounds eager to be let in on whatever's making me smile so ecstatically.

I shrug. He stares at me for a second, waiting for something. He finally frowns and turns back around in his seat. I keep forcing the smile. I want to die so badly.

The announcements come on. Everything seems fuzzy, and I wonder how much longer I can carry on faking like this. I feel like a can of soda that's been shaken and shaken and shaken. Explosion is eventual.

"Attention all T.A.G. members," Kevin says on the screen. "Rehearsal is cancelled for today due to illness. It's requested that you please continue to practice your acts at home."

"Well, that's awesome," Monk says. "If I hear one more note from Jordan, just *one* more…"

He trails off. I just nod.

"Seriously," he says, concerned now. "You doing okay, man? You look like you've been crying…and your smile's sorta freaking me out a bit."

"I'm winning," I mumble quietly.

"Huh?"

"I'm fine," I lie. "Everything's fine."

The bell rings, and I rush ahead of Monk. I need my friends, but I can't talk to them about anything at all right now because I know they won't understand. Even if they *do* understand, I know they won't *really* understand.

Sarah was with us at Grandpa's grave, she saw what Jordan did not just to Grandpa but to *us*. She was broken apart in tears and demanding to know *why* Jordan would do what he did—this perfect and merely misunderstood "great guy" she'd fallen for so wholeheartedly.

Jordan's not in English class. His mom is at her desk, looking somehow even witchier than usual. She doesn't even glare at me when I unleash my dopey smile in her direction.

I go to my desk, and before my butt's even in the seat, I overhear a conversation that pulls me out of Hell and extinguishes the fire.

"What an absolute *bitch!*" Stacy says. "I mean, who the hell just *ghosts* someone like that? Who's seriously *that* much of a psycho?"

"Right?" Taylor says sadly, shaking her head. "No face-to-face breakup, no phone call, just a 'goodbye' text? She's unhinged. I've always known she was unhinged."

"She's a *slut!*" Stacy says, fuming now. "Poor Jordan."

"Poor Jordan," Taylor agrees.

"I mean, he's got a total heart of gold! He deserves so much better than what that skank did to him!"

"He was crying on the phone last night," Taylor said. She starts to tear up. "I called him, and…I've never heard him cry like that before. It breaks my heart."

"He should never have taken that whore back," Stacy says. She repeats, "Absolute *bitch!*"

And just like that, the smile game ends.

It washes over me, the absolute beauty of it all and what it signifies, how all the pain from Sarah's betrayal was over nothing at all.

No, not nothing—it was over *art!* Beautiful, cruel art. Her masterpiece. Her perfect revenge on Jordan, revenge that none of the rest of us could ever have gotten on him. Absolute, calculated viciousness.

I can't help it. I'm suddenly so overwhelmed by relief that I start to laugh.

Stacy and Taylor just stare at me as I nearly fall out of my seat, doubled over and loving Sarah to death all over again.

Chapter Twelve

"**A**bsolutely *brutal*, Sarah!" Clive says, applauding wildly with a cigarette between his lips. "Well done! I'm so proud of you, you goddamn black widow she-devil!"

It's nighttime now, two days later. We're up in the tree, all of us together again. Clive's been pouring his praise on Sarah since the moment she showed up on her bike, and it takes everything in me not to kiss her right here and now.

She smiles toward the ground, looking only slightly proud of herself.

"I had to tell him," Monk explains to her, shrugging apologetically. "Sorry, but it was just too beautiful not to share."

"Absolutely *brutal!*" Clive repeats, and laughs to himself as he blows a cloud of smoke. "You have *no idea* how close I came to slapping you when I heard you got back with him! For real, I thought you were the dumbest chick in the universe! But that's some medieval justice shit you pulled on him! Seriously, you're my new hero."

"Let it go," Sarah says, waving a hand. "I'm not proud of it. I just wanted him to feel what he made me feel."

"You've absolutely perfected the art of destroying a person. Teach me your ways. I am your humble student, oh she-devil."

"I mean, you probably had to do some real dirty work to make the whole act believable," Monk says. She doesn't answer, but just climbs up onto a branch and stares at her feet.

"Oh, she *definitely* banged him again!" Clive says, shaking his head at her in admiration. "You cruel and wonderful beauty."

They finally let the subject drop, and it's quiet for a while.

It feels like things have dried up a bit in the short time we've spent apart, like none of us even know what to say to each other as we crack open beers from the half-empty 24-pack Clive brought with him, stolen from his Dad. We nod to one another and exchange little smiles, but I know we all feel the strange disconnect.

The awkwardness disappears rather quickly when Kevin breaks the silence. For once, surprisingly, I absolutely *love* him for opening his mouth.

"I found a date for prom," he says. He's sitting in one of the lower branches and drinking from a flask.

"That's awesome!" Sarah says. She sounds relieved to have the spotlight off her. "Who is it? Do we know her?"

Kevin grins sheepishly, and he takes a deep swig before answering.

"Mandy Ferguson."

Clive and Monk spit their beer simultaneously, showering Sarah, Kevin, and I from the above.

"*Mandy?*" Clive asks. "Wow...did you catch her with a doughnut on a fishhook, or did you have to harpoon her?"

Sarah throws her empty soda bottle at Clive, glaring a silent warning at him. Kevin lowers his head.

"I used to play chess with her after school at the library. We're pretty good friends," he tells us. His cheeks turn pinkish-red, and he adds, "I whistled at her when she was walking by this morning. Thought it was something you might've done."

"You...whistled...at *Mandy Ferguson?*" Monk asks, sounding genuinely perplexed.

"Maybe that's the manatee mating call," Clive says.

I smile at the four of them, watching Kevin's face grow redder and redder as the one-sided battle continues and Sarah tries to keep the peace. I think about throwing in a few comments of my own: *There are plenty of other fish in the sea, Kev...if she didn't already eat them all. How much did you have to spend on a net that big?* I keep my mouth shut, though. It's just nice seeing them all happy again.

There's been one thing that makes smiling a whole lot easier, and that's the look of complete misery on Jordan's face, which I take as reassurance there's *some* justice in the world. Every time I see him he looks increasingly broken-hearted, and I'd be lying if I said I don't relish every detail, from the dark bags under his eyes to the noticeable weight loss. He still goes about critiquing everyone's acts during T.A.G meetings, but when he does there's an emptiness in his eyes that betrays his complete vulnerability with Sarah in the room. I see him glancing at her during the longer acts, and sometimes tears start to well up in his eyes, making him a spitting image of one of those puppies shown during pet abuse commercials. Is he suicidal yet, I wonder? That'd be pretty cool, I guess.

"So, are you taking Movie Theater Chick, Clive?" Monk asks, burping as he drains his first can. "You've been stalking her long enough, you might as well make a move."

Sarah laughs. "You seriously don't even know her name yet?"

"Who cares about her name?" Clive asks. "Look at her body!"

"You're going to die alone someday."

He waves a dismissive hand.

"I'm not taking anyone. Leaves more room for opportunity."

"Ah," Sarah says, nodding. "You're too scared to ask her, huh?"

Clive ignores the comment. He lights his third cigarette and blows a large smoke ring down at her.

"And you?" he asks. "Who do *you* intend on spending the night with now that Anus is out of the picture?"

Sarah looks completely caught off guard. A chill fills the air around us all, as if mentioning Jordan around Sarah is an unspoken taboo. Leave it up to Clive to throw a cold water balloon at a sick person.

"I don't know," she answers, looking down and toying with her bracelet. I can imagine the thoughts racing through her mind: life's deleted scenes of what would've and could've been the perfect night with someone she'd been so in love with. "Maybe I just won't go this year either."

"Bullshit," Clive says firmly. He cocks his cigarette at her like a chiding nanny. "Jordan's not going to ruin you fun. You'll go if one of us has to tie you up and drag you there ourselves."

"Though she might like that too much. Being tied up and all," Monk says, grinning.

"You might just have to," she says, smirking back at the two of them. She shrugs. "Okay, so I go. Who do I go *with*? Everyone in this town sucks."

"Oh, I have a feeling you'll find someone," Clive muses.

Someone kicks me roughly in the shoulder, and I nearly fall off the branch as I whirl around with a surprised shout. Monk stares down at me intently, snapping his eyebrows toward Sarah as he mouths something unclearly. I shrug, asking for a clearer explanation.

The next thing I feel is Clive's empty beer can hit me on the head, and I look upward to yell at him. He winks encouragingly, pointing a finger from me to Sarah and mouthing the same thing a little slower. He makes an 'o' with one hand and wriggles his other index finger in and out of it.

My stomach lurches with understanding, and I feel the hair on the back of my neck stand on end. I shake my head back at him wordlessly, feeling my chest go cold with fear as my cheeks grow hotter. Sarah's not seeing any of this, too busy staring at the graves. I remember every time I've wanted to ask Sarah out in the past but couldn't because she was with someone else. I also remember all the times talking to an invisible "her" in my room, romanticizing the moment like I could ever really have the balls to go through with it. When will I *ever* get another opening like this? More importantly, how can I *not* call myself a pussy if I don't ask?

But what if she says no? What if I look like an idiot— what the hell would I say after that? How would we ever be able to talk again, or—

"Oh, for Christ's sake, just ask her!" Monk bursts, startling me from my thoughts. Sarah looks away from the graves, and her eyes settle on me. I feel myself shrink inside as I realize I now have no choice in the matter.

"Would you want to go with...me? Maybe?" I ask. Right away I'm mentally hitting myself for adding 'maybe' before she even has the chance to say it.

For a second her expression doesn't change—she just stares at me the same way, like she's waiting for me to laugh or give any sign of joking.

"I was just thinking," I recover, "since neither of us have a date yet, it would be fun if we just went as—"

"You'd really want to go with me?" she interrupts, and my tongue's frozen before it can speak the word 'friends.'

Monk sighs dramatically. "No, he's *kidding* with you— just say yes!"

The corners of her lips jump at his sarcasm, and if my imagination isn't fooling me her cheeks are having a colorful reaction. She shrugs, looking down at the grass and thoughtfully scraping the bark off the tree with her thumb nail. My mind's never felt tenser: if there really is a purgatory, it must feel like waiting for a girl's answer during moments like this.

"You know, Trey," Clive purrs deviously, "My ex from two years ago, Katie Werble, just broke up with her boyfriend today. I think I could hook the two of you up, if you want. Her body's okayish, but she's got a tongue like a dog…"

I hear a loud swallowing sound, and when I look toward Sarah again the look of indecision has vanished from her face. She looks sharply up at Clive and then out over the cemetery again. Then, putting on a decisive smile that lights up her whole face, she looks over at me.

"Sure," she says. "It'll be fun. Two good friends out having fun."

The released tension in my throat comes out as a hoarse laugh, and I feel the corners of my lips stretch from ear to ear. No fireworks light up the sky. No angels come down with harps and shining lights. Nonetheless, this feels more important than anything in the world right now, like God created everything else just as a footnote for this moment. Above us, Clive and Monk whistle and clap like school children, having finally found their source of entertainment for the night.

Chapter Thirteen

One week later. I don't notice how loud I'm humming to myself until I look up from my dinner plate and see my parents staring at me, forks lowered and jaws stuck mid-chew. I force my legs to stop shaking and pull a quick smile, trying like hell to regain control of myself. From the corner of my eye I see 4:37 flashing on the microwave clock, less than an hour and a half until the Rock the Arts Festival. Damn the sun for being such a busy bastard, rising and falling faster than a Disney pop star's career.

"Are you drunk?" Dad asks me. I laugh, but I don't think it does much for my case. Mom leans forward from across the table and wrinkles her nose at me, sniffing for either liquor or marijuana. I only wish I had a bottle of whiskey hidden away somewhere.

I'm freaking out.

I run through the story again in my mind, fumbling for the words like I have been all day. I thought I had it locked down perfectly, but now the hubris is starting to wear off. It's like this whole time I've been holding a piece of gold only to find out now it's just been a hardened turd all along, the worst damn story I've ever written. Meanwhile, on top of all the anxiety, I'm still bouncing off the walls thinking about Sarah and me, and every few minutes or so my concentration is interrupted by prophetic visions of me dancing with her at prom, being *her man* for the night, sitting on the couch with her at Monk's after-party, and maybe *kissing* her. I can't concentrate on any of it, high or low.

I.   Am. Freaking. Out.

Monk and Kevin are supposed to come pick me up soon. I have almost no time to get myself together.

"I'll be up in my room," I tell my parents, standing abruptly and sweeping my remaining half-plate of spaghetti into the trash.

Mom shouts after me, "You sit back down and *ask* to be excused!"

"For Christ's sake, he's almost in college," Dad says. "Let the man off his leash."

He waves me away with a tilt of his hand, returning to his dinner as Mom stares daggers at him.

I take the stairs three at a time, already whispering the story rapidly to myself before I even reach my bedroom door, trying hard to just let the story be and not revise everything about it. Why didn't anyone tell me it sucked so badly?

Mom and Dad know nothing about my part in the show. Unlike Monk, whose parents have probably been feeding his confidence all afternoon, I want my parents completely in the dark about all this. It would feel too weird reading one of my stories in front of them, even with hundreds of others in the audience.

I dig through my dresser drawer, making a last-minute decision to just wear a black t-shirt and jeans. I turn to grab my shoes from under the bed, and I nearly scream when I see a large gargoyle sitting outside my window.

Its hands and eyes are pressed to the screen, staring in at me, and it smashes its fists against the window as I turn around.

"Ha! Totally got you!" the monster says, and I recognize the voice as Monk's. I move a few inches out of the light to see him better—then I jump again. There are heavy shadows under his eyes, complimenting the black dye he's put into his wild hair and the white coat covered in fake blood. I smile at the spectacle.

"What the hell's this?" I ask, opening the window and letting him in. "You look like you just got hit by lightning!"

"It's art, jerk," he grunts, and he raises a makeup-thickened eyebrow at me. "And what are you supposed to be, a stage lackey? You're hardly dressed up."

"I'm every famous storyteller who ever lived," I answer, and I puff my chest out in false bravado. "A total mess."

He rolls his eyes, cocking his thumb behind him.

"Let's get going."

I climb out onto the roof behind him, closing the window behind me. A sickening feeling rises in my stomach as I reach the edge of the roof. I watch as Monk go first, no fear whatsoever as he hums the music of *Razor's Edge* to himself. Taking a deep breath, I get down to my haunches, reaching to grab the end of the ladder...then I stop and reassess. I start to go legs first...then stop again, glancing down. I haven't had a fear of heights before, and it's like I'm someone else.

Monk's already on the ground, arms crossed.

"Pussy," he says. He walks toward Kevin's car. I groan to myself, ashamed of my fear...then the ladder creaks as

I put a foot on the first rung, and I double my speed toward the ground.

The fairgrounds are on the other side of town behind Elm Street and Hancock, surrounded by cheap apartment complexes with railroad tracks running behind the grandstand. Most of the year, it's a place used for having sex, smoking weed, drinking in small groups, and meeting with "pharmaceutical dealers." But during the county fair and the Rock the Arts Festival, the town brings in food vendor, carnival games, and puke-inducing rides that seem on the verge of falling apart.

On the sidewalks of every street by the fairgrounds, we see the true animals of Caedes. Parents drag their kids by the ears as they talk into cellphones, cars everywhere disregard oncoming traffic and cut ahead of each other for cheap parking spots, and teenagers from other schools in the county come out of the woodwork wearing anything from liberty spikes to leashes as they garner sickened looks from the senior citizens wearing Gucci polo shirts and the much-larger redneck population wearing trucker hats and flannels. It's pretty beautiful, I think, the way they all come in through the same gate like a dirty needle into a vein.

Kevin curses like a sailor as he becomes progressively liberal with his horn and middle finger.

"Can you believe this?" he says as we finally leave the pay-to-park lawn and enter through the main gates. "Ten dollars just to *park*? What a rip-off!"

Monk slaps him on the back, smiling around at the fairgrounds.

"Cheer up, Kev," he says. "They say every time a toll booth rings, a demon gets its wings. Your ten dollars is like charity."

Kevin blows a deep breath, taking off his glasses and rubbing a hand down the side of his face.

"I need to find Jordan," he says. "He wants me to set up cameras for the show."

"No problem there," I tell him, staring off at all the rides as I walk. "Just look for the guy throwing a length of rope over a rafter."

Monk laughs, and we shove ahead through the crowd, barely avoiding a group of five-year-olds running with squirt guns. Kevin walks off with his hands in his pockets.

Monk and I reach the basement to the outdoor stage, out in the middle of the open horse track in front of the grandstand. I see Sarah across the room, and I immediately get the urge to go speak to her. I fight it, though. Too much, too soon. Play it cool. It's hard not to notice the perfect shape of her body, though, in the tight black leotard she's wearing...

"Attention all T.A.G members!" Jordan's voice echoes from across the room. I turn and see him standing with his arms opened, smiling wide as he runs his eyes over everyone. He's dressed in a puffy white shirt, one with over-indulgent frills down the chest and sleeves that extend to the tips of his fingers. With his bangs flattened down over his eyebrows, he looks like a cross between a sad collie dog and one of the Three Musketeers.

"I just want to tell you how proud I am of all your hard work and dedication this year. You're all very talented and gifted people indeed, and you've done a great job at zeroing in on your individual weaknesses and fine-tuning your acts for the show." He glances down at his feet and exhales loudly, and when he raises his eyes again they linger on Sarah. "We all have those areas that need fixed sometimes, you know? Some of us more than others. That said, I'm very happy to be quarterbacking this endeavor."

You son of a bitch, I think. I want to burn you to the ground and piss on your ashes.

He clears his throat loudly, re-affixing his smile before glancing around the room again and clapping his hands together.

"Okay," he continues, "I'm going to read off the order of the show one last time so we can get everyone lined up by the stage entrance. Then the show can begin!"

I don't pay much attention as he draws a folded note card from his pirate shirt. I look at Sarah, bothered like hell by the sudden distance in her expression. What is she thinking, I wonder? Something changed just now, something small but detectable nonetheless, something ugly I can't put a finger on but can only attribute to Jordan's presence.

She was in love with him, I remind myself. Was. Past tense. She's allowed to be uncomfortable. That's all it is. Discomfort being around a shitty, unbearable, backstabbing, sonovabitch ex in an equally shitty and unbearable costume.

I find my place in the very back of the line, only slightly bothered by the fact that Monk and Sarah are in the very front but absolutely annoyed by the blonde pair of she-trolls in front of me, girls who talk in short wheezes and have something nasty to say with every breath. They're definitely two of the girls responsible for spreading rumors about Sarah after the breakup. I wish I had a snot rocket in the chamber for them both.

I watch Monk mime through his entire act off in the shadows while Sarah stands with her arms crossed behind Jordan, who's at the head of the line. Every few seconds he turns his head like he feels her looking at him.

The room quiets down briefly when the door behind us opens and we all turn to see the superintendent walking toward us with Principal Jones in tow, each of them dressed to the height of unnecessary ballroom fashion with black suits and white gloves. They both wink and wave at students as they walk by, tipping their bowler hats to one or two. They're not even halfway down the line when Jordan ambushes the superintendent with a handshake, eyes lit up like he's meeting Christ in the flesh.

"Mr. Felton, thank you so much for coming down here, sir!" he says. "I know you're a very busy man, and I really appreciate getting the chance to meet you. Can I get you a water? We have a cooler of pop too, if you'd like one."

Mr. Felton smiles warmly, waving a hand. "No thank you, I—"

"I'll go grab you one," Jones says. He starts a slow-jog past Jordan, patting him on the shoulder. If I were to guess I'd say he's as far up Felton's ass for recognition as Jordan.

"I'm never too busy to meet an ambassador of our community's future," Felton continues. "Mr. Jones was just telling me some very interesting things about you and your group. Tell me a little more, would you? I'm always happy to hear what's going on in the schools."

Jordan's overwhelming excitement is the instant death of whatever interest Felton may have had: right away he starts talking like there's a time bomb set to explode under his tongue, flying through an explanation of how he runs the group, what inspires him as an artist, how his goal has always been to help others reach their peaks, how he's aspiring to be part of something big in the future, and *yaaaaawn!* Felton's stare loses its charming twinkle after a minute of this droning, and when his eyes flick quickly toward his watch he abandons the façade and just starts nodding.

"That all sounds so enrapturing, Mr. Renus!" Felton interjects the second Jordan stops to catch his breath. "Your mother must be very proud of you for all your hard work and dedication—those are both key attributes to a good leader. If you'll excuse me, I need to make my way onto the stage."

"Wait, please, just one second!" Jordan interrupts, and he hold a finger up before turning to Sarah and pulling her headphones out. My stomach tightens as his arm glides casually around her waist.

"Mr. Felton, I'd like for you to meet one of the greatest highlights of our group," Jordan says, smiling wide, "Sarah Hilligoss!"

Felton looks up and down at Sarah, studying her unsurely before re-affixing his political smile and offering his hand to her. Sarah's expression has similar subtext: *who the hell are you and why am I being inconvenienced?*

"Sarah's one hell of a dancer," Jordan testifies, placing a hand on his heart. "I mean, she could blow way past any cheap diva on MTV if she wanted to, no doubt about it!"

Felton nods silently, and in a moment of what *must* be confused emotions I notice Sarah's cheeks turn an embarrassed shade of red.

"A dancer, huh?" Felton asks. "That's really great. I see kids your age on TV turning into celebrities all the time because of little hobbies like that. Do you sing as well?"

"Like an angel," Jordan answers for her. The look she gives him is the perfect photograph of confusion taken out of a textbook: *is* he just sucking up to her in the lamest way possible, or is he really being sincere with his lavish compliments and celebrity treatment?

"What's he talking to *her* about?" one of the trolls in front of me scoffs to her friend. I shrug, keeping my eyes locked on Jordan as I think of how much better a depressed frown suits him.

"Tonight may just be your dance to fame," Jones says, returning to Felton's side with a bottle of water. "There are always talent scouts from colleges at these things. This could be the big break for both of you!"

A look of nervousness overcomes Sarah's expression. The second Jordan sees it, he takes instant advantage.

"You'll do great, babe," he says, giving that ratty smile of assurance that's only forgivable from someone you're actually close to, *not* someone who should be out shopping for straight razors and cyanide.

"Well," Felton says, clapping his hands together. "Let's get this show on the road, kids. Mr. Renus, I trust you're a well-versed young fellow when it comes to events like these. I'll go on first and introduce you and your group, then you'll do whatever it is you do, and the show goes on from there. In lieu of having any sort of dress rehearsal to prepare properly, we'll play things by ear if anyone gets weak knees."

"I'll pull them off at the first sign of stage fright," Jordan promises. "I'd hate for anyone to embarrass themselves too badly."

Oh Jordan, I think to myself as I watch him flash his Good Guy smile, *I hope you choke to death and die shitting yourself.*

The superintendent smiles at the two of them and walks off toward the entry doors with Jones inches behind him. Jordan watches him go until he's completely out of sight, and when we hear the shrill electronic sound of a stage microphone being moved and Felton begins greeting the audience, we know the show has begun.

"Alright everyone, nobody move from the lineup!" Jordan shouts, rushing toward the closet in the corner and pulling out an old television.

"We're being recorded?" a redheaded boy screeches. Jordan sighs at him.

"Yes, but it's a closed line, meaning only this set can pick it up. Don't get all nervous."

He dicks around with the wiring in the back, and after a moment of fuzz the screen shows a slightly skewed picture of Felton and Jones shot from somewhere at the head of the stage.

"Perfect!" Jordan says. He stands with his arms crossed, his eyes glued to the screen and Sarah's eyes glued to him and my eyes glued to Sarah. Why's she looking at him so intently? Christ, what am *I* looking at so intently? I'm acting like a fool again. There's nothing on her mind about getting back with him.

I pull my eyes away from them and focus on the screen instead, finding the quality less 'perfect' than judged: with all the static and echo, Felton might as well be talking with a mouthful of cotton. Jordan manages to hear his own name, however, and at the sound of it he grins and bolts toward the door, combing his hair back as he does so.

"Here we go! Wish me luck!" he says.

"Break a leg!" I tell him.

The confident look evaporates from his face as he turns his head toward me, and I see beautiful confusion, plain as day. I hold a thumb up to him. Peace, Jordan: I'm your pal. Get on stage like a good little puppy—I'll watch your bone for you while you're gone.

He nods back at me, forcing a smile, and jogs down the tunnel toward the stage where a loud applause greets his appearance. The second he's out of sight I walk toward Sarah.

"Can you believe this lineup?" I ask her. She whirls surprisingly when she hears my voice. She must have been deep in thought.

"Yeah," she says, nodding. "Pretty pathetic, right?"

"Pathetic," I repeat, savoring the sound of the word coming from her. "Are you coming out to the graveyard tonight?"

"Why? Is something going on tonight?"

"Nothing, really. I just figured we could all celebrate, you know? The end of the show and everything. Maybe you and I could do something beforehand."

"Something like...?"

"I don't know, maybe we could go bowling, or catch a movie, just...you know...you and me."

I've seen corny date movies with smoother lines than that, but I hold my eyes steady nonetheless, willing myself not to mess up. She doesn't smile, not exactly. Her eyes just sort of look to her side and then to the floor and then back at me.

"Let's wait and see what happens," she says. "Prom's in a few days and I'm still busy picking out my dress. We'll talk later, alright?"

'We'll talk later,' I repeat in my mind. Nothing to worry about. No red flags. It's not like she's going to take me aside later, put on that really soft sort of don't-want-to-hurt-your-feelings expression I dread so much, and clarify, in simple terms, that she's still in love with Jordan no matter what he did and I'm always just going to be a friend. Nope. Nothing to worry about.

I nod, satisfied enough with the vague response. There's silence in the room as the audience's applause dies down. I hear Jordan from the TV, but his voice is loud enough from the stage.

"This is an original poem I wrote about war and its devastating cost to innocents everywhere. It's called 'Autographed by Gunfire.'"

Monk makes a sarcastic and flamboyant hand gesture. "Ooh, how edgy!"

Sarah laughs, and so do a few others around us. I look around, enthused, and notice a few people at the end of the line scowling at the joke, just as others in class would scowl when we spin the morning announcements to our liking.

The thought gives me a sudden bright idea, and when I turn to communicate the message to Monk he winks at me with a grin on his face, already having the same idea in mind. Our education in homeroom has finally becomes valuable!

Jordan begins: *"The beautiful diva walks the land with a grin on her guilt-ridden face, her gut bouncing, her talons trembling, as she puts the world in its place."*

I gesture for Monk to take the honor. He tilts his head thoughtfully at the screen.

"'Hits orphans in the face?'" he booms, furrowing his brows.

"She walks with care, missteps here and there, wipes out countries with no regard for life's essence. Wherever she goes, havoc flows, and blood is spilt from her short-term pestilence."

I whisper loudly, "Clyde, didn't your Uncle Ronnie have blood in his piss too?"

Clyde's lips tremble as he stifles a laugh, looking over his shoulder at the girls behind him stretching for their aerobics act. They're hiding grins too, though, growing less interested in their own preparation and more intrigued by our backstage show.

"When she steps on a burr she cries like no other, stumbling tearfully as she holds her cut toe. Though the wound is small her eyes turn black, and the aggressor within her grows."

"Y'know," Monk says, "I'm getting a very clear image of Jordan's mom. *She* sure moans like no other in the sack."

"She looks for enemies with eagle eyes, mistaking pleas for savage war cries. If she jumps at a shadow an entire city dies, and she carries on with only self-love in her eyes."

I give a low critical hum, opening my mouth to compliment Jordan's adoration of 'liberal lies' and 'fat turd pies'. But before I can speak a word, Sarah interjects.

"I always knew Jordan was a genius," she says, blinking with a look of complete worship on her face. "Who else can write an entire poem from the word 'bullshit'?"

I don't think I've ever been more aroused by Sarah than I am right now. Once again, everything feels *right* somehow, like this moment and everything in it was long prophesied. I feel my cheeks flush as I grin at her, and when she laughs it becomes imperative that I make her laugh even harder with whatever I say next.

"While the diva runs with vengeance in mind and storms through all in her path, she signs her name in the fans she kills with bullets as her autograph."

Jordan steps back from the microphone and smiles at the audience, holding his hands to his side and taking a deep bow. Before I can even begin to come up with something funny, a loud applause from the audience blasts the volume of the television straight to Hell. Even with the screen shaking I can still make out the wide, confident smile on Jordan's face and the redness of life being restored in his corpselike cheeks. A few of those behind us clap as well, cheering him on as though they too were in the stands, shouting his name. I gape back at them, fully convinced they've all gone mad, and I forget about our own mini-show of destroying Jordan's lyrics.

His poem should've gone down in flames. He was supposed to die of embarrassment on stage and *stay* dead inside forever. It's the justice I've been waiting for, the reward for my patience and all this fake smiling. How are they all clapping? What sick, sad Hell is this?

There's something very wrong with a town that shows any respect whatsoever for a piece of crap like that poem, a work of 'art' Jordan didn't even show us during rehearsals for fear that we would offer our opinions as freely as he spews his. Any second this could turn into a zombie film and I wouldn't be surprised—mindless zombies don't scare me half as much as brainless followers.

Monk takes the moment from me when he sees I've got nothing.

"Huh," he says. "Sorta a lame ending, don't you think? I mean, it's got a lady going around capping people, but no verse about her tits? I'm not impressed."

I don't even realize the figure coming back through the door is Jordan until I turn fully and see his proud smile charging at us. The audience has stopped clapping, and now the superintendent's back on stage talking.

"I've got them all warmed up for you, Sarah!" Jordan says, suddenly right behind her and rubbing her shoulders. Sarah swats his hands away and walks toward the entry door, cracking her neck to both sides and stretching her arms and legs as she goes.

"Say, Jordan," Monk says, clearing his throat loudly. "You think you can teach me how to write poetry like that sometime? The way you stood up there and read with such...*passion!* I mean, *how* does a genius like you get up every morning?"

The sarcasm in his voice goes unnoticed. Jordan pats Monk on the back.

"Stick to what you're good at, Theodore," he says. "With a lot of work, you might even be an okay actor someday."

Monk brushes the hand mildly off his shoulder, keeping his smile calm and relaxed. Sarah appears on the television, and after looking around at the audience she turns her back to them and waits for the music to begin.

"I don't know why she's so nervous," Jordan says. "Her and I have been through her routine a hundred times now. She could breeze through it in her sleep, I bet."

I straighten my jaw as I glance at him and then look away again, reminding myself before I can get angry that

Sarah's already given her verdict of him: *pathetic*. If he's really in denial this bad, I'll get front row seats to watching his spirits shatter before the night's over.

The soft music begins from the speakers, crackled and distorted by the bad sound system. Sarah's body moves reflexively to the sound of it, waving and bending with master fluidity. She turns the stage into a canvas and her body into a paintbrush, manipulating the music like soft clay and making it and extension of herself, detailing her art with the slightest change of her facial expression.

"Uh-oh," Monk says to Jordan. "Looks like you might be upstaged after all."

Jordan shrugs.

"She would've done better with a different song, like I kept telling her," he says. "No one cares about interpretive dance or any of that 'soul searching' music. A sexier dance to a popular song would've been a way better choice."

I tell myself he's wrong. So, so wrong. He wouldn't know 'art' if it came into his bedroom in the middle of the night and painted its name in blood on his ceiling. Sarah's going to blow their minds by the time the song ends, and when she bows the applause will be so loud the floor will shake.

But when the song ends at the flick of her wrist, and she bows so low that her hair sweeps the floor, I discover I'm the one who's wrong. So, so wrong.

The audience's report is a dull clap at best, nothing compared to the wild applause Jordan received. The cheering is so low that I can make out the words of a little boy in the stands crying for his parents to buy him more cheesy nachos. Sarah lifts her head back up when the applause dies quickly and pushes her hair back before giving a pitiful wave to the unappreciative bastards and leaving the stage.

"Told you so," Jordan says. He jogs back out the doors, exiting as Sarah re-enters.

"You did great," I tell her right away. "For real, Sarah, that was awesome!"

She shrugs, and the not-quite-smile of five minutes ago returns to her face.

"Thanks," she says quietly. She looks back toward the screen with crossed arms, watching as Jordan flirts with his audience and announces "a selection from the Broadway musical *Razor's Edge*, performed by my good friend Theodore Munkowski!"

"Oh crap!" Monk gasps. He rubs his hands together, taking a deep breath. I touch both his shoulder and Sarah's, cracking a smile as they both look at me—then I kick him in the shin.

"Get your ass out there and show those swine what art is!" I tell him, and I nod at Sarah. "*Clearly* they need some re-education."

He blows a deep breath outward, hardening his expression as his shoulders straighten. The doors fly open as Jordan bursts back into the room, and when he sees Monk standing with us his eyes go wide.

"Theodore, you're on!" he hisses. "What are you waiting—"

He's silenced by the loud, guttural roar that makes everyone in the room jump in surprise. Monk's eyes are large and maddened now by the infamous spirit of the London barber he's become the vessel for, and his nostrils flare as he storms past Jordan and kicks through the stage doors.

"I had him!" he yells, voice booming through the television set. Everyone stares at the screen, fascinated, watching him as he stands on stage shaking in pure madness as the accompaniment catches up. "I had him! His neck was there beneath my hand! I had him! The man was there and now he'll never come again!"

I glance around and find that not one pair of eyes is watching anything but the screen—Monk's got everyone eating out of his hands less than a minute into his act. Even Jordan, who's watching the act closely for the slightest mistake to criticize, is silent.

"Looks like Monk knows exactly what he's good at," I mutter to him, swelling with pride on Monk's behalf. Jordan shrugs.

"Holy crap!" Clyde gasps as Monk pounces off the stage and into the audience.

"Alright!"

Swish!

"You sir!"

A man shrieks in surprise.

"Ready for a shave? Come and get a close shave for free! You sir!"

Another shriek, this time a woman's.

"Too sir! With blood you shall pay!"

"When the hell did he rehearse this?" Jordan complains. It's hard to tell if he's outraged or envious, but I tell you, it's damn enjoyable.

"About the same time as you rehearsed your act, I suppose," I tell him. "I like his, though. It's at least creative."

He rolls his eyes, trying his hardest to hide what's surfacing in his expression. Pictures are playing in my head, doubling the satisfaction: a child throwing a tantrum in a toy store...a snake choking on its own tail. He turns toward Sarah, smiling stupidly at her.

"So," he says to her, "I talked to Mr. Felton on the way offstage and he said he was really blown away by your dance. I'm meeting him and Mr. Jones after the show, and I think that if you came with me maybe they'd—"

"Go away, Jordan," Sarah sighs, leaving him with his mouth hanging mid-word. He doesn't move, though. He just stands there, looking confused as if maybe he'd misheard her. She continues, "I'm not your girlfriend. I'm not your friend. There's *nothing* between us anymore. Now leave me alone."

His eyes seem unsure where to look as she continues staring at him: back at her cold stare or down at the floor? It's harsh to watch this so intently, and I know I'm going to Hell for it because I'm laughing on the inside while his soul is being shattered to bits.

The moment of Jordan's heartbreak ends appropriately: in a halfhearted round of applause. Monk's act ends with a loud bellow, and Sarah turns away from Jordan with total finality. His lips tremble as his hand comes up to stop her, like he wants to say something but forgets the words. She walks away before he can gather his thoughts, heading toward the table of food in the back of the room. The others in line watch as she goes, paying more attention now to the live soap opera than to anything on stage. I follow after her.

"Fuck, Trey, leave me alone for five seconds!" she shouts, turning around. She stares at me like I'm *not* me, like I'm someone she barely knows at all and just wants gone. "You're smothering me, okay? I don't want to talk to you right now! Seriously, five seconds!"

My mouth hangs open, but I have no words at all. I watch her wipe her eyes and storm off.

The small crowd of onlookers stare at me. Someone pulls at my sleeve.

"Trey," Clyde says. I turn toward him, feeling all at once like I'm having a heart attack yet already dead. Clyde's next in line to go on stage, and he's shaking terribly.

"Calm down, man," I mutter quietly, still looking backward toward Sarah.

She's sitting behind the snack table, arms hugging both legs and staring emptily toward the floor in front of her. I feel that iron fist closing over my heart again, and I think, 'This isn't real. None of what just happened *really* happened.' Every instinct in me tells me to go comfort her, to say something to make everything better, to get back to what was literally *just*, moments before, so perfect. What the hell just happened? What the hell did I do wrong?

"I can't go on," Clyde says, jerking his head wildly back and forth. His pupils are just tiny specks in his green eyes, and his bottom lip trembles as his mouth hangs open.

"What do you want?" I ask him, annoyed. "Just get on stage and do your damn stand-up act!"

"These jokes..." Clyde says, holding up the note cards he'd been muttering to himself in line. He looks at them now like they're a wad of used toilet paper. "Jordan edited a lot of the bits I'd written, but I threw away all his edits and brought my own jokes along just to piss him off and show people *my* comedy. But now...damn, dude, I'm freaking out!"

He's sweating in panic, and it occurs to me that no matter what I say to him he's not going to budge from this spot, at least not willingly.

On stage, Jordan mutters his introduction to Clyde's act, barring tears from his voice as he calls him one of CHS's greatest comedic minds. I want to go tell Sarah how 'pathetic' Jordan looks right now—I want to hear *her* say it again!—but Clyde shoots me a final look of desperation, begging silently for mercy.

"Damn it," I sigh. I push Clyde aside roughly. "Take my place in the back of the line. If Jordan says anything about it, tell him you were puking in the bathroom and I offered to take your spot."

His face lights up, and he throws both arms around my neck and squeezes tightly. I shove him away and he runs off. Monk walks back inside, greeted like royalty by everyone. His face is lit up...and then he sees me walking in a daze, and it all disappears. He asks me something, sounding concerned, but I don't hear a word he says. I pass by him and walk down the hall toward the oppressive silence on the other side of the stage door, where the audience waits.

What do I say when I get out there? Where's my script? Is it in my—*yes*, here it is, in my pocket! I unfold it and skim the long paragraphs one final time, wishing like hell I'd made the font bigger. I push through the stage doors when I'm only halfway down the first page, and right away I'm greeted by the scorching heat of several overhead lights and the stares of two-hundred men, women, and children in the audience. So many people: old people, young people, fat people, short people. I've stepped into a Dr. Seuss poem, a canto of Hell that Dante skipped in his descent.

There's a strange smell in the air as I step over bundles of wire duct-taped to the floor. I may or may not have just farted. I stop at the very front of the stage and tell my left hand to bring the microphone stand closer while my right hand turns my script back to the first page. It goes terribly wrong: my brain loses contact with my limbs and both hands scramble upward at once, and the script goes flying from my right hand into the front rows of folding chairs.

Don't panic, I hear Grandpa tell me. *A good writer doesn't panic—will you listen to me, damn it? You can pull this off. If Jordan's little poem can put a spring in the audience's pants, so can a half-assed story.*

"I'm Trey," I say, dipping my mouth closer to the microphone and flashing the all-important *confident smile.*

"I'm a fiction writer. The story I'm going to tell you takes place in the Garden of—"

A loud, wet cough from a man in the front row stops me.

Enemy fire! Never pause for them! Fire back, kid! Grandpa shouts

"—Eden, just after Adam and Eve were banished from Paradise for discovering temptation. Outside the garden there was nothing but wasteland, just as the bible tells, but there were also creatures risen from...*ahem!*...from..."

I stop abruptly again, feeling myself start to slip. I search my mind frantically for the rest of the sentence, but I can't even *see* the story I my mind like I'm always able to. Sarah's voice is playing over and over in my head, and the fist squeezing my heart is growing hotter and hotter.

All I see are the hundreds of eyes watching me, some of which set above crossed arms as they listen intently, others wandering around in boredom or focused on the hot piece of ass three seats down from them. Screw it: I skip ahead to the closest bit I can remember.

"Adam and Eve stood listening to the sharp cacophony from the demons' laughter, and when Eve heard the sound she was put under a trance. She took a sharp stone from the ground and slit Adam's throat, fertilizing the soil with his blood."

A man five rows deep, sitting with a girl who could pass for either his wife or his eldest daughter, makes a loud sound of revulsion as he shifts in his seat.

"When she was freed from the trance Eve saw what she'd done and wept. Without the seed of Adam there'd be no future for mankind, and without a man she...she'd surely suffer at...she'd surely suffer at..."

They're still talking. Not just whispering anymore but leaning over in their seats and holding full-on conversations. What are they saying about me, I wonder?

Nasty things, I bet, the sort of things a parent would whisper to their kids after walking past a meth addict on the street.

Tracks change in my mind and send me somewhere black—what am I even doing up here, trying with these people? They don't grasp the story at all. They don't know creativity. They don't know 'art.' These are the same people who love Jordan and remain silent for people like Sarah. They didn't even give Monk's act a good enough response.

Whatever happened is because of *them*. They did this. They changed her and ruined everything that was great. They killed everything good, them and everyone like them.

Pictures flash through my mind as I find myself in Wonka's boat, going deeper and deeper down this dark tunnel:

The camera staring up at me a few rows into the audience, feeding my image onto the screen backstage.

Grandpa dying horribly of cancer, alone in his bed and disregarded by his daughters.

Sarah sucking Jordan's dick in the wings of the auditorium, the same auditorium I've been rehearsing this trashy story in for the failed task of winning her over.

The audience's eyes going wide as they pour applause onto Jordan, validating every grandiose belief he already has about himself.

Are they all—

"—out of your fucking minds?"

The talking stops, and a collective gasp—wrapped around a loud belch—replaces the sound. Realization of what I just said hits me. How long have I been talking out loud? What did I even say?

The shock doesn't take me down: instead it breaks open my cage, freeing me. I reach into my pocket and touch

Grandpa's ring, feeling not just reassurance, but *permission*. These aren't people in the audience; they're nothing but marionettes with dry-erase faces, obeying their master's hands. Felton comes up behind me, putting an arm around my shoulder and pulling me away as he mutters an apology to the audience with an embarrassed smile. There's a terrible heat in my veins, worse than I've ever felt before. It touches everything from my toes to my face, and when it hits my mouth it manifests into something terrible.

Gunfire opens from my mouth.

"You people think you know what art is?" I roar, throwing Felton off me and startling those in the audience who've stood up to leave. "You love it all, don't you? You fucking *love it* when some no-talent dickhead stands up here and reads some lame ass poem that he probably didn't even write, but you belch back at everyone else! You bunch of stupid ignorant hick nobodies!"

Felton tugs at my arm, nearly jerking it out of its socket, but I kick back at him. He puts me in a headlock and wrestles the microphone out of my hands.

"Folks, we're going to take a very short intermission while we fix a few things backstage, if you'll please—"

"You want something full of shit?" I yell into the microphone. I turn myself around in his grip, reaching down to unbuckles my pants and pull them down. Not making sense now. *Blur*. Everything's blurred. The only thing moving inside me is blind rage. My pants hit my ankles, but my underwear only comes down halfway before Felton grabs my arm in what feels like a vice grip. Camera lights flash as my bald ass makes its debut and sings one long-winded note at the audience. Felton pulls me up off my feet and hurries back toward the stage door. I scream and thrash out with my feet, kicking a speaker and knocking a large stage light over in a shower of sparks that makes the audience cry out. As soon as we're out of the audience's view, Felton punches me in the stomach.

"Shut the hell up!" he hisses into my ear.

The rage begins to die as soon as I'm dragged away from the angry, mocking faces. Now there's nothing but emptiness in the long dark tunnel, letting my mind whirl freely. I let it take me where it will, unable to make sense of or escape from the madness. In my blurred vision, I see Grandpa standing off in the distance, one hand hiding his face as he shakes his head sadly.

Chapter Fourteen

"**W**hat the hell were you thinking?" Felton roars.

This has become the chorus between verses in an ungodly song as I'm shuffled from one person to the next. A sickening feeling eats at my stomach, replacing the rage that's hung me out to dry. All that's left is fear and the taste of something sour rising up my throat.

Felton and Jones lead me by my arms toward a separate room backstage, away from all the others. The two of them bark furiously at me the whole way, quieting their voices only as we pass the line of gawkers. I hear Jordan's voice at close proximity, talking to Felton in a very soft and concerned voice. I don't look at him—I know my temper will light up like gasoline if I do—but I look to the side and see Monk and Sarah standing alongside the rubbernecking crowd. They both stare at me without a word, but the silent message I read in their expression is worse than whatever they want to say: *What the hell were you thinking?*

Time skips and suddenly I'm sitting in a small, closet-like room, staring into Felton's unforgiving expression from across a desk. Every few seconds his lip quivers as he mutters something, cracking his fists every time he blows a heavy breath toward the floor. Jones paces back and forth with a cellphone to his ear, and when he hangs up he sweeps the bottom of his jacket back and puts both hands on his hips, tilting his chin down at me with one eyebrow raised.

An hour ticks by like this, and I stare down at the wooden rings in the desk. Then the door opens and the silence is broken as my parents walk in. Dad regards me apprehensively. Mom asks what's going on, and Jones takes them both to a corner and offers a very drawn-out explanation filled with euphemisms: *"a few foul words...," "he disturbed some folks in the audience..."* Then he trails quietly into the specific details, and when I look up from the table I meet Dad's glare. I want to look away or blink, but I can't. My body isn't *my* body right now, and it's like I'm watching everything through someone else's eyes.

Felton continues talking, looking between my parents and I as he gestures with his hands and grimaces over and over between words. His tone starts to drop, becoming increasingly apologetic as he gets to his point, and though I can't hear the words he speaks I know exactly what he's saying by the hushed sort of cry Mom gives. A heavy silence follows, despite Mom's crying and Dad roaring back at both men about "process" and "working this out."

"What the hell were you thinking?"

Mom hisses the words into my ear the whole way back to the parking lot as she and Dad rush along with me held between them like a kindergartner. The grounds are still crowded with people out having fun, oblivious to anything that just happened at the show. Every few seconds, though,

I see someone stop and grimace at me. Someone throws a fountain drink, aiming for me but hitting Dad's back. He and Mom just stare straight ahead.

The second we're all in the car Dad speeds off toward home, staring straight ahead the entire way with unblinking eyes, knuckles turning white from gripping the wheel so hard. I watch him carefully, waiting for the big explosion. Despite Mom being the one doing all the yelling and threatening, it's Dad and his restraint that scares the hell out of me. The radio is on low, and I can hear the lyrics to some strange and ugly pop song.

"What the hell were you thinking?"

Finally, the magic words pass through Dad's lips, sighed wearily as he stands at the kitchen counter with an open bottle of vodka. This is the first time I feel expected to answer, but I can only manage to shrug as I look up at him.

"You know the church is going to find out about this," Mom says. "What do you think Pastor Dan's going to say? We'll be the laughing stock of this town because of your little stunt! Do you have *any* idea how this will affect our reputation?" Tears start rolling down her cheeks, and she squeaks, "how will I ever show myself in public again?"

I may be a rotten, spoiled bastard at times, but I hate seeing my mom cry as much as the next guy. I wrinkle my eyes at her, trying to get my apology across without opening my mouth—God knows I'll mess things up more if I try talking. Somehow, though, she doesn't decipher the look the way I intend.

"You think this is funny?" she screams. I shake my head, but she's already made her mind up. "Do you care about anyone besides yourself? *Do you?*"

"Leave him alone," Dad grumbles, staring calmly into his bottle. Mom snaps her head at him, blinking in disbelief.

"*"Leave him alone*"?" she repeats. "Just what are you doing to help? Get up and...do something!"

His head pivots slowly up at her, and when he blinks I see it again: that look of a pissed off bull holding itself back—*waiting* to strike.

"And what do you suggest I do?" he asks. "By all means, if you think screaming his ears off is going to accomplish something, keep at it. You're doing a great job."

I lift my head, thinking maybe he's going to have mercy. But then he looks at me, and I see nothing but disgust in his features.

"Maybe that's the best approach, though," he continues. "I've tried speaking to him like a man, but he's obviously not ready for that. He's still irresponsible. A little boy. He deserves a little boy's punishment."

He puts the bottle down, apprehending me as he takes a deep breath and hitches his pants up by the belt.

"Go to your room," he says decidedly.

"Go to his room?" Mom repeats. "What is he, ten?"

He pays no attention to her, keeping his gaze only on me.

"I can't fix whatever's wrong with you, no matter how much I wish I could," he says. "You're nearly a man, and if you want to continue acting childish, *you're* the one who's going to feel the repercussions. I can only show you where you're heading and hope to God you make sense of things on your own. Go upstairs and wait for me there."

"And I want a hundred sentences written by the time he gets there!" Mom adds quickly. "*'I will never misbehave or abuse my parents' trust ever, ever again.'*"

I gape at Dad, nervous about such a light punishment. He shakes his head at me.

"I don't know what the hell you were thinking," he says, "but it's time to grow up."

*

Suspended for three days. No prom. A whole audience of people who probably think I'm the world's biggest asshole. In short, everything sucks and I wish I was dead. At least if I was dead I could talk to Grandpa, actually hear *him* and not just thoughts of what he might say, cheap imitations of the real thing.

I'm lying down on the stripped mattress in my bedroom, ruminating over all of it and how much of a screw up I am. I lost control, and now I'm stuck in the smoldering wreckage. I shouldn't have even been in the damn show, just like I shouldn't have ever joined T.A.G. or told some stupid story that made me believe in myself or feel somehow closer to Grandpa, pretending to be a writer when all I've ever been is a faker.

I try to close my eyes and sleep. But sleep is impossible.

I'm losing it all over again. I want to scream and let it all break out of me; I want to shatter completely like I did in the back of Kevin's car. But I can't even do that much. I feel paralyzed even though I'm shaking all over, and every few seconds my mind shows me everything that's gone wrong, all the ways everything is completely broken and won't ever be okay again, and I can't turn it off or shut it up.

I think of the way Sarah looked at me. It was like nothing good or loving had ever existed between us at all.

Hours pass before I notice the large and uneven paint stroke on the ceiling above my bed. I don't know how it's escaped my attention all these times I've been here, how it looks directly down on me and watches my every twitch. It's untrustworthy. It's accidental. It's confrontational. It dominates my attention.

I tilt my head to one side, and the curved stroke becomes a smile; The Great Blank greets me.

"Well hello there," it says.

The thumb on my left hand twitches behind my head. I'm in Shawshank Prison, surrounded by The Sisters with no Morgan Freeman to procure me a rock hammer. I force a smile back, assuming the best way to avoid being shived in prison is to befriend your dangerous cellmate. I also have nothing else to look at aside from the bed I'm lying on. Mom and Dad stripped the room of everything, right down to the last thumb tack holding up the posters on my wall. This means no computer to type with, no pencils to write with, and no paper to crumple and throw. My only living company for the next three days is Hector, and he's already blown me off to go sleep in his cave.

There's nothing for me to be afraid of; I've fought The Great Blank several times in the past and won. I've spent several hours staring at a blank Word document on the computer screen, fighting word-by-word to finish a damn story without letting The Great Blank euthanize it with writer's block. The only difference here is manifestation: he stares at me from every wall in the room, every spot on the floor, and every skewed paint stroke on the ceiling.

"C'mon, Trey. Be courteous," The Great Blank says. "Pass some time with me: pretend I'm Monk or one of your other friends and tell me how you're feeling. I'm not going anywhere any time soon. You can open up to me."

Why the hell didn't Dad yell at me the whole time he was up here? He barely even made eye contact as he emptied the room. I wish he would yell and get it all out of his system, all the anger I've built up in him over the years which he doesn't even vent in small doses. No; instead he looks at me like a doctor on *E.R.*, throwing a promising look back at me as he exits the room like I'm a patient with cancer and he's been charged with finding a cure.

It's getting dark now, and in a few minutes, I'll be alone with the four-walled boogeyman. Hope of escape is futile:

Dad even nailed down my window and changed the lock on my door so it locks from outside.

"You have no idea how long I've been waiting for this," The Great Blank says. "You've grown a lot over the years. You've been steeped in the real world for so long: the fading friendships…the dying dreams …the dead friends…"

"Shut up," I grumble, flipping over onto my side to stare at Hector. I feel The Great Blank smiling around me—all four teeth seem to move in closer, and the tongue I'm lying in laps up the sweat from my back.

"…talking back to your bedroom walls," he finishes. "Do you really think you're well, Trey?"

The show re-plays in my mind, and although I try to stop it I experience every emotion all over again in ultra-slow motion.

The way she looked at me, that single cold look as she told me to leave her alone. I should've never asked her to prom, it was way too much and it was like cocaine to my imagination. Why did I ever tell Clive and Monk how I feel about her? Why couldn't I just bury it somewhere deep inside and let her be a friend and nothing else, the way she probably sees me and has *always* seen me?

It doesn't matter that I said anything, though. I'm looking back, putting every moment I've ever spent with her under a microscope, and I was practically *leaking* feelings for her, leaving a big wet stain with every smile, every small gesture that I'd built up and up so much in my head, convinced it was all perfect and everything would be okay because she's the one for me, and she *must* feel something similar.

I'm an asshole for loving her. I messed everything up; I tried too hard and believed too much, and now she probably hates me, too. She could never love me. I'm broken in more ways than she is, and she knows that because she's witnessed it firsthand, how I completely lost my mind not once, but *twice*. I could've just let her be, but I had to go and reach too far, imagine too much, really believe anything in life could ever work out the way I hope.

And what exactly is my excuse for being this messed up? Sarah lost her mom to breast cancer and then lost her dad to suicide, and she's still able to act normal, or at least hide the dark stuff that eats her up inside. I have no idea how any of her pain feels. The only person I've ever really lost was Grandpa, and even that's enough to kill me inside.

I can't deal with anything. I'm broken. I wish I wasn't broken, but I'm broken. And all I can do is ruin whatever's around me.

"I know," The Great Blank says, "how about a song to cheer you up, hmm? *'Humpty-Dumpty stood on a stage, Humpty-Dumpty had a great rage. All the heavy drinking and all his lost friends couldn't put Humpty together again.'"*

I close my eyes as I go on and on mumbling to myself, trying to ignore the voice, telling myself it's all in my head and I'll come down from this craziness. The song remains the same as The Great Blank continues to taunt me, but the voice changes every time I see another face in my mind watching me up on stage. Grandpa sings. Sarah sings. Dad sings. Mom sings.

Eventually, I do fall asleep. But when I dream, I see the horrible thoughts all over again, and there's nothing I can do to stop them.

Chapter Fifteen

Day one of suspension—before I even open my eyes I know it's going to be a miserable day. I feel it in every inch of my body. I force a smile as I get out of bed, though, stretching like I would on any other morning and pretending I have something to stretch *for* besides lying around all day. Grandpa would tell me to play the smile game, so that's what I'll do. Smile through the pain.

As soon as I've rubbed the sleep out of my eyes I notice an assortment of objects next to the door: two buckets, a roll of toilet paper, a bowl of cereal, and a glass of milk. Not a cup of coffee; I'm starting the morning with *milk*.

Score one, miserable day.

I approach the two buckets, eyeing the milk warily like an old enemy of the breakfast table. One bucket's full of hot water and has a washcloth inside it. The bucket closest to the roll of toilet paper is empty. I hear the bathroom calling out to me from across the hall as Mom or Dad flushes and heads downstairs to the breakfast table. Through the air vent I smell eggs and bacon cooking, and there's coffee brewing. I hear Mom telling Dad about her errands for the day, running around town for groceries and such. Dad mumbles back responses, and I know he's only half-listening by the sound of him turning the newspaper in his hands. I listen to all this for ten minutes and there's no mention of me whatsoever, not even a sigh from Mom.

I walk around the room, circling the bed thirty-seven and a half times before I hear a car starting outside and look out the window to see Dad leaving for work. Mom will leave shortly too, and they'll both be gone until five or six. I'll be alone for nine hours without even the faint drone of the downstairs television to keep me sane.

The hours crawl by slowly, and I'm stuck in my thoughts.

I try thinking about happy things, memories that will *surely* make me feel better and take away a bit of the pain. I think about the time Grandpa—

"Who's dead," The Great Blank says.

—took us all out for ice cream after school. It was almost a year ago, in the middle of the hottest part of Summer, and we couldn't eat the ice cream cones fast enough before they melted in our hands, and Sarah—

"Who doesn't love you," The Great Blank says.

—grabbed her half-melted ice cream right out of her cone and smashed it into my mouth, initiating a full-on ice cream food fight on the picnic tables outside the shop. There were plenty of other people out there, families with kids and old people under umbrellas, so it was only a matter of minutes before we got kicked off the property. I chased Sarah around the picnic tables, watching her laugh as she dodged each handful of ice cream I threw at her, and I was feeling electric inside, like—

"It doesn't mean anything at all," The Great Blank says.

—everything in this moment was great and nothing could ever take that playfulness away from any of us or destroy what we all shared. Afterward, with melted ice cream running down our faces and shirts, we walked home to Grandpa's and sprayed each other with a hose in the back yard. Then we sat, soaking wet, out on the front porch, and Sarah sat on my lap and took a picture of the two of us. I was smiling like an idiot, high on the moment and on copious amounts of sugar.

I think of this happy moment, desperate to feel something good from it, some semblance of peace. It only hurts worse, though. Those days are all gone. Grandpa's gone. And soon, high school will be over, and things will never be exactly the same as those good days.

"I know how we can pass the time together," The Great Blank says. In my mind I feel him running a hand over an assortment of torture devices. "Let's talk about Sarah more, shall we? She dominates every train of thought any other time, doesn't she? Hmm...where shall we begin?"

Concerts I've been to. Past family reunions. Fights at the dinner table. I search for *anything* to fill my mind with but thoughts of Sarah. I'm ashamed to even picture her face.

"Let's take a trip down memory lane for a moment. That ought to help us evaluate your losses with closer precision," The Great Blank says. "Tell me about the moment you think you fell for her, the time when you became the knight and she became your princess. Tell me that fictional gem."

"Shut up."

"You need to believe me, Trey. Christians call me the Devil...writers call me writers block...but what have I ever done but insist on the truth? When have I ever stopped you from telling a story that was going to become successful anyway? When have I ever pointed out flaws in you that others wouldn't discover in due time? I'm trying to help you now: your obsession over Sarah is going to take you to bad places—worse places than you could ever dream. Give up on her while you can. Drive her as far away from you as possible *now* so that when high school ends you're not still pining over her every second of the day, wondering who she's with and if you ever even cross her mind. School ends in a month. Let the poor girl go. It'll never be what you want it to be, loser."

Status updates. Photo postings. Relationship statuses. I think of all the times I've agonized over whether or not to type a comment on various videos she posts from YouTube, or what the difference in implications is between a smiley face and a winking face at the end of a text message. It's not obsession, it's...

"It's not love, either," The Great Blank says. "What you consider 'love' is just a collage of photo-shopped memories with her, spliced together by how you *want* to remember each memory."

"She agreed to go to prom with me, didn't she?" I demand.

"Yeah, but were you her first choice or just a default? And even if you weren't stuck in here during prom, how do you think the night would have turned out with her? You'd have been a nervous wreck. You'd be playing possibilities of how every exchange of words between the two of you would affect the rest of your lives, and at the end of the night you'd end up home alone after all the parties thinking about what you *should have* said. It's not even typical. It's...pathetic."

"Fuck you!"

"Yelling at your subconscious mind: also *pathetic*."

I can't take this anymore. I grab the cereal bowl off the floor and slam it as hard as I can against the wall, shattering it. The Great Blank laughs as I drop to my knees and search among the shards for the largest piece I can find, something I can use to pry the damn window open and get the hell out of here.

"I've got a feeling this won't be the last time you'll be rummaging around for a sharp object in your life," he says. "Your ending's already been decided. Why not take one of those shards and do the honest thing with it? Life's never going to be what you want it to be. Everyone you love is either going to die or get tired of you."

I rush toward the window and start wedging the piece of porcelain between the small sliver of space in the window. When it's partway in I start to pry gently, praying to any God available for help. Nothing happens. I pry harder.

"Come on. Quit running from the truth and talk to me," The Great Blank taunts. I look over my shoulder around the room, feeling eyes closing in on me. All I see is Hector, pressed up against the glass of his tank.

"You're already caught in the sticky web you've built, Trey," he continues. "Give in to me."

"Eat shit!" I yell, voice strained by the force I'm putting into the makeshift lever. I need to get out of here. Now.

Suddenly the shard pushes down a little easier, loosening the nails just barely. I grin like a wolf, licking my lips as I gouge the shard deeper. Just a little more and I can fit my fingers—

It snaps in half in my hand, and part of the fragment splinters into my palm. A sick feeling rises in my stomach as I see my chance of escape denied. The Great Blank— the giant, ferocious spider of my nightmares—just hums.

"No, Trey ca-an't always ge-et what he wa-ants," he sings. *"He ca-an't always ge-et what he wa-ants."*

My old comrade returns: the bubbling rage in my stomach who dug me into this situation and now promises a way out, talking about salvation as he digs deeper and deeper.

"But if he dies someti-ime…"

My fists knot as my lips tremble. I can't help it anymore. I start punching the wall as hard as I can, over and over until the skin tears off my knuckles. I want to scream but can't even find words to do a scream justice.

"…he'll fi-ind…"

I'm in Hell I'm in Hell I'm in Hell I'm in Hell!

"…it's better to blee-eed!"

Chapter Sixteen

The rest of Friday passes. I bandage my hand with one of my socks, since I don't want to tell Mom or Dad about the smashed bowl or The Great Blank and all his taunting.

Mom and Dad eat dinner downstairs, and when Dad comes up to give me a plain bologna sandwich without cheese or condiments, he doesn't say a word. He does let me out long enough to take a dump, since there's no way he honestly expected me to go in a bucket. Even as I sit on the toilet, thankful for the briefest escape from my bedroom and The Great Blank, I still hear its voice talking to me.

"Everyone you love will either die or get tired of you," it repeats over and over again.

I flush and walk back to my room. Dad locks the door behind me.

I sit on the bedroom floor, trying to drown out all the bad thoughts. Nothing works. And when I fall asleep around 2 a.m., I dream of Grandpa's house.

The house is empty in my dream. Every trace of Grandpa and all our bonding madness has been taken away, and all the walls in the house are blank and the holes are patched over. It smells sterile, like a hospital room, and as I walk from room to room I feel something following close behind me, breathing down my neck and making the air freezing cold.

I can't turn around to see what's following me, because it scares me to death and I know I'll die if I see its face. It brought me here, and I'm not allowed to leave until I see what it wants me to see. I'm its prisoner, and if I try to run, it'll grab me by the back of the neck with its sharp nails and force me onward.

I arrive at the staircase leading up to Grandpa's room. I hear him up there, crying out in unbearable pain like he's being tortured. The beast behind me pushes me forward.

"Go," it says. Its voice is haunting and unnatural, like a cold wind that merely *sounds* like a voice.

Grandpa screams my name from upstairs, and the thought of seeing him up there scares the hell out of me. I can't move, and the beast claws at my back, urging me onward.

"Go," it repeats. *"See."*

I take the stairs slowly, one by one. With every step, I hear Grandpa scream again. There's no trace of the Grandpa I know in these screams, none of his humor or madness or glee for challenging life with a mocking smile. There's only pain and fear.

"I don't want to see him!" I tell the creature behind me. "Please don't make me. I can't see him like this. I can't."

The creature lashes at my back again.

"Go," it repeats. *"See."*

I arrive at the top of the stairs.

And there he is.

He's the same parody of an actual person that was in his casket at the funeral home, made up into someone neat and clean and almost doll-like. I scream when I see what's been done to him.

His body's been hacked apart at each joint and reconnected with ropes made of barbed wire and veins. He's help upright by strings attached to both arms and the top of his head, and they jostle his body up and down, causing more pained screams.

Whatever demonic hands are holding his strings suddenly whip his whole body forward, and when he flies at me his outstretched arms hit me in the chest and take me to the floor. He screams in absolute agony.

"Trey…" he weeps, snot and tears running from his face like a scared child. "Why did this happen to me? What's going on?"

The strings holding his body are suddenly replaced by a large assortment of I.V. tubes and drip bags. The enormous needles jammed into his wrists and elbows tear his flesh as he's yanked upright again.

He's dressed in soiled bedsheets, and now his face is gaunt and pale, decomposing as he speaks.

"It should have been you!" he shrieks. "Why couldn't it have been you, you miserable shit! You deserve this! You!"

The skin melts from his face, and husks of flesh rain to the floor from his bared bones as he continues screaming.

"It should have been *you*, Trey!" he screams. "It should have been *you!*"

*

I wake up in a cold sweat, and it takes me a long moment adjusting to the darkness to remember where I am.

The Great Blank remains silent, and he's like that for the rest of the night. He doesn't need to speak, though. I lie awake the rest of the night, crying and shaking and wishing it *had* been me and not Grandpa.

Chapter Seventeen

Saturday comes, and I'm a total wreck. I didn't sleep all night. Any time I started to drift off, I'd hear Grandpa's voice again, screaming that horrible accusation: *It should've been me.*

It wasn't him. It wasn't. It wasn't him.

But I can't stop hearing his screams.

I keep telling myself it wasn't really him in the dream. I know he'd never say something like that to me, and the dream was just all the bad thoughts catching up to me subconsciously. It was just a dream. I'm not crazy. The Great Blank isn't real. None of this is real.

*

7 p.m. It's prom night.

This can't be the same night me, Clive, and Monk have been planning in the back of our minds all year. There's no beer here, no mindless yelling and havoc-wreaking and yowling at the moon to the sound of AC/DC playing in Kevin's car.

None of us went last year when we were Juniors; it all seemed so lame, and we just hung out in Grandpa's living room and drank and danced as *Bride of Frankenstein* played on a large projector screen. But this year was going to be something special. We *had* to go this year, if only to mock all the pageantry.

They're out there doing their own thing right now—Clive will be casting his hooks all night, flirting with several different girls and being rejected by all of them, Monk will be like a magnet to fun, drawing everyone else in and sniffing out the after-parties like a bloodhound, and Kevin will be the first man his size to dominate a whale without the use of harpoons and nets.

Christ, I wish I was out there with them, having the time of my life come hell or high water. Just being around to see the last of our great, epic blunders together would be enough for me, no matter how my own night ended up.

I ignore the jealousy as I watch the first of many scenes of debauchery out on the street. A black sedan whips around the corner, going something like fifty miles an hour and crashing its back end into the neighbor's curb. From the moon roof, a Junior named Christopher Campbell shouts at the top of his lungs with his eyes closed and his arms raised above him in a V-shape.

The windows in the back seat are open, and from my high vantage point I can see the girls in the back and their dates, one of them doubled over with laughter as her enormous breasts nearly pour out of her loose, low-top dress and her hair only *bends* in the wind from enough hairspray to make chemical warfare a reasonable assumption of her intentions. The car disappears down the street and it becomes silent again, and even though I grin at the thought of all the DUI's and public urination citations soon to come, I feel The Great Blank breathing down the back of my neck again.

The torture continues relentlessly as the sound of fun outside escalates. Hours pass, every minute feeling more and more like my last minute alive. No kidding, either. He doesn't stop talking to me, no matter how hard I bang my head against the wall or try drowning him out. I tell myself there's an off button to all this, that I'm a completely sane person who's in control of his own mind.

"Your Grandpa would be ashamed of you," he says. "You really messed *everything* up. Such high hopes for you...all wasted. Jordan would've made him proud."

"You're not real," I tell him. I press my face against the mattress, plugging my ears as if it'll do any good. The Great Blank just grins from inside my eyelids.

"You really should be nicer to me, Trey—I only want the best for you," he says. "Now, tell me about Sarah. Tell me *everything*."

I resist at first, wrestling to keep silent in my mind. Sarah's the perfect girl for me, that's all I *need* to know. She's beautiful, but she's *more* than just a body, she's...her eyes, they just...whenever she talks, I feel something different in the pit of my stomach, and it's *not* just lust, its—

It's futile. I explode internally, and shards tear the mental barrier to bits, and like a sinner shouting "hallelujah" to the Lord, I let it all bleed out.

I tell him about my pathetic hopes for what prom would be. I never even went out and got a tuxedo, and I was just going to go in jeans and a t-shirt because that probably would've been fine with Sarah and might've even made her smile. I tell him how I pictured us dancing to whatever crappy music would be playing, how Clive, Monk, and Kevin would've joined in the sarcastic display of whatever dance everyone else was doing, and we'd all somehow manage to get booted from prom within an hour.

We'd all go the graveyard, and maybe the others would even bring their dates with them, and we'd have one of our wild nights freed from worry or grief or any of that ugly stuff. And maybe, at the end of the night, I'd kiss Sarah. And she'd kiss me back, because in this delusional fantasy of mine she really *does* love me, and she's *always* loved me, and we're meant to be together like this forever.

I tell him about the dream I had the other night, where Sarah's lying on her back and my head is down between her legs. I tell him about how the lights in the sky kept changing like a kaleidoscope and how the Virgin Mary statue in Grandpa's back yard with Paul Stanley's makeup painted over its face sang "Strutter." I confess the sick proportion of these dreams over any others, how there's only ever me and *Sarah*. Never the other girls from school or any internet models. Only *Sarah*, each and every goddamn time. I tell him how exhausting it all is, how I despise myself for it all, how I've always hated the crybaby emo kids on album covers but how I see one every time I look in the mirror. These are ghosts of high school Past, Present, and Future because this is the same whiney idiot I've ever been: the same sensitive, ready to blow, crybaby—

"Enough!" I scream.

The Great Blank shuts up suddenly, perhaps surprised by the outburst. In a sudden moment of clarity, I realize exactly what I must do.

I knock the mattress over as I rush to my feet toward the shards of the broken bowl on the floor, and I grab the biggest piece I can find and squeeze it as tight as I can. It digs into my hand, collecting a pool of blood in my palm.

"What are you doing?" The Great Blank demands. "Don't kill yourself yet, we're just getting to know each other."

"You're not real," I growl at him, throwing the shard aside as the well of red ink fills. "If I'm going to go insane, I'll do it on my own. Now *be quiet!*"

I dip my finger into the well, and like the first caveman to interpret his surroundings on a wall, I draw the ugly bastard on the wall and force him to face me—two wide eyes, a large red clown nose, and an open 'o' mouth.

"Stop it!" he commands. "No one sees the All and Powerful Wizard! *No one!*"

I step back and admire my work, grinning savagely as a familiar electric feeling runs through me. I stare into the eyes of the demon, one who's now trapped right in front of me where I can take him head on. No more running. No more hiding in the walls or in my head.

He starts to say something—some new secret of my self-consciousness, a gem of self-loathing—but before he can get a word out, I smack the pool of blood against his mouth, silencing him behind a crimson scribble.

I turn away from my would-be executioner, finally able to ignore him as he fights to get a single word out. My eyes fall shut, and the bed rushes up to meet me. This isn't victory yet and I know it. It's okay, though, I think. I've heard everything the worst parts of me had to say…and now I know, I guess. I'm going to be okay. Probably. I haven't completely lost my mind yet. I can rebuild whatever I've wrecked.

I fall asleep. It's the only solution for the moment. Vegetate.

I don't know how long I've slept before I get the rude awakening of a loud knock. I roll over and groan, lifting my head just enough to look at the bedroom door through squinted eyes. It occurs to me that Mom and Dad are probably watching Nicholas and his friend again, and the two kids are probably just playing games by knocking on the door to my dungeon.

I lie back down, ignoring them. Sleep…I just want to sleep right now, go back to that pleasant dream I was having, whatever the hell it was. It's pitch black in the room, and I don't want to stay awake in here while everyone else is out at a party...

"Wake up, lazy ass!" a voice behind me hisses.

Definitely not Nicholas.

My eyes snap open at the familiar voice, and when I roll to the other side I see Sarah perched outside my window the same way Monk was a few nights ago, save for the fact that she's holding onto the sides for dear life. Her pale expression floods with relief when I stand up and walk toward her, wondering if this is even real or if I'm just making stuff up again.

"I've been knocking on your window for twenty minutes!" she whispers loudly, eyes wide and annoyed. "What are you, deaf?"

I don't answer. I simply stand and study her from the other side of the window, captivated like never before. Her shoulders are bare except for the thin spaghetti straps of her red dress, and she's wearing black leggings covered in white skulls. She has mascara and crimson lipstick on, and a small black cross is drawn below each eye.

She squeezes her fingers into the small gap I made under the window, biting her lip as she tries to dig her hands deeper for more leverage as she pulls upward. The veins in her neck surface from the strain, and the labor of her arms makes what's visible of her cleavage move in response. After a few seconds of trying, she scowls at me.

"Why don't you go grab a camera and record this so you can watch it later too?" she asks.

My eyes widen as I snap out of it and fumble for an apology, bending at my knees and fitting my fingers in with hers the best I can. We push together, leveraging both our bodies under the window. The nails are tough bastards to loosen, holding as if they've been rooted there forever.

Then they start to wiggle, and finally the window shoots upward as they let go.

Several minutes seem to pass in the space of thirty or so seconds. We stand looking at each other, no pane between us. She breaks the moment first, grinning wide as she looks me up and down.

"What's with the birthday suit?" she asks.

I look down at myself, not knowing what she means at first—then all the blood seems to rush from my face as I realize in horror that I'm naked except for my boxers. I rush to hide myself, childish as it feels, and I seize my clothes off the floor as she hurries inside behind me. As I dress in the dark I notice her looking around the empty room.

"Wow. That's…interesting," she mutters, looking at the smiley face made of dried blood on the wall. I lower my head, deciding to let her make whatever she will of it. What sort of explanation can I give, anyway? *The walls started talking to me about you, so I fought back*?

"What are you doing here?" I ask instead, avoiding the topic completely. She turns and looks at me strangely, like I just asked what color grass is or who the hell Bruce Springsteen is.

"It's prom night," she answers. I puzzle over the answer, staring at her as I gesture helplessly around me. She shakes her head at me, glaring icily as she takes a few steps forward.

"Oh, you'd better believe you're still taking me out!" she says, stabbing me with an index finger. "You're not getting out of this that easily. Let's go, we're going to be late."

"What time is it?" I ask, looking out into the darkness where there's no longer a peep to be heard.

"Three-fifteen," she answers. "We need to get going if we don't want our dinner to get cold."

I have no idea what she's talking about, what the hell she's doing in my room and talking as if it's the middle of the day and she didn't just break in through my window. For the life of me, I can't even picture how she got up the nerve to climb up here, given her fear of heights.

"I can't go anywhere," I tell her, half-smiling as I shake my head at her. "I'm…grounded."

The words fall flat, sounding even lamer than they normally would—if I'd heard myself say it on tape I'd swear to Christ and all his angels that it was an imposter imitating my voice. Sarah's quick to snag the answer before I can salvage dignity from it.

"Ooh, you're right!" she says, looking sarcastically over both shoulders. "The whole town's going to be waiting for you out there, ready to pop out of the bushes the second you set foot on the sidewalk. We should *really* be afraid!"

All I can do against such logic is shrug toward the floor. She sighs and takes a step closer to me, lacing her fingers in with mine.

"Do me a favor," she says as I look up at her. "Quit worrying, grow your balls back, and come out with me. Okay, Rapunzel?"

She has perfume on, something flowery and somehow erotic. There's whiskey on her breath.

"You've been drinking," I say. She rolls her eyes and laughs.

"Whoa," she says, holding her hands out defensively. "You're not seriously going to lecture *me* about drinking, are you? *You?*"

"No. I just didn't think you drink. Like, at all."

"I don't," she says. "But I wanted to tonight, and I can do whatever I want. Are you coming or not?"

She stares at me in a way that pretty much tells me she'll win this argument no matter what I say. Even if I tried to look away, those bright green eyes would only follow, and I know from experience that she'll eventually get to the point where foot-stomping and slugs to the shoulder will take place of her words. It's funny how in any other situation, in some other room that doesn't reek of B.O. and doesn't have a face drawn in blood on the wall, this would all feel sort of sexy.

"Alright," I say, smiling a little as her eyes light up. She lets go of my hand and moves quickly back toward the window, stepping carefully outside onto the slanted rooftop. An invisible foot kicks me in the ass when I throw a cautious look back at The Great Blank's cadaver. *Don't you dare think twice about this*, I tell myself. I'm not sure which will prove the bastard right, though: going with her or ignoring her completely.

"Everyone you love will either die or get tired of you," I hear him say.

Screw it.

I step barefoot out the window, feeling a breeze crawling up the knee holes in my jeans as I squat beside Sarah and close the window behind me.

I watch her descend the ladder until her face is out of sight, and then she's walking across the lawn. When she turns and sees me still standing at the top of the ladder, she throws her arms out impatiently.

"Hurry up, or I swear I'll start singing at the top of my lungs," she says. Her voice is loud enough already, and it makes me wonder how much she's had to drink and how early she started. I motion for her to be quiet, walking carefully toward the ladder.

"Oh, you did *not* just hush me!" she says. Then she belts out loudly, *"Treeeey! Come out and dance with me todaaaay! Let's go far awaaaay!"*

A light across the street comes on. I see the silhouette of someone looking out their window.

My face sizzles as I rush down the ladder.

"Keep your voice down!" I whisper as I run across the lawn. I can't help but laugh, though. She sways back and forth on her feet, smiling wide. Her eyes are so bright, and she's got that big and dorky grin with dimples on either side of her crimson lips.

"Look what I brought," she says, lifting the handle of a large picnic basket. There are two fading bears printed on top of it. Grandpa's basket.

She opens the lid, tipping the basket so I can see the large assortment of cheeseburgers, French fries, and other fast food from all across town.

"It's about time," I joke.

She fakes a frown and whips a cheeseburger at me. It misses my head and opens across the lawn.

"Let's go," she says, grabbing my hand and pulling me along. "We've got a dance to catch."

"Open your mouth," Sarah says as we walk half-sideways, laughing every time one of us trips over the broken sidewalk or stumbles into the empty road. I grin as I obey her, and she grabs another French fry from the *Burger Joint* bag in her hand and draws her arm back. It hits me below the eye when she throws it, and like a circus seal I pull my head back and catch it in my mouth. She claps loudly, and by this point I don't even bother telling her to quiet down. I gesture for her to hand me the basket.

"My turn," I say, and she opens her mouth eagerly. I break a fry in half, determined to make this one count after missing the last four times. I see her eyes light up suddenly, catching something that I don't. Before I can giggle in agreement that yes, this is *so* damn cliché, my foot oversteps the curb behind me and I yell in surprise as I fall backward on my ass.

She cries out with laughter, covering her mouth with both hands to keep from waking up the entire street. Any other time I'd be worried as hell about someone's lights turning on from inside one of these houses and a friend of my Mom or Dad running out to see what all the noise is, but I honestly don't give a crap. I laugh right along with her as I scramble to pick up the food that spilled.

She reaches into the basket and takes out a tiny bottle. She stops long enough to chug the whole thing, and she makes a disgusted face as she tosses the empty bottle into someone's yard.

"I don't understand why everybody goes to the big places for prom dinner," she says, popping a fry into her mouth.

"There's no fun in it," I agree. I bite into my second cheeseburger, and for the twentieth time I look around at our surroundings, trying to figure out where she's leading us.

"So, where's this dance at, exactly?" I ask. Her eyes twinkle, and she shrugs.

"Somewhere special," she answers. "We're almost there."

I grumble under my breath, playing it like I'm annoyed by all this mystery, but inside I'm giddy with anticipation. I play with the notion that her Aunt Mary is out of town for the weekend...her entire house all to ourselves. But Sarah lives on the other side of town, not over here by these dark woods, all these—

Shit! I look around once again at all the tall, uncut grass and the unkempt look of the surrounding houses, and suddenly I know *exactly* where we are and where we're going. I run ahead of her, growing more and more excited as I recognize the tall wrought-iron gates at the end of the block with the dim yellow streetlight illuminating the arched entrance, surrounded by trees on all other sides. I feel strange staring at it, slowing my steps as if approaching it for the first time. I grin widely as I hear Sarah coming up behind me. I look over at her and she smiles, spreading her hands like a modest artist.

"I figured that since the others would be out tonight we could have the entire graveyard to ourselves," she says, twirling on her feet and giggling as she trips and falls to the grass. "I'm a genius, right?"

I'm speechless, like some young romantic in a Shakespeare play who's forgotten his all-important lines at the apex of his career. There's no response good enough for all this.

"Damn," I half-laugh, half-sigh. For as short as it is, it feels strong enough, proper for the moment.

Sarah loops one arm underneath mine, and we enter our silent dance floor together. I don't feel like I missed a goddamn thing tonight after all, locked in my room while all the others follow the cattle call to dance in a high school gymnasium, imprisoned to regulated fun. They wave and smile with their dates as they walk through a crowd of parents and teachers at the entrance door, but that's all just for tradition sake. This, however, is *ours*. I don't need the flashing of cameras or the boo-hoo-hooing of my parents to validate how this moment feels.

She leads the way forward, dragging me excitedly by the hand toward our tree. The branches have all been strung with colorful Christmas lights, trailing off into an outlet near the caretaker shed. The soft glow catches her eyes as she smiles back at me, caught up in her own drunken excitement.

She throws her arm around my waist and squeezes me tight as she holds her phone out in front of us.

"Picture time!" she says. "Let's do a serious one first, okay? Three...two...one!"

She takes the picture, her face pushed up against mine and my arm awkwardly around her waist.

"Okay, now a cute one! C'mere."

She puts her lips against my cheek, pushing them out like a chimpanzee. I stick my tongue out and cross my eyes. She takes the picture, and then she jumps up and down excitedly as she holds her phone between us.

"Oh my god, look at you!" she says. She reaches up blindly and strokes my cheek, then turns to look at me. "You're handsome."

"And you're drunk," I tell her. I smile, though, hopefully hiding my own excitement. *Handsome.*

She sticks her tongue out and blows loudly, waving a hand.

"Get off it, old man," she says. "I'm not drunk. If I were drunk, could I do this?"

She lifts one food off the ground and leans forward with her arms splayed out. After a second of balancing and sticking her tongue out at me, she starts to teeter, and her arms pinwheel as she starts to laugh. I grab her shoulder before she can fall.

"You sound like Clive," I tell her. She stares daggers at me.

"Don't you dare compare me to Clive. I'm not a total alcoholic like he is, okay? I just wanted one night of fun after the past few weeks. Are you going to be on my case all night? Seriously?"

I hold my hands up in surrender.

"Fine. I'll stop. Just…maybe go easy on it?"

She pats my cheek as she walks past me.

"Don't tell me what to do. I can do what I want, okay?"

"Okay."

"Come on, let's sign our names!" she says, pointing toward the base of the tree. She drops to her knees and feels around the grass until she finds a small pocket knife. She flicks it open and hands it to me. "You sign for us," she says. "I have horrible handwriting. I'll grab us some juice."

I shrug and take the knife, carving out small bits of bark in awkward straight lines as she walks toward a large punch bowl hidden behind Grandpa's grave. Aside from playing with Legos, I'm a terrible craftsman—the capital 'T' I carve is slanted, like an ugly birthmark on the tree we've spent so many nights in. Whatever; it's a style choice.

"So," I ask, "how did the rest of the show go after I left?"

She snorts sarcastically, reminding me that "left" isn't the most accurate way of describing my departure.

"Terrible," she answers. "You completely killed it."

The knife slips and nicks my thumb.

"Crap," I say. I drop the knife and reflexively bring the wound to my lips.

"Don't worry about it," she says, handing me a cup and leaning her head back against the tree as I work. "The whole thing was stupid anyway, just another excuse for Jordan to show himself off to the town and look good for the cameras." The corners of her lips rise into a smirk. "You should've seen him squirm! Oh my god, it was, without a doubt, the greatest thing I've ever seen! He looked terrified, and the audience wanted his blood!"

"What did he do?" I ask. "Get back up on stage and yell 'April fools'?"

"No, he tried to improvise another poem there on the spot," she answers. She lifts a hand theatrically and exhales, "*Life Among Roaches!*"

I laugh loudly at this, all too easily picturing poor Jordan trying to calm the lynch mob I'd left in my wake. This is the first bit of pride I feel over my actions, the silver lining in the toilet bowl.

"Nobody else wanted to go on afterward," Sarah continues. "A few others tried to go on after Jordan got a hot dog thrown at his face, but it felt like a riot would break out any second. I wish you'd seen it."

"Must not have been a good image to the talent scouts his mommy invited," I say, taking a large gulp of the spiked juice.

"Actually, Monk got a call from one of them."

Red juice showers the air in front of me as I spit and turn to face her, wide-eyed.

"Get the hell out of here!"

"If you don't believe me you can ask him yourself," she says. "Monk says the scout was from an acting conservatory in Chicago. He keeps saying it's nothing big, but you know how bad of a liar he is, even for an actor. Every time he's brought it up he's gone on and on about all the famous actors he knows who went there. Clive says if he hears one more sentence about it from him and he's sewing his lips shut."

She smiles, staring straight ahead now. The happiness I feel for Monk is fleeting, however—there's something absent about the way Sarah's telling me all this, like she's simply listing the natural order of things rather than telling of a modern miracle.

"So…you're not happy for him?" I ask. She shoots me a glare.

"*Of course* I'm happy for him!" she says. "Monk's more passionate about his work than anyone I've ever met, and if any one of us deserves this little bit of luck it's him!"

I lower my head ashamedly. Strike one for a good night. Sarah sighs heavily, rubbing above her eyebrows with her fingertips.

"The talent scout was a friend of Jordan's mom," she explains carefully. "The only reason Jordan invited him to the show was because the little weasel must have thought that if I got the scout's attention I would somehow still be connected to *him*."

"Okay…so?"

She rolls her eyes. "Don't you get it? Now that *Monk* got the scout's attention, Jordan can talk his mom into putting a bad word in about him. And *even if* the scout won't listen—" she says, cutting me off before I can argue, "—the school won't take Monk if he gets into any trouble with you."

"With *me*?" I ask, taken aback by the accusation. She quickly throws a hand up before I can stand to my own defense.

"Look, I don't mean that you would *purposely* do anything to ruin this for him," she says. "It's not about you, not really. It's about what's been going on *because* of you since you've been gone."

I look at her warily, feeling something slimy and foul rising from the pit of my stomach.

"I've been gone for two days," I tell her. "What the hell could have happened?"

"Well, there's been a lot of talk since the show," she says carefully.

"Screw it," I say, waving a carefree hand. "People can say whatever they want about me. I made a big mistake, I'm sorry for it, and now I'm ready to get back to life as normal."

"But it's not just about you anymore!" she repeats, and she slaps a hand to her forehead. "You're not listening. I'm trying to explain, and you're not listening."

"Then explain slower, like I'm stupid or something," I tell her. I notice my hands suddenly quaking at my sides. "Just tell me what's going on. What happened back at school?"

She's silent for a long moment.

"A lot," she says. "And you're not going to like any of it."

An image of the mob rushes through my mind—a thousand Great Blanks jeering at me from the audience stands, this time wielding torches and pitchforks to avenge their father. I force the image away as Sarah continues.

"Things have changed back at school since the show. Yesterday, before the morning announcements even came on, Mac Gallagher flushed a cherry bomb down every toilet in the fourth-floor men's room."

"That old trick?" I ask, dubious. "How many movie clichés did he sift through before settling on that one?"

She shrugs.

"I heard the explosions all the way from Mrs. West's room on the other side of the building. Everyone thought the school was being shot up or something. I mean, with everything on the news about that stuff happening, you can't imagine the looks on people's faces—it was like we were all wondering who had just been killed. Mr. Jones came running out of his office, yelling for everyone to stay put in their rooms, but when I snuck out to take a peek…" She stops for a second, freeing a small, nervous laugh. "There was a toilet seat half-buried into the row of lockers outside the bathroom."

I smile patiently but twirl a finger for her to get on with it.

"The police came and had everyone line up in the gym to have their attendance re-taken," she continues. She takes a deep drink from her cup and flinches at the taste. "Long story short, they found out it was Mac and everyone started shitting bricks—the police left the room and the entire faculty guarded the exits to keep everyone in, and while Jones walked around shouting 'stay calm, stay calm,' Felton just snapped! He marched around screaming at everyone to shut up and sit down, and he got so flustered with Steffen Grady that he threw him up against the wall and started screaming in his face."

I groan. "Where do I come into the picture?"

"Well, it only took them like ten minutes to find Mac, sitting by the creek next to the band practice field. When they brought him inside he was grinning from ear to ear, nodding his chin at people as he passed them like he was some sort of rock star. It was sort of suffocating, watching and waiting to see what was going to happen to him." She pauses and shrugs at me. "Sort of like how it felt when you got pulled offstage."

"So what happened to him?" I ask, ignoring the burger and fries turning in my stomach. "Did he get suspended too?"

She shakes her head gravely, and mutters, "Expulsion."

"What?" I shout. I wince, thinking of what little I even know of Mac but feeling injustice on his behalf.

"Kevin overheard Jordan talking about it after school in the TV studio," she explains. "Felton decided to make an example of him. I mean, after that school shooting on the news a while back, and after what you did on stage—"

"How can you even pair what I did with school shootings?" I ask incredulously. I'm shaking even worse than before.

"It's what Mac yelled when he was led away," she says. She stares at me sympathetically, and when she speaks again she stares down at the grass, opening her mouth just enough to be heard. "He yelled, 'For Trey.'"

I'm frozen for a moment. I can't even make a fist as I picture the entire student body turning to one another, pairing me with the school's newest felon and imagining us planning together like bunkmates. Going back on my previous thoughts of injustice: that little asshole deserves to be fed to lions.

"You didn't just explode on stage when started yelling about art," Sarah says. "You lit a fuse. And I bet it's not going to stop here."

"How could you know that?" I ask defensively, wishing like hell I didn't already know the answer. "People are probably already Facebooking about how Mac and I are two dumbasses who got what they deserved. No one in their right minds would latch onto this!"

"You're wrong," Sarah says. "You already had a group of supporters before Mac did what he did. He was one of them."

"Supporters?"

"Some people are talking about you like you're their hero. I mean, you went on stage and pretty much gave the middle finger to the entire town while going on about art. You said what everyone else in T.A.G. wanted to say about Jordan's bullshit. Oh, and you *mooned* the audience!"

I shake my head. "I'm not proud of any of that."

"No, it was totally punk rock!"

"It was?"

"Just about everyone in T.A.G. loves you for it. You totally destroyed Jordan's baby right in front of him. Kids I've never heard *speak* in homeroom talk on and on in your defense the second someone even whispers your name. The way they argue so passionately for you, making up all these crazy explanations for why you said what you said…it's really sort of impressive."

"But I'm messed up in the head!" I shout defensively. "I don't know what the hell I was saying! I could've recited the goddamn national anthem for all the control I had!"

She smiles for some reason, like she's remembering all the idiots at school crafting rigorous speeches at the pulpit, using *my* name in every sentence like we grew up together. It's not funny, not any of it. I don't know how the hell she can smile at anything while I've got this creepy feeling under my skin.

"Laugh it up," I tell her, forcing myself to stay calm. "I'm not going to take part in any of this. If they all want to use what I said to justify their own drama, they can knock themselves out with it. Hell, if they want more crap to throw up on a banner, I can dig some old emo poetry out of my desk drawer, along with all the other dumb shit I've spewed when my head wasn't clear."

Her smile fades.

"I'm sorry," she says. "Really. I know you didn't do any of it on purpose. But...are you telling the truth?"

"About what?" I ask, half-laughing through all the mixed emotion. "Not wanting to be the leader of some sort of 'rebellion'? Hell yes I'm serious! I've gotten myself into enough trouble."

"And you won't let Monk get involved?" she presses. I wave a dismissive hand.

"He won't want any part of it," I tell her confidently. "If anything, we'll record whatever goes down and put it online for others to laugh at."

She nods.

"I'm glad you're at least being reasonable," she says after a moment of silence, watching me as I she takes a giant swig of her drink. "I don't know what I was expecting."

I grin wolfishly, looking to provoke her.

"Go on, say it," I tell her. "If I really wanted to, I could flip the whole school upside down, couldn't I? I could have people eating out of my hands, ready to do anything I said: goose-stepping, funny moustaches, all of it."

She laughs hard at this but slugs me in the arm as I finish off my drink.

"Well, Hitler *was* a failed artist before he was a dictator and mass-murderer," she muses, then looks at me with mock-suspicion. "How's *your* art going?"

"Failing," I answer. "Another reason I should stay off stages, I suppose?"

She shakes her head.

"You couldn't handle the responsibility of being a madman, even if you are a little stupid sometimes."

"Stupid?" I repeat, blinking dubiously and then snapping my fingers. "Oh, right! Like the way *Jordan* was stupid for blasting the country with his shitty poem in front of a town full of war veterans?"

"At least he got a good response," she says. I clap my hands together.

"Well there you go: *he* can deal with all this crap, make whatever he wants out of it. He knows how to make an audience buy into his agenda just by throwing a few pretty words together."

She shrugs and looks down at the ground.

"He's easy to be fooled by," she says. Then she adds, "I really thought he cared about me. Then he went and desecrated Grandpa's grave. How can someone tell you they love you and then hurt you like that? Am I an idiot?"

I shake my head.

"You're not an idiot," I tell her. "He's the idiot for taking you for granted. And it was pretty awesome how you broke his heart right back."

Her smile seems forced as she reaches up clumsily to wipe her eyes. She's careful not to ruin her makeup.

"You mess with my friends, you mess with me."

"Well, if someone ever dumps on *my* grave, just go ahead and stab them," I tell her.

Her eyes seem to brighten, and in the thin bit of moonlight that breaks through the treetops above us her entire expression seems to glow. Part of me reawakens within, that bastard werewolf that howls to please her in every way possible. The entire conversation is forgotten to me as she looks into my eyes, smile fading into something more serious, and I start imagining a hundred ways this could *happen*, right here, under the moonlight...

And then my stomach rumbles loudly, breaking the complete silence with a sound like a lion being kicked in the balls. My eyes go wide for that long, drawn out moment, and my cheeks feel like they're on fire. She stares at my stomach, her mouth hanging like she's transfixed by some strange, hidden talent.

"Damn..." she says under her breath, blinking with a look between amazement and humor. My stomach rumbles again, and her fingers shoot over her mouth as she laughs uncontrollably. After a sick, eternal minute of shame, the laughter becomes too contagious to ignore, and I start cracking up too, embarrassment be damned.

"Come on, let's dance!" I say, grabbing both her hands. Her drink splashes between us as she gawks at me strangely and stumbles forward.

"Dance to what? There's no music!" she laughs. I shrug.

"We'll make our own," I answer.

She gestures, clearly waiting for me to make the first move. I would never do this sober—never ever, not even on my mother's life. But in this half-drunken state, free of the need for excuses and completely alone with her aside from row after row of the departed, I swing my arms from side to side and kick my feet up and down.

Sarah stares at me blankly.

"What do you call that?"

"Dancing," I tell her.

I grab her hands and pull her toward me, forcing her to join. She twirls under my arm, and we double over with laughter and bow to one-another before shifting into a mock-waltz. I lace my fingers together, doing a wave-like motion with them and bouncing from foot to foot.

"Bet you never knew I was a professional dancer, did you?" I say, pointing a finger to the sky and tucking one arm behind my head. She gets a kick out of that, and she shakes her head at me with her face in one hand.

"Come here," she says, and takes my hands in hers. She dances steadily, guiding my arms to whatever silent beat she's making up. "Loosen your shoulders. Just relax."

I let her guide me through the dance, the perfect idiot student.

We continue dancing until we run out of cliché dance moves and energy in general. We don't stop moving completely, but rather fall into one another, hands entwined as we dance slowly toward the dwindling punch bowl. We fill our cups and I chug mine in half a second, hovering on that fine line between buzzed and drunk, feeling pain in my cheeks as my grin spreads uncontrollably.

Sarah pauses in mid-sip and throws a quieting hand toward me.

"What's that?" she asks, cupping a hand to her ear and listening intently to our silent audience. "A slow dance? Well…"

"You can't be serious," I mutter. Her answer is straightforward enough: her hands move to my shoulders, and the sudden absence of space between our bodies pulls my hands toward her hips like a vacuum. The moonlight in those eyes…damn it. I sway with her, stepping the feeble step of either a desperate romantic or a cripple trying not to fall over.

"Stop," she whines, moving my face back toward hers as I stare off toward the gate. "We're alone, okay?"

"What if the others come?" I ask, thinking of what Clive or Monk would say if they stumbled upon this.

"You didn't seem too worried when you were dusting off the Elvis moves," she reminds me. I shrug. "What's on your mind?" she asks. I inhale shortly as I open my mouth to make up an answer, any answer but the truth.

"It's just this story I've been working really hard on."

"Liar," she says. The conviction in her eyes kills any hope of me fooling her. I lick the inside of my lower lip, trapped here with her arms around my neck and mine around her waist. Could Hell be so pleasant?

"I was thinking about us," I say truthfully, wishing that saying something quietly meant you weren't saying it at all.

"Okay…what about us?" she asks.

This is the romantic moment where my mouth opens as a song like "Kiss Me" plays from the skies above. This is the moment where the silky words of a professional romantic escape my lips like a pre-recorded message.

If only real life could be cheated so easily.

"I…well…you know…I've been thinking a lot," I answer.

"Congratulations, that means you do have a brain!" she says. She repeats, "What about us?"

"Well…we've known each other for a long time…"

Je-sus! my mind groans. *Are you trying to tell her how you really feel about her, or proving to her you read chic-lit and watch corny soaps late at nights?*

"And…?" she presses before I even realize I've stalled again.

The way she's looking at me, it's like she knows what I want to say. It's like she's an actor who knows what's coming next in the script. Her hands are moving up and down my shoulders, gently massaging them. Her eyes are bright, and somehow, I think, desperate. God, she really must be drunk. Dancing with me like this. Being so suddenly flirty.

I think of The Great Blank's prophecy. *Let the poor girl go. Everyone you love will either die or get tired of you.*

Her face moves ever so slightly closer to mine, until I can feel her breath on my lips. I brace myself for pain.

"I'm really glad we're such great friends," I tell her.

The look in her eyes changes. She stares at me for a second, and it's like I just killed something. The space between us grows again, and she taps her fingers against my side.

"Everything we've been through together," I continue, hating myself, "I'm glad we both know we're there for each other. And that nothing can mess up our friendship."

She looks so caught off guard and confused. I want to take back everything I just said, go back less than a minute and damn The Great Blank's words.

Then Sarah smirks.

"Trey," she says quietly. "Are you seriously trying to friendzone me right now?"

"No," I say. "I'm just saying…I'm glad we're such great friends. I wouldn't trade your friendship for anything else."

"You're a terrible liar," she says.

"I'm not lying. You…mean a lot to me."

"Uh-huh," she says. She laughs at whatever face I'm making. "Why can't you just relax?"

"I am relaxed."

"Whatever." She looks at me, amused. Then she laughs again and rests her cheek against my chest. "I love you, weirdo."

Rewind…play. Pause. Rewind again…play again. Pause again. I analyze every syllable and movement of her expression as the same twisted confusion I'm feeling appears in her eyes.

She loves me…loves me…she…

"I love you too," I say, finally.

"Dance with me a little longer, okay?" she asks. Her voice is quiet. "I just want you to hold me for a bit."

"Okay," I tell her. Her hand moves to my arm, and she rubs it gently as we sway back and forth.

"You're so warm," she says.

My mind's racing again. I try to shut it off, because it's ruining the great moment and telling me to worry when I know I shouldn't feel worried at all. No one else would feel worried right now. I wish I wasn't broken, that I had the "off" switch everyone else seems to have.

"You remember that time Grandpa let me cut his hair?" Sarah asks. I nod. The memory's like a life raft, and I latch eagerly onto it.

"He let you give him a mohawk," I say, smiling. She nods. Her hand is moving up at down my arm still, and then it's on my belt.

"And he wore it up in spikes for a month," she says, and she laughs weakly. I feel her finger tracing the inside of my belt. Her hand travels slowly toward the center of my back, and then toward the front of my belt again.

Shut up, brain. Just shut up and let me be here right now.

"Hey Sarah?" I ask. Her hand stops, and she tilts her head up at me. There's uncertainty in her eyes, and I think there's a silent question in them. I ask mine first.

"Do you think you'll ever get sick of me?" I ask. She scrunches her eyes at me, humored again. "I mean it," I say. "I mean, I'm broken. I never know what the hell I'm doing. And I think I might be going crazy."

She smiles, and recites, "Crazy can sense crazy."

I think of the backseat of Kevin's car, my meltdown on stage, The Great Blank and everything it told me. Does she see all that when she looks at me? Does she really know how messed up I am?

"I just don't want to lose you," I tell her. "I don't want you to ever regret knowing me."

I don't know why this hurts to bad to say out loud. It makes me feel stupid and weak, and I can hear an audience heckling me in my mind.

She stares at me for a long moment again. Once more, I see doubt in her eyes. Her hand moves back from my belt to my side, but her fingertips barely touch me now, like her hand's unclear what her mind's trying to tell it. I wish I was in her head, then I could know for sure what I really mean to her, whether she's here with me right now because she wants *my* company or if I'm just circumstantial. I know she still loves Jordan, no matter what she says, and that the pain is still in there somewhere. That's why she's drinking, trying to shut the pain up and bury it. What does that say about this moment and how she keeps looking at me?

"I'm never going to get tired of you, Trey," she says seriously. "And I wouldn't change a thing about you. Ever."

She touches my cheek, and our awkward swaying stops as she looks up at me. My insecurities are burning. The questions won't stop.

The night air brushes us, either complimenting the moment or telling us to get the hell out of here, to take our dance floor elsewhere and leave this land to the dead. Something in my fingers, an electric feeling at the very tips, takes control. I find myself making counter-clockwise circles in the small of her back. She pulls tighter to me, and now her hands are on my chest and there's a nervous feeling in my stomach, like I'm about to break again, but it urges me onward.

Like a deer caught in headlights, I stare down into her bright eyes, seeing something in them that suddenly reaches back wholeheartedly.

I kiss her.

Our eyes shut, and she moves her soft lips against mine, killing something inside of me and bringing something better to life. Our breathing collides as our mouths readjust and lock again. My lips begin moving faster against hers, kissing her the way I've only dreamt of, feeling something new and strange take control as the fist squeezing my heart lets go and I'm suddenly *here*, in this moment, and nowhere else.

Her lips part in a sudden smile, and I'm kissing nothing but teeth before she holds a quick hand up and pushes herself away.

"It's like you're trying to eat my lips!" she laughs. I feel my cheeks flare, and I mutter an apology, not even realizing how lame it sounds until she giggles. "Stop acting so nervous," she says. "We're alone."

"Okay."

I kiss her again, but I slow down this time. I let her take the lead, following her lips and tongue with expert timing. There's music playing in my mind like none I've ever heard, a full chorus of alto angels, baritone demons, bass Gods, and soprano spirits singing disharmoniously. The tune makes no sense, like the composer threw everything he'd ever written into a shredder and taped the pieces together into a Frankenstein monster. But the chaos feels *right*.

She pulls tighter against me, and my hands move innocently up the back of her dress. The tempo of our lips rises, and without stopping, she backs up enough to pull my t-shirt up over my head and I lower the straps of her dress down over her shoulders.

Our clothes hit the ground.

And then so do we.

It's four-thirty in the morning before we make our long walk back home, her hand in mine. I feel like Christ, and everything we walk past catches my appreciation, glowing with sudden beauty I've never noticed in my previous condition. The pools of light from the street lamps, the bushes we pass, every crack in the sidewalk…it's like they're all there just for our pleasure.

Or I'm just drunk and exhausted.

We don't speak. Neither of us have said a thing since she sat her head up from my arm and walked over to the punch bowl, slipping her underwear back on and then just sitting silently with her back against the tree until I came over and sat beside her. She hugged my arm and put her head on my shoulder, and we just sat there like that for a while, looking up at the moon in the sky and around at the graves, perfectly silent.

I look over at her as we come to my house, squeezing her hand gently in mine. She looks over at me with a tired smile, and she squeezes back as she takes my other hand. The silence loses its novelty, then it becomes awkward, void of *something* one of us is supposed to say. I lick my lips, fighting the urge to bounce on my toes, then I lower my head and kiss her again.

"I should probably head inside," I say as we part again. I don't know why I say it—I don't have anything to do except lie in bed and think of the past few hours. She hums agreement, still moving her hands up and down my shoulders. I truly don't want this moment to end. I could happily stand here like this forever with her in my arms. It ends, though, as she slips her arms away and takes a few steps back, wearing an uncertain smile.

"I'll see you," she says. I nod and lift a hand like a neighbor about to wave goodbye. I dismiss the hand quickly and walk toward the ladder, still looking at her.

"I'll…see you," I return. What a line. I quickly add as I set my foot on the bottom rung, "Thank you."

I wince as soon as I say it and have the sudden impulse to kick my own ass. And then she's gone, walking down the sidewalk, and my night ends just as quickly as it began.

I undress again and lie down on the bare bed, then I stare up at the blank ceiling and replay the entire night in my head down to the smallest detail. The euphoria still feels like a second layer beneath my skin, and I hold onto the feeling tightly, convinced it'll disappear if I don't focus on it. This could be what magic feels like, the buzzing under my flesh. I think of all the pain, loss, and insecurity. All the questions that won't go away. The craziness and loss of control. It's all lead me *here*.

Nothing can ever go wrong again.

Chapter Eighteen

When Dad opens my bedroom door and tells me I'm "free to go," I question how many days have actually gone by between my time with Sarah and now. Sunday, Monday, and Tuesday have somehow come and gone, and I feel taped back together inside. No nightmares. No pain.

I've spent the last three days planning in my head, outlining the entire book about the cannibalistic pastor-clown and picking apart every detail. It's perfect, I think. It'll fall apart again the moment I try to put it all on paper—I'm not an idiot like Jordan, and I know better.

I need a pencil and a cup of coffee. Cup after cup of glorious, beautiful black coffee.

"You can put your stuff back in here later," Dad says. He looks at the bloody smiley face on the wall, and from the look on his face as he opens his mouth, I know he's about to lose his mind at me.

"I'll scrub the wall when I get home," I tell him.

"What the hell is this?"

I struggle to think of an explanation but end up just shrugging. He stares at me, realizes I'm not going to say anything else, and sighs.

"You can paint the room for me this Summer," he says. "Your punishment's not over yet. I'm putting your ass to work when you're not at the slaughterhouse."

"I'm working there? Like, for sure?"

"Goddamn right," he says. "I'll start you a few weeks after school."

I sigh. "Great."

"And tell Clive I'll hire him, too, but I'm firing his ass the second he shows up drunk. I know who his dad is."

"Clive doesn't drink," I lie.

He gives me a stern look as he hands back my cellphone, then he walks out. I smile at The Great Blank's corpse on the wall, victorious as I stand in the open doorway.

"I beat you," I tell it. I hold up a middle finger.

I celebrate in my mind as I shower: I've tamed The Great Blank, all on my own terms. He's malnourished, starved of all the thoughts that have plagued me for weeks and weeks. As soon as I get my posters back I'll cover the bloody remains, and I will get away with murdering the mental mutineer. Grandpa would be proud, I think.

"Breakfast is on the table if you're hungry," Dad says from outside the door as I towel off. "Get a move on, though. Theodore and Clive have already dug into the pancakes."

I pause in mid-motion, caught off guard. Have they come to see me early, before I'm even back at school? A wide grin spreads across my face as I imagine Clive bringing a quart of Jägermeister for an early-morning celebration of my freedom. I know he has menthol cigarettes with him, which honestly sound like the best thing in the world right now.

Sure enough, there they are sitting patiently on the sofa when I get downstairs. Clive lifts a can of Coke to me in greeting, and Monk barely nods at me over the screen of his laptop. Clive stands, grinning devilishly over my shoulder into the kitchen. He licks his hand and runs it through his hair, which is tied back in a high pony tail.

"Check out that ass!" he whispers, eyes lit up. I furrow my brows and look behind me, where I see Mom bent over as she unloads the dishwasher. I shoot Clive a dirty look but can't hold back a laugh. So we're right back where we left off after all. Nothing's messed up.

"Damn, if I'd known I was missing an all-out attack on authority, I would've gone to the stupid artsy-fartsy show," Clive says. He claps me on the back, looking proud as hell. "I've taught you well, young Padawan."

"Yeah, it was pretty stupid," I tell him. I quickly change the subject.

"I heard you got a call from an acting school," I tell Monk.

"Uh-huh," he says back, not even glancing up from his feverish typing. He's staring down at his computer screen with total attention, absorbed in whatever site he's on. I look at him, taken aback by the lack of enthusiasm in his voice and the determined look on his face, wondering if things have already gone south. Clive peers at me.

"How did you hear about that?" he asks. "We didn't even know until the day after the show."

Crap. Mud in my tracks. There's a strange feeling in my head as I scramble for an answer— the entire night with Sarah is probably playing like a film in my expression.

"Never mind that," Monk says, shooting an open palm up. Keeping his eyes on the screen, he motions us toward him. "You need to see this, Trey—you're going to shit yourself!"

On the list of possibilities, I'm expecting: a) the finalized acting reel he's been putting together since Freshman year, or b) a fan page dedicated to rumors about Johnny Depp's next role. He moves aside so I can sit, and as he and Clive drop down at either side of me I stare at the screen, baffled.

"Facebook?" I ask. "What's so special about..."

Then I notice my name, over and over again in paragraph after paragraph of comments. I scroll down the page to read them all, but it's like they're endless. *'Right on, Trey!'* says one, signed by Christopher McMurray. *'Anarchy 4-Ever! Screw the system and its rules!'* says another, signed by Tony Moore. I scroll back to the top, already gnawing at the inside of my cheek as I consider the implications and what Sarah told me. I see my name again, right above my crappy yearbook picture with a crown drawn in marker over my head.

"*'TreyBellion?'* " I read, my lips breaking in and out of an unsure smile. "What's this?"

"My sister did it last night," Monk says excitedly, pulling the laptop across the coffee table to scroll around. "Look at the numbers, man! A hundred and twenty-five members in, like, twelve hours! There are even posts from kids in other counties!"

I nod robotically. I thought Sarah was just being dramatic when she told me how serious this was; I was expecting just one or two overly-involved kids in the school who needed a cause to piggyback their own angst onto.

This is insanity. Pure insanity.

"Who came up with the name?" I ask, keeping my eyes on the screen. I need to know who to kill first.

"Nobody knows who came up with it," Clive says. "It sort of just came up around the school and stuck. Catchy, right?"

"No."

I scroll down the page, reading more comments. *"Jordan's a bag of dicks!"* says one. Not wrong. *"They can't suspend us all!"* says another, from a girl I recognize from the T.A.G. group. *"Speak your mind! Express yourself however you want! Art is subjective, and what Trey did was a self-aware performance piece about that exact point!"*

I fight a grin. Wrong, but somehow harmless. It makes me look smart, if anyone's dumb enough to believe it. Maybe I'm worried over nothing.

Then I scroll further, and I see a selfie of Damien Hunts holding up a piece sign and sticking out his tongue. I point at the screen, gaping dumbly from Clive to Monk.

"My face is on his shirt," I tell them. "Why is my face on his shirt?"

"Pretty cool, huh?" Monk says, mistaking my expression for enthusiasm. "He brought a bunch of them in on Friday and has been selling them. Some people even wore them to prom."

"And now you get an automatic detention if you're caught wearing them," Clive adds. "You're on a banned t-shirt. Total rock star."

"My face is on his t-shirt," I repeat quietly.

It's an extreme close-up of my meltdown on stage, and I look stupid as hell. Below, in fiery red letters: *"Screw this whole town!"-Trey Matthews.*

I didn't even say that...

"You guys want something to eat?" I ask, stumbling over Clive in a quick move toward the kitchen. I need a cup of coffee. God, it's been so long since coffee.

Monk furrows his brows at me.

"Wait a second, don't you want to type something? Some sort of public statement?" he asks, turning the laptop toward me.

"Umm…no. I mean, not just yet, you know?" I say, and for some reason I force a smile as a take another quick series of steps toward the kitchen. "I'd rather just get through the first day back and see how it goes from there. You guys want something to eat?" I ask again.

The two of them exchange baffled looks as I bolt out of view, rushing toward that God-blessed pot of ecstasy on the burner. I feel Mom and Dad's eyes looking at me as I grab a mug and fill it to the brim, downing a large gulp before I even consider how hot it must be. I close my eyes as I swallow quickly, ignoring the pain, and I smile at them as I pull out a chair and stuff my face eagerly with eggs and bacon. I look up when I stop hearing their forks scraping against their plates, and they're both staring at me strangely.

"What?" I ask, spewing a nice chunk of egg back onto my plate. Mom grunts and returns her attention to the newspaper she's holding. Dad, however, gives the old 'fatherly doctor analysis,' peering at me as a he shoves a forkful of food into his mouth.

"You feeling okay, Trey?" he asks. I take another quick gulp of scorching hot coffee.

"I'm fine. Why?"

He continues studying my expression, searching for God knows what. My hand tightens around the coffee mug, but I smile back coolly. Nothing to hide. No worries. First day out of Hell—*I'm ecstatic, Dad!*

"Just wondering," he says, and he drops his gaze back toward his plate. I clear my food in about a second flat and rush the plate toward the sink as I down the rest of the coffee.

"You know, it's really no problem if you need a ride back today," Dad continues, keeping his tone all soft as he scoops more egg. "My office is just around the corner."

"I said I'm fine!" I snap suddenly, whirling around as I grab the thermos from the top shelf. A glass falls and shatters at my feet.

"Jesus!" Mom shrieks in surprise, jumping in her chair. Everything goes silent as they both stare at me, Dad with his fork halfway to his mouth and Mom with her eyes wide and her jaw hanging as if she's going to yell something but doesn't have the words yet.

"Sorry. It slipped," I say quietly, and I set the thermos down and start picking up shards of broken glass.

They put my face on that dumbass t-shirt.

TreyBellion...

I hurry back through the living room, seizing my jacket and shoes as Clive and Monk watch my every move in silence.

"C'mon," I mutter, opening the front door a crack and looking over at them. Without a word Monk stuffs his laptop into his shoulder bag and the two of them follow me outside toward Monk's car.

I try to smile as I look up at the sun, feeling fresh air blow over me from the rolled down backseat window. I imagine how the day will go, how everything will be back to the way it was in no time and how anyone who even mentions the night of the festival with gusto in their eyes will be blown off as a creep by the general masses.

As the car takes off, though, I hear laughter coming from my bedroom window, taunting my halfhearted optimism. The Great Blank has risen from the dead, and it's out for my blood.

Chapter Nineteen

"**P**lease rise for the saying of the Pledge of
Allegiance. I pledge allegiance—"
    I look at Monk from the corner of my
eye, waiting for the sign of our usual game
to begin so I can finally feel a bit of normalcy. He stares
straight ahead, though, no sign of games. Everyone's
staring straight ahead at the television.

"—of the United States of America, and to the
Republic—"

"He'll get what's coming to him," I hear someone say
under their breath. I get the strange feeling of eyes moving
toward me, watching my every move.

"—nation, under God, indivisible—"

"…wonder what he's thinking of now…"

"…hero, seriously dude…"

Can't be talking about me. I'm imagining this. I'm not
that important; I'm no one.

"—liberty and justice for all. You may be seated."

Everyone sits. I look down at my pile of notebooks,
humming to myself and taping my pencil at my side. Kevin

rattles off the lunch menus as Chris Fauver gives his account of Friday's incident to someone else across the room in whispers, stealing a quick glance at me in mid-sentence. The other announcer says lifeguarding lessons will be held after school—Damien Hunts whispers to Alex White about a meeting of their own after school, also looking at me in mid-sentence. I grind my molars, thinking only of lunch and cheesy burritos, maybe even treating myself to a Coke from the vending machine, more caffeine before I get home and chug another pot of coffee.

I've seen five people wearing those stupid *TreyBellion* t-shirts since I got here. I want to chop Damien into little pieces.

"Psst!"

I glance toward Damien and Alex and my grip tightens on the pencil I'm holding. Damien pulls a note from his pocket with a discreet look over his shoulder, and then, flashing his eyes at me, he drops it to the ground and kicks it under the desk toward my feet. I pick it up, staring into Damien's eyes and wondering what sort of good can come from a kid named after a horror movie anyway, wondering why his mother didn't throw him into a dumpster the second she saw the disgusting look in his eyes as a baby.

'Meeting after school today behind the bowling alley. Big plans for tomorrow. Everyone's anxious to hear your opinion. Need a ride?'

I read the note twice, disbelieving. I crumble it and throw it back at him. Katrina Lee turns her head toward me from next to the teacher's empty desk as the girl she's talking to stares daggers at me. Other eyes shift toward me, ever-so-casually. I lower the note, biting my tongue to hold back an explosion big enough to make the day of the festival look like a Sunday church sermon. Monk looks up from a pad of paper he's scribbling something on and notices all the eyes focused on me. He snorts loudly.

"What the hell are you staring at, Katrina? There ain't no McDonalds over here!" he says. The fat girl's cheeks flush red with embarrassment as others laugh, and she sinks into her seat. From the fury in her rabbit-faced friend's expression, I assume she's crying. More blame. More hate in my direction. More madness I have both everything and nothing to do with.

"Screw them," Monk mutters to me, still glaring at the two girls and flashing a warning stare to everyone else. "I'll walk with you to the meeting just in case, man," he says, nodding confirmation to the two jackasses I'd like nothing more than to strangle. I stare blankly back at him. He asks me, "Are you feeling okay? You don't look so good, man."

Snap back into focus. Take in reality again. Let go of Damien's skinny little neck in my imagination. Stop beating invisible fists against Monk's face. I put my head down on the desk.

"Trey," Damien whispers loudly. I keep my head down. Can't blow up again. Can't make this worse for myself.

A crumbled ball of paper hits the back of my head.

"Hey man!" Damien whispers. "Hey!"

I tighten my arms around my head, shutting myself off from everything. It's for their protection, not mine. I've got a mouthful of verbal bullets, and I'm afraid of unwanted casualties if I start firing again.

Someone suddenly shoves me, and it's hard enough to move my desk loudly across the floor. I spin around, pencil raised high.

"What the hell?" Monk shouts, shooting to his feet and standing between me and Katrina, who's being pulled back by Damien and Alex.

"My family was at that stupid T.A.G. show!" she shouts furiously. "You think they're all idiots, huh? You think you're *so* much smarter than everyone else?"

I open my mouth to tell her no, that I've never seen her family and frankly don't give a damn about them.

But Damien speaks first.

"*Of course* they're stupid, if they're offended by free speech!" he shouts triumphantly. "I bet they *loved* Jordan's song, though!"

"It was a poem, dumbass! Were you even there?"

"I'm *here*, right *here!*" he says, throwing his arms out at his side and standing up on his seat. "What are you gonna do? C'mon, hit me!"

"Sit down," I moan miserably, hiding my face behind my hands in embarrassment.

"This is a rebellion against censorship!" Damien continues loudly, addressing the whole class now. He jabs a finger at Katrina. "People like her want to shut people like Trey and me up! They want to control how we all think and how we choose to express ourselves!"

"There is no goddamn rebellion, you stupid asshole!" I shout, on my feet now. "Sit the hell down or I'll slit you open!"

Katrina gasps.

"He just threatened me!" she shouts. "You all heard him! Trey just threatened me!"

"We didn't threaten anyone!" Damien shouts. "*You* and people like you threatened free speech!"

"There is no *'we'*!" I say. "What the hell are you even talking about? When did I say *anything* about free speech and rebellion? Don't any of you see how stupid this is?"

It's like they don't even hear me. Monk shoves Katrina back, and Damien cries out maniacally as he jumps onto her back and latches on. The whole homeroom seems to erupt with loud arguments, and nothing I shout stops it.

The teacher walks back into the room, and his whole expression drops as he beholds the chaos. Katrina and her friend have Damien pinned to the floor now, and she's wailing on him with both fists as he cries out *"Free speech! Free speech!"* like a willing martyr to a made-up cause.

A few others pull Damien free, and he smiles with blood gushing from his nose and mouth.

"She hit me!" he tells the teacher. "You have to send her to the office! I bet she won't be suspended, though, because this whole school's full of hypocrites!"

"He started it all!" Katrina yells, pointing a finger at me. "He threatened me! You all heard him threaten me!"

The bell rings suddenly, and I run out of the room before anyone can say anything else. I forget to grab my notebooks from under the desk, and I don't even care.

This is all so stupid, I think as I run, shoving past others and noticing more *TreyBellion* shirts beneath smiling faces.

What the hell did I do? What have I accidentally created?

I keep my head low, dodging any contact with anyone on my way to English class, muttering apologies to every foot I step on, avoiding eye contact at all costs. I blast the radio in my mind at full volume, drowning out everything, even the cesspool of juicy rumors and stories I usually love sifting through. Today I just want to live in silence.

I saw a Sophomore girl wearing a white belly shirt with *"Censor me!"* written sloppily in red marker. I saw an idiot with a scruffy neck beard and a half-shaved head reciting crappy poetry in the middle of the staircase, holding everyone up when he saw me and started waving both hands overhead excitedly. At least two people have called me a fag or an idiot as they passed in the halls, swatting my books out of my hands or doing loud and sarcastic impressions of my meltdown, adding crybaby tears to it.

I saw another kid from Spanish class, someone I've literally *never* heard speak at all, walk past me with 'Art' written on one cheek and 'Chaos' on the other.

I hate this. I hate all of it. If I see one more shirt with my name on it, I'm going to reach down someone's throat and pull their guts out.

I'm down the third-floor staircase, apologizing my way toward Mrs. Renus's class, when someone catches my attention.

"How was the weekend, Trey?"

I snap my head up and see Billy Graham shuffling up beside me, dividing his attention between the book in his hand and where he's walking. He sounds sincere, but I don't give him benefit of the doubt. At this point I don't know if I'm capable.

"Eat shit," I snarl at him, staring coldly into his eyes. Right now, he's Jordan and Monk and Damien and everyone else all twisted into one. Right now, he's the wide bull's eye for everything I've wanted to say all morning. He stares back at me, dumbfounded.

"Asshole," he says, raising an eyebrow at me as he moves on. I have a quick change of heart the second he steps away, though. Suddenly I *need* him to talk.

"Billy, wait a second!" I call, catching him by the back of his shirt. He turns and gapes back at me, unsure what to expect. I don't blame him. "I'm sorry, man, I...I'm just sort of a wreck today. Lots of stuff on my mind since last week."

He frowns. "Why? What happened?"

"What do you mean? You don't know?" I ask. Is that cracking in my voice? The sound of desperation?

He shakes his head. "My whole family was on vacation last week I've been re-reading for the quiz today." He holds up his copy of *Fahrenheit 451*. "Why? Did I miss something? And did I see your face on a t-shirt earlier?"

He's the miracle child. The last sane person in a world gone mad. I could hug him if only he wasn't staring at me like I'm some sort of crazy person.

"So...you didn't hear anything about the festival? Or Mac and...stuff?" I ask, twitching at the corners of my lips. He shakes he head.

"I don't care about that crap," he says. "Who lotta assholes in that crowd. Speaking of which, doesn't Jordan run that group? What are you doing hanging out with him?"

Once again, I could hug this kid. I could worship him. I could wash his feet, nail him to a cross, and wear him around my neck.

I spill the beans quickly, recapping everything I've said and heard as if my lips had a motor behind them. I feel refueled as I vent my frustration, how Jordan read his crappy poem, how I lost my temper on stage, how I got suspended from school and how everyone here is either eying me as a leader for something I want nothing to do with or staring at me like I'm a bomb ready to go off. I'm breathing hard by the end of the whole story, and the hallway's empty as the bell rings to tell us we're late for class. Billy raises his eyebrows, as disbelieving as I am as he shakes his head back and forth.

I stare at him anxiously, waiting for this beautiful miracle child to tell me something helpful and profound, some bright and shiny "Aha!" revelation that escaped me until now and can fix all this madness.

Billy simply shrugs. He laughs to himself.

"Damn, man," he says. "Your life sucks."

And then he walks off.

I'm rushing toward lunch when Clive catches up to me in the locker bay.

"Slow down, bastard!" I hear him pant, holding one hand to his chest pocket to keep his cigarettes from bouncing out. "You're walking like you've got a demon on your tail."

"Worse," I groan, staring toward the remaining few people in the hallway. "Paparazzi."

He furrows his eyebrows at me.

"Come again?"

To tell the truth, English class was pure hell, being stared at like either a terrorist or a revolutionary by everyone but Billy, who seemed like he couldn't care less. I got detention from Mrs. Renus for being late, along with a lecture in front of the entire class about my timeliness and how "even *you* ought to know better, Trey."

As if in response to the sentiment of *"They can't suspend us all!"*, she gave out seven other detentions in the space of 45 minutes, smiling pleasantly the whole time. It was dead silent by the end of class, and I've never loved the witch more. She still looked at me like she wanted to murder me and defile my body, but that was alright. Clive didn't even bother showing up to class.

Then there was gym class immediately after, where I saw a flash out of the corner of my eyes in the locker room as I was changing into my shorts. When I spun around with my pants halfway down, I saw Cory Kassir running off with his phone in his hand. Later in class, as girls checked their phones, I saw laughter hidden behind several hands and eyes moving toward me.

I feel violated. Now I'm checking over my shoulder constantly, waiting for either a camera or a fist to the face.

"This has to be how celebrities feel after making a bad movie," I brood out loud. "I wish I'd never gone to that stupid show. I hate everything about all of this, man."

"Oh, quit your bitching!" Clive dismisses, smiling wide and pushing me against a locker. "You're famous now! A regular Lee Harvey Oswald! Think of the possibilities."

He keeps walking. I stay glued to the spot.

"What are you talking about?" I demand.

"The rebellion, man!" he answers excitedly. "I mean, damn, I thought I'd be your second-in-command in this thing. Half the schools eating out of our hands! Do you have any idea how much we can screw with people between now and graduation?"

I breath slowly in and out through my nose, telling myself to count to ten. It doesn't help at all.

"Trey!"

I look toward the sound of the high pitched, wheezy voice and see Damien from homeroom running excitedly toward us, grinning wide. He has toilet paper jammed up both nostrils.

"Hey man!" Damien says. He shifts his gaze between me and Clive, exhaling an awkward sort of laugh. "So, good news! I just talked to Justin, who talked to Ralph and Peter in Spanish class earlier, and they're bringing Peter's older cousin Steve, who has a *ton* of fireworks in his garage, to the meeting tonight! Great, huh?"

Clive groans, unimpressed.

"I said 'fart bombs,' not 'fireworks,'" he says. "And what's the deal with the spray paint? Did you tag the stage at the fairgrounds yet?"

Damien's mouth opens, and he looks suddenly embarrassed. He slaps himself in the forehead.

"Damn, I totally forgot about that part! I'll get on it after school, I promise!"

Clive claps his hands together.

"Get on it. And why don't I see any fliers hanging outside the principal's office? Don't tell me you're a coward."

"I'll get to it right away!"

"Good. And don't forget to post pictures of yourself doing it *all across* social media, alright? Leave no doubt in anyone's mind that you're guilty! That'll really stick it to them."

"Oh, hell yeah! Great idea!"

Clive bows sarcastically.

I stare at Damien. I stare at Clive. I nod at them both, mustering as much composure as sanity will allow as I clear my throat.

"Stay the hell away from me. Both of you."

"But wait!" Damien cries, throwing a hand up and stumbling after me as I hurry away. "I need to get your approval on the t-shirt designs I made this morning! I was thinking maybe you could sign them all once they're printed, and we could put everyone's names on the back of them! Like a jersey, right?"

He brings an armful of books up from his side and removes the top one. Below is a fluorescent yellow pile of cloth, which I lift between thumb and forefinger the way I'd lift a used tissue.

The shirt unfolds, and when I spread it open in front of me, the word 'anarchy' leaps out at me—large and obnoxious red print, slanted haphazardly from either a faulty printer or a douchy artistic touch. Below this monstrosity: my picture. On stage, at the show, mouth wide and eyes blazing hellfire.

"So, what do you think?" Damien asks excitedly, standing so close to me that his filthy body odor invades my nostrils. "I know it's not much just yet, but I'm still working on adding some effects. How awesome would it be if we added, like, a bright red horizon in the background? Or something like a crowd of silhouette hands reaching up at you? Or a row of broken prison bars around you, or even—"

I spring at him before I can stop myself, pulling the t-shirt taut in my hands as I topple him to the ground and wrap it around his neck. He cries out and lashes at me as I strangle him, but it's a pitiful effort. I'm going to pop his head off his shoulders.

Clive pulls me away quickly, before I can do any serious damage, and he stands between us as Damien rushes to his feet.

"Stop using my damn face for your bullshit rebellion and stop putting words in my mouth!" I shout at him, struggling against Clive's tight hold. Damien turns his attention up at Clive, looking suddenly lost and confused.

"But you said he'd love this!"

"Shut up, Damien," Clive says between his teeth. Damien's mouth hangs open, and his eyes go back and forth between the two of us.

"You told me he'd—"

"Damien," Clive says quietly. It's the tone Dad uses when he's on the verge of going nuts, the perfect calmness before the great storm. He steps around me and towers over Damien, jetting one hand underneath the books in Damien's arms. Loose papers, t-shirts, and textbooks go flying everywhere, and Damien lets out a pitiful cry.

"Get out of here," Clive says. "*Now.*"

Damien scrambles backward, forgetting all his supplies and bolting toward the other end of the hall, looking backward as he goes. I stare at him, then I stare at Clive's expression, then I stare at the open t-shirt lying on the floor. It all clicks together in my head, the horror of it all.

"You," I say. "You bastard."

I shove him back as hard as I can, barely moving the wiry bastard. My face is contorted into a shape I've never felt it make, something special saved just for this particular degree of rage.

"You look upset," he says.

"You started all this, didn't you?" I demand.

"I didn't think it would work so damn well, though!" he says. Not apologetically; proudly. "I heard about what happened at the show, and I thought about how we could turn it into something awesome."

"You think this is awesome for me? Seriously?"

He rolls his eyes.

"See, this is why I didn't want to tell you right away," he laughs. "I figured once you actually saw things here, you'd get excited about the possibilities! For real, man, why are you so pissed?"

"My face is on t-shirts!" I yell. "People are putting words in my mouth!"

"Yeah, so?" He shakes his head, lost. "What's the issue?"

"It's annoying!"

"Okay," he says, holding both hands out in surrender. "Maybe I shouldn't have spread the whole *TreyBellion* thing—"

"*You* came up with that stupid name?"

"—but look how well it worked! People are totally losing their shit! It doesn't matter what they think you said or how they want to interpret it, we've got everyone at each other's throats! It's hilarious, right?"

"I'm going to kill you. I'm going to go home, grab the sharpest knife I can find, and I'm going to kill you with it."

His idiot smile only grows wider.

"What about Monk? Was he in on this?" I ask.

"I didn't tell him I started it, no," he says. "But look how excited he is about it! He thinks he's fighting for 'art' or something, but he sees how we can mess with everyone!"

"Mac got expelled," I tell him. "You want Monk to get in trouble, too? You want *me* to get in trouble?"

"Oh, no, not *trouble!*" he says sarcastically. He sees the face I'm making, and he makes an attempt to stop smiling so proudly. "Look, man. We're graduating soon. We're probably all never going to be together the same way ever again, and I just thought it would be great if we had one last big prank together. Like we used to do when Grandpa was alive. Something that celebrates *us*, all of us and all the fun shit we used to do together."

He sounds so suddenly sincere that I forget I want to stab him. There's a desperation in his voice, an eagerness for me to get the big joke and understand.

"You're using *my* name and *my* face," I tell him. "If you want this phony ass rebellion just to mess with people, why not use your name? You started all this when you spread those pictures of Jordan's mom all over school."

"Yeah," he concedes. "But *you* went on stage and ranted like a lunatic. It struck a chord, man. It works better than anything I did. You mooned an entire audience and shouted about 'art.' In a way, I mean, you were kinda asking for this, right?"

Now I want to kill him again. I can picture my hands around his throat, squeezing and squeezing...

"Are you retarded?" I demand. "If you think I'm okay with playing along with this—"

"Oh, shut up!" he yells. "*Waaaah! Wah! Wah!* That's all you do, all you're really good for! Christ, make a decision and stick to it every once in a while, will you?"

"I didn't ask for any of this!"

"Grandpa would've seen the fun in all this," he continues. "He would've laughed like hell and *congratulated* us all for turning the whole school upside down for even a few days! Why can't you see that? And it's because of something *you* did!"

"Bullshit!" I snarl.

"Bullshit?" he repeats, shoving me back with both hands. "Who's the one who went up on stage like he was the king of the world and tried to put everyone else in their places like *he's* got such a great grip on things? Jesus, man."

He shakes his head in disgust.

"I thought you'd love all this, that you'd really get it. You're just another damn hypocrite. You're *worse* than Jordan, you know that?"

"*Screw you!*"

I barrel into him, connecting my shoulder hard into his stomach and running him backward with all my might, taking him by surprise up until the top of my head rams a locker door. With the opportunity provided, he wraps a hand under my armpit and whips me around, and the breath in my lungs is suddenly gone as he pins me with one forearm and punches me in the stomach.

"Let me go…" I breath, prying his arm away the best I can. "I swear to God—"

"What?" Clive laughs. "You'll chase me down the street and have another mental breakdown? Christ, *listen* to what I'm saying here! You have the school at your fingertips, and you're complaining like it's a bad thing! Nobody's getting hurt, nobody's doing any real damage, and you've got your tits in a knot because people are using your face? For real?"

He lets go of me and I crumble to the ground, coughing heavily and holding my stomach. I'm shaking all over. I can still see his wide, mocking grin, and with what's left of my energy I throw one last punch.

"What a waste," he mutters, shaking his head as he avoids the swing easily.

"Look around you," he repeats, gesturing toward the school in general. "It's already in motion, and it's not like

we can stop it now anyway. Do what you want, but I'm
going to keep fucking with people."

He shrugs helplessly, and then he walks off.

"Bastard!" I yell after him, my voice gurgled and
deformed.

"Pussy!" he yells back. I watch him round the corner of
the locker bay, and when he's out of sight I try sitting back
up. My head falls back against the locker behind me. I
want to rip something into pieces, anything at all. I want to
scream.

"Trey?" someone calls from my left side.

I turn my head and see a scrawny kid with long blond
hair hanging down his forehead and enormous front teeth.
He gapes at me with large, spectacled eyes, then walks
cautiously toward me.

'Oh, gorsh!' I imagine Goofy from the Disney Channel
saying as the boy comes closer, moving slowly down to
his knees and reaching a nervous hand to somehow
console me. I'm tempted to snap it off with my teeth and
spit it back at him, but my entire body feels locked up.

"Shh...hey, it's okay...it's okay," he coos to me,
patting my shoulder again and again. I stare, unblinking,
back up at him. He takes his hand away from my shoulder
takes a cellphone from his pocket.

"Can I get a selfie?" he asks.

Without waiting for an answer, he puts his head next to
mine, holds out a peace sign, and sticks out his tongue.

Then he snaps the damn picture.

Chapter Twenty

I skip detention—oh, rebel I am!—and take a different way home than usual, wary of anyone following me as I take the long trek through the upper streets rather than cutting through the marching band field. My eyes are glued to my feet as I walk fast as I can, more of a halfhearted jog than a walk. I saw Monk waiting for me by the second-floor doors, so I left through the gym on the first-floor, praying he didn't see me. I don't want to talk to anyone right now—I need quiet! I need to think, quickly. What's my next move? How am I going to deal with tomorrow, when I come back to the same scene and Damien the Little Anti-Christ shows me another stupid flyer or t-shirt with my name attached to quotes that aren't mine?

This game isn't for me. This Frankenstein monster is made from *their* spare parts, not mine! I'm just the doctor who gave the monster an electric shock and then became its servant!

As I turn down Whittlesey Avenue it occurs to me that maybe if I go to Grandpa's porch and just sit for a while, something will pop up in my mind. I've always done my best thinking there, I think. I'll stop along the way to get a pack of cigarettes, and then I'll sit and smoke the whole damn thing while I think.

My phone vibrates, and I nearly walk into a stop sign as I dig it from my pocket. Monk's name glows on the front, and I groan loudly.

"What?" I answer.

"Get your ass outside, man!" he shouts into my ear. "We're going to be late for the meeting! Do you have notes prepared? I have a few ideas to run by you."

Shoot me, shoot me now, God, right in the brain, splatter my thoughts, stop these films, stop stop stop—

"Meeting's cancelled," I tell him, surprising myself with how normal my voice remains. "I got detention. I'm just walking to the room right now, so I should probably—"

"Mrs. Wagner's out sick today, all detentions got switched to tomorrow," he says, amused. "Half the guys in the group got detention today for one thing or another. Now come on! We're doing this together, right?"

Damn it, Monk, why are you doing this to me? I've always been good to you, haven't I? Can't you just walk off the chessboard with me and let these people burn themselves to the ground?

Then the only true God arrives on the scene to save me.

I hear the car behind me before I whirl on my heels and see it, tires squealing as it blows past a stop sign. It's right when I turn around that the Holy Messenger—a overgrown dickhead from the football team—leans out the passenger window and yells, "heads up, faggot!"

He whips a cheeseburger at me, and it hits me hard in the left temple, splattering all over my eyes, nose, mouth, and shirt. I stumble sideways from the impact, blinded by either ketchup or blood. The phone slips from my hand as the bastards in the car howl with laughter from the end of the block. I stare at them for a long second, reaching a total melting point inside that I'm not sure a human being is capable of suppressing. The car idles, and I see them all laughing at me, taking pictures with their phones and recording. I prepare myself to yell, *"Get back here, you sons of bitches, so I can I'll tear your guts out and show them to your whore mothers!"*

"Trey, are you still there? Trey?"

Monk's voice shouts at me from the phone on the ground, stealing my attention and bringing sudden enlightenment to the situation. There are more guys in that car than just the driver and the assailant—strong, steroid-juiced douchebags who probably jerk off to thoughts of hitting people on the football field. Picking a fight with a group of them would be like standing in front of a wrecking ball. I can't afford an ambulance ride, nor another mental explosion.

I turn my head away, swallowing my pride along with whatever landed in my mouth, and the car rolls away with fresh issues of laughter. I pick the phone back up.

"Something came up. I'll talk to you later," I say. I hang up without waiting for a response, and I shut my phone off.

Going to Grandpa's house is out of the question now. I can't sit on the porch looking like I just raped Ronald McDonald, not without neighbors noticing me and asking questions.

I walk home, fast as I can, trying to wipe all the condiments out of my hair and eyes as I peel a pickle slice from my left temple.

As soon as I reach my house I rush through the front door and toward the staircase, not looking anywhere but forward. I hear the rustle of a newspaper lowering from in front of Dad's face in the living room.

"Are you okay?" he calls after me as I reach the top of the stairs and bolt toward my room.

"Never better," I answer. I walk straight into my bedroom door, and like a toddler, I remember that I need to turn the handle first.

"Hey, get down here and talk to me," Dad continues, concern building in his voice the way it always does. I hear him rising from the couch, coming toward the stairs.

"I said I'm fine!" I shout, and I slam the door behind me as I go about stripping off all my clothes and wiping my face and hair again with my t-shirt. I rush across the hall, naked as hell but not caring, and into the bathroom. I turn the shower on and step in. Cold water, full-blast—I inhale sharply at first and then just relax into it. Exhaling. Inhaling. Exhaling. Inhaling. I sit down and turn the dial toward hot, as far as it will go.

Tomorrow will be here in no time—that punctual bastard! I'll be back in homeroom with Monk talking in my ear and notes being kicked toward me and whispers from both sides of the war and more drama I don't want— all for a meaningless 'rebellion' against nothing in particular! A bunch of lame assholes who all want to feel that what they're doing is *oh so important!*

And here I am, rebelling against rebellion: a one-man rebellion! I hate it all, and I hate Clive for starting it but *especially* for comparing me to Jordan.

I don't know if he was right or not, and that's what bothers me most as I sit on the shower floor for the next half-hour. I can't ask Grandpa what he thinks of all this because he's dead and it's just us now, and I can't even hear his voice in my head to guide me or tell me if I'm messing myself up by overthinking all this and being so bothered.

The water's cold again by the time I get out. I don't bother drying off, but instead rush back across the hall, thinking about my bed. I open the door to my room and see Sarah standing at my dresser, looking at some ugly photo of me at a family reunion. She turns and sees me dripping wet in the doorframe, covering myself suddenly with both hands, and my eyes go wide as a smile spreads across her face.

"Hey there," she says, emphasizing the awkward inflection and milking the moment for what it's worth. I gape at her, cheeks burning hot enough to save Dad a month's gas bill.

She holds up the steaming mug in her hands.

"Your dad made me coffee. You took forever in there."

I don't say anything. I just stand there, dripping all over the floor.

"I didn't tell Monk or Clive you'd be here," she says.

"How did you know I would be?" I ask. She shrugs.

"Just a feeling, I guess. You weren't outside the school anywhere, and I tried texting you. I figured you were trying to avoid people."

I swallow hard, sucking in a deep breath as I look down at myself.

"Umm…could you…?" I twirl my finger at her. She laughs.

"Trey, I've literally had your dick inside me. It's not like I haven't seen it."

"Yeah, but…" I can't finish the thought. I stand there silently.

"Fine," she sighs, and turns back toward the open window.

"Okay," I tell her once I've put on a pair of underwear and jeans from my dresser. She turns back around as I pull a t-shirt over my head, and she starts walking around my room, studying everything like this is the museum of my life.

She smiles as she grabs the bundle of sheets at the edge of my mattress, and she dances her eyebrows.

"You need help putting these back on?"

"Why are you here?" I ask, skipping whatever else you're supposed to say when you've had the longest day of your life and a hot girl appears unexpectedly in your bedroom. She drops the sheets.

"Fine. I'll leave. Bye," she says, and moves toward the door.

"No!" I say quickly. "No, it's just been…today's been a little crazy and, well…I'm still feeling whiplash from it. I'm sorry. I'm really sorry. Will you stay? Please?"

I flinch at how desperate my voice sounds, but from the way her smile resurfaces I doubt she even notices. She comes close enough to reach out and stroke my forearm, and with that beautiful, witchy magic of hers, I'm back to feeling like another anonymous high school jerk. It's cosmic disorder, bouncing between being this lucky one second and feeling close to breaking down the next. We sit down on the edge of the bed, and I run the tips of my fingers mechanically up and down her back.

"So, what do you feel like doing?" I ask her. Not in a dirty way or anything, I just can't stand the monotony of sitting here so quietly. She shrugs.

"I dunno," she says. There's an excited flicker in her eyes. "Do you have any videogames? I bet I could kick your ass at Mario Kart."

"I don't play videogames," I admit, shrugging apologetically. She spreads her hands and starts looking around the room again. She points at the bloody face drawn on the wall. "What's with this?"

"I got into a fight with Clive today," I say, avoiding her question. She looks at me inquisitively, all ears. I wave it off. "It's nothing, though. Everything's cool. We were just fooling around."

I don't know why I don't just come clean with her. I could tell her right now why my brain is wound so tight, why I can't just relax and let this all blow by. I'm back to thinking about what Clive said, and my fists clench at my sides.

"Did you hit him?" she asks. I shake my head, still stuck in the re-run of violent emotions.

"It was nothing. The whole day was fine. It's nothing, really."

She scrunches her face. Her hand fires out and punches me in the arm.

"Damn!" I shout, grabbing the spot on reflex. "What was that for?"

"You're obviously upset about something!" she says. "There's a drawing in blood on your wall and you're shaking all over!"

"Well, you didn't have to hit me!"

"Aww, you want a band-aid for that or a tampon?" she asks. "I'm asking you to talk to me, and you're shutting down. I hate that. Are you going to talk, or do you want me to leave?"

I gape back at her, taken completely off guard. She shakes her head at me and stands up, walking back toward the door.

"Wait!" I shout, grabbing her wrist as I stand. I lose my balance, though, and I take her to the ground with me as I fall. The floor shakes, and she groans, rubbing her elbow. She pushes her head off my chest.

"Nice move, Romeo," she says, and playfully straddles me torso. "You're pinned. Now talk to me."

"Fine."

I take a deep breath, still pulling it all together in my mind, the pecking order of where to even begin.

I tell her everything, all about the miserable day, the people with my face on their shirts, Clive's part in it all. I go on and on about it, how angry I am at him, how this is all his fault and I don't want a single damn part of it.

She nods when I finish venting. She looks impossibly calm about it all. It makes me feel somehow calmer.

"Clive's an idiot," she says. "And the t-shirts are...wow. Just wow."

"Yeah."

"But this is all going to blow over. You know that, right? People are latching onto it now, but how long can it really go on? They all want to feel like they're part of something, that's all. Just keep ignoring it."

"Monk's already all in on it," I tell her. "He's going to mess up whatever he's got going with that theater school or whatever."

She shakes her head.

"He's smart. He'll come to his senses, and maybe Clive will, too, once he gets bored with it."

"Yeah...maybe."

I feel a little better than before, now that it's all off my chest. It all still sucks...and I'm still pissed about every last bit of it...but I'm not shaking anymore. Sarah's right. It'll all blow over.

"You want to go see a movie?" I ask. She smiles.

"I thought we could just lie here a while. I mean, you *are* the notorious leader of a school-wide 'rebellion.'"

"Yeah," I laugh. "Dangerous man, right here. You might get a cheeseburger thrown at you."

"I could go more for pizza."

I lean over and kiss her on the forehead. She turns and kisses me on the mouth, first just a quick kiss and then longer, and her arms are around me and I start to carry us backward toward the bed. She pats my stomach and pulls away again.

"No, for real," she says. "I'm hungry. Feed me."

*

We walk downtown without incident, and I wear a hoodie and sunglasses even though Sarah tells me it makes me ten times more suspicious looking and twenty times less attractive. She keeps checking her phone as we walk and talk, and each time, she gets quiet and I awkwardly lead us back toward conversation.

"Someone blowing up your phone?" I ask. She shakes her head and quickly pockets it, giving a forced 'everything's fine, I'm fine, you're fine' sort of smile.

"No, just scrolling," she says. I saw text boxes from the corner of my eyes, but she changes the subject. "What movie are we seeing?"

"No idea. I don't really care, I just want to sit in a theater for a while."

"Probably another remake," she says. Then she checks her phone again. She looks anxious about something. I tell myself to ignore the bad feeling in my stomach.

We get to the theater, and both movies playing have already started. Since neither of us really cares, we get two slices of pizza and head into the better of two options: *Attack the Pack II: Bloody Dawn Rising*.

There's nobody else in the theater when we walk inside. We sit in the very center of the auditorium. Sarah checks her phone again.

"No phones in the theater," I joke. She doesn't even smile. She takes a handful of popcorn and shovels it into her mouth.

There's a shirtless dude on the screen giving some longwinded and overwritten speech to an army of other shirtless dudes as fire blazes in the background and super serious music plays. I think it's supposed to be a scene from the fourth book. The guy giving the speech is supposed to be a 900-year-old vampire with one eye missing and a heavily-scarred face. Instead, it's a pop-star-turned-model-turned-actor. Damn adaptations…

I try to get immersed in the movie, but it doesn't seem possible. I've only taken a few bites of my pizza.

"Want the rest?" I ask Sarah. Her phone's down between her legs, and she's typing quickly. I ignore it.

"Sure." She takes the slice, and I put my arm around her. She doesn't move, and my arm suddenly feels awkward there.

"Something wrong?" I ask. She shakes her head and puts her phone in her pocket.

"No," she says. She leans against me in her seat and smiles up at me. I kiss her forehead. We stare at the screen.

My mind wanders. I'm thinking all over again about Clive and *TreyBellion*, and the stupidity of it all. My name's on it. I'm its author, its owner. And it's just another bad adaptation.

We watch another forty minutes of vampires fighting vampires. Time travel is involved somehow, but it's like the screenwriter never even read the book series. A character that died in the first movie (but not until the *eighth* book) is suddenly back for inexplicable reasons, and from the way the music swells dramatically as he walks onscreen, I assume it's supposed to be some sort of fan service to people who actually read the series. It does nothing for me.

Sarah stands.

"I'm going to the bathroom," she says. She squeezes my hand and walks toward the back of the exit. I see her phone already in her hand again.

It wouldn't be so bad if the rebellion at school actually *meant* something. If it all had something coherent to say. Something I'd want my name on. But everyone seems to have their own idea of what's going on. And to Clive, it's just another prank, an attempt to revive Grandpa's spirit so that all of us can pretend he's still here somehow and we're okay.

A vampire rips another vampire's throat out with his teeth. There's no blood. The camera cuts away, and everything's only shown as shadows on the cave wall behind them. No blood or extreme violence in a movie about vampires.

If there was a way to make the rebellion really mean something, and we could all be together at the head of the madness...

"How do we reclaim the Stone of Xanthar, the one thing that can end the 400-year vampire war with a snap of one's fingers?" the vampire leader asks a room of soldiers. "As you all know, the stone is guarded by our enemy, and we aren't ready for a fight that big! We blah-blah-blah, blah-blah-blah-blah. Blah? Blah."

I rub my eyes tiredly. Tomorrow I'll have to go back to school. I'll have to hear more about *TreyBellion* and whatever it means to whoever's talking. I'll have to put up with it until the school year finally ends. And it won't mean anything at all to me.

"Blah! Blah-blah-blah-blah! Blah? Blah?"

"Blah!"

"Blah?"

"Blah!"

"Hold on, hold on, hold on!" Grandpa roars. "Why don't we just use the Holy Stone of Whogivesadamn to jump to the third act of this stupid movie? Ooh, or maybe one of us can conveniently discover some hidden ability that lets us mind control our enemy, or some other convoluted garbage?"

I look up at the screen, and there he is, seated among the vampires. They're all dressed in heavy black armor and battle garb, and he's wearing two pillows duct taped to his body and an umpire's mask.

"Tell me you didn't pay money to sit there looking depressed," Grandpa says to me. The vampires continue talking, and he walks toward the screen, staring down at me. "Play the smile game, kid. We're prisoners to the things we can't smile at."

I shrug, speechless.

"Hang on a sec," he says. He takes off the mask and shakes out the thin gray mohawk he didn't even have when he was buried. Then he walks through the screen toward me.

"I'm gone less than two months and this whole theater falls to hell," he says, amused. "And you've seen better days too, kid. You look like you just got bashed by the Hulk, not gonna sugarcoat it."

He walks through the theater and stops to glance back at the movie behind him.

"Adaptations are a bitch and a half, aren't they?" he asks. "If you're gonna do one, you'd better do it well."

"Everything's out of control," I tell him. "I don't know how to fix it. You're not here anymore, and I don't know what to do."

"You could kill yourself," says one of the vampires onscreen. His face is blank now, just an empty white space. "Everyone you love will either die or get tired of you."

Grandpa gives him the finger and lifts one leg to fart loudly.

"You're messing with the wrong kid, pal," he says. "Trey's strong. He's got it upstairs where it really counts."

"He'll mess it up somehow," The Great Blank says. "He always does. He's cursed to fail. Cursed to disappoint."

Grandpa shakes his head and waves dismissively.

"Ignore him," he says, plopping down in Sarah's seat beside me. "I've beaten him before. Everyone has."

I can smell his rotting stench. When he smiles, I see a maggot wriggling between his teeth. The iron fist is back in my chest and it hurts terribly.

"I miss you, Grandpa," I tell him. "Everything sucks without you around. I don't know what I'm doing anymore, and every time I *try*, really, really *try*, I just mess everything up."

"Oh, that's quitter talk," he says. "I'm here now. I crawled through six feet of dirt and there's a rat up my ass, so what do you need me to tell you? That everything's going to be okay?"

I nod.

"Well, tough," he says. "Life gets hard, and then it gets harder. No one's coming to your rescue, and your ship's not coming in to take you away."

I choke out a laugh.

"Thanks. That really helps."

"Help yourself," he says. "You're a bright kid. You're all bright kids. I never gave you anything you didn't already have inside you."

"You made life better," I tell him. "You brought us all together, and you made life fun when nobody else cared. I wish I was wherever you're at."

"Spoiler alert," he says, "someday you will be. Someday you'll be dead longer than you were alive, and you won't know what it all ever meant."

The image on the screen changes. Suddenly the vampires are running through school hallways, wearing my face on t-shirts and waving flags with meaningless symbols and chanting about rebellion.

"Now," Grandpa says, "what are we going to do about all this? You miss having fun and feeling in control of yourself. How are you gonna do it?"

"I have no idea," I tell him. "Tell me what to do. What would you do?"

He winces at the desperation in my voice, and it makes me feel small and ashamed. This isn't a dream. This isn't a hallucination. He's really sitting here next to me and looks so disappointed.

"I don't have any answers for you, Trey," he says sadly. "I can't tell you what's right or that the pain and self-doubt will ever stop. I don't control your life, and I'd never presume to do so."

"Then why are you here?" I demand. "Why even bother? I've been dying for you to come back, or to give me some sign that you're still here, and all I get from you is 'tough'? Just tell me what to do. Please. Tell me what to do."

Grandpa sighs. It's quiet for a long moment. He dances his fingers up and down on the armrest.

"You're breaking my heart, kid," he says finally. "You're torturing yourself, and I never wanted that for any of you."

"You died," I tell him. I'm crying now, and when I try to stop it, it just hurts worse. "It's not fair. It's not right. We never even got to say goodbye to you until you were already gone. I just want to go back. I want the dreams to stop. I want to feel okay again."

"You will," he promises. "Pain keeps coming and coming, but you've got to find a way to smile through it. That's the only way."

On the screen, one of the vampires is dressed as Jordan. He's giving some longwinded speech to others as they sit on choir risers in an auditorium, and whenever one of them opens his mouth to speak, he cuts them down with a heavy sword.

Grandpa stands up suddenly. All at once, I'm losing him all over again, reliving that horrible pain.

"Don't leave us," I beg him. "Stay. We need you, Grandpa."

"My time's done," he says. "Yours isn't. You'll figure it out, Trey. I believe in you, I really do. And I'm so, so proud of all of you."

He starts to walk away. Then he stops suddenly, and he reaches into his pocket. He pulls out the chess piece that I left on his grave.

"This is yours," he says, and throws the King piece onto my lap. "You'll find a way to enjoy life. Then things will get hard again, and you'll feel more pain and all that horrible stuff you can imagine. And you'll figure out how to be happy then, too. You can do it, Trey. I believe in you."

He smiles down at me. Suddenly he isn't a rotting corpse anymore, and the decaying smell is gone. He's just Grandpa, the Grandpa I remember. The smiling maniac who saved us all.

And then he's gone.

On the screen, the vampires are going on again about their war. I stare at the screen, searching for Grandpa.

A few minutes later, Sarah walks back in. She looks at me funny as she sits down. There's no King piece in my lap anymore, just crumbs from the popcorn. I stare up at the screen, seeing an entirely different movie playing from the projector in my mind. I feel something new inside, some kind of fire.

"Did the movie get good or something?" Sarah asks. I shake my head, dazed. "Are you okay? You look dizzy or something."

Everything's coming together somehow. The pieces suddenly fit, and I know it's Grandpa's hand moving them into place. I bite my lower lip, forcing my thoughts to the surface. I don't want that sad, cold shower tomorrow.

"You remember how I told you I didn't want anything to do with these freaks at school and their rebellion?" I ask. She groans.

"This again? Oh my god…"

"I'm not so sure now," I tell her. "They're using my face. My name."

"So, laugh it off and move on!" she says. "Trey, we're *graduating* in a few weeks! Is this really bothering you that badly?"

"Yeah," I tell her. "Look, I'm not saying 'let's blow up the school' or anything like that. But if people are going to run around school with my face on their t-shirts, and if they're all going to try to make some sort of cause from something I said, I want it to really be *my* cause. I want it all to mean something. I want it to be something we're all proud of."

She rolls her eyes.

"Wow. Clive really got to you."

"I'm not talking about random pranks or just causing chaos for the sake of it," I tell her. "I'm talking about something real. Something that won't get anyone hurt. I want to take back what's ours."

"What does that even mean?" she asks.

So, I tell her. Everything I'm seeing unfold in the beautiful new adaptation only I can see on the screen. I open my mouth and it's like I'm back on stage that first day at T.A.G. rehearsal, letting something strange and somehow wholly formed spill out of my mouth. I talk fast, growing more excited as it all comes together.

I can see it all. I know what we have to do. And it's going to be beautiful. It's going to be stupid, something others might not get or claim as "revolutionary." But it's going to be *ours*. Our adaptation.

Sarah stares at me for a long moment after I've finished, her expression unreadable. She flinches when I reach out and take her hand in mine. This could be it. This could be the moment she finally realizes I'm not just 'crazy,' but actually *crazy*, someone she was wrong about all along and is having second thoughts about having in her life.

I'm out of words, though. Out of explanations. All I can think to do is hold onto her and hope that my eyes communicate the rest.

My cheeks burn, and I'm mentally naked for a long moment, stripped of any disguise I could hide behind. She must sense this, because she squeezes my hand and suddenly smiles. She might see me for what I really am, and somehow, miraculously, she doesn't look bothered by it.

"Wow," she says.

"Yeah."

"Do you think it would work? I mean, it sounds cool and everything, but it's *a lot*."

I shrug. It might all blow up in our faces, granted.

"We'll be giving everyone what they want," I tell her. "Everyone feels special, no one gets hurt, and we all get one last big game together before graduation."

"And it screws over Jordan," she adds. She sounds neither pleased nor displeased, but she looks down at her black phone screen.

"Are you okay with that? I mean, I know things are still fresh. It's okay if you're not okay."

"No no no," she says quickly. She smiles again, but her enthusiasm seems somehow forced now. "He deserves it. He brought it on himself."

I nod. Good enough. I try not to think about the phone and what it might mean. She's with me on this. She's with *me*.

I bring my lips toward hers, eyes half-closed in that goofy sort of pre-kiss expression…then her hand hits my chest and stops me, and she pulls her face back with a sarcastic laugh.

"Later," she says, grinning as disappointment and embarrassment fight for control of my facial muscles. "First I at least want proof that you have some sort of plan."

I turn my head and groan.

"Text Clive and the others," I decide. My stomach turns as part of my mind returns to the locker bay where he had me pinned so easily. I force the feeling away. "Tell them to meet us at Grandpa's house in an hour or so."

I stand up, running every idea for how to pull this off through the gauntlet of probability. Sarah throws a handful of popcorn at my face when I look back down at her.

"I said I'm with you on this, *not* that I'd be your secretary," she says. "Why do you want Clive around, anyway? You just said you two are fighting."

I shrug, still sketching the whole idea out in my head.

"If we're going to pull everyone's strings, I'm going to need Clive there with me. He's better at that than I am."

She shakes her head.

"Let's be realistic: it's *your* strings Clive will be pulling. Unless you put him in his place."

"I'm not afraid of Clive," I tell her. "It's nothing. It's just, you know, a guy thing."

She sighs miserably.

"Boys," she laments. She starts texting them, though. I stare at the movie on the screen. It's back to vampires fighting vampires, all CGI and bad makeup. Our adaptation will be better. We'll take this 'rebellion' and make it something great. Grandpa believes in us.

I reach in my pocket and put on the ring.

How exactly does one rebel against a rebellion? I never thought I'd have to think about that, or that anything I ever said or did would ever be of much consequence.

Then again, less than a week ago, I never would have have thought I'd be yelling at my bedroom walls or facing drive-by cheeseburger assaults.

"Sit back down," Sarah says, patting the seat next to her. "We have an hour."

"You seriously want to watch the rest of the movie?" I ask. She smirks, then she looks around at the empty theater, the closed door behind us, and the vacant projector room above us. She dances her eyebrows at me.

"Nope," she says. She grabs my belt straps with two fingers and pulls me closer, repeating, "Sit back down."

I sit, filled with a sudden nervous energy. She straddles my lap, arms up over my shoulders and looking down into my eyes for a long moment. She looks around the theater again, then, decisively, she drops her phone to the ground.

Our shirts come off. Her forehead's against mine. Then her lips are against mine. Then her bare hips are against mine.

Like a nostalgic sign from the universe, we're back to making noise over bad movies in a theater.

Chapter Twenty-one

Clive's already on the porch smoking a cigarette when we get to Grandpa's. I saw the 'For Sale' sign at the edge of the lawn as soon as Sarah and I rounded the corner, so I've had a few moments to brace myself before the house comes into full view. The blinds are gone from all the windows, showing the completely emptied rooms.

There are two overflowing garbage cans outside the garage, which I can only assume are filled with all Grandpa's "worthless" memorabilia.

His daughters must have returned to finish the job and to collect whatever else they felt was due to them.

Sarah squeezes my hand gently as we stand at the edge of the lawn, and we both stare in silence at the slaughtered home. I look up toward Grandpa's bedroom window. The creature from my nightmare isn't there, nor is Grandpa's weeping phantom. It still hurts, though.

"Take it in," Clive calls to us. He spreads his arms at the house behind him. "It's dead. Long live home, right?"

The fake cheerfulness isn't convincing. He stomps his cigarette and immediately lights another.

"We can dig stuff out," Sarah says to me, looking toward the garbage cans. "I'll keep all of it in my room, if you guys want. We can go through it all."

I shake my head. A dozen bags or so are clustered around the cans. Plastic shrouds for dead memories. He's not in those bags.

"We don't have to," I answer. "Is there something in there you want to find?"

"I already have his picnic basket," she says. She lets herself look at the bags only a second longer before forcing a halfhearted smile and squeezing my hand again.

"So...is this a thing now, or what?" Clive asks, gesturing at us with his cigarette as we walk across the dead grass. "Damn, Trey, you packing a footlong down there, or what? Mister Steal-Your-Girl. Good for you two."

I ignore him. Honestly, I still don't even want to see him. He used my face and my name for his idiotic prank *TreyBellion*. If I don't look directly at him, maybe the hellhounds in my chest won't start barking for his blood.

"Nice day out," he says.

There's no hint of subtext in his voice, nothing apologetic or even vaguely bothered by the tension. The way he's just smiling down at the ground, taking in deep breaths of smoke and watching the shapes he makes as he blows them out, you'd think this was natural to him. He counters my silent scowl with a raised eyebrow, and he offers the pack toward me. I take one. I even let the son of a bitch light it for me.

I sit on the porch beside him. He starts clicking his tongue in boredom, looking around at nothing in particular.

"So…" he says after another minute of silence. "Here we are. You write anything good lately?"

I shrug silently, and he flicks his cigarette and sighs, dissatisfied with the monotony. I agree completely. We can't have this awkward silence any longer. The situation is in desperate need of resolution, and by the grace of God, inspiration strikes me.

I copy his motion, flicking my cigarette toward the neighbor's house and then cracking my knuckles.

Then I punch him as hard as I can, just above his waistline.

Silence is shattered by his loud 'whoop' as his hands fly toward his gut and his body folds forward, eyes bulging. Sarah's attention snaps toward us, and she reaches out to pull me back. I push her arm away gently, standing as Clive gets to his feet. He's still holding his stomach miserably, but he waves me forward.

"Is that it, then?" he asks, spitting a yellowish wad of phlegm. "I thought you had a little more in you. Bitch."

My fists tighten, ready to hit him again and again until that stupid grin disappears. But then I shake the feeling, knowing I won't get much more of an apology out of him.

"We good now?" he asks, already lighting another cigarette. I nod.

"Yeah. We're good."

Sarah shakes her head at us.

"Dumbasses," she mutters.

Kevin's car pulls up a few minutes later, and he and Monk join us on the porch.

"You never showed up at the meeting," Monk complains to me. "It was such a shit show, man. We didn't even talk about anything. It was just a bunch of idiots talking over each other. I don't think anyone even knew why we were meeting."

"Surprise, surprise," Kevin says. "But I bet they all felt pretty cool talking about 'anarchy' and stuff, huh?"

"If I hear the word 'anarchy' one more goddamn time today," Monk says, "I swear I'm going to punch someone right in the dick."

"Blame Clive," Sarah says. "He's the one who got everyone riled up with this fake 'rebellion' stuff."

"What?" Monk and Kevin ask in unison. Clive spreads his hands at them.

"I won't apologize for art," he says. "As far as I'm concerned, this chaos is my masterpiece."

"I hate you so much right now," Kevin says, shaking his head. "All these dumbass symbols and slogans you've got everyone spreading around…it makes my brain hurt. It's literally *that* stupid."

"People like edgy symbols. Doesn't matter if they know what they mean or not."

"Someone spray-painted a cross made of dicks on the gym doors," Kevin says. He claps his hands sarcastically. "Congratulations. Real groundbreaking stuff."

"It's not even fun," Monk says. "I thought this whole thing was supposed to be about free artistic expression or something. It's just a costume contest to see who can *look* most rebellious."

"Trey and I have an idea how to fix it," Sarah says. "Well, *he* has an idea. But it's a good one."

They all look at me, and I say a silent prayer. Grandpa, please be with me.

"We can't fix it all," I tell them. "People are going to do what they're going to do, and there's no stopping that. But we can get whoever will listen to help make something cool from it. Not just us, not just people from the T.A.G. group, but anyone who's actually interested."

Sarah smiles. "One last big prank together," she says. "One last big game before we graduate."

Clive blows lip music at us.

"Umm, excuse me, but that's exactly what I've been saying. Trey went all PMS on me."

"The chaos part is good," I tell him. "People want to feel involved, and they want to feel heard. Jordan's pissed off just about everyone creative at the school, changing their work to suit his idea of what art is. If this really is *TreyBellion* or whatever, that's what I want it to be about. Not just showing anarchy symbols and fighting over bullshit."

"It doesn't have to mean anything cohesive," Sarah adds. "It's just everyone showing who they are."

They stare at me like I'm speaking witchcraft, and Kevin grimaces at the idea like he's holding back a hundred logical objections. My smile doesn't go away, though, as the images play over and over in my head. I picture crowds of people breaking out of the high school hellhole, a wad of pus rocketing out of a social zit.

It's exactly what Grandpa did with his life, and what he'd always encouraged us to do. Pure freedom. Stepping out of the norm.

"*Mental* anarchy," Sarah clarifies. "Not chaos for the sake of chaos. Just pure, unrestrained expression of what we're each longing to create."

"Just imagine it," I say. "An army of us breaking our shells all at once, like a bomb of creativity with no one editing from over our shoulders, no audience telling us what's good and what sucks."

Whatever enthusiasm Monk lost after his 'rebellion' meeting seems to have returned. His eyes light up as he claps his hands together.

"Hell yes!" he says. "*That's* what I want! *That's* what this should've all been!"

"Sounds like just a re-do of the T.A.G. show," Kevin says. "How exactly are we going to do that? We'll have to get a venue, print flyers, organize acts…"

He trails off when Sarah lifts a hand to stop him.

"We already have a venue," she says. "And a captive audience. And all the acts we'll need."

"We do?" Clive asks, surprised.

Grandpa, I think, *I know you're here with us still. You gave me this idea, this last big game for us to play together. And it's damn perfect.*

I nod, and I smile wide at Kevin.

"Do you still have the keys to the school?"

We spend another hour discussing it all, excitement building until even Kevin's smiling from ear to ear. We laugh together, trade insults as we plot, and feel that warm and beautiful type of crazy that may or may not be Grandpa's spirit embracing all of us as he shouts his own enthusiasm.

By the time we split for the night, we all know our jobs. Monk and Sarah have a list of people to contact and sell the plan to, and Kevin and Clive have copies of the school keys to make.

The next day at school, we start spreading the word.

And the response is overwhelming.

Chapter Twenty-two

We spend the next day organizing, getting everyone who wants to be involved all on the same page about what we're doing and why. I expected a lot more questions: *How is this all going to come together so quickly? Won't we all get into trouble? What, exactly, is any of it going to accomplish that's worth the risks?*

A few people outright say no. They tell us how great the idea is, and how they wish they could get involved, but, y'know, the risks...

But most of the T.A.G. group is on board. The idea of putting on *their* show with *their* art trumps any worry of what they stand to lose. Jordan took away their voices. He edited them down until it was no longer *their* work they were presenting at the show. It's not as pretty and punk as spray painting anarchy symbols around the school and shouting heatedly about 'rebellion,' but it's a chance to take something back.

Mental Anarchy. Unapologetic creativity and performance.

My temper flares a few times throughout the day. A few people are still wearing those damn t-shirts, almost like it's a moment of pride for them when they get detention for it. They look so smug and self-righteous in their costumes, and it makes me a little sick. I want to yell at them, demand to know what it all even means to them as I pummel their faces with a heavy textbook.

But I don't lose my mind. Even when I hear Jordan loudly alert his mommy in class when he sees someone wearing a *TreyBellion* t-shirt, I keep my temper in check. I keep Grandpa's ring on my finger, reminding myself of what lies ahead tomorrow morning. I don't even hit Damien when I see him passing out flyers that say "Keep rebelling! They can't fight us all!"

When I get home, Mom tells me I have mail on the counter. It's from The Northwestern Hills University, the only college I bothered applying to because it's where Sarah said she's going. I open it as I drink my fifth cup of coffee.

"What's it say?" Mom asks. She looks needlessly anxious on my behalf; this college accepts just about anyone.

"I got in."

"That's great! I'm so proud of you!"

I shrug and hand her the letter.

"We'll go out for dinner when your dad gets home!" she says.

I leave her with the letter and go up to my room. College seems so far away, and I wish it actually was. I want more nights in the graveyard, in our tree, staying out all night. All I want to think about the rest of tonight is tomorrow morning. It's all that really matters, not some validation from a college acceptance letter.

I nap. We eat. Mom and Dad tell me how proud they are, like I'm doing anything worthwhile. I nap again.

At 3 a.m., I head to the graveyard, ready to pull the pin from our grenade and watch the rebellion blow up.

Chapter Twenty-three

Sarah's late getting there, but the others are already up in the tree with celebratory beers in their hands. I see them before they see me, and I stand at the edge of the graveyard just watching them for a second.

Music is playing from Kevin's phone, some indie rock garbage that's driving Clive visibly crazy and causing him to go on one of his rants, much to Monk's entertainment. Monk's already in his stage makeup and costume, and there's twice the blood down the front of his shirt as there was at the T.A.G. show. Clive's phone rings suddenly, and he jumps down from the tree branch before answering it. I watch as he paces around between the graves, talking animatedly to whoever's on the other end, either berating them or just loudly busting their balls. He smiles as he talks, though, his own best audience member. I stare at Grandpa's gravestone, and somehow it doesn't make me sad right now. He's here, and I can feel him watching over us from someplace I can't put a name to.

They all look happier than I've seen them in a while, more like who they were before Grandpa told us he'd be gone soon. We've all had happy moments since then, sure, but it finally feels like we're fully back to who we were. Maybe I'm being too sentimental and overthinking things again, or maybe it's excitement for the final grand prank we're about to pull off together. Monk or Clive will throw me a beer when they see me approaching, and somehow, I know it's the only beer I'm going to need tonight. I haven't felt the fist in my chest all day, and The Great Blank hasn't said a word since that day at the movie theater. It's hard not to feel that something significant has happened.

I've never really been one for religion, and I usually have more questions about it than I do answers, but it feels like something beautiful and holy's taken hold of us. I don't know that it's God, or if there's any sort of divine plan in all the pain we've been through in our lives. It would be a tough sell for Sarah, I bet; she's lost more than any of us. All I know for sure is that right now, to me, it feels like everything that's happened to us all has led us here, and it's where we belong.

Someone throws their hands over my eyes from behind, and I shout loudly in surprise. I turn and see Sarah cracking up.

"Scare ya?" she asks. I nod.

"You're like a tiny goth ninja," I tell her. I stare at her outfit, probably longer than appropriate.

"See something interesting?" she asks.

"Nah," I say. "Just you."

And it's 100% *her* I see. No ugly sports hoodie, no fake smile. She's got her war paint on: fake blue lashes with sharp and precise makeup around her eyes, crimson lipstick with glitter, red and blue slashes painted from one side of her forehead to the opposite side of her jaw. She's wearing a spiked collar around her neck, and a torn and frayed black jean jacket with dozens of band patches. She even has her heavy black boots and her smiley face leggings.

"Is it too much?" she asks self-consciously. I shake my head.

"You look perfect," I tell her. "You're officially the mascot of our rebellion."

"Hooray," she says, waving her hands overhead with mock enthusiasm. She smiles wide, that impossible smile that seems to touch her whole face and come from her soul. I don't know why every detail feels so suddenly significant, or why I'm so suddenly energized by this "holy" feeling of everything being right.

I charge at her, and she shouts as she throws her hands up playfully and half-turns as I wrap my arms around her and take us both to the ground.

"Get off me, jerk face," she says, slapping at my chest and pushing me sideways. I let her roll me over, and I look up into her eyes as she sits on my hips and pins both my wrists with her hands, giggling victoriously.

She dips her face slowly toward mine, and as I close my eyes and go to kiss her, she lightly headbutts me and pulls her face away again.

"Come on," I groan. She laughs and lies down against me, wrapping my arm around her waist.

"You should be nicer to me," I tell her. "I got accepted to Northwestern Hills today, you know."

"Oh *wow*!" she says with mock amazement.

"I know, I know. I'm truly an amazing individual. All shall bow before me."

"Yes, m'lord." She's quiet again, and I stroke her lower back as we look up at the stars together. In the background, I hear Clive still talking loudly on the phone while Monk cheerfully sings the song of a murderous barber.

"Jordan's going to be at Northwestern, too," she says quietly. I don't answer; I just keep staring up at the stars in silence. She turns toward me and stares at my blank expression. "He's been texting me. I told him I didn't want him to change his plans and that I didn't want *him* at all."

"Uh-huh."

"Are you mad?"

I shake my head. "There's nothing to be mad about."

"I know," she says. She continues, "He has this delusional idea that we can work stuff out, and that the breakup isn't permanent. I told him to leave me alone, but he keeps trying to get me to talk."

"You want me to kick his ass?" I ask seriously.

This makes her laugh. I'm not sure how to take that, so I laugh along. She puts a hand on my chest.

"He'll move on," she says. "He's just so used to getting what he wants."

"You miss him, though."

She's silent.

"It's okay," I tell her. "You were with him for a while. You don't have to pretend anything's easy."

"Trey...stop talking."

I nod. We stare back up at the stars.

"I want to stab you in the face sometimes, you know," she says. I shrug.

"My face is very stab-worthy, I guess."

"Just stop talking for a bit. I just want to lie here with you."

"Okay."

We're quiet for another few minutes, and she rubs my chest with one hand.

"I hope we always stay crazy," she says. "All of us. I never know what I'm doing, and that scares me sometimes."

"Nobody knows what they're doing," I tell her. "I didn't know what I was doing when I went on my rant."

She nods, and it's back to silence for another long moment. There's an ant crawling across her arms, and I smash it between my fingers. She looks up at me again with a serious expression.

"You're not going to change, are you?" she asks. "We'll always stay crazy together?"

I lean forward and kiss her forehead, pushing her hair aside with one hand.

"Crazy 'til the end," I promise. I hold out a pinky, and she grins as she wraps it with hers. I stare down into her eyes, feeling like I'm about to say something else but not knowing if it's right. Do I really want to say it, or am I just high on the moment?

She sits up.

"Race you to the tree," she says, and when I lean forward on my palms, she pushes me back down and laughs as she takes off. I chase after her, and she starts running at a comically slow pace, kicking her feet up to her butt. She touches the base of the tree and sticks her tongue out at me when I reach her.

"Cheater," I grumble. She laughs, slapping playfully at me as I put my hands on her waist. My fingers lift the bottom of her shirt, stroking lightly just above her hip. I press my mouth to hers, and her eyes shut as she puts her arms up over my shoulders.

Monk calls down at us, "Oh, my god, you two are going to make us all barf!"

"For real," Kevin says. "Get a room."

"We have a tree," I tell him. He rolls his eyes.

"Great, you're both finally here," Clive says, walking back toward us as he pockets his phone. "Everything's set with everyone," he tells us. "People are meeting us outside the school in two hours. That should be enough set-up time, right Kev?"

"Teachers start showing up around six or six-thirty," Kevin says. "As long as we're quick and no one screws around, it should be enough time."

"How are we going to keep people from coming in while we set up?" Sarah asks.

"There are chains and door barricades in the janitor's closet," he says. "No one gets in until we're ready."

"And guess who the idiot to let them in is going to be," Clive says proudly. "Trey's best friend and biggest fan: Damien."

"Good," I tell him. "Maybe he'll take the blame. Just make sure he doesn't have any fireworks or other stupid crap."

"I've got that kid wrapped around my finger," Clive says. "He won't do anything unless I tell him to."

"I'm still going to hit him."

"And I'll hold his arms back while you do it," he swears.

Sarah's hand suddenly reaches down my front pocket, and I jump in surprise.

"Hey! Whoa!" I yelp as I try wriggling away. She laughs and pulls her hand away again, and I see my Grandpa's ring on her middle finger."

"Looks pretty badass on me, right?" she asks, holding her hand out for us to admire.

"Umm…yeah," I say. "Now give it back." I lunge toward her to grab the ring, and she pulls her hand to her chest defensively. She pushes out her lower lip.

"C'mon, let me wear it!" she says. "Just for tonight. I should wear something of my boyfriend's, right?"

Clive groans loudly. "Jesus, already with the labels. Run, Trey."

Sarah sticks her middle finger up at him.

"See?" she says. "It even looks cool when I flip people off! Let me wear it."

I wince, already feeling weird without the ring in my pocket.

"You'll give it back tomorrow?" I ask.

"Pinky swear," she says, and holds her finger out. I sigh, nodding in defeat as I look at the ring on her finger. She plants a wet kiss on my cheek, and I smile despite myself as I wipe it off.

"Boyfriend, huh?" I ask. "Does that position come with any added benefits?"

"You can walk me back to my bike," she says.

"Wait, you're leaving already?"

She nods. "I think I left my phone in my room. And maybe I'll get a quick nap before meeting you guys there."

"She's totally going to be late," Clive says.

"Will not! I'll set three alarms."

"Sure, sure," he says. "Trey, come shotgun a beer with me. We need to celebrate the end of your perpetual loneliness."

I pick an empty can up and throw it at him. He bats it back, and it flies past me and hits a gravestone.

"Your escort," I say, holding my elbow toward Sarah. She takes it in both hands and we walk back toward the gates. Clive retches loudly behind us.

"Hey, can I have one of those eyelashes?" I ask. She scrunches her face at me.

"Why?"

"You get to wear my ring, I get to wear one of your fake eyelashes."

"You're weird, you know that?"

"The main character in the movie adaptation of *A Clockwork Orange* was wearing one. Looked pretty cool on him."

"Aww, you just want to think of me every time you blink," she says. She takes off one of her lashes, though. "Close your eyes for a sec."

I do it, and I feel her sticking it to one of my eyelids.

"Beautiful," she says when she's done. She smirks. "Do you want me put makeup and lipstick on you, too?"

"Get outta here," I tell her. She sticks her tongue out at me and gets on her bike. "Don't forget. Five a.m."

"You don't have to keep reminding me," she says. "I can remember stuff."

"I know."

She leans forward on her seat and kisses me on the lips, then she squeezes my face in her hand as she looks at me.

"You make a pretty handsome rebel," she says. I don't know what to say, so I just nod. Standing here now with her, seeing the streetlights reflected in her eyes…it's like I've just woken up from a bad dream. None of the other stuff from the past few months matters.

She pedals away, and I watch her go until she rounds the end of the block.

I smile to myself. Once again, it's like everything else in life, all the good and the bad, has led me to this moment. I feel stupid thinking about it, but it's there in my head. It's all real.

"Trey!" Clive shouts at me. "Come chug a damn beer, you pussy!"

I walk back toward the others. I feel…good. I feel right.

Setup is a raging headache from beginning to end. When we arrive at the school, there are 12 others in total, including Damien. They're all standing out in the band practice field in plain view of the road near the school, and though it's unlikely anyone will pass by at this hour, it's always a possibility that some nosy neighbor will see the group gathered and alert the police.

Thank God for Clive, who becomes a drill sergeant the moment we arrive. He calls for everyone to move their cars the hell out of the school parking lot, and once everyone has parked a few streets away and reconvened, he gets them all inside and into the auditorium.

As soon as we're inside, Damien immediately tries to take control of the group, first calling out a huge thank-you to everyone for arriving and then waving his hands and yelling for everyone's attention. Clive shouts only once for the whole group to shut up, and everyone's silenced like a whip's been cracked across their backs. He gives out very quick directions, walking through the group and assigning tasks person by person. Everyone nods along anxiously, some of them wringing their hands like they're having second thoughts while others bounce on their feet, completely amped up for the big show.

Two minutes later, Kevin walks the group out through the second-floor stage doors and starts placing people strategically around the school. We've already unlocked the band practice room, and they quickly borrow all the equipment we'll be needing: guitars, a full drum set, amps, etcetera.

Damien stands waiting for orders. When he realizes he hasn't been given a task yet, I see him nursing a dying smile.

"What about me?" he asks, hopeful. "I brought fireworks! Do you want to, like, place them around the school or something?"

"No," I tell him. "We have a very, very special job for you."

He smiles wide again.

"Oh, hell yeah! What can I do?"

"You get to sit down and shut the hell up until we tell you otherwise."

"It's a very important job," Clive emphasizes. "And only you can do it."

Damien's mouth opens like he wants to argue or pitch better ideas, but Clive claps his hands together loudly.

"Sit, boy. Heel," he says, and points to a chair in the front row. The look of utter dejection on Damien's face is ten times more satisfying that I imagined. It almost makes me forget to check the time on my phone.

"She'll be here soon," Monk says. "Just give her time."

I nod, pretending it's no big deal. My thoughts are already running away, though. She's with Jordan again; she went directly to him after meeting us at the graveyard, and she's telling him about everything because it turns out she loves him after all, and nothing he ever does to her or says to her will ever change that...

Piss off, I tell The Great Blank silently. She's just late. She's always late.

I watch Damien squirm miserably in his seat, arms crossed. I picture everything in my mind, how it's all going to play out. It's both a gift from Grandpa and a perfect tribute to him: revenge for everyone who's ever been told their art isn't good enough, or who's been censored by people like Jordan and his mother, or who are slowly sinking in doubt that the world will ever let them be who they are inside. Crazy can sense crazy; I have no doubt that everyone who showed up this morning, regardless of how well I know them or how little I care about them, is crazy like us.

In front of the second-floor entrance, we have a kid named Thomas Haggerson setting up a drum set to play wild and free, fast and furious.

In the center of the commons on the fourth floor, Ashton Reilly is setting up an amp for his electric guitar, and he'll play an ongoing punk rock solo that Jordan called "disjointed" and "weak sauce." Corey Harms will aid Ashton's performance by screaming improvised lyrics into a megaphone, all the sickest and darkest stuff he can come up with.

Over the P.A. system in the principal's office, Clyde will tell every single joke that Jordan deemed "too offensive" or "tasteless" for the T.A.G. show.

In the center of the lunch room, up on a table, Corrine Albertson will read pages of poetry that didn't even makes it past T.A.G. auditions because she has a terrible stutter.

In the gymnasium, Gunnar Hart will shoot apples off Tyler Green's head with a bow and arrow from the gym supply closet, while Caitlyn Ellis juggles fire on the second-floor balcony overlooking the room. Heavy metal will be blasting from the stereo Mr. Evans keeps in the gym office, an assortment of music Caitlyn assured us will "melt some faces off!"

In the study hall room on the third floor, Casey Hodder is artfully stacking textbooks from classrooms into the shape of a tall middle finger.

And while all this is going on, Wes Cooper and others will be roaming the school with their cameras, recording everything and everyone's reactions as they enter the chaos. Chances are, the whole thing will be shut down within an hour or so, and teachers will be running around the school and barking orders for everyone to stop what they're doing *immediately*, while students entering the building will either laugh at the explosive display of unbridled madness or join in somehow.

I'm picturing mosh pits erupting, but maybe that's too optimistic. It's doubtful anyone will do anything but record the acts on their phones and post their reactions to social media so that everyone will know how interesting their lives are.

And the grand topping on everything is Damien. Not only will he be the one to remove the barricade from the second-floor doors and likely get murdered by an incoming stampede, he'll also take all the blame.

I look over at Clive, who's dutifully typing on his phone and occasionally looking up at Damien. It didn't take Kevin long to hack Damien's Facebook account; you'd be surprised how easy stuff like that really is. Post after post, typed by "Damien" will link him to organizing all this chaos. Given how he's been shouting gleefully about "anarchy" around the school and handing out t-shirts, it'll be easy to pin the blame on him.

A lot of us will get detention or in-school suspension, I bet. Our parents will be called. There will be an emergency assembly later this afternoon or tomorrow morning. We'll get yelled at by the principal and possibly even the superintendent. Jordan will watch smugly as we're all berated, viewing it all a big and messy failure, blind to the subjectivity of art.

We made sure everyone involved knows the risks. Thankfully, they're all the same type of crazy as we are, and it makes me wish for a moment I'd discovered these people sooner so they could've joined in all our late-night meetings at the cemetery and played our wild and stupid games around town. Our little family could've been so much bigger, all this time.

Half an hour passes, and I keep looking at the clock on my phone. Finally, I give in and text Sarah: *"Where R U?"* And then I try calling her. And then I try calling her again. And again.

Clive sits at the end of the stage with his feet dangling, crumbling up wads of paper and throwing them at Damien.

"Damn, this is going to be a wild ride," he says, and lights a cigarette. He blows a smoke ring toward the ceiling, and Monk snatches the cigarette from him.

"There are smoke detectors in here, dumbass!" he shouts. Clive waves a hand.

"Relax, would you? We're already going to get in trouble. We're not going to get in *more* trouble just for a bit of smoke."

Monk groans, and then he starts pacing back and forth across the stage as he recites his lines from *Razor's Edge*, slowly getting into character and slashing the air in front of him with the straight razor he brought. He'll stalk the halls of the second-floor locker bay, performing the musical and staying in character all the way until the inevitable ending to our fun. Hopefully, he'll remember to pocket the razor as soon as he sees a teacher approaching.

Kevin eventually re-enters the auditorium.

"Everything's all set to go," he announces. I can hear the echoes of drum beats and guitar riffs when he opens the door.

"All the entrances chained up?" Clive asks.

"Yep. Only one way inside."

I nod, trying to smile enthusiastically but unable to shake my anxiety. I check my phone again. No response at all from Sarah.

"Teachers will probably start arriving soon," I tell them.

"Then we'd better get our special little helper to the door," Clive says, jumping down from the stage and walking toward Damien. He flicks his cigarette at him. "C'mere, idiot. I've got a real job for you."

Damien jumps up, looking suddenly enthralled to be included in the fun. Poor, poor Damien. He should never have put my damn face on t-shirts.

The two of them exit the auditorium through the second-floor doors. I try calling Sarah again. My foot is moving restlessly against the floor.

"Not gonna lie," Monk says, abruptly ending his pacing, "I'm getting a bit nervous. I mean…I've never done immersive theater like this before. It's a lot."

Kevin shrugs, looking humored.

"If you're that unsure of your acting skills, *Theodore*, then by all means…" He twirls a finger toward the exit doors. Monk stares daggers at him.

"No. No, I can do this," he says, taking a deep breath and shaking his arms at this sides like he's warming up. "I'll make this the best damn performance of my life!"

"Attaboy," I tell him.

Another ten minutes or so pass. I keep trying Sarah's phone.

"The hell's the matter with you?" Clive asks when he re-enters and sees me pacing.

"Nothing," I mutter. I put my phone back in my pocket.

Over the P.A., I hear a sudden shrill ring and then the sound of Clyde saying, "Testing… Testing… Uno, dos, tres…"

"Gorgeous," Clive says, spreading his arms toward the school in general. "Absolutely gorgeous! Our last big hurrah! Whoo!"

He cups his hands around his mouth and starts howling like a wolf. Monk joins in, and then dives onto Kevin's back and rides him around until Kevin finally joins in as well. I try to smile.

"I want to go have a look," I tell them.

"We still have plenty of time to go," Clive says.

"Yeah…I just want to have a look."

He shrugs, and I leave them all to their howling as I take the steps two at a time toward the second-floor exit. Something's wrong; the iron fist is back in my chest, and it's searing hot now. All my internal alarms are going off, and I can't tell if the sudden anxiety's due to my excitement for the big show or the idea that *something* terrible has happened, something unaccounted for in all our planning…

I walk down the halls, taking deep breaths and trying to calm myself. The cacophony of noise echoing through the school is just as chaotic as I imagined. Every blank spot on the hallway walls seems to call after me, mocking me: *"Something's wrong,"* The Great Blanks taunts. *"Something's wrong, Treeeeey!"*

I give the thumbs-up to Ashton and Corey as I pass them upstairs. They're already in full force, lost in their performance. Corey's screaming something into the megaphone about dead babies and wolf teeth, but I can barely understand a word he's saying. Somehow the lack of understanding makes my anxiety worse, and I break into a jog.

Corrine is up on the lunch room table, already shouting her poetry to an audience of empty chairs. I check the gymnasium, and quickly confirm no one's on fire and no one's skull's been impaled by a flying arrow.

Over the P.A., Clyde says, *"What do you call a smelly hole filled with twenty sausages? Jordan's mom on the weekend!"*

It occurs to me suddenly that Damien is behind all this worry—he's done something stupid, or he changed our plan without asking. I picture him lying on the floor with his bloody stump of a hand held against his chest, staring blankly up at the ceiling in shock as fireworks keep erupting around him.

But when I arrive at the second-floor entrance, completely out of breath, he's just standing dutifully near the doors.

"I'm getting bored," he complains when he sees me. "For real, man, let me go do something fun! We still have plenty of time, just let me tag a few lockers or something!"

I shake my head at him, too out of breath to even argue. I look out through the glass doors. The parking lot's still empty. Teacher's haven't even started to arrive yet.

"Are you feeling okay?" he asks me. I don't know why, but the question pisses me off incredibly, and when I turn to face him, I shove him hard into the wall.

"Shut the hell up," I tell him. The terrible feeling inside me has to go somewhere, has to be pinned on someone. "Just...shut the hell up! And never put my damn face on a t-shirt again!"

I turn around and run toward the shop class, convinced someone's decided to incorporate power drills and other tools into their act. I'm imagining arterial blood spraying across the drum set as Thomas plays on and on despite a saw blade stuck in his neck. But there's no sign of disaster as I round the end of the hallway and see him playing wildly, spinning one drumstick overhead as he hammers the drums with the other.

I see new signs posted around the halls as I continue running through the school, telling myself I'm just having another brief episode and it'll pass quickly. The signs read "Art is what you make it!" and "Screw your rules!" and "Trey, there's something wrong! Something horribly, horribly wrong! This was all a mistake and you're to blame!"

Over the P.A., Clyde says, *"Jordan's mom is so fat that she has to use the car wash to shower!"*

Streamers made of paper towels and toilet paper litter the hallways, too. As I run by an unraveled roll of toilet paper toward the fourth-floor computer lab, I see that it's actually The Great Blank's mouth, and it's smiling at me.

Stop it, I tell myself. I fill my mind with good things, all the things that make me feel like nothing could ever go wrong again: that night in the graveyard with Sarah, seeing Grandpa again in the movie theater, drinking with Monk and the others only a few hours ago as we celebrated the event that I *should* be enjoying right now...

That's it. The alcohol. I told myself I'd only drink one beer, but Clive kept handing them to me and I was too stupid to say no. The anxiety's just excitement, and the alcohol's fooling me into thinking otherwise. I'm overreacting. The Great Blank isn't real.

But I am real, he insists.

I make my way back down to the auditorium, walking now and forcing myself to smile at my stupidity. I'm not used to things working out, that's all it is. I'm expecting disaster, because most things since Grandpa's death have *been* disasters, and my mind's just having trouble accepting that everything's finally going right.

"Jesus, dude," Clive says when he sees me. I look down and see the pits in my shirt are soaked with sweat.

"Everything's good!" I tell them, sounding probably too relieved. "It's all perfect! *Whoo!*"

I start howling at the auditorium ceiling. The others don't join in; Monk approaches me calmly, holding out a steady hand.

"You should drink some water," he says. "You're looking a little...scary."

I don't know why, but I laugh loudly at this. Then I feel my phone vibrate, and my hand shoots into my pocket to grab it. Sarah's name glows on the screen, and my heart pounds as I answer.

"Shit!" she says. "Shit, shit, *shit!*"

"It's okay," I tell her. "We're all here in the auditorium."

"I'm on my way! I'm pedaling as fast as I can!" she says, sounding out of breath.

"Shit!" she says again. "I'm so sorry I'm running late! I had my alarm set, but my phone was on vibrate!"

"It's okay," I tell her again, more and more relieved by the second. "Don't rush, there's nobody even in the parking lot yet. Take your time."

She hangs up. I can't help but smile to myself, and I shake my head as I collapse into a seat.

"What's going on?" Monk asks.

"Sarah's on her way. Her phone was on vibrate."

"Hah!" Clive says triumphantly. "I told you she'd be late!"

"She's on her way," I say again. I smile up at the ceiling. I haven't had much sleep, and I'm running on fumes. The alcohol surely didn't help. All that running around was over nothing.

Clive hands me a cigarette, and I smoke as we all sit there watching Monk get back into character and stalk around the room menacingly. Clive heckles him and says loudly that after today he's going to have even *less* respect for musical theater. Monk leaps onto the chair in front of him and starts singing the lyrics even louder, slashing toward Clive's face.

After a while, I check the time again. It's six now. Teachers should be arriving soon.

"I'd better get out there," Monk says finally, walking toward the exit. "Wish me luck!"

"Break your legs, or whatever," Clive calls to him.

The sound from outside the doors is growing louder and louder, as if everyone's anticipating the start of the big show. My heart's beating faster now, too. It's all coming together. Grandpa made this all happen, and he's so damn proud watching over us, cheering us on from wherever he is now.

Clyde's endless stream of jokes abruptly stops mid-sentence, and we all hear him shout loudly in surprise.

"Trey!" his voice yells over the P.A. The fear in his voice is palpable; my insides seem to suddenly freeze.

"Trey! You guys! There's something going on outside!" he shouts. *"Holy shit, you guys!"*

I'm already out of my seat and running toward the second-floor doors before Monk and the others move.

"I think there's been an accident!" Clyde shouts.

I'm running faster and faster, slipping as I step on a half-unraveled roll of toilet paper and crashing hard into a locker. Pain erupts in my elbow, but I ignore it, and all I can hear suddenly is The Great Blank's laughter.

I can hear the others behind me as I push past Damien and remove the barricade from the second-floor doors. My heartbeat is pounding in my ears, and I can hear the sound of someone screaming as I run outside and down the cement stairs toward the parking lot.

"Trey!" Monk calls from behind me. I can barely hear him; all I hear are the anguished screams from across the lot.

I see an old red pickup truck near the entranceway. Its front end is smashed into the brick sign reading "Welcome to Caedes High School!" Smoke is coming from the front end.

An old man in overalls is collapsed against the side of the truck, screaming as he stares helplessly at something ahead of him, eyes wide in terror.

"No…" he says between screams. "No, no, *no!* Oh Christ! *No!*"

I stop running suddenly. I listen to the man shout and weep as he buries his face in his palms and then stares straight ahead again, toward the road in front of him. Bushes near the entranceway hide whatever he's staring at.

My feet don't want to move forward any more. I hear Monk and Clive say something from behind me, and I hear something like recognition and then terror in their voices. They run ahead of me toward where the man in overalls is staring.

Monk stops and turn toward me, putting his hands out to stop me as my feet keep carrying me forward on their own accord. I can't hear anything anymore. There's only a loud ringing in my ears as I move closer and closer, ignoring Monk's hands as he tries urgently to stop me. I see Clive up ahead, but it's like he suddenly isn't Clive at all, just a pale statue staring with its mouth fallen open.

I reach the entranceway.

I see the bicycle first. It's bent in the center, and the front wheel is still spinning slowly. There's blood pooled beneath it, blood from the body I can't yet see.

I try to stop myself from walking any further, every nerve in my body screaming with dozens of exclamations points. The ground feels like it's moving beneath my feet.

I see the face smeared down into the gravel road, long brunette hair fanned out in all directions, one half soaked in red. Through all the blood, I can make out a pink streak.

Several things seem to happen at once as I stumble closer and closer. My knees give out from beneath me, and my palms suddenly hit the ground as everything in my stomach flies up from my mouth. Everything seems to blur together; I'm everywhere and I'm nowhere, and time no longer exists.

I see the heavy black ring on the corpse's left middle finger.

And then the whole world ends. I don't even hear myself screaming.

Chapter Twenty-four

G randpa warned me once that drinking should be treated like a marathon and not a sprint.

Start slow, he said. *Alcohol's got legs, and that monster will catch up to you quick.*

The funeral is at noon. Four hours from now. The black suit and tie that I've been wearing since last night is damp with sweat, and there's puke and snot on one sleeve. The near-emptied bottle of Jameson stares up at me from my left hand, promising me it'll save me if I just keep trusting it. My head is against my bedroom floor, staring toward the sky outside.

Can you hear me? I ask the sky silently. She doesn't answer. She doesn't climb in through my window to take me dancing somewhere.

The bottle stares up at me.

The door creaks open, and I hear Mom's careful footsteps as she walks into view. She stares at me worriedly, the same way she did each time she came in throughout the night, three hours ago, six hours ago, nine hours ago. I look toward her and blink. I can't hear what she's saying this time, something else that's gentle and well-meaning but also confused and cautious.

She carefully sets another plate of chocolate on top of Hector's tank and then stands there a long moment, looking down at me with red and tearful eyes. I want to get up and hug her tightly. I haven't wanted to hug her or dad in a long, long time. And now my body won't let me do it.

Mom leaves the room, closing the door gently behind her. After a few more minutes of looking toward the sky and looking for any sign of Sarah's face in the clouds, I force myself slowly to my feet. The room's spinning worse than it was last time. I take the plate from Hector's tank and open the window. I dump the comfort food out onto the roof with the last four platefuls.

The bottle shouts something up at me, still in my hand. I nod at it, and I take another deep gulp. Then I collapse onto my bed.

I don't know where the last five days went. I don't know how I've made it through school on the days I didn't skip. I've been drunk more than I've been sober. Dad's tried to stop me a few times, intercepting me in the kitchen as I go for another of his bottles, calmly telling me that it's not going to help. I nod each time, staring down at the floor and mumbling something like agreement as he hands me a glass of water instead. Each time, he tells me to get some rest. He tells me to eat something, and he asks if I want to come out of my room for a while. I mumble something, whatever it takes to end the conversation. Each time, he hugs me. He says he's here for me.

I keep finding my way back down to the kitchen. One way or another, I keep finding bottles in my hand.

I close my eyes, and I'm suddenly back on the ground outside the school parking lot. I hear the man in overalls crying as police cars and ambulances come, telling them how he only looked down for one second to grab his coffee and how he didn't even see the girl on the bike until his truck hit her.

She'd been rushing toward the school on her bike, probably not expecting anyone to be on the road yet since the sun was barely up. Rushing toward our big stupid rebellion.

A crowd eventually gathered as students and faculty began to show up in their cars and officers fought to redirect traffic filled with people staring and asking what happened. I sat there in the grass with Monk, Clive, and Kevin, listening to all these people ask questions and shriek 'oh my God!' and make sounds like they were going to be sick. Sarah's body was taken away. It seemed like everyone in the crowd had their phone out to take a picture. I swear to God, I even saw someone taking a selfie.

I throw myself sideways off the bed and lurch toward the trashcan, pulling it up to my face in time to catch most of what comes out. I wipe my mouth and start crying again.

Everyone you love will either die or get tired of you.

I shouldn't know how any of this feels. I shouldn't. It's not fair. I'm a kid in high school—I should be thinking about college, fretting about getting all my things in order and having anxiety about future plans. I should be dreading my Summer job and how it will affect time with my friends. I should be sitting on the couch with my girlfriend, one arm around her shoulder as we watch a movie and talk mostly about little things, making the other one laugh when it's really *us* who needs a laugh to stop our thoughts from destroying us internally.

I shouldn't be thinking of her lying in a casket and wondering what she looks like right now. I shouldn't be thinking of how someone else is applying her makeup in a way she'd never do it herself, presenting her in death as someone she never was in life. I shouldn't be thinking of how her face probably had to be stitched back together from where it was pulled from her skull by asphalt.

I hear the bedroom door creak open again.

"I don't want any chocolate!" I yell.

"Take it easy," Dad says softly. "It's just me."

I don't look up from the floor, but I get the mental image of him standing there in the doorway, staring down at me with a concerned expression.

"Get out. Please," I whisper. He ignores me; there's no sound of movement.

"I see you've helped yourself to more drinks," he says quietly, casually. I growl, suddenly annoyed so badly that I'm able to fight back more tears and sit up to face him.

"Like father, like son, right?" I sneer. This will *not* be some father-son bonding moment. This will *not* be some big connecting point between us.

But at the same time that I'm feeling this anger, another part of me is feeling shameful. A small voice tells me that someday Dad will be dead, too. Him and Mom. And by the time I realize they really do love me like they say they do, and that I really love them with all my heart and wish we'd spent more time together, it will be too late. Everyone I love will either die or get tired of me.

He swallows audibly and starts looking around the room as he takes a deep breath inward.

"How's your spider doing?" he asks, crouching down in front of the tank. Conveniently, he's right at eye level now. "Is he molting still?"

"Dad," I say quietly. "Please get out. Please."

He looks over at me, grimacing in a way that I guess is supposed to convey sensitivity and understanding. Then he does the worst thing I can imagine: he takes a step closer on his haunches and leans forward to hug me. He keeps his arms around me for a long time, patting my back gently. He's waiting for me to cry, or to confess everything I'm fighting to keep buried inside. I don't hug him back, but I grip the bottle tighter in my hand.

"You don't have to talk about it if you don't want to," he says, still hugging me tight. "You don't. I'm here for you, though. None of this is easy. I love you, Trey."

And someday he'll die or get tired of me.

I'm going to hit him. I'm going to break the bottle over his head if he doesn't let go of me and leave while he can. I don't want to be hugged anymore. I don't want to be loved by anyone, ever, because I want everyone to be safe.

I push him gently away and turn my back to him, looking toward the dozen or so brownies lying out on the roof outside my window. I take another heavy gulp from the bottle and hear Dad scoot back against the wall, sighing. He stays purposefully silent, waiting for me to break open and start pouring all the bad stuff out. He's here for me. He wants to help. He wants to take the pain away. I love him, and someday he's going to be dead and I'll wish I never felt anything at all.

"You can't make me feel better," I tell him. "You don't know what any of this feels like. I want you and Mom and Grandpa to stop trying to help me. Stop telling me I'll be okay."

He stares at me the same way Mom did, mouth partway open like words are trapped in his throat. I suddenly realize I mentioned Grandpa, and I imagine the psychobabble parent talk that's going through his head right now, the worry for my mental health. He opens his hands at me, suddenly the Father, Son, and Holy Ghost all at once, insisting I let him in.

I turn suddenly and whip the bottle across the room. It explodes against the wall in a goldish-brown spray of glass and whiskey. Dad falls back in a panic, shielding his eyes with his hands and staring at me with his mouth agape.

"Get the hell out of here!" I scream, pain pushing against the back of my eyes and throat as I stagger toward him. "You don't know anything, alright? You didn't know Sarah, you didn't know Grandpa, and you don't know a goddamn thing I'm feeling!"

He doesn't move from his spot on the floor, not even when I'm shouting straight down at him. He just stares up at me, eyebrows raised. I want him to scream at me, tell me what a worthless and selfish piece of garbage I am and that I deserve to suffer alone, and that I don't ever have to worry about losing a loved one again when he eventually dies.

But his eyes stay locked on mine, and he doesn't look angry. He just looks sad for me, pained on my behalf.

I totter from side to side on my feet, staring down at him and feeling his unyielding empathy like a crashing wave. I feel something rising in my chest, some dreadful feeling of guilt and apology. I want to fall down and hug him tight. I want to open up. I want to tell him that he's my dad and I love him and I never want to lose him or Mom or anyone else, even though I'm an ungrateful little bastard who deserves his curse.

He stands up slowly, though, still keeping eye contact. I don't want to cry, but I feel tears running down my cheeks anyway.

"Okay," he says. He back away toward the door, looking down at the floor as he exits and starts to shut the door behind him. Then he looks up at me again. I wish he wasn't crying too.

"You don't deserve to feel any of this," he says quietly. He adds, even quieter, as he shuts the door: "I'm sorry, Trey."

And then I'm alone again. I collapse back onto the bed, holding my head in both hands and feeling a sudden sickness.

I look out the window again. Clouds move over the sun, hiding it for a moment and turning light red. Maybe pink.

"Where are you?" I ask. No one answers. Neither of them comes to me. The Great Blank doesn't even speak to me.

Chapter Twenty-five

I insist on going to the funeral alone, even though Mom and Dad both offer go with me for support. I tell them I'd rather just be alone, and by this point the anger and frustration have left me completely, leaving me empty and exhausted. I want to hug them both and tell them I'm going to be okay. I don't want to lie anymore, though. Dad offers to at least drive me to the funeral, and I tell him I'd rather just walk. He tells me I can borrow one of his suits, since the one I've been wearing looks lived in. I nod, relenting. He looks so happy to even do that much for me.

I walk there with my hands in my pockets, staring down at the cracked sidewalk as cars pass by, hearing the occasional radio pop song from opened windows. Monk and Clive have been trying reach me all morning, and for the past three days. They love me, too. And someday they'll also be dead.

People dressed in black walk silently up the staircase toward the opened wooden church doors. It's an enormous building, the type of place you might picture when you think of a Catholic church, lots of narrow stained-glass windows and a tall peaked roof with a cross on top. Looking at the place, I feel immediately apprehensive.

The man with a plan lives here. The man whose plan involved taking Grandpa from us, and then taking Sarah. I look up at his sorrowful expression in one of the stained-glass windows. I want so badly to believe in him just so I can feel comforted. He can be here with me *and* not really be here with me. I wouldn't need to tell him anything that's gutting me from the inside, because he already knows it all, and he made me, and I can love him without ever fearing that he'll die or get tired of me like everyone else I love. I want to believe he's out there, and that he's not just a glass image.

Everyone seems to have their eyes downcast as they gather inside and find their places in the pews. Lots of students from the school are here, as well as a few people from the failed rebellion that ended in multiple detentions and in-school suspensions. I'm sure our punishments would've been worse if not for the tragedy that had taken place.

I don't say anything to any of them. I look around at all the stations of the cross painted on the walls, and up at the tall domed ceiling with intricate gilded patterns. Everywhere in the room, there's too much of everything, too many altars with various colored candles and too many flowers and paintings and bird baths with holy water inside. There's no room for The Great Blank here, and that's at least comforting.

Then, staring back at me as I look directly ahead, there's the casket. The lid is open, and through all the flowers and decorations near the pulpit, I can see the pale skin of Sarah's hands folded over her chest. Her Aunt Mary is standing alone beside the casket, dressed in a black skirt and a jacket that makes her seem somehow small and frail. Her hair was dyed blonde the last time I saw her, months before Grandpa died, but it's greying now.

I don't want to go near the casket. Not yet. But I don't want Sarah's aunt to be alone up there. She took care of Sarah after all the horrors of losing both her parents. She never tried to change Sarah, and she was always proud of her for exactly who she was. I barely know her, but I love her for it.

She hugs me when I approach, and I pat her back the way Dad patted mine earlier. I somehow stay composed, incredibly aware of the open casket that I can't let myself look directly at just yet.

"How are you feeling?" I ask. It's a stupid question. She shrugs, dabbing her reddened eyes again and blinking toward the floor.

"Part of me still feels like she's here somewhere. Alive," she adds, and the tears in her eyes grow a little heavier. "I keep remembering her as a little girl. Just a scrawny thing playing hopscotch with her dad in my driveway. Things changed so fast. I never thought things could change so fast."

I swallow, unable to look away as she keeps wiping her eyes and breathing in deeply. She forces a smile as she turns to look at Sarah, and she brings the handkerchief to her face. My hands are trembling in my pockets. It's the inevitable moment, and I'm terrified of what I'll see in there.

"She looks so at peace, doesn't she?" Mary asks, fresh tears in her voice.

There's ice in my chest and a sick feeling in my throat. I tell myself to stay together, to be brave on Sarah's behalf, but I want to turn and run. It won't be Sarah in there. It won't be her beautiful smile and dimples. It won't be her devilish expression, her sarcasm, her personality. It won't be her staring off into her own private world, creating something in her head to put onto canvas and release into the world. No; it will be another artist's crude rendition of who Sarah was. A doll. A prop. Just like at Grandpa's funeral.

I turn toward the casket, eyes looking at the floor first, delaying as long as possible. Then I look up, and my breathing stops like I've been thrown into a cold pool.

I see Sarah lying in there, surrounded by the white padding. Her brunette hair is perfectly straight, and the pink streak hasn't been dyed to suit anyone else. She's not wearing dead person's lipstick, or dead person's eyeliner, or dead person's clothing. She's just *her*. Perfectly *her*. The gashes and cuts in her forehead and scalp are completely hidden, as if by magic. She doesn't look dead, just still, calm, like she's only resting in her red dress and leather jacket. She's even wearing her boots with the smiley face stickers on the sides.

I stare at her, feeling a million different things hit me at once as everything seems to grow dark around me. Sadness, relief, anger, hope…too much at once, too much to process. I'm afraid that if I breath too loudly or make any noise at all, I might wake her up, and she'll be upset at first and then smile as she says something like "I was just resting my eyes, I swear! My alarm didn't go off…"

I start crying. Really crying. I feel myself breaking down, and everything is shaking and all I can feel is Sarah's Aunt Mary set her hand on my shoulder as she tries to comfort me.

"She's in a better place now," Mary says. "We have to believe that."

Any second, Sarah's calm face will break into a grin. Any second, I'll catch the smallest movement from within the casket, the shallowest breath, the tiniest twitch. Less than a week ago her lips were pressed against mine and I felt her warmth against me in the empty movie theater. I want to hold her hand again, but I know that if I do so it will just be a cold mannequin hand I'm touching. An empty shell.

I turn abruptly and walk away, back through the pews and toward the church doors. I see Clive and Monk on my way out, and Monk tries to wave me down before standing and working his way toward the aisle. I keep my eyes on the floor and move faster, determined to get out of this church and back to my bed and my bottle.

"Trey," he says. He says it a few more times, and I'm almost at the door when an old man in glasses stops to intercept me.

"Excuse me," he says, touching my jacket and pointing behind me. "I think there's someone trying to get your attention."

I nod. Slowly, I turn and look up at Monk. I haven't spoken to him or the others at all since the accident.

"Hey," Monk says, voice quiet and throaty as he walks closer. He looks like how I feel, eyes tired and red. He looks torn down from the inside. I don't say anything. Suddenly we're hugging, sobbing into each other's shoulders.

"I'm sorry," Clive says, hugging me the same way when he approaches. I shake my head.

"Don't be sorry," I tell him. "You didn't do this. Nobody did this."

He has a look on his face like he wants to tell me differently, like he has so much more to say and he's barely keeping everything bottled up. He gestures vaguely, opening his mouth and closing it again. He shakes his head.

"Fuck," he says. "This is so fucked."

All I can do is nod.

Across the room, I see Jordan sitting beside his mom. He looks miserable, even worse than I'd seen him at the

T.A.G. show. He stares straight ahead, looking like someone in shellshock. His mom is texting something on her phone, and when she says something to him that I can't hear, his lips hardly move at all in response. He lets his head fall forward onto the pew in front of him, and he sits like that as his mom glances around the room until she spots someone she knows, and she waves animatedly and hurries to go greet them.

"Let's sit," Monk says. I follow him and Clive back to the pews, wishing I was anywhere but here. We're barely seated when I hear a strange choking sound from Clive, and when I look over at him he's crying into his hands. Monk says something I can't hear, something that's supposed to sound soothing and assuring, I guess. But he's crying too. It makes me die inside, seeing my friends like this.

Kevin shows up just before the service begins, squeezing awkwardly past people's knees toward where we're seated. He doesn't say anything at all, no kind words or expressions of mourning. He just stares toward Sarah's casket the same way I do. Maybe he's also watching for movement from within.

We're all together. All five of us. Our last big event together before graduation.

I only half-listen to whatever the pastor's saying during the service. It's all bible verses and hopeful messages about the life beyond this world, something that's probably pre-scripted and ready to deliver at every funeral he's ever spoken at. Same words, different cast members. Same bible verses, different name inserted. Praise God, Amen, Hallelujah.

I look at Sarah's Aunt Mary as she weeps openly into her hands as the pastor speaks about Sarah's life, a very generalized collection of details condensing her entire existence and value into less than two minutes. Someone's phone goes off during this, and the eulogy is interrupted by a loud and obnoxious ringtone that somehow gets a laugh from a few people.

Others go up to speak. Sarah's aunt speaks first. She talks about how Sarah's "been an oddball since the moment she popped out of her mom," and how she was so uniquely herself in everything she ever did, everything she ever created. She looks down at Sarah's still body as she speaks and pauses to recompose herself when the tears start to come again.

"My niece was the most inspiring person I've ever met," she chokes out. "She lived with me. She made me laugh when I needed it. She made my house a home. And she was never, ever afraid of the world. She always knew just what she was doing."

The pastor takes her hand as she walks back to her pew, and she looks behind her again at the casket. She's praying for something to undo it all, I think. She's praying for a miracle, bargaining privately with God, thinking of the impossibility of Sarah's sudden death. I want to run and hug her. I want to be there for her, look out for her on Sarah's behalf, treat her as family even though Sarah and I had only just started dating and her aunt probably has no idea.

I stay in my seat, though. I feel trapped here. Every thought I have—all the happy memories with Sarah, all the times I made her smile—just brings more pain, and I can't escape it.

The principal goes up next, and then a few students from the school, and then one of Sarah's cousins I've never heard of. They all tell us their own version of who Sarah was, and none of it's right. None of them knew her, not like we did. Kylie Reed, who absolutely hated Sarah and never had a single nice thing to say about her, goes up to speak. She talks about how she wishes they'd been closer and that she was "such an amazing person, a true sweetheart." Then she breaks into tears and goes running toward the back of the church, sobbing uncontrollably as everyone turns their heads to watch her exit.

I wonder what Sarah must be thinking, wherever she's at. She's probably laughing, maybe making some sarcastic comment like "Oh! I never knew our *one* conversation throughout all of high school meant so much to you, bestie! I'll always miss how you called me Little Orphan Annie when my parents died. Good times."

I sit there listening, trying to fill in Sarah's commentary in my head as more and more people who never really cared about Sarah go up and tell the congregation what a great person she was. It's enough to make me smile at first. And then I cry all over again, because I know she's not really here anymore.

Days pass in my room, but it feels like the funeral never ended. I think about it constantly. I hear Sarah's voice in every thought I have. I don't get much sleep, but whenever I do, Sarah's somewhere in my dreams, and I wake up crying. Mom hears me screaming one night, and she comes rushing into my room with Dad. They both sit with me, listening to me cry, hugging me tight as I tell them all about Sarah and what she meant to me and how I'll never get her back. I tell them I want to die.

They don't say anything, but just hug me tighter. I try to explain to them in a choked voice that Sarah was the only girl I'll ever love, the only girl I'll ever *want* to love, and that she meant everything to me, and anyone else I ever meet or fall in love with will just be a reboot of her, a poor impression of the original. They don't say anything to this either. I don't think they understand a word I'm telling them. But they're there for me on those rough nights, and they assure me they'll always be here for me.

The last day of school comes. At the end of the day, the principal calls all the Seniors into the commons, and he gives a short and sentimental speech about how the world is ours for the taking, and how our best days are ahead. Green Day's "Time of Your Life" plays over the intercom.

Commencement. Family dinner. Photos. Graduation parties. More photos. Fake smiles all around. Congratulations all around.

I'm dead inside, and I don't think I'm ever coming back. All I'm doing is running out the clock until the day I get to be where Sarah's at. I play the smile game, and when Dad asks how I'm doing, I lie and tell him I'm fine. Somehow, people start believing my smile.

At the end of each night, I'm back in my room, alone at my desk, staring at a blank Microsoft Word document. Unable to create. Drumming my fingers idly on the keyboard. Waiting for something, anything at all.

Neither Sarah nor Grandpa come and talk to me.

Chapter Twenty-six

I'm staring at my computer screen, scrolling through Sarah's Facebook page and looking at all our old photos. School's been out for a month. It's just after midnight, and I'm sore from packing boxes full of pig parts all day at the slaughterhouse. I spent the whole shift thinking of Sarah and trying not to cry, just like every other shift I've worked. Clive doesn't start working for another week.

I find the picture I'm looking for.

It's of her, Grandpa, and I sitting together on Grandpa's back porch, less than a month after we'd all started hanging out. Sarah has a cup of coffee to her lips but is smiling with a sort of shocked expression at what Clive said from behind the camera. I'm covering my mouth with one hand while Grandpa's making a wide-eyed crazy expression and holding bunny ears behind my head.

I remember the second before that photo was taken, how my stomach rumbled loudly from all the fast food and coffee I'd had as we all went pranking around town, passing out flyers for a concert we'd completely made up at a venue that didn't even exist. Sarah heard the sound and started laughing, and my cheeks felt like they were on fire and I couldn't think of anything to say. Clive shouted, just before taking the picture, "Trey just crapped himself!"

Monk and Kevin weren't around that day. I wish they'd been there, because no matter how many times Sarah and I tried to recreate the moment for them, cracking each other up as we retold it, it just wasn't as funny as it was right at that perfect moment.

Grandpa and Sarah are gone. The good times are all gone. I loved them both more than life itself, the same way I love Clive and Monk and Kevin.

The pain hasn't even started to go away. Someday I'll lose everyone, and I'll probably hurt just as bad every single time. Or maybe I'll die suddenly, hit by a random driver just like Sarah was, and they'll all be in pain because of me and I won't be able to comfort them.

I wonder if we all end up becoming the voice in someone else's head when we're gone.

I turn off the computer. I turn off my bedroom light. Then I collapse into bed, staring up at the blank ceiling for two hours or so, wondering if the pain will ever really end and what it's all supposed to mean.

Somehow, I fall sleep.

*

In my dream, I'm in the middle of a blank Word document, and I'm nothing but two bold black letters forming a capital 'ME.' A giant black line blinks in and out of existence—blocking me, freeing me, blocking me, freeing me, over and over again. I have no eyes to look around with, not human eyes, but I feel The Great Blank all around me, and I know that he's eaten me alive. Somewhere far outside myself, I'm aware of a pair of hands rested on a keyboard, and when the hands start typing, I feel myself moving. I start running forward, trailing words behind 'ME,' creating something beautiful that fills me with absolute happiness like I've never felt, something that tells me I'm more than just 'ME' and that what I've surrounded myself with will never be erased. And then the giant black line swoops in and takes everything away, diving down at random words like a bird of prey and stealing the meaning from everything that's behind me. I try creating again, running forward as fast as I can, trailing more words and rebelling against my aggressor. But he just keeps taking, and taking, and taking. Somewhere far away, I feel the stranger's hands moving swiftly at the keyboard, pushing me onward, promising an end to everything and the restoration of all the things I've lost. I have no choice; I keep running forward, no matter how many times the black line takes something away.

And then I wake up

*

My alarm wakes me up. It's 3 a.m., and without even pausing to turn on a light or put on a fresh set of clothes, I climb out my bedroom window and down the ladder. I rub my eyes tiredly as I trudge across the front lawn and down the quiet street.

I look at my phone as I walk, all the text messages from earlier that day. Promises to my friends. Promises from them. Long blocks of text with every bit of what we're feeling and how awful it is. We haven't seen each other much the last few weeks, but we've been reaching out throughout the days. It's time.

Twenty minutes later I'm at the cemetery, and I hear noises coming from our tree near Grandpa's grave, laughter and loud conversation and empty cans being thrown. I hear Monk singing drunkenly. I hear a sarcastic comment from Clive, followed by a quick correction from Kevin that makes them all three laugh again.

Whatever conversation they're having stops abruptly when they see me approaching, and I smile awkwardly up at them with tears running down my face. I stand at the bottom of the tree for a long and silent moment, looking up at their faces with new appreciation for every last detail. I don't have words right now, and I don't think I'd say them even if I did. Someday we'll all be gone. Someday soon we won't have these nights anymore. There's not much time left.

I lift myself up onto the bottom branch, sitting in my normal spot. Clive reaches down with an open pack of cigarettes, smiling as he lights the one between his lips.

"Cig?" he asks.

I nod quietly, drying the last of the tears from my eyes as I take one out and light it. Monk hands me a beer, and I take a small sip as I look down at Grandpa's grave and then toward where Sarah's at, not too far from our tree. I feel absolutely certain about nothing in particular, but there's a feeling of absolute certainty nonetheless.

"Screw it," I say to myself. I chug the rest of my beer and throw the can at Monk, who bats it out of the air and shouts something nonsensical, some sort of gibberish that makes us all four laugh for some odd reason. Clive mimics the sound, waving his cigarette like a wand, and then we're talking about the new movies at the theater and how awful they all sound. We immediately decide to go see them, and we'll get pizza at the theater so Clive can stare creepily at the hot girl behind the counter.

I look around at them, the friends I have left, so full of life right this moment no matter what's hurting us all inside. It's the only rebellion that really means anything to us anymore: moving onward even though we feel like we can't. It's our art, every moment we're able to laugh when all we feel is pain. It's our collective middle finger to whatever comes at us next, no matter what it might be or what it might take away.

Because we're crazy. And when we die, we'll die crazy.

THE END

Acknowledgements

Writing is hard when you don't have people to pick you up when you're at your lowest. Fortunately, I'm surrounded by people who've helped me rebel against The Great Blank and find ways to smile. Crazy can sense crazy, and these people are the craziest.

My parents and family are first, of course; it'd be a real dick move to leave them out, right? Mom, Dad, my stepdad, and all my siblings, cousins, grandparents, aunts, and uncles have all been there for me. In particular, I want to thank my Grandma and Grandpa Kennedy, my Uncle Ed, my older sister Shannon, and my cousin Hayley.

This book wouldn't be possible without my friends and their specific brand of craziness: Brittany and James Hill, Samuel "Audioflesh" Capozziello, Brent Winzek, Jaclyn Zajac, Jason West, and Trevor Tieche. You guys rock.

A big thank you to Amy Casey, who did the wonderful cover art for the e-book and understood just what I was going for.

Thank you to all my teachers over the years, but especially Lucas Ostrowski. You tolerate me.

Thank you to the artists who've influenced me and are always willing to give advice: Adam Green, Joe Lynch, Steve "Uncle Creepy" Barton, Joe Knetter, Jeff Strand, PJ Starks, and Ben Liebsch.

And, finally, thank you Syler Will. You were taken from us too soon, little brother, but you showed me what strength truly is. You're the voice I'm thankful to always have in my head.

About the Author

Chase Will is from Coshocton, OH, where some of the kindest people in the world live. He loves horror movies, punk rock and metal music, theater, and powerlifting. He's written for several horror websites, including Dread Central, Scare Tissue, and CryptTeaze. Visit www.ChaseWill.com.

Made in the USA
Monee, IL
04 May 2022